# The Hunt for
# BILLY JACK

# The Hunt for
# BILLY JACK

Brian Oeffner

Copyright © 2017 Brian Oeffner.

All rights reserved. No part of this book may be used or reproduced by any means, graphic, electronic, or mechanical, including photocopying, recording, taping or by any information storage retrieval system without the written permission of the author except in the case of brief quotations embodied in critical articles and reviews.

LifeRich Publishing is a registered trademark of
The Reader's Digest Association, Inc.

LifeRich Publishing books may be ordered
through booksellers or by contacting:

LifeRich Publishing
1663 Liberty Drive
Bloomington, IN 47403
www.liferichpublishing.com
1 (888) 238-8637

Because of the dynamic nature of the Internet, any web addresses or links contained in this book may have changed since publication and may no longer be valid. The views expressed in this work are solely those of the author and do not necessarily reflect the views of the publisher, and the publisher hereby disclaims any responsibility for them.

Any people depicted in stock imagery provided by Thinkstock are models, and such images are being used for illustrative purposes only. Certain stock imagery © Thinkstock.

This is a work of fiction. All of the characters, names, incidents, organizations, and dialogue in this novel are either the products of the author's imagination or are used fictitiously.

ISBN: 978-1-4897-1127-4 (sc)
ISBN: 978-1-4897-1128-1 (hc)
ISBN: 978-1-4897-1126-7 (e)

Library of Congress Control Number: 2017909719

Print information available on the last page.

LifeRich Publishing rev. date: 6/16/2017

This book is dedicated to the memory of Ron "Legbone" Hagge.

# Chapter 1

It was a beautiful June day in central Iowa. The flowers were in full bloom and the grass was as green as the frogs Jim used to catch as a young boy. The air was fresh and clean and the aroma from his cup of coffee was a smell he had missed many mornings during his 24 years in the military. Jim had been home for about six months now since retiring from the Army and life was good. He was thinking about knocking a couple of items off of his 'Honey Do' list when his cell phone rang.

"Hello, this is Jim."

There was a slight pause before the voice on the other end said, "Hi, Jim. This is Samuel Littlebear, Billy's dad."

"Well, hello, sir. How are you doing?"

"I'm doing well, thank you, but I have a problem and want to know if you can help me?"

"I'll sure try," Jim replied. "What is it, Mr. Littlebear?"

There was another pause before he answered, "Jim, Billy is missing. He went up to Canada fishing three weeks ago, and never returned. He was only going to be gone for a week, and I'm sure he would have called if he decided to stay longer. His mother and I are worried, and we don't know what to do. I was hoping that maybe you could give us some guidance on how to proceed."

Jim was instantly worried. He knew Billy was not the type of person to say he would be home in a week and then not come home or call. Billy truly loved his parents and would never put them through something like this. Jim didn't want to show his concern and get Billy's family even more worked up, so he tried to downplay the whole thing.

"Well, sir, my first thought is that Billy found a great fishing hole and decided to extend his stay. Maybe his cell phone doesn't work up there—or maybe it's lost or broken and he can't call you. Maybe he thought his cell phone was working and thinks he left you a voicemail message. We both know he can handle himself in any situation that comes his way, and his military survival training will kick in if needed. Maybe he got into a fight in a bar, was thrown in jail, and is too embarrassed to call home. I guess there are all kinds of possibilities as to why he hasn't returned home, so I hate to jump the gun and think the worst. Have you filed a missing person's report or contacted the authorities?"

"No. I wanted to contact you and see if you'd heard from him and could give me some advice on what to do next."

"Well, here are my thoughts," Jim replied. "You contact the local authorities and file a missing person's report. Make sure they contact customs at the Canadian border, and see if he did cross into Canada and when. Then, check to see if he reentered the United States. At least then we will know what country he is in now. Do you know if he went with anyone or was going to meet someone up there?"

"He said he was going alone but he might look up an Indian guide on one of the lakes. I'm sorry, but I don't know the name of the guide or the lake," Mr. Littlebear replied.

"Well, sir, would anyone else know which lake he was going

to or the lake the guide was on? Maybe one of his buddies or his new girlfriend?"

"How did you know about her?"

"I keep in touch with the team as best I can," Jim replied. "Billy called me a couple of weeks ago, and asked if I wanted to go to Canada fishing with him. I told him I couldn't get away right now and would have to take a rain check. Anyway, Billy mentioned that he had met someone. He wouldn't say much about her, but I could tell by his voice that he really liked her. Do you think that maybe they had an argument or something and broke up? Maybe Billy just wanted to get away for a while."

"I don't think so, Jim. She calls the house every day and asks if we have heard from him. I asked her if they had a falling out and she said absolutely not. She said Billy gave her a beautiful necklace before he left and told her he loved her. She said she loves him very much and has never felt this way about anyone before. She was crying on the phone, and I believe in my heart that she was telling the truth. Billy told her that he would call her as soon as he crossed the border and was back in the U.S. That was three weeks ago, and no one has heard from him since. Jim...... I'm really worried."

"Well, sir, you make some phone calls and see what you can find out. I will call the team and see how many of them can take off on such short notice and go to Canada with me. I would like for all of us to meet at your ranch and come up with a game plan before we head out. I'm thinking we could meet at your ranch on Friday and go over our game plan before we leave for Canada. Maybe Billy will show up while we are at your ranch. If that happens, we can just have a party and return home. How does that sound to you?"

"Jim, that sounds great," Mr. Littlebear replied. "I will pay you what I can."

"No, sir," Jim replied. "Don't worry about that. You just concentrate on talking to customs and to his buddies and girlfriend and find out if anyone knows the name of the lake or the town where he was planning to go. You may have to contact the sheriff's office and get them to verify that he is missing before you can get any information from his credit card or cell phone companies. When we get there, we can pitch some tents behind your house or get some cheap motel rooms in town, so don't worry about any lodging or food on our behalf."

"You don't know how much I appreciate what you are doing," Mr. Littlebear said.

"Not a problem, sir. Billy is like a brother to all of us, and I'm sure he would do the same if one of us were missing. You just find out all the information you can, and we'll see you in a few days. I'm sure we can find him."

"Okay. Thank you so much."

"Okay, Mr. Littlebear. Call me if you hear from Billy, or if anything changes. I'll see you soon. Goodbye, now."

"Goodbye, Jim," Mr. Littlebear replied.

After hanging up the phone, Jim sat quietly for several minutes and tried to process the information he had just received. He knew that Canada was a big country with thousands of miles of wilderness, and finding a missing person up there could be a real challenge. He was hoping Billy would show up in the next few hours, and he would get a phone call from Mr. Littlebear telling him to cancel the mission. Something inside told him to prepare for the worst.

Jim, known to his team as 'Tunes', was the team leader. He'd grown up in a small town in Iowa and joined the army right out of high school. His father and grandfather had both been in the army, and Jim always loved listening to their stories. Jim's grandfather had served with the Thirty-Fourth Infantry

Division in the Iowa Army National Guard when the unit was activated for WWII in February of 1941. The Thirty-Fourth Infantry Division saw a lot of combat and was later recognized for amassing 517 days of front-line combat—more than any other U.S. division. His grandfather served proudly and was awarded two purple hearts for injuries sustained in combat, along with numerous other medals.

Jim had been a great athlete in high school and loved playing football. He wasn't big enough for college ball, so he stuck with his original plan to join the army. His military schools included Basic Combat Training, Infantry, Airborne, Pathfinder, and Ranger. He'd attained the rank of sergeant before his enlistment was up. He'd thought about making a career of the military, but after much consideration, decided to leave the army for a few years, get a college education, and become a commissioned officer if and when he decided to return to the army.

He attended Iowa State University in Ames, Iowa, and really enjoyed college life. He had met a girl in high school who had stolen his heart. She was a freshman his senior year, and he never got up the courage to ask her out before he graduated from high school and joined the army. He learned through one of his buddies that she would be attending Iowa State University after she graduated, and that was all Jim needed to help him decide which college to attend when he got home. They dated during college and were very much in love, but drifted apart their senior year and went their separate ways.

Jim had joined Army R.O.T.C. and was commissioned a second lieutenant upon graduation. He attended the Infantry Officer's Basic Course at Fort Benning, Georgia, and decided to make the army a career. During a tour in Afghanistan, he was assigned as a team leader for a special operations group, and that was where he met the guys who would become his best friends.

Jim was a musician and played the guitar, piano and harmonica. He loved all types of music and played in a couple of bands during his high school and college years. He was playing the guitar in the barracks one night when a guy asked him if he could play any oldies. Oldies were what Jim grew up on and he immediately broke into a song by the Beatles, then Credence Clearwater Revival, then Santana, then the Grass Roots, and this went on and on for over an hour. One of the guys was heard saying, "Jim sure can play some great tunes". And that is how the nickname 'Tunes' came to be.

One of the last missions the team was assigned in Afghanistan was a very close call. They were ambushed and pinned down and it didn't look good for the team. They were outnumbered four-to-one and had it not been for a patrol of German soldiers being in the area and responding to the gun fire, the whole team might have been killed. The Germans just happened to come in behind the terrorists and the bad guys decided to run rather than fight. The team thanked the Germans, then held hands and thanked God for watching over them. This close call was probably the deciding factor that led to all of them retiring when the tour in Afghanistan ended. Many of them had already been thinking about retirement because they all had over 20 years of military service and were eligible for a pension and free medical care for the rest of their lives. Every member of the team had given many years of his life to the military and they all decided it was time to leave. When their tour ended in September, all of them were out of the military by the end of the year.

Jim had gone home to Iowa and was enjoying civilian life. His wife, Patti, was many years younger than him and had a good job. He missed the military, but enjoyed being home with his wife and two dogs and was making the adjustment to civilian life without any problems.

Ron Hardin, better known as 'Dawg', was the first sergeant of the team. He was from Colorado, and his military career was very similar to Tune's. He was the toughest member of the team and was built like an NFL linebacker. His leadership skills were second to none, and the guys would follow him anywhere. He would never make someone do something that he wouldn't do himself, and the team always respected him for that. He would have been a great officer, but he got into a fight early in his career and as luck would have it, broke the jaw of another soldier that just happened to be the nephew of the post commander. He was busted down two ranks, but allowed to stay in the military. This of course ruined his chances of applying for Officer Candidate School and meant that he would have to remain an enlisted soldier throughout his military career.

Dawg was an avid hunter before joining the military and raised some world class hunting dogs. He kept photos of some of his dogs inside his locker and this led to his nickname, 'Dawg'. He liked the nickname, and became good at doing dog impressions, like growling when he got mad, or turning sideways and lifting one leg when he took a pee. He had a great sense of humor, but could be the most intense person you ever met when it was time to get serious. There was an old saying that went, 'When the going gets tough, the tough get going.' This pretty much described Dawg to a tee. He was one person you were glad was on your team.

Dawg's father owned a construction company and Dawg went to work for him when he returned home. Dawg enjoyed working outside and liked building things, so he was really enjoying the job. His dad wanted him to work on a crew for a year or two and get some experience before becoming a crew leader. Dawg agreed as long as he got to pick the men that would be on his crew. His dad agreed and Dawg was looking forward to the day when he would be the leader of his own crew.

Leon Bjorkren, better known as 'Swede', was the weapons expert of the team. He was from a small town in Oregon and grew up hunting and fishing. His uncle owned a gun shop and Leon worked at the shop for many years before joining the army. He had forgotten more about guns than most people will ever know in their lifetime. He was a great wrestler in high school and made it to state wrestling tournament 3 years in a row, but could never get past the second or third round. Like every high school wrestler, he wanted to be state champion more than anything, but just couldn't quite get there. After graduating from high school, he worked at the gun shop full time and planned to buy the shop when his uncle retired. He had a girlfriend his last two years of high school and she was the love of his life. He planned to marry her and raise a family and eventually become the owner of the gun shop. She was on board with this and life was good.... Until one day when he caught her in bed with one of his best friends. Leon was supposed to be out of town for a gun show, but came back early to surprise her. He surprised her alright. He was so rattled by this experience that he joined the army and left town. He gave up his dream of owning the gun shop, because he never wanted to see his ex-girlfriend or ex-friend ever again.

Leon got the nickname 'Swede' not because of his last name, but because one time in Afghanistan the team was on patrol and stopped at a compound occupied by a bunch of soldiers from Sweden. The Swedish soldiers were just sitting down to eat dinner and they graciously invited the team to eat with them. Jim wanted to get some information from them on one of the villages the team would be passing through the following day. It had been a long day for the team and they were all very hungry, but whatever the Swedish Soldiers were cooking had a horrendous odor and the team politely declined. Except for Leon. He took a whiff and said, "Wow, lutefisk". He scarfed down two plates and would have eaten more if it were not for the team having to leave. Some of the guys wanted to give him a crude nickname after watching him eat the lutefisk, but the team decided the name Swede would work and always remind them of the night they watched him eat food that smelled worse than a dead camel.

Leon had inherited the family farm and was keeping busy fixing up the place. He knew he would have to get a job someday, but for the time being, he was enjoying working on the farm and doing a little fishing every chance he got.

John Jamison, better known as 'Wiz', was the electronics expert on the team. Wiz was from Nebraska and had been a great basketball player in high school. He was 6 feet 3 inches tall and only weighed about 175 pounds. He loved playing basketball and led his high school team to the state tournament, but his family were all die hard University of Nebraska football fans, and he didn't get much respect for playing basketball. After graduating from high school, he went to a trade school that taught computer repair, and John graduated top in his class. He was up on all the latest high-tech stuff and this led to the nickname, 'Wiz'. Although he was a good kid, he got in with the wrong group of people and he soon started breaking bad. He was at a party one night that got raided and Wiz was caught with some marijuana in his possession. Back in those days, if it was your first offense and you were truly sorry for what you did, the judge would sometimes give you the option of joining the military rather than prosecuting you for possession of drugs. Wiz was lucky and was offered this option. He joined the army to avoid the drug charges.

After getting out of the military last fall, Wiz bought a house in Omaha, Nebraska and started up a computer repair business. Things were going very well and he already had three people working for him. He had made some new friends and was really enjoying life as a civilian.

Fred Fiddelke, better known as 'Boom', was the explosives expert for the team. He grew up in Wisconsin where his parents owned a fireworks business. He got interested in fireworks at a very young age, and when he found out that the army trained soldiers to work with explosives, it was only fitting that he join the army and become trained in Explosive Ordinance Disposal (EOD). He was trained in the construction, deployment, disarmament and disposal of high explosive munitions. Boom loved his job and was very good at it. His knowledge of explosives saved the team many times in Afghanistan and he was highly respected among the team members. He was the smartest member of the team and had an extremely high IQ. He would have been an excellent lawyer or CEO of a large company, but wanted a job working with his true love, explosives. He naturally got the nickname of 'Boom' because he loved blowing things up.

Boom moved back to Wisconsin and was working for his parents in the fireworks store. He wasn't sure if he wanted to take over the business when they retired or do something else with his life. He was thinking about joining a 'Bomb Disposal Squad' and started looking into the qualifications needed for one of those jobs. He parents could always sell the fireworks business when they were ready to retire if he found a job he liked.

Steven Good, better known as 'Dancer', was the ladies' man of the team. He was a very good-looking guy and was always on the prowl for beautiful women. After going through a nasty divorce, he was looking for a way to meet girls and one day decided to give dancing a try. He took some dancing lessons and soon discovered that he was a very good dancer. He had an incredible sense of rhythm and the instructor told him he was born to dance. Dancer would go out to night clubs with his buddies and after a couple of beers, get up the nerve to ask a pretty lady to dance. After she and her friends saw how well he could dance, he was in like flint. Ladies would often ask him to dance, so he spent most of the night on the dance floor and did very little drinking or talking with his buddies. The ladies he danced with would often ask him if his friends could dance and he would always tell them that they could, so the guys enjoyed going out with Dancer and getting to dance with some of the girls that were waiting their turn for their next dace with Fred Astaire.

Dancer grew up in New York City and was the only 'big city' guy on the team. He had more kids in his high school graduating class then most of the team had people in their whole town. Apparently, he asked a girl out one night that turned out to be a gang leader's girlfriend. The gang leader found out the next day that Dancer had asked his girlfriend for a date and went into a rage. He put a contract on Dancer's head and gave the order, "Find him and bring him to me". Luckily, Dancer found out about the contract before they located him and snuck out of town. He joined the army a few days later and left for good.

Dancer had been through the army military intelligence school. He had always been an analytical guy that asked a lot of questions. After his divorce, he analyzed ways to meet women and one of them happened to be by asking them to dance. So, he signed up for dancing lessons and the rest is history. Dancer also went through the army's training to become a certified hand-to-hand combat instructor. He felt that if he ever went back to New York City to see his family, it might come in handy. This motivated him and he became proficient in close order combat.

Dancer went back to New York City to spend some time with his family, but didn't want to live there for the rest of his life. He was putting new shingles on his parent's house and was going to paint the house and finish off the basement before he left. He was enjoying the time with his family, but didn't have any friends there and didn't care for the large crowds. He had spent 22 years in the army and was tired of the 'Hurry up and Wait' thing. He wanted to move out west and meet a nice woman and settle down where it was peaceful and quiet.

Scott Wilson, better known as 'Shades' was the interpreter for the team. His father was a politician and Scott initially got the nickname 'Shady' because his father had gotten caught up in some dirty politics. Scott always had a love for sunglasses and somewhere down the line his nickname was changed to Shades (which Scott liked so much better than 'Shady'). He had been through the Army's Linguistics School and was fluent in Arabic, Pashto and Dari, the latter two the most common languages spoken in Afghanistan.

After a couple of combat missions in Afghanistan, the team agreed that the most important things to mission success were: Good training, proper weapons, a good interpreter, and an explosives sniffing dog. Shades knowledge of Dari and Pashto were invaluable to the team in Afghanistan. The team had classes on the customs of the Afghani people, but really only knew a few words. Shades was fluent in their language and that saved the teams butts several times.

Shades was from Delaware and had wealthy parents. His parents objected to him joining the army, but he did it anyway.

He had always loved speaking foreign languages and taught himself to speak Spanish and German by taking online courses. His ability to learn foreign languages and his high intelligence were the reasons he was selected to attend the army linguistics school.

Shades was currently living back in Delaware but hadn't found a job yet and really wasn't trying. He was taking some 'online' management courses and was going to start looking for jobs when he finished the training.

Gary Westberg, better known as 'Big' was the dog handler for the team. He was from Arkansas and was an avid outdoors man. He was an excellent bow hunter and always carried a bow and arrows with him on missions. His main weapons were his M4 rifle and Beretta 9mm pistol, but he carried the bow and arrows in his ruck sack just in case the team ever needed them, and there were a couple of times when they came in very handy. An arrow through the heart of a terrorist on guard duty was sometimes the best way for the team to get in close and use the element of surprise on the rest of them. The team referred to his bow and arrow as the 'Silent Killer'.

Big was a dog lover also, and had raised blood hounds as a young man living in Arkansas. He had gone through the army's K9 handler school after joining the army and graduated top in his class. His German Shepard named 'Buck' was trained to sniff explosives and had saved the lives of many soldiers and local nationals in Afghanistan. Improvised Explosive Devices (IED's) were a common weapon of the Taliban. They would usually bury them on major roads or trails and then detonate them when NATO forces or locals that they thought were sympathetic to the infidels passed by them. Buck's keen sense of smell could sniff them out and the team would mark them and call in the EOD team, or let Boom dispose of them. Most of the time it was too dangerous to try to dig them up, and the team was usually on a mission and needed to keep moving, so they usually just let Boom put some explosives on top of them and detonate them. You never knew how much explosives were buried in the ground, so every explosion was different. But Boom was always like a young child on Christmas morning when he got to blow something up.

Big and his dog, Buck, were best friends and were very seldom apart. They slept together at night and were together all day long. If Big got up in the middle of the night to pee, Buck got up and went with him. That is probably the way most dog handlers are with their animals, but Big and Buck seemed to have a special love for each other and when Big retired from the military, he put in the paperwork to keep Buck and it was approved.

Big was 6 ft. 4 inches tall and weighed 250 pounds. As a young boy, he was nearly a head taller than the other kids in his class and he got the nickname "Big" back in grade school. He had a tremendous appetite and someone once said that he would eat anything that didn't eat him first. This was proven to be untrue when he passed on the lutefisk that night in Afghanistan and watched Swede eat it like pudding. He was strong as a bull and most of the time had a very pleasant disposition. He didn't get riled too often, and this was a very good thing, because he could be a real handful to get calmed down when he got upset. Dawg was the only one on the team that was tougher than Big and had proved it to Big a couple of times.

Big had moved back to Arkansas and had started a dog training business. His friends had thrown a 'Welcome Home' party for him when he returned and he met a young lady that had quickly stolen his heart. Life was very good for Big and he was really enjoying life as a civilian.

Lyle Johnson, better known as "Doc" was the medical expert on the team. He had been through the army's medical training center and was very proficient in emergency first aid. He personally saved the lives of several wounded U.S. soldiers in Afghanistan, usually by putting on tourniquets to stop the bleeding before they bled to death. He was a very caring, good-natured fellow that people liked to be around. The team always felt better going into dangerous missions just knowing that Doc was with them.

Doc was from Arizona. Both of his parents were medical doctors, and during his senior year in high school, they were pressuring Doc to follow in their footsteps and go to college and then medical school. Doc wasn't sure this was what he wanted to do with his life, so, much to his parent's dislike, he decided that he was going to do a tour in the army before making up his mind on what career path to follow. He did tell them he would enlist to be a medic and that might help him make up his mind about being a medical doctor after finishing his army tour. Well, Doc liked being a soldier so much he re-enlisted several times and ended up doing 21 years' active duty army. He was now retired from the military and working as an Emergency Medical Technician on Life Flight helicopter rescues.

The final member of the team was William Joseph Littlebear, better known as "Billy Jack." Billy's dad, Samuel, was a descendant of the Lakota Indians, and his mother Linda, was a white woman. The most famous Lakota Indian was Chief Crazy Horse, and Billy's dad had some great stories about Crazy Horse that were handed down through the generations.

Billy was a handsome man, with pitch black hair and beautiful brown eyes. He was proud of his Indian heritage and never tried to hide the fact that he was a half-breed. He grew up on a small farm in South Dakota. He loved the outdoors, and as a child, you would only find him inside when it was time to eat or time for bed. He would have slept in the barn with his horse and dog if his mother would have let him. His father taught Billy a lot about nature when Billy was growing up. They would spend weekends camping down by a nearby stream and Billy's dad taught him how to live off the land by catching fish, trapping animals, and which plants were edible and which ones would make you sick.

Billy was a good student in high school and well-liked by his classmates and teachers. He was a great football player, but didn't get a college football scholarship and his parents didn't have the money for him to go to college, so after high school he got a job working construction. It was a decent job and Billy was doing very well at it, but he wanted more out of life and one day, decided to join the army. Since he loved the outdoors, he volunteered to be branched infantry, and went to basic combat training and advanced individual training at Fort Benning, Georgia.

Years before he joined the team, one of his army buddies watched the movie, "Billy Jack" and later gave Billy that nickname. It stuck, and somewhere down the line Billy got a black, flat brimmed hat, like Billy Jack wore in the movie. The hat looked great on him and Billy wore it whenever he could. He probably was wearing the hat when he disappeared in Canada.

# Chapter 2

Jim spent several hours making phone calls to the team to let them know the situation, and to see who could go to Canada to help search for Billy Jack. Everyone could go except for Dancer and Doc. Dancer didn't have a current tourist passport to get across the border into Canada, and Doc had to attend his niece's wedding the coming weekend. Jim asked them if they would be available to go to the Littlebear ranch and do some snooping in town if the team didn't find Billy in a week. They both were available and would wait for Jim to contact them with the go-ahead.

So, seven members of the team were going to meet at Billy's parent's house on Friday, three days from now. Jim was planning to split the group up into 2-man teams so they could cover more ground, but since he had seven people going, he really needed one more person to make four 2-man teams. He decided to ask his brother-in-law, Mike to go along. Mike was a great guy and Jim thought the world of him. Mike had done a few years' active duty military when he got out of high school, then got out and joined the Iowa Army National Guard. Mike was a good soldier and stayed in the guard until he hit 20 years of service. This qualified him for a military pension when he reached age 60. Mike was currently working as a cement truck driver, but was getting tired of it and was looking for another job. He had some vacation time coming, and was thrilled that Jim asked him to go on the mission. After calling his wife and getting her approval, Mike phoned Jim and said he was good to go.

Jim knew that the team wouldn't approve of Mike going with them if this was going to be a dangerous mission, but as far as he knew, they were just going to Canada to find Billy Jack. And Mike was going to be on Jim's team, so he was sure the others would be okay with his decision.

Jim had been to Canada bear hunting several times and had a permit to bring a shotgun across the border into Canada. In Canada, they use deer slugs in shotguns for bear hunting rather than rifles. Deer slugs have better knock-down power at close range and the slugs don't travel as far as rifle cartridges, which make them much safer. Jim would stay at a lodge where the owner had several tree stands placed in the woods. Shortly before bear season opened, the owner would start baiting the stands by putting food scraps out close to them. The bear's keen sense of smell would quickly locate the food and the bear would have a nice meal. The lodge owner would continue putting out food scraps so the bears got into the habit of going to get the food when they got hungry. It's a practice called, "baiting" and it is perfectly legal in Canada.

One time in Canada, Jim was sitting in his tree stand about an hour before dark and fell asleep. He had been up early that morning walleye fishing and never got to take a nap in the afternoon like he usually did before going out hunting. Anyway, as he was sleeping in the tree stand, he awoke to a shaking feeling and looked down to see a big black bear about half way up his tree stand. Jim was startled, but his military training kicked in and he instantly grabbed his shotgun and blew a hole into the bear's head, which was about 6 feet below Jim's feet. Jim had taken a sandwich with him into the tree stand and only ate about half of it before he dozed off. The bear had eaten the table scraps and was still hungry. He smelled Jim's sandwich and was going after it. Anyway, that's the story the lodge owner told him. Jim still thinks the bear was going after him. One thing for sure; Jim never took food into a tree stand with him again after that night.

Fishermen are allowed to take shotguns with them to Canada if they filled out the paperwork and got a permit prior to crossing the border. Jim already had the permit and knew he could get some shotguns into the country without any problem. Rifles and pistols were a different story, so the team would only have shotguns and some bows and arrows. Jim was positive the shotguns and bows would be sufficient for anything they would come across.

Jim and Mike left home on Thursday morning and got a hotel room around seven-thirty that night in the town closest to the Littlebear ranch. They wanted to get some sleep and get to the ranch early in the morning to get an update on the situation and to greet the other team members as they arrived. After checking into their rooms, they met in the hotel bar for a sandwich and a few beers. They finished their first beers and Jim ordered the next round.

"I would like to get two more cold ones here when you get time, sir," Jim said to the bartender.

"Coming right up," was the reply.

"Thank you very much," Jim said as the bartender brought their beers. "How long have you been working here?"

"Well, I'm the manager and I've been here for over 20 years now."

"Do you by any chance know a fellow named Billy Littlebear?"

"Well, I know who he is, but don't know him well. I grew up in this town and remember reading about him in the local paper. He was a great high school football player, then joined the army a couple of years after he graduated from high school. I saw him here one night about a month ago."

"Well, I'm Jim, an old army buddy of Billy's and this is my brother in law, Mike."

"I'm Pete. Nice to meet you guys" the bartender said as he shook hands with both of them.

"Nice to meet you as well, Pete," Jim said. "Do you remember if Billy was alone that night or if he had anyone with him"?

"Oh yes, I remember, he had a very attractive young lady with him. They sat in the corner table and had dinner and a couple of glasses of wine. I usually leave around nine every evening and let my assistant manager close up. When I left, they were talking and laughing and really seemed to enjoy each other's company."

"Well, thanks for the info, Pete. I think we better get something to eat. Could you bring us a couple of menus, please?"

"You bet," Pete replied as he grabbed two menus from behind the bar.

Jim and Mike ordered sandwiches and couple more beers. Mike was excited to be going on an adventure with Jim and had talked most of the day during the drive to South Dakota. He couldn't help but ask Jim the question they had talked about most of the trip.

"So, have you come up with any more ideas as to what happed to Billy?" Mike asked.

"I really don't have a theory at this time," Jim replied. "When we get the team together tomorrow morning, Mr. Littlebear will give us all the information he has and we will brainstorm ideas on what we think might have happened and courses of action for us to take to find him."

"Well, I'm sure the logical thing to think is that Billy was in an accident or had an encounter with some wild animals," Mike said. "So, I have been trying to think of what else besides these two obvious things might have happened to him and I came up with the possibility that Billy might have been traveling through some rarely traveled woods to get to a remote fishing lake and stumbled across something".

"Something like what?"

"Maybe a meth lab, or some escaped convicts, or a mafia hideaway, or something like that," Mike replied.

"Well, that is possible", Jim said. "But I tend to think he might have gotten caught between a mama bear and her cub, or his boat hit a rock and started taking on water, so Billy had to swim to an island, or something like that. But, if my theory is correct, I just can't understand why no one has found his abandoned vehicle and called the authorities to report it. Anyway, Billy's disappearance really has me confused and I don't have a strong feeling one way or another."

When they finished eating, Mike asked, "So, you want to have another beer and keep discussing the possibilities?"

"No thanks. I'm ready for some shuteye. Tomorrow will probably be a long day and we both should get some sleep."

"What time do you want to meet in the morning?" Mike asked.

"I plan to get up around six and work out for an hour. You can join me if you like?"

"Thanks, but no thanks. I get enough physical activity back home."

"OK, then let's meet outside by the pickup at 7:30 and we'll stop at a café and get some breakfast on our way to the Littlebear ranch."

"Sounds like a plan, "Mike said. "I'll see you in the morning."

"And please don't stay up all night watching TV or playing video games. You need to be alert tomorrow for our meeting."

"I'm going to bed as soon as I finish this beer."

"OK. Good night, Mike."

"Good night, Jim."

# Chapter 3

Jim and Mike arrived at the Littlebear ranch around nine o'clock Friday morning and were the first ones there. The team started showing up about an hour later, and they were all there by noon. Mike ran into town and brought back a couple of buckets of chicken and Mrs. Littlebear whipped up some potato salad and lemonade for lunch. Jim had told everyone to hold off talking about Billy's disappearance until the meeting, so they made small talk and caught up on what everyone was doing now that they were out of the military. After everyone had finished eating, Jim decided it was time to get down to business.

"First of all, I would like to thank everyone for coming today. We are going to let Mr. Littlebear speak first and bring us up to date on the latest information he has, then we will brainstorm possibilities of what might have happened to Billy, and courses of action we can take to find him. I brought an easel and some butcher-block paper. Dancer, I'd like you to write our ideas on the paper for everyone to see, and Wiz, I'd like you to take notes on your laptop." Both of them acknowledged Jim and shook their heads that they were ready to go. Jim said, "Mr. Littlebear, you have the floor, Sir."

Mr. Littlebear stood up and began to speak. "You don't

know how much this means to Billy's mother and me, and we both thank want you from the bottom of our hearts." He hesitated for a minute and the team could see he was getting choked up, but he quickly regained his composure and began to read his notes from a piece of paper. "Billy left home around 6 A.M. on Saturday, June 2$^{nd}$. He told us he was going to Canada fishing and would be gone for one week. He was driving his Jeep Wrangler and had his dog, Kota, with him. He named the dog Kota because we are descendants of the Lakota Indian tribe. I contacted customs border patrol and was told he and Kota crossed into Canada through International Falls, Minnesota at 7:07 P.M. that night. Tomorrow it will be four weeks since he crossed into Canada. I checked with his credit card company, and was told he bought gas and some groceries at a convenience store in Vermillion Bay, Canada on Sunday, June 3$^{rd}$. That is the only purchase on his credit card and at this time, the only location we can prove that he was at in Canada. Billy didn't trust credit cards and seldom used them. I'm sure he took plenty of cash with him so he wouldn't have to use his credit card."

Mr. Littlebear continued, "He took a tent with him and was going to camp out rather than rent a cabin. He was concerned Kota might not be welcome in a cabin and said he preferred sleeping in a tent with Kota at his side. He wanted to look up an Indian guide on one of the lakes and his girlfriend remembered he referred to the guide as 'Barefoot Joe'. I think that name will help you find the guide so you can determine if Billy met with him before he disappeared. That's all I can think of at this time."

"Mind if we ask you some questions?" Jim asked.

"Go right ahead," was the reply.

"Do you have current photos of Billy, the jeep and Kota?" Dawg asked.

"Yes, I do. Sorry I forgot to mention that. And one of the photos of the jeep shows the license plate number," Mr. Littlebear continued.

"Great," said Dawg. "What about his girlfriend? Is there anything she could tell us that might help?"

"Well," Mr. Littlebear said. "She wanted to meet you guys and I told her I would call her and let her know what time she could come out to the ranch."

"Why don't you call her now?" Jim said. "I think we would all like to meet her and see what she has to say."

Billy's mom spoke up, "I'll give her a call right now and see if she can join us."

"Thank you, ma'am," Jim replied. "What else can you tell us about his dog, Kota?" Jim asked.

"Billy found the dog in the woods one day," Mr. Littlebear replied. "At first, Billy thought it was a wolf, but as he got closer, he could see it was a dog. It is an Alaskan malamute. The dog was starving, dehydrated, and had been severely beaten. Billy brought him back to the ranch and nursed him back to health. I didn't think the dog would live, but he pulled through. They became best friends and rarely did Billy go anywhere without that dog. I think the vet determined he was about four years old."

"Do you know if Billy had a chip put in the dog to help identify him if he was lost or stolen?"

"I don't think he did," replied Mr. Littlebear. "But Billy had a special identification tag made for his collar and I saw a photo of the tag in Billy's desk when I was searching through it the other day. You can take the photo with you along with the other photos."

"Great," said Jim. "And just to be safe, one of us will contact the vet after our meeting and see if he has any information that might help us identify Kota. Did you hear anything back from the Canadian authorities when you filed the missing person's report?"

"Yes, I heard back from them, but they didn't have much information. They said that they checked the local police departments around Vermillion Bay and Billy wasn't in any of the jails nor had anyone reported finding his jeep or dog."

Billy's mom came back into the room and said, "Angela was waiting for the call and will be here in about 15 minutes."

"Great," Jim said. "Let's take a quick break and resume when Angela gets here."

Angela Paulsen was a beautiful young lady, with blonde hair and a terrific smile. She looked like she was in her 20's, but knowing Billy was 42, she was probably in her mid-30's. She was a guidance counselor at a local high school and she had met Billy when he came to talk to her students about his military experiences. The school had a veteran come in every year and talk to the students that were interested in joining the military. Billy had been retired from the military for a few months and was asked to come in and tell about his military experience and let the students ask him questions about the military. Billy and Angela hit it off right from the start and Billy finally got up the nerve to ask her out on a date. She accepted and they quickly fell in love.

After Angela was introduced and hugged everyone in the room, Jim spoke up. "Angela, do you have anything to tell us that may help us find Billy and is it OK to ask you some questions?"

"I do have a few things to say and I would be glad to answer any questions," Angela replied. "Billy and I have been dating for about three months and I have fallen deeply in love with him. He is so special and caring and I have never met anyone like him before. He said he felt the same way about me and these last three months have been the happiest days of my life. I brought some recent photos of us for you to look over. I came out to the ranch at 6 A.M. the morning he left for Canada. I surprised him and gave him my favorite stuffed animal, a teddy bear that lies on my bed, to take with him to remind him that I love him and am counting the hours until he comes back to me."

"I also took a photo of him packing the jeep, so you can see a bunch of the items he was taking with him. After giving him a long kiss and Kota a big hug, my eyes filled with tears as they drove away. And I have not seen or heard from him since. That's all that I can think of at this time, but I will be happy to answer any questions you may have for me."

Wiz was the first to speak, "Angela, would you have an ex-husband or boyfriend that may have been jealous of your feelings for Billy and may have wanted Billy to disappear?"

"Well, I was married about 12 years ago, but my husband was killed in a car crash 2 years after we were married. A truck driver apparently fell asleep at the wheel, crossed the center line and hit my husband's vehicle head on. I was an emotional wreck for quite some time. I finally started dating about 5 years ago, but never found anyone that I really liked until I met Billy. As far as the last two guys I dated, one moved to California over a year ago, and the other got married and moved out of town. So, my answer to your question would have to be no."

"How about your family?" Wiz asked. "Could any of them be upset about you dating an American Indian?"

"I'm not real close to my family anymore," Angela answered. "My parents were best friends with my husband's parents, and all of them blamed me for his death. The accident occurred a day before my 25th birthday. My husband was out of town and going to return on my birthday. We had scheduled a romantic dinner and then we were going to meet up with some friends for drinks and dancing. Well, my husband decided to come home the night before to surprise me, and got into the accident on the way home. Apparently, his parents thought I must have told him to come home that night rather than get some sleep and drive home in the morning, but that is not true. Anyway, the truck driver also died in the crash and my husband's parents needed someone to blame, so they picked me. And my parents chose to support their best friends rather than their daughter, so we have drifted apart over the years. I also have a younger brother that has been in trouble with the law most of his life and I only see him when he needs to borrow money or needs a favor from me. I have only seen him a few times since I started dating Billy and didn't tell him I had met someone, so I don't think he even knew about Billy."

After a few moments of silence, Wiz said, "Thanks for sharing that with us, Angela."

"Angela, can you tell us anything about the Indian guide he was going to look up or the name of the lake where the guide worked?" Boom asked.

"Well, I remember he said he planned to go to Canyon Lake and try to catch some muskies. Someone told him that they had gone to Canyon Lake to fish for walleyes and caught more muskies than they did walleyes. Billy said walleye was his favorite fish to eat, but he had never caught a musky before, so he was going to try Canyon Lake for a couple of days and see what happened."

"And, someone else had told him about an Indian guide named 'Barefoot Joe' that was a guide on a lake close to Canyon Lake and Billy planned to look him up if he got time. Apparently, this 'Barefoot Joe' never wore shoes even in the winter and his feet were very tough and weathered and looked like an old baseball glove. I guess he was a great fisherman and knew how to catch fish when no one else could. Billy was going to try to find him and speak with him, but he said it wasn't a big priority and if the fish were biting on Canyon Lake, he would probably keep fishing rather than spend a day looking for the guide."

"Wow, I'm glad you remembered the name of the guide and the lake because that gives us a place to go after we check out the convenient store where he used his credit card," Jim said.

Wiz spoke up, "I just looked it up on the internet and Canyon Lake is about 20 miles from the convenience store in Vermillion Bay."

"Wiz, can you look up the names and phone numbers of all the resorts on Canyon Lake?" Jim asked.

"Sure," Wiz answered, "But Billy was going to pitch a tent so why would he even stop in at one of the resorts?"

"Well, my guess is Billy had to rent a boat somewhere, and I know the resorts will rent boats if they have some extras," Jim replied.

"Good thinking, Tunes" Wiz said.

"Tunes?" said Angela, as everyone laughed out loud.

"Yeah, Tunes," said Jim. "I'm an old guitar player and someone gave me that nickname many years ago. We all have nicknames that we go by. We couldn't use each other's real names on our missions in Afghanistan for fear that if the bad guys found out our names, they could possibly find out where we lived and get to our families. So, we started using nicknames only and now we pretty much just use them out of habit. So, what's your nickname, Angela?"

"Well, Billy called me 'Wiwasteka', but he never told me what it meant."

Everyone looked at Mr. Littlebear and he paused slightly before saying, "That's what I used to call Billy's mother when Billy was a young boy. Wiwasteka means beautiful woman."

Angela's eyes instantly filled with tears, and Billy's mom hugged her and led her out of the room and into the kitchen.

After a couple of minutes of silence, Jim spoke up, "Okay, let's start discussing ideas of what may have happened to Billy. I'm sure you all have thought a lot about this the last few days, so please give me your thoughts and we'll discuss them as a group. Let's start on my left with Dawg and go around the room so everyone has a chance to speak."

"Well," Dawg said. "I did some research on the internet and have given this a lot of thought. I'm sure Billy would have had Kota with him if he was exploring or looking for a remote lake, so I really don't think he would have surprised a momma bear and her cub as long as that dog was with him. And he is smart enough to make noise when walking through bear country so he doesn't sneak up on them. So, he was probably talking out loud to Kota or singing a song or something to make some noise and alert any bears that might have been in the area. My guess is that he fell off of a cliff or down a ravine and got injured. He would have had to break his back or something more serious, because a broken leg or something less severe wouldn't stop him from leaving."

"Also, my research said that nights in Canada are much more dangerous than daytime. So, let's say he fell and injured his back and couldn't walk. He probably cut himself in the fall also, which means bleeding, and the smell of blood at night in Canada is very, very dangerous. And, as much as I hate to say this, Kota could attract wolves, and a pack of hungry wolves could be deadly to both Billy and Kota. So, my theory is he fell off a cliff or into a hole and was injured enough that he couldn't escape."

After a few seconds of silence, Jim asked, "Any comments on Dawg's theory?"

"Yeah, my thoughts were very similar to Dawg's," Shades said. "And I added that maybe he got caught in a bear trap. Even though bear traps are illegal, that doesn't mean they aren't still being used. And if the people that placed the illegal bear trap came to check on the trap and found Billy caught in the trap, they might have decided it was better to dispose of his body rather than pay a fine or go to jail."

"Interesting," Jim said. Any more comments on this topic?" Hearing nothing, Jim said, "I think a fall is more probable than a bear trap, but let's keep moving on to other ideas and we will come back to this when we review the final list. Okay Big, you're next."

"Well, since there are no poisonous snakes in Canada, we can rule that out. But I really don't think Billy would have fallen off of a cliff or gotten caught in a bear trap. He was much too sure footed for that. I have to think he went up against the meanest animal on earth."

"You think my ex-wife was in Canada?" Dawg said. "Da Bitch," everyone said in unison as the room filled with laughter. Years ago, Dawg had gone through a nasty divorce, and every time he mentioned his ex-wife, he would always say, 'Da Bitch', before he continued. Well, the team picked up on this, and every time Dawg mentioned his ex-wife, the team would all say, 'Da Bitch,' in unison with Dawg.

Jim explained this to the others so they would understand. Everyone needed a good laugh and Dawg had sensed this. Even Mr. Littlebear had a good laugh at this one.

Big continued. "I just think it has something to do with bad people, and not animals or Mother Nature."

"So, do you have any theories to back up your thoughts," Jim asked?

"Well, Mr. Littlebear told us that Billy was probably carrying a lot of cash. And, since his jeep has never been located or reported, maybe someone robbed him for his money and vehicle."

"That is my main theory also," said Shades. "We really need to get the title of the vehicle and give the VIN to the Canadian authorities so they can start looking for it."

"I believe the title is in our safe. I'll get it for you after the meeting," Mr. Littlebear said.

Jim commented, "Mike, this is a good time for you to tell your theory."

"Sure," Mike said. "I tend to think it's possible that Billy was walking to a remote lake through some scarcely traveled woods and stumbled across something that people didn't want him to see. Maybe a makeshift campsite for poachers, maybe a hidden cabin for criminals on the run, or maybe a meth lab. He may have discovered something and someone had to stop him from leaving for fear he might tell the authorities what he had seen."

"Comments on Mike's theory?" Jim asked.

"That makes a lot of sense to me and I think is more probable than him getting killed by a bear or a pack of wolves," said Big.

"I agree," Shades commented.

"Probably the best theory so far," Dawg added.

"And that would explain why no one has reported an abandoned vehicle or stray dog," said Jim. "Either he is being held prisoner, or they killed him and hid the body. I would like to think that he is being held prisoner until they finish whatever they are doing, and they will let him go when they leave. Any other comments on this topic?" Jim asked.

Hearing nothing, Jim said, "Okay, let's keep moving. Swede, what are your thoughts?"

"Well, having grown up in Oregon, I have driven to Canada several times. The main roads in Canada are not the best, but the side roads are extremely dangerous. So, not only are the roads narrow and poorly maintained, you have to watch out for falling rocks, moose and bear crossing the road, sharp corners, and drunk drivers. Canadians really like to drink, and you probably would too if your favorite sport was hockey." Everyone chuckled and nodded their heads in agreement.

"My thoughts are Billy might have swerved to miss a moose and driven off a cliff, or into a lake, or down a steep ravine. And it was on a rarely traveled back road where no one could see the vehicle, so no one has reported it."

"Great possibility," Jim replied. "What do you guys think?"

"That makes a lot of sense to me," Big said.

"Yes, it does," Dawg added. "And that means we will have to search every road around Vermillion Bay and look into ravines where someone could have driven off of the road."

"Dawg is right," said Shades. "There is going to be a lot of territory to cover."

"Then cover it we will," Jim said in his 'command' voice as everyone nodded in agreement.

"Okay, Wiz, I know you have been busy taking notes, but do you have any other scenarios to add to the list," Jim asked?

"Well," said Wiz. "Nobody mentioned the possibility of an alien like in the movie, 'Predator,' and nobody mentioned any outer space phenomenon like in the movie, 'The Blob', and nobody..."

Jim interrupted, "Okay Wiz, I got your point.....again."

The team was all chuckling except for Mike, so Dawg decided to explain it to Mike. "A few years ago, we were brainstorming ideas like today and Jim told Wiz he needed to start thinking outside of the box. Well, we found out that Wiz doesn't take criticism very well, because Wiz starting thinking way outside of the box, and sometimes even outside of our solar system."

Mike had a big grin on his face as several members of the team were laughing.

"Wiz, once again let me apologize if I offended you when I asked you to think outside of the box," Jim said.

"Apology accepted," said Wiz. He continued with, "I tend to lean towards Mike's theory that Billy stumbled onto something he wasn't supposed to see and ended up in the wrong place at the wrong time."

Jim commented, "Okay, thanks Wiz. Anyone have anything different than what we have on the flip chart?"

No one spoke up, so Jim continued, "Well, here is what I think our plan of attack should be. There are eight of us, so we will split up into four two-man teams. Dawg and Swede, Big and Shades, Wiz and Boom, and Mike and I will be together. Each team can decide whose vehicle they want to drive to Canada. I highly recommend you take a pickup or SUV. Since we know Billy was at the convenience store in Vermillion Bay, we will find a campground close by for our command post. Every morning, each team will head out and search a certain area on their map."

Jim continued, "We will hit the towns and resorts first, handing out missing posters of Billy. If we don't get any leads within a few days, we may rent a helicopter to fly us around and see what we can from the air. This will also help us locate any remote lakes or cabins not on the map. If we don't find any clues from the air, we will start combing the woods and marking off the areas we have covered. Any questions?"

"Yeah, I have a couple," Wiz said. "Is the Canadian law enforcement agency going to be involved in any part of our search?"

"Well," Jim replied, "they have received the missing person's report and are looking for Billy or anyone using his passport to cross the border back into the U.S. We might be able to get them to help with a search party or get some divers to check the bottom of a lake if we find clues to tell us that Billy was in the area."

"So, unless we find some good clues, they aren't going to do much to help us?" Dawg asked.

"That's pretty much it," said Jim.

"Well," Wiz spoke up. "That leads into my second question. If we stumble across something in the woods and find some evidence that Billy was there, and the evidence leads us to a cabin or a group of people we think may have had something to do with Billy's disappearance, are we going to call the Canadian authorities or handle it ourselves?"

"It depends on the situation," Jim replied. "We'll make that call if and when the time comes. Canada is not a combat zone. We don't have a license to kill like we did in Afghanistan. And the last thing we want to do is get someone on the team hurt or killed or sent to prison because we put our noses in something instead of waiting for the authorities. Is everyone clear on that?"

The team all answered, "Clear, Sir" out of habit. Anytime Jim asked if everyone was clear on that, they knew he was serious about something and wanted to drive home a point so there would be no misunderstanding if and when this circumstance ever occurred.

"And one more thing," said Jim. "I didn't want to mention it earlier when Billy's mother and Angela were in the room, but now that they are not here, I can talk about it. The Yellow Lab dog that is tied up in the backyard, well that is Big's dog, Kadence, or Kadie for short, and she is going with us. Big, I'll let you explain it to the team."

"Okay, thanks Jim," Big said as he stood up and prepared to address the team. "You guys know I have been a dog trainer for years and went through the K-9 handler school in the army. Well, after I retired and went home last winter, I was contacted by an organization and asked if I would be interested in training cadaver dogs. I found out that a search and rescue dog is trained to find living humans, but not to detect decomposing flesh. So, in cases where a dead body will likely be the outcome, cadaver dogs are used rather than search and rescue dogs. Cadaver dogs are trained to detect the scent of decomposition that rises from the soil, very similar to the principal of how a dog knows where he buried a bone in the backyard. I looked into training cadaver dogs and decided to give it a try."

Big could see everyone was listening intensely so he continued, "I had to go through an extensive background check and finally my license was approved. I went through several weeks of training in Texas and then started my own training program in Arkansas. I have a special permit that allows me to get human body parts from morgues to train the dogs. It's very controlled and I have to account for each body part I get or I could end up in prison. These dogs are mainly used to find bodies and help solve crimes, but they are also used to find bodies in buildings after fires or when devastation occurs like with the Twin Towers."

Big could see the team was listening intently as he continued, "Kadie just completed training and was the highest scoring dog in the group of six that just finished the 12-week course. She is also one of the smartest and most gentle dogs I have ever worked with. I got permission to bring her along and see how she performs in a real-life scenario. She will be with me, but if any of you discover clues and think Billy was there, I will bring her to you and we will do a thorough search of the surrounding area. I truly hope we don't have to use Kadie, but Jim wanted me to bring her just in case. Do you guys have any questions?"

"Will there be a problem getting Kadie across the border?" Wiz asked.

"There shouldn't be a problem," Big replied. "I called Customs and they gave me a list of things to have done prior to crossing the border. It was mainly that her shots were up to date and I have the papers from her vet that shows she is current on everything, so there shouldn't be any issues."

"Dawg, are all of your shots up to date?" Swede asked as everyone laughed.

"I'm up on all of them except for the 'Bad Joke' shot," Dawg replied. "One more bad joke like that and I'm likely to bite the person who said it," Dawg said as he growled and barked a few times.

"Down, boy," Jim said with a grin.

"Hey, if you brought Kadie with you, where is Buck?" Wiz asked.

"Buck is staying with my girlfriend," Big replied. "I wanted to bring him, but decided it would be easier to leave him home since Kadie was coming along. And, my girlfriend has a female dog that Buck is sweet on, so she should help keep his mind off of me for a few days."

"I just hope Buck doesn't get his heart broken and turn into a mean dog for the rest of his life like Dawg has done," Swede said as everybody laughed.

Dawg gave Swede a dirty look as Jim said, "Okay, let's get back to business."

"Maybe we should bring some shovels with us just in case we have to do some digging," Boom commented.

"I've got some in my pickup," Jim said. "Anybody else have any more comments?" Hearing nothing, Jim continued, "Well, we need to go into town and get some things done before we leave for Canada tomorrow morning. I've got an assignment for each team as far as where to go and what to do. Then we'll meet up for dinner at 1800 at the local steakhouse. The address is at the top of your list. After eating, we will split up again and each team will hit the local bars and snoop around for any info they can find."

"Also," Jim continued, "Dancer and Doc are available to come to the ranch next weekend and can stay for a week or two if necessary. I will call them from Canada and let them know how we are doing and if they are still needed. They will be working with local officials, doing some snooping in town and helping out Billy's parents anyway they can. If by chance we do find Billy's body, they will help get the paperwork to bring him back to the U.S. and help with funeral arrangements. We will stay with Billy's body until it is returned back home. Any questions?" Hearing nothing, Jim continued. "All right then, I'll pass out the lists and see you at the steakhouse in a few hours."

# Chapter 4

The steakhouse was a nice little mom and pop restaurant. Mr. Littlebear had reserved the meeting room in the back so they could be alone and continue discussing the mission. Everyone was there by 1800 to include Angela and Mr. and Mrs. Littlebear. The teams had picked up the 'Missing' posters, gotten Billy's dental records, talked to the vet to see if Kota had a chip placed in him, and spoke with the local law enforcement agency as to whether or not they had any update on Billy's disappearance. Jim's checklist was complete and they were ready to head for Canada in the morning. When the waitress started to take orders, Jim noticed that Angela just ordered a salad.

Jim asked if she wasn't hungry and she replied, "I'm actually very hungry, but I'm a vegetarian and there isn't a lot of non-meat choices in this steakhouse."

Mr. Littlebear spoke up, "vegetarian is an old Indian word for bad hunter," as the room exploded with laughter.

After everyone had finished eating, Jim decided it was time to speak. "Wiz, do you have an update on how we are going to communicate with each other in Canada?"

"I do," Wiz said. "I purchased some chips to put in our cell phones rather than buy new cell phones in Canada. Just pass your cell phones to me one at a time and I can put them in right now while we are talking. These chips are only good for one month, so after 30 days, you will not be able to make any more international calls. And, the fee's will go on your individual cell phone bills, so don't be calling one of your buddies in Afghanistan unless you want to pay big bucks on your next cell phone bill. The charges will be for incoming calls as well, so call your families and tell them not to call you in Canada unless there is an emergency. Keep the calls short and use the phones only when necessary."

Dawg spoke up, "I hope I don't get any calls from my ex-wife." "Da Bitch," everyone except Billy's mother said out loud as the room again filled with laughter.

After the laughter quieted, Jim continued. "Did everyone bring a tourist passport or a pass card with them?" Everyone shook their heads in agreement. "Make sure you have your passport and a photo ID ready to hand to the customs agent when you reach the border. When they ask where you are going, tell them you are going to Vermillion Bay or Canyon Lake fishing. Do not say you are there looking for a friend. Also, you are only allowed to bring one case of beer or one bottle of booze per person into Canada. If you have more than that, you will have to pay. Be totally honest with them, because if you tell them you only have 2 cases of beer and they find 3 cases of beer when your vehicle gets selected for a random search, you are in big trouble. Not only will they perform a thorough search of your entire vehicle which could last a couple of hours, you will have to pay a large fine. Is everyone clear on that?"

"Clear, Sir," was the response. "Great", Jim said. "But knock off the 'Sir' crap. I want your response to be 'Clear, Jim', or 'Clear, Tunes', when I ask you that question. Is everyone clear on that?" "Clear, Sir" again was the response as everyone laughed out loud.

"It looks like some old habits are hard to break," Dawg replied as Jim just smiled and shook his head."

"Moving right along," Jim continued, "Mr. Littlebear said we can leave any vehicles that we aren't driving to Canada at the ranch until we return. So, let me ask each team right now, who is driving their vehicle and who will be leaving a vehicle at the ranch?" Jim asked.

"I'm driving my Dodge pickup and Swede is leaving his Yugo at the ranch," Dawg replied as everyone laughed.

"It's a KIA Soul," Swede commented as he looked at Dawg and shook his head.

"Sorry, man," Dawg replied. "All foreign cars look e the same to me."

"Okay, let's keep moving," Jim said.

Big spoke up, "I'm driving my SUV since I have Kadie's kennel in the back of it, and Shades will be leaving his new Camaro at the ranch."

"I hope nothing happens to that new Camaro while we are gone," Dawg commented.

"Unlike you, I carry insurance on my vehicles," Shades responded.

"Well, I've seen you drive Shades," Dawg replied, "and believe me, you need insurance."

"Okay, you two knock it off," Jim said. "Now, who else is driving?" Jim asked.

"I'm driving my pickup and Wiz is leaving his Hybrid at the ranch," Boom said.

"And I'm driving my Chevy pickup with a topper on it," Jim replied. "So, Mr. Littlebear, we will be leaving three vehicles at your ranch."

"No problem," Mr. Littlebear replied. "I will show you where to park them in the morning."

"Okay," Jim said, "before we break up and some of you head out to talk to people at the bars, I would like to propose a toast." Everyone raised their drinks and waited for Jim's comments. Jim raised his glass, looked towards the sky and said, "Billy, we don't know where you are, or what you are doing, but we are coming to find you. To Billy," Jim shouted.

"To Billy," everyone replied before taking a drink.

"Okay, "Jim said, "Let's meet up back here at the restaurant at 10 P.M. Mike and I will stay here and talk to the restaurant owners and customers. Mr. and Mrs. Littlebear and Angela, you are welcome to stay with us as long as you like."

Mr. Littlebear spoke up, "I would like to speak to the team before you leave in the morning. I have an Indian prayer I want to say to give you safe travels."

"Well, sir, some of us are camping in your backyard and a few of the guys have motel rooms here in town, so how about we meet up at the ranch at 7 A.M. and have a brief meeting before we depart?" Jim asked.

"That would be great," Mr. Littlebear replied.

"Okay, then you two have a good night and we will see you at seven tomorrow morning," Jim said.

"I will be there also," Angela said. "I will probably stay here for another couple of hours and then I'm going home to bake you guys some cookies to take with you on your trip."

"Well, that's part of the soldier's creed," Jim said. "We never leave a fallen comrade behind, and we never turn down homemade cookies." Everyone laughed as several people got up and headed for the door.

Jim and Mike spoke with the restaurant owners, cooks, and bartenders, but didn't get any new information. Some people knew of Billy, but no one was close to him and hadn't seen him within the last month. They even talked to some of the customers, but no luck there either. They left a couple of missing posters with the bartenders and he stuck the posters up behind the bar. The posters had Mr. Littlebear's and Jim's phone numbers on them, and they were hoping someone would call if they knew anything about where Billy was going in Canada. They knew it was a long shot, but maybe he had spoken with someone at a gas station or in the grocery store and they would remember if he said anything about his upcoming trip to Canada.

After a couple of hours of mingling with no luck, Jim and Mike ordered another beer and went back to sit in the meeting room and wait for the others to return. Angela had been visiting with one of her friends out in the main part of the restaurant, but she soon joined the guys in the meeting room.

"So, Angela," Jim said, "Is there anything else you can think of that might help us find Billy?"

"I can't think of anything right now," she said. "But I have the list of all of your phone numbers and I will call you if I think of something."

"Great," Jim replied. "And maybe you can help Dancer and Doc if and when they arrive here next weekend."

"I will be glad to," she replied. "I have to tell you guys this. I pray every day that Billy comes home to me. I miss him so much it hurts. I just can't understand why God is punishing me so severely. I try to be a good Christian and do what is right, but things just don't seem to work out for me. First my husband was taken from me in a car wreck, and now Billy is missing, I just don't know how much more I can take."

Mike instantly spoke up, "Angela, life is hard and we all go through difficult times, but you must never lose your faith. When times are bad, you must continue to trust in God and pray to him to take away your troubles. You must stay strong and keep your faith. He will take care of you."

"Well said, Mike," Jim commented.

"Thank you, Mike," Angela replied. "I'm trying to stay strong. It's just that so many bad things have happened to me in my life, and now I am worried that you guys won't find Billy, or that one of you could get killed and not come back…..and I really don't know what I can do to help."

"You just stay strong and keep praying," Jim said. "That's the best thing you can do to help us. And keep talking to people in town that were friends with Billy or might know something about his trip. I plan to call Billy's parents with an update every night and I can call you also if you want me to. And please call me if you find something out or remember something that might help."

"Thank you guys so much," Angela replied. "Could I hug both of you before I go home and start baking cookies?"

"I never pass up a hug from a beautiful woman," Mike said as he gave Angela a big hug.

Then Jim spoke as he was getting hugged, "Angela, Billy is like a brother to us, and since you are the woman that captured his heart, you are now part of our family also. You have my word that we will do everything we can to find Billy and bring him home to you. You have a good night, get some sleep and we'll see you in the morning."

"And don't forget the cookies," Mike said. Angela smiled at them, then turned and headed for the door.

After she was out of the room, Jim said, "I sure can see what Billy liked in that woman, she is a sweetheart."

"Roger that, Tunes," Mike said with a smile. "I think we have time for one more beer before the team starts showing up for the meeting."

"Roger that, Mike," Jim said with a smile. "Your turn to buy my friend."

Mike ordered a couple of beers and the two of them sat in the meeting room waiting for the guys to return.

"Is there anything you can tell me about the guys on the team that I should know about?" Mike asked.

"Well, there is a couple of things I was going to talk about on our drive to Canada, but since you asked, I might as well bring them up now. First of all, we don't cuss or swear. We had different team members over the years, and one of them was very religious and was offended by all of the swearing some of the guys were doing. He brought it up and we discussed it as a group. We couldn't find any good reasons to swear, but came up with a lot of reasons why not to swear. So, instead of just telling everyone not to swear anymore, Wiz came up with the idea that we would use swearing as a key to tell other members of the team that something wasn't right."

"For example, one time while on patrol, we stopped and took a break to hydrate ourselves. Dawg saw movement in the rocks and didn't want to say something out loud for fear that we could be ambushed before we knew what hit us. So, he started swearing. We all picked up that something wasn't right and we were in danger. We didn't know what it was, but since Dawg was the one doing the swearing, we knew he must have seen something. After he had alerted us with his swearing, he turned to us and quietly said, "Movement in the rocks behind me. Dive for cover on the count of three. One, two, THREE," and everyone dove for cover just as some bad guys opened fire on us. We returned fire and threw a couple of hand grenades into the rock piles and the battle was over in a few seconds. We killed four of them without taking a casualty."

"Wow," said Mike.

"So," Jim said, "If you swear by accident, you always apologize by saying, 'Pardon my French' or 'Sorry about the language', or something like that."

"Got it," Mike said. "What else can you tell me?"

"Well, Dawg is a great guy and one of my best friends, but here is something you should know about him. His brother, Robert, died of cancer when he was in his 20's. Robert was married and had a young son named Randy. After Robert's death, Dawg helped raise his nephew, Randy, and the two of them became very close. When Randy graduated from high school, he wanted to join the Army to be like his uncle, even though Dawg discouraged this and wanted Randy to go to college. Well, Randy didn't listen to Dawg and enlisted in the Army and went through all the infantry schools that Dawg had gone through years before. Dawg was so proud of Randy and they called or emailed each other nearly every day. Then one day, Randy's unit was notified they were being mobilized to Afghanistan. Randy was so excited, but Dawg was very worried. Well, the unit was only in Afghanistan for about a month, when Randy's vehicle hit an IED. Randy was badly injured, and it took nearly 2 hours to get him out of the vehicle and medevac'd to the field hospital. He died later that night."

Jim hesitated for a few seconds, then continued. "Dawg took it very hard as would any of us, but after that, he seemed to develop a real hatred for terrorists and seemed to enjoy inflicting pain on them whenever he got the opportunity. He gut-shot a couple of them one day when I felt he could easily have fired a kill-shot. We had been ambushed and a couple of them were trying to work their way in closer when Dawg shot them. I spoke with him about it and he said he was firing center mass so he didn't miss them. Well, I know he is an expert shot and I think he just wanted them to suffer for a while before they died. I don't think we will run into any terrorists in Canada, but I wanted you to know this so you don't talk much about IED's when Dawg is around. Boom could talk about IED's and explosives all day long, but all of us know to keep that subject to a minimum when Dawg is present."

"Thanks for the heads-up on that, because not knowing what you just told me, I'm sure I would have asked Boom some questions about IED's in front of Dawg."

"Well, now you know not to swear and not to talk about IED's or explosives in front of Dawg."

"Got it," Mike said, as some of the team members walked into the meeting room.

Within minutes, they were all there and Jim gave each team a chance to brief what they found out. No new clues from any of them. Jim knew it was going to be hard just to find Billy, and the chances of finding him alive were slim to none. The team had lots of tough missions in the past, and this looked like it was going to be another one of them.

"Okay," Jim said. "Let's call it a night. Everyone needs to get some sleep and be at the ranch by 0700 tomorrow morning. Please keep the skirt-chasing, dancing, drinking and fighting to an absolute minimum. It's a long drive to Canada tomorrow and everyone needs to be alert. I'm heading for my tent back at the ranch. I'll see you all in the morning."

# Chapter 5

Everyone was at the ranch by 0645 the next morning. Mrs. Littlebear had home-made cinnamon rolls, coffee and juice waiting for them. After eating, Mr. Littlebear rose and spoke to the team.

"First of all, I want to thank all of you again, for everything you have done already and everything you will be doing in the next few days. It is so very important to us, that you find Billy and bring him home, even if he is dead. You see, we believe that Billy's spirit cannot find the way to the afterlife if he is lost. In the old days, we didn't believe in burying our people under ground because we believed the spirit couldn't get out and travel to the heavens when it was buried under dirt. Now, we believe that the spirit leaves the body during the death ritual, or funeral as you call it, so we can now bury our people underground. But, until Billy is found and a death ritual is performed, his spirit cannot travel to the afterlife. If you don't find him, his mother and I will sell the ranch and spend the rest of our lives in Canada looking for his body. He is our only son whom we love with all our hearts, and we owe him that. I hope you can understand our ways."

After several moments of silence, Jim said, "We may not

totally understand your ways, but we respect your beliefs and we will do everything we can to find Billy and bring him home."

Mr. Littlebear replied, "Thank you," and then said, "I would like to say a prayer now before you leave." Mr. Littlebear then lifted his hands to the sky and spoke these words; "Oh, Great Spirit, whose voice I hear in the wind and whose breath gives life to all the world, hear me now. These men need your strength and wisdom on their journey. Give them safe travels and help them to remain calm in the face of danger. Give them a successful hunt, so they can find our son and bring him home to his family." He lowered his hands and hugged his wife, then Angela, then Jim and the rest of the team. After that, he turned and slowly walked into the house. The team got into their vehicles and drove out the lane as Angela and Mrs. Littlebear waved until all of the vehicles were out of sight.

Jim was driving his Chevy pickup and Mike was riding with him. After several minutes of silence, Mike spoke up, "You know Jim, I drive a cement truck for a living. I truly love my wife and my family, but my life is so boring compared to what you guys have done in your lives. I have to tell you that these last two days have been fantastic and we're not even to Canada yet. I love mystery and excitement and I'm really enjoying this. Thank you so much for asking me to go along."

"I'm just glad that Karen gave her approval for you to go with us," Jim said.

"Well, she is a good woman and I think she knew I needed to get away for a while," Mike replied. "I really need to do something special for her when I get home. I'm open for ideas, so let me know if you think of something I can do to thank her. Something really special and out of the ordinary."

"Well, right now my thoughts are on the mission," Jim said,

"But remind me again on the way home and we will brainstorm ideas until we think of something she will really like."

"Sounds like a plan, Stan," Mike said. "So, Jim, can I ask you some questions about Afghanistan?"

"Sure," Jim said. "We've got about 12 hours of driving time, so fire away."

"Well, I know you emailed us newsletters every month or so, and they were very interesting, but you never got into any details or specifics on what you were doing over there. I'm sure you weren't at liberty to tell us much, but now that you are retired, can you at least share some things with me, like what you really did over there?"

"Sure. We were one of several teams that had the mission of going into small remote villages to see if there were any Taliban in the village or if there were any signs of people making IED's."

"Wow. That sounds really dangerous."

"Everything is dangerous in a combat zone," Jim replied. "Our commanding General used to tell us every morning that the Taliban wake up with one thing on their minds, 'kill an infidel'. An infidel is a non-believer, so any non-Muslim was considered an infidel to them. Well, we had air support and about 40 combat soldiers in reserve in case we ran into trouble. Shades spoke the language fluently, so when we went into the village he told them that we were only the lead element, and if they were hostile to us in any way, the main body would come into the village shooting and there would be many people killed. This always seemed to get their attention. Shades would ask the village leader if there were any Taliban in the village and we always got the same answer, 'No.' And we would always ask if anyone in the village was making IED's, and they would again tell us, 'No.'"

"So, we would tell him we wanted to look inside some of

the buildings just to be sure. They never liked this, but we said if they didn't let us look inside the buildings, we would believe that they were hiding something and we would call for the main body to come in and do a much more thorough search of every building in the village. So, they would always let us go through the buildings."

"Did you ever find anything?" Mike asked.

"Well, we never found any Taliban. I'm sure they were there, but they looked like everyone else in the village and the ones that we had wanted posters on were never in the villages while we were there. We even showed them the wanted posters and Shades asked if they had seen the person in the photo. Of course, every answer was 'No', even though the person in the photo was the nephew of the village leader and slept in the village every night. But occasionally we would find weapons or signs that they were making IED's."

"What kind of signs?" Mike asked.

"Well, we all had IED training and Boom was a subject matter expert on explosives, so we were looking for things like; switches, power sources, detonators, the main charge (explosives) and containers to hold the explosives. Some of the things like switches and detonators are easy to hide, so we mostly found signs that they were making home-made explosives when we found fertilizer or chemical containers, bags, jugs, 55-gallon drums, diesel fuel, mixing bowls, respirators, and of course the odor that came from mixing these chemicals."

"That reminds me of my all-time favorite TV series, 'Breaking Bad,'" Mike said.

"That was a really great show," Jim replied, "but these guys weren't near as smart as Walter White."

"I'm sure of that," Mike said with a laugh. "So, what did

you do when you found some of those things used to make explosives?"

"Well, we didn't do anything at the time, but we reported it to our higher headquarters and they set up surveillance on the village and tried to catch them bringing in supplies or taking out IED's."

"So, looking for Taliban and IED's was your main mission?" Mike asked.

"It was at first," Jim replied, "but a young American soldier got captured by the Taliban and then our mission changed to finding him."

"Was that the soldier the Taliban released a few months ago that was on the news?"

"That was him," Jim replied.

"So, what was the story on that?" Mike asked.

"Well, I'm not sure what really happened, because we got different stories from higher headquarters when we asked for that information. At first, we were told he fell behind in a patrol and got captured without the rest of the patrol knowing about it, and later we were told he had just gotten off of guard duty and was on his way back to his hooch to get some sleep when they took him. And when I asked for more information and what really happened to him, I was told that it wasn't important and our mission was just to try to find him. Later, the Taliban admitted they captured him and even sent photos of him to prove it. They said they would release him if the U.S. released some of their friends being held at Guantanamo Bay. Of course, this isn't something our government easily does, so he was held captive for a few years until he was released a few months ago."

"Well, didn't I hear on the news that they have determined that he just walked off of the compound and was willingly captured?" Mike asked.

"That's what it sounds like. And the last thing I heard was they were trying to decide whether or not to label him a 'deserter' and send him to prison for a long time."

"So, after he was captured, the hunt for bad guys and IED's was dropped and you were just looking for the captured soldier?"

"No," Jim replied. "Looking for the soldier was supposed to be our priority, but it was just another part of our mission. We felt they gave us the mission of finding the soldier just to satisfy the press and the soldier's family. The military could say that they had people out looking for the captured soldier every day, but we knew our main mission was to find Taliban and IED's. We felt very strongly that the Taliban took the soldier across the border into Pakistan, and since we were not allowed to cross the border, our chances of finding him were pretty slim."

"So, what do you think should happen to him."

"Well, I have mixed feelings on this," Jim replied. "Several soldiers lost their lives searching for him, so if the courts determine that he intentionally deserted, part of me thinks he should be sent to prison for life or even executed. But, another part of me thinks he must be mentally unbalanced to do something like that and he now has to go through life knowing that good men died trying to find him because he did something totally stupid."

"I see your point. And the fact that he was held prisoner for several years may have been punishment enough for the court system."

"I guess so," Jim replied. "I'm curious to hear the final verdict on this case."

"So, let me ask you this, Jim. Weren't you worried about walking into an ambush when you entered a village?"

"Well, actually the villages were safer than the mountain paths that connected the villages. The people in the villages knew we were coming a long time before we got there, so there was plenty of time for them to hide the IED stuff and for the bad guys to slip out the back way and hide in the hills until we were gone. And they knew that if they ambushed us in the village there would be a lot of deaths when our reserve forces showed up. So, our most vulnerable spots were on the narrow trails with mountains or cliffs that we had to take between the villages. That was where we usually got ambushed."

"Interesting," Mike replied. "Well, here is another question that I have wondered about. What is the difference between the Taliban and Al Qaeda?"

"That's a good question. Both of them are terrorist organizations with Islamic roots," Jim replied. "The Taliban was started by a group of religious students during the Soviet invasion of Afghanistan. The term Taliban is an Arabic word, meaning 'Student'. We were told that a teacher named Mullah Mohammed Omar and his students were so enraged by an incident of rape and murder of an innocent family traveling to Kandahar that they decided to take action against the men that did it. So, the Taliban was formed on the basis of rage and vengeance. The Taliban believe in a strict interpretation of Islamic laws and that violence is needed to enact it. They are mostly located in Afghanistan and Pakistan."

"Al Qaeda was formed by foreign militants in several places around the Middle East. The basic ideology of Al Qaeda is to establish an Islamic state through the concept of offensive Jihad, which is armed warfare. They want to get rid of socialism and nationalism because they consider these as non-Muslim concepts. Al Qaeda consists mainly of Sunni Muslims who practice Wahhabism, which is considered to be the most extreme and violent form of Islam. When Osama Bin Laden went to Afghanistan to help fight the Soviets, he became the leader of Al Qaeda and it grew much stronger under his leadership. The agenda for Al Qaeda is to go global and eradicate any kind of governance in the world and replace it with the rules of Islam."

"Wow. I'm impressed. So, basically, they are very similar organizations, both wanting change through terrorist activities, with the Taliban mainly present in Afghanistan and Pakistan and Al Qaeda being a global threat?" Mike asked. "That is a pretty good understanding," Jim said. "And what about the new terrorist organization called 'ISIS'? Mike asked.

"I don't know much about them," Jim replied. "I think ISIS stands for the Islamic State of Iraq and Syria, but I'm not sure on that. I believe they used to have close links to Al Qaeda, but in 2014 they had a falling out and Al Qaeda cut all ties with ISIS. And they are known for their brutality and violence. That's about all I know about them at this time," Jim concluded.

"I know this is kind of personal, and I know you don't ever talk about this, but did you ever lose any team members in Afghanistan?" Mike asked.

"We did" Jim replied. "I don't like to talk about it, but I will give you a quick run-down and then we can talk about something else. We lost a few people early on before we really knew what we were doing. They were great guys that gave their lives for their country. We lost the first two soldiers to well-hidden IED's. Shortly after that, we got Big and his dog Buck on our team, and we never lost anyone to another IED. We lost the next two soldiers from small-arms fire when we were ambushed. After that, we requested better air surveillance of the terrain and mountain sides when we had to travel though a mountain pass with steep hills or rugged terrain. We would send in the coordinates of the trail we planned to take and one of the planes in the sky would zero in and look closely for bodies with infrared heat sensing cameras and let us know if the pass was safe to travel."

"So, you could request surveillance of an area before you entered it?" Mike asked.

"Sure," Jim replied. "We got it nearly every time we requested it and it really helped. Several times the 'Eye in the Sky' found bodies hiding in the rocks next to the route we planned to travel. Then they would zoom in to try and make a positive identification as to whether they were bad guys or just goat herders. About half of the time they were bad guys, so when positive identification was made, rockets were sent in a short time later and terminated the bad guys. Then, our team would go in and take photos of the bodies and write the report. We had to do this so the Taliban couldn't lie and say that the Americans killed an innocent family with women and small children in it."

"So, the Taliban would tell lies to turn the locals against you and win them over to their side?" Mike asked.

"In a second," Jim replied. "That's why it was critical for us to get in right away and get photos for the report. We were also looking for letters, maps, laptops, and things like that to turn into Army Intelligence."

"So, what if the 'Eye in the Sky' wasn't flying or was in another area and couldn't get you a report of the terrain?" Mike asked.

"It depended on the mission. We might wait for them, or take another route, or just go slow and anticipate an ambush. Several of our team members had been to 'Sniper' school, so we always had a couple of sniper rifles on the team and we would send a sniper and a spotter on ahead of us to get to high ground and set up overlooking our route. They would get in position and observe the terrain as best they could. When they felt it was clear, they would call us and we would move out. They would provide cover for us during our movement. This was time consuming and still dangerous, but better than going into an area without any surveillance report."

"So, when you were ambushed and the team killed some bad guys, what did you do with their weapons and ammunition?" Mike asked.

"Usually, we would take the weapons with us and blow up the ammunition. In the beginning, we would just break the weapons against rocks and bury the pieces, but they always seemed to find the broken pieces and then they would use the pieces of the weapons in IED's. So, we decided it was better to just carry the weapons with us and turn them in later. Sometimes, if there was a large supply of weapons and ammo, we could get a helicopter to come in and take everything away, but that depended on what choppers were available, the terrain, the risk, etc."

"Did you ever find any good intelligence?" Mike asked.

"Well, they never gave us any feedback after we turned the stuff in, so I really can't answer that."

"So, what scared you the most while you were in Afghanistan?" Mike asked.

"Probably not what you think," Jim replied. "I was the team leader, and my biggest fear was making a mistake and getting someone killed. We were a very close-knit team, and if someone would have been captured or killed because I made a bad decision, I'm not sure how I would have handled that. I realize we were in a combat zone, and all of us could die any day, I just didn't want it to be from something I did wrong. Do you understand what I'm trying to say, Mike?"

"I do," Mike replied. "And I respect you for that. I remember one time on a promotion board I was asked the question, 'What is more important, caring for your people or preparing your people?'"

"Wow. That's a great question. So how did you answer it?" Jim asked.

"I thought about it for a few seconds, and I answered that preparing your people was more important. They asked me why I gave that answer and I said that preparing your people WAS caring for your people, because the better trained and prepared they were for any situation, the better chance they had for success."

"Great answer. Did you get the promotion?" Jim asked.

"Yes, Sir. I was promoted to sergeant," Mike replied.

"Well then Sergeant Mike, why don't you kick back and get a couple hours of sleep so you will be wide awake when you relieve me from driving for a couple of hours?"

"Sounds good to me," Mike said. "Wake me in a couple of hours or when you need a break."

"You got it," Jim said, as Mike reclined the seat and closed his eyes for a nap.

# Chapter 6

Jim enjoyed the drive through northern Minnesota. It was a beautiful day and the scenery was majestic. It was easy to see why they called Minnesota the land of 10,000 lakes. It seemed like there was a lake around every turn and you never went more than a few miles without seeing another lake. The team stayed in contact with each other on their cell phones and they decided to meet up for lunch at a small town a few miles down the road, so Jim woke up Mike. Mike had taken about a two-hour nap and woke up refreshed and hungry.

Dawg and Swede were the first ones at the restaurant and were standing outside waiting for the rest of the team. Jim and Mike joined them outside and stretched while waiting for the others. Wiz and Boom were the next to arrive followed by Big and Shades a few minutes later. Big told Shades to order for him as he wanted to take Kadie for a walk and give her time to go to the bathroom before he joined the team in the restaurant.

The lunch special of fresh walleye was excellent, and the home-made banana cream pie for dessert was just as good. Jim asked the waitress as she was picking up the pie plates, "how far is it to the Canadian border, Miss?"

"About two hours," she replied.

"Thank you," Jim said. "The food was excellent." She smiled and walked away with a stack of dirty pie plates.

Jim spoke up, "I would like everyone to pitch in $100 for our community food fund. Also, I would like everyone to buy a case of beer or a bottle of liquor to take across the border. Only one case of beer or one bottle per person. After we get across the border, we'll stop at a bait shop and buy our fishing licenses. It's about a 4-hour drive from there to Vermillion Bay and I want to get there before dark so we can set up camp. I think we will wait until morning to visit the convenience store, so after setting up camp you guys can do some fishing or go into town or whatever you like. Just remember rule number one, no one goes anywhere alone. If one person goes, someone else goes with him. We are already looking for one of our team members and don't need to be looking for another one. Is everyone clear on that?"

"Clear," was the response.

"Great. Now, when we get to the border, there will be several lines of vehicles waiting to go through customs, so we will not all cross at the same time. I've written down the directions to the bait shop and we'll meet up there." He passed out the directions and commented, "Remember, don't say anything stupid to the customs agents or you could get selected for a random vehicle search and that could hold us up for a couple of hours. Make your calls home before we get to the border and remind your family not to call you in Canada unless it is an emergency."

Everyone gave Jim a hundred dollars and he put the money in an envelope and wrote 'Community Food Fund' on the outside of the envelope. "We will all do the shopping together, so if you see something you like for breakfast or dinner, you can throw it in the shopping cart. Each team will eat lunch on their own and be back at camp for a community dinner."

The scenery on the two-hour drive to the border was filled

with Norway Pine and White Birch trees, with a lake every few miles. "This sure is beautiful country," Jim commented.

"It sure is. Is Canada a lot like this?" Mike asked.

"Somewhat. Only more rugged terrain and more dense forests. One time, one of my buddies and I were going to a neighboring lake to catch some Lake Trout. We took our boat about 18 miles up Canyon Lake, then pulled it ashore and were walking through the forest to get to the other lake. Well, we got into some of the thickest woods you can imagine and lost the trail to the other lake. Sometimes we were only a few feet apart and couldn't see each other. And sometimes the trees were so dense, that they blocked out the sun and it was dark like night time. And the mosquitos were unrelenting. We had to keep moving and waving our arms just to keep them away. When we stopped to talk, or catch our breath, there would be over 100 of them on our face and arms."

"Wow, what happened?" Mike asked.

"Well, we gave up on finding the lake and decided to head back to the boat, but we were lost and couldn't find our way back. My friend was a very religious guy and we stopped, held hands and prayed. We had just finished praying when we heard a train whistle. Railroad tracks run right along Canyon Lake and we headed in the direction of the whistle. Sure enough, we soon found Canyon Lake and our boat. We were tired and sweaty, but thankful to be back. We headed back to our cabin and slept most of the afternoon."

"So, you have already had an eventful experience in Canada and now you're heading back for another one?"

"Well, I'm truly hoping that this one turns out to be 'uneventful'," Jim said. "I would sure like to find Billy alive and unhurt, spend a couple of days fishing, and head back to the U.S. That's what I'm hoping for, but realistically, the chances of that happening are pretty slim. Even if Billy found out Angela was cheating on him or something like that, he wouldn't just leave and not come home. He loves his parents too much to put them through this. We really need to find out what happened to him."

The team got through customs without any trouble and met up at the bait shop. The bait shop was busy as always, so they had some time to do some shopping and put Billy's 'Missing' poster on the bulletin board. They were ready to head for Vermillion Bay after about 30 minutes and met outside by their vehicles. Jim gave a quick safety briefing before they left.

"I know all of you are safe drivers, but be extra careful for moose, bears, falling rocks, narrow roads, and people trying to pass in non-passing zones. Let's all stick together, but leave plenty of room between your vehicle and the vehicle in front of you. We have about a four-hour drive to Vermillion Bay, but will make a pit stop in about 2 hours. Any questions?"

"Yeah, I have one," Dawg said. "What did I do to get stuck with Swede? He's been farting like a pack mule ever since we left the ranch."

Everyone was laughing as Swede spoke up, "I probably shouldn't have eaten that double order of onion rings last night at the steakhouse."

"So, Swede," Wiz said, "You can eat lutefisk all day long and it doesn't bother you a bit, but onion rings make you fart?"

"Yeah, my stomach has never been able to handle onions," Swede replied.

"You knew this and still ate two orders of home-made onion rings?" Dawg asked.

"I said my stomach can't handle them, I didn't say I don't like them."

Everyone was laughing as Jim said, "Just be thankful it's nice outside and you can leave the windows rolled down."

"And that is the only reason Swede isn't riding in the pickup box," Dawg commented.

"Swede, you do remember that Dawg is known for paybacks," Jim said.

"Oh crap," Swede replied.

"You better sleep with one eye open," Wiz said as everyone laughed out loud. Dawg just looked at Swede and smiled.

"Alright," Jim said. "Time to go. Mike and I will lead since I know the route." Everyone got into their vehicles and followed Jim as he pulled out and headed north.

After a few minutes of driving, Mike said, "Dawg sure is a character, isn't he?"

"That is putting it mildly," Jim replied.

"You probably have a lot of good stories about him, don't you?"

"You can say that again," Jim replied.

"Can you share one or two of them with me?"

"Sure," Jim replied. "One time in Afghanistan our team was assigned to help train the Afghanistan National Army or A.N.A. President Obama wanted to build up the A.N.A. as quickly as possible, so the A.N.A. could provide security and the U.S. could pull its military forces out of Afghanistan. Well, in an attempt to quickly build up the A.N.A., the vetting process, which is the background check of the Afghan men joining the army, wasn't getting done properly. In Afghanistan, you can't go to a computer and run a background check on a person like you can in the U.S. When an Afghan man volunteered to join the A.N.A., they would send someone to his village to talk to the village leader or one of the elders about the man to find out if he was associated with the Taliban or Al-Qaeda. If the report that came back said he was a good man and not associated with either of these terrorist organizations, the man would be allowed to join the A.N.A. Well, a lot of village leaders lied about the men, so many bad people were allowed to join the Afghan army."

"I think I saw a report on '60 Minutes' on that very subject," Mike said.

"You probably did," Jim replied. "Because after a bunch of these 'bad guys' were allowed to infiltrate the Afghan army, they started turning against the NATO forces that were training them and killed a lot of good soldiers. These attacks were called 'Green on Blue' or 'Insider Attacks', and for a while, these 'Insider Attacks' were killing more NATO forces than IED's or ambushes."

"That is unreal," Mike said.

"They actually stopped training for a few weeks until they could do a more thorough background check on some of the Afghan soldiers, but some documents had been falsified, so many of the soldiers passed the background check and were allowed to stay in the army and when the training started up again, so did the attacks."

"Wow," Mike said. "So, our soldiers were getting killed by the Afghanistan soldiers that they were training?"

"They sure were. At first, most of the killings happened on the ranges after they were given live ammunition. One minute, the Afghan trainees would be firing at targets, and the next minute they would turn and open fire on the instructors or range safety personnel. We then reduced the number of instructors and range safety personnel on the ranges and started putting a sniper in the range towers overlooking everyone on the range. The few instructors on the range wore body armor and carried a loaded M4 rifle to defend themselves."

"Did that end the attacks?" Mike asked.

"Well, it slowed them down for a short time, but then they

came up with a new tactic," Jim replied. "We only gave them live ammunition when they were on the firing range, the rest of the time they carried their weapons, but without any ammunition. Well, they started stealing ammo from the ranges or sneaking it into camp, because the attacks started coming at any time of the day or night, not just when they were on the ranges."

"So, you had to be alert anytime they were carrying a weapon?" Mike commented.

"That's right," Jim said. "And that was nearly all of the time."

"And what did you do?" Mike asked.

"We had them go through a metal detector several times a day, we didn't let them have a magazine in their weapons and all weapons had their bolts locked to the rear so we could see they didn't have a round chambered."

"Did that help," Mike asked.

"It helped reduce the attacks, but it didn't stop them. The people doing the vetting process needed to do a better job on background checks and stop letting terrorists join the A.N.A."

"So, did they do it?" Mike asked.

"Finally, after many innocent soldiers died from these attacks someone way up the ladder said, 'Enough is enough' and they started doing a better job with background checks. The bad news was that by the time they got fed up with the attacks, the A.N.A. was at around 300,000 soldiers and many bad guys had already joined. So, they had to go back and start doing background checks on the soldiers that were already in the A.N.A. and it was a real mess."

"So, how does Dawg tie into all of this?" Mike asked.

"Well," Jim said, "As Dawg was training the A.N.A. soldiers, he noticed one of them was very secluded and acting strange. Dawg started watching this guy very closely and got the interpreter to talk to him and see if he was okay. The interpreter said he was just a quiet person but Dawg had a gut feeling that this guy really hated Americans and was just looking for the opportunity to kill as many infidels as he could. Well, Dawg decided to come up with a plan to test the man's loyalty. One night he took a bunch of ammunition apart, poured out the gunpowder and replaced it with sand. He put the ammo back together so you couldn't tell it was a dummy round. He then filled a magazine with these dummy rounds and put it in his M4 rifle."

"Later, he stopped the Afghan soldier and told him he was chosen to go on a midnight ambush and kill some Taliban soldiers up in the mountains. He told the soldier to be ready to go in 15 minutes and said he would get him some ammunition before they left the compound. Dawg then said, "Why don't you take mine now and I will get some more ammo before we leave," as he pulled the magazine of dummy ammo out of his M4 and gave it to the soldier."

"What happened then?" Mike asked.

"Well, as you can imagine, the soldier loaded the magazine into his rifle as Dawg was starting to walk away. Dawg heard him say something and stopped and turned around. The soldier was pointing his weapon at Dawg and had a smile on his face. He said some words in Dari and pulled the trigger. Nothing happened. He ejected the round and chambered another one. He again pointed the weapon at Dawg and pulled the trigger. Again, nothing happened. Dawg had been right about this guy and instead of pulling his pistol on the man, he ran at him and tackled him like an angry Dick Butkas. He then broke a few bones in the soldier's body before security showed up and took the soldier to the stockade."

"Wow," Mike said. "So, did the other A.N.A. soldiers believe the story when Dawg told them what happened?" Mike asked.

"Well, Dawg thought the Afghan soldier would turn on him like he did, so he had an interpreter and an American soldier hiding behind some fuel barrels and watching the whole encounter, giving him two witnesses to verify exactly what happened."

"So, Dawgs instincts probably saved the lives of several American soldiers," Mike said.

"You got it," Jim answered. "A lot of soldiers are alive today because of something Dawg did at one time or another in his military career."

"Amazing," Mike said. "I've only known the guy for two days and already have a lot of respect for him."

"That's good," Jim answered. "He deserves every bit of it."

The team stopped at a convenience store after about two hours of driving. Everyone had filled their vehicles with gas in the U.S. before they crossed the border, so it was just a stretch and pee break. Big threw a tennis ball for Kadie to retrieve a few times and they were back on the road within 15 minutes. Wiz had located a campground within ten miles of Vermillion Bay and they were going to try it for at least one night and see if they liked it. They really only had two main conditions for the campground; close to Vermillion Bay and not too crowded. They wanted some privacy for their nightly meetings.

Jim and Mike were in the lead vehicle. They were talking about the annual Iowa – Iowa State football game coming up in a couple of months. Mike was a Hawkeye fan and Jim a Cyclone fan and they always liked talking about the 'Big' game. One of Jim's friends from Northwest Iowa had a son that was going to be a starting linebacker for the Hawkeyes this year and Jim planned to watch every Hawkeye game just to see Traver play.

"So, do you cheer for the Hawkeyes as long as they aren't playing the Cyclones?" Mike asked.

"I do now, since Traver went to Iowa. Before that, my two favorite teams were the Cyclones and the team playing the Hawkeyes," Jim said with a smile.

"Ha – ha. You're funny, Jim," Mike replied.

Do you remember a guy by the name of Bryce Paup?" Jim asked.

"I sure do," Mike said. "I remember him playing at the University of Northern Iowa before he went to the NFL. He was a great linebacker."

"Well," Jim said, "Traver is a lot like Bryce in my opinion. I was in the military with Bryce's brother and he used to give us updates on Bryce. Bryce played football at Scranton, Iowa and went to UNI after he graduated from high school. He was a great player at UNI and was later drafted by the Packers. He was a very good player in college, but really became a stud in the pros. He was selected to the Pro-Bowl four times and in 1995 was named the NFL's Defensive Player of the Year. I know Traver has a good head on his shoulders, is very athletic, and has a great work-ethic. I think the only thing that will keep him from playing pro-ball would be a career-ending injury."

"Hey, now we can watch Hawkeye games together and both be pulling for the Hawks," Mike said.

"As long as Traver is in a Hawkeye uniform and they aren't playing the Cyclones," Jim said.

"What about after Traver graduates?" Mike asked. "Then I'll probably be a fan of whatever NFL team drafts him," Jim said.

"But will you still be a Hawkeye fan?" Mike asked.

"I'm not a Hawkeye fan now," Jim said. "I'm a big fan of Traver Silverstein. There's a big difference."

"You're right," Mike said. "So, are you still going to bet me a case of beer that the Cyclones win the big game?"

"Of course," Jim said. "You can consider that an annual bet."

"Then don't forget that I drink Bud Light," Mike commented.

"Now you're the funny guy," Jim said as they both laughed out loud.

After a few minutes of quiet, Mike spoke up, "I would like to know more about Billy. What else can you tell me about him?"

"Well," Jim said, "Billy was a great guy. He and I were battle buddies or team members on several missions, like you and I are now. I've never known a man with more integrity than Billy. Maybe it's part of the Indian culture, but he always told the truth. For example, a woman wouldn't want to ask him if the dress she had on made her butt look big, because Billy was going to give her an honest answer. If someone asked him a question that he didn't want to answer, he might say that it was personal and he didn't care to answer the question, but he would never say something that wasn't true."

"He was a little on the quiet side, but would speak when he needed to. He was a great listener, and had a great memory. I would often take him with me to meetings to help me remember what was said. He loved nature, and he loved animals, but most of all he loved his family. He was proud of his Indian heritage and spent a lot of his free time reading about it. He could talk for hours about Chief Crazy Horse, Sitting Bull, and some of the other great Indian Chiefs. He hated how the government had taken Indian land and put them on a reservation. He read a great deal about General George Armstrong Custer and how his over-confidence and poor leadership decisions lead to the massacre of his soldiers. He would eagerly volunteer to take the point on our patrols saying that since he was part Indian, he could see and hear better than the rest of us. He probably could, but I believe he took the point because he wasn't afraid to die and didn't want any of us to get hurt."

"Everyone on the team loved him like a brother. He had a

girlfriend back home when he graduated from high school, but she dumped him when he joined the army and I don't think he ever found anyone again until he met Angela. I think those two would have made a great couple and it will be heartbreaking if something awful has happened to Billy and they don't have an opportunity to get married and start a life together."

Jim was a little choked up and paused a moment. Then he said, "You heard Billy's dad say that they believe his spirit won't get to the afterlife until the burial ritual is performed, so if we don't find him, his dad and mom are going to spend the rest of their lives in Canada looking for Billy's body. Now I ask you, is that love or what?"

"That is true love," Mike replied.

# Chapter 7

When they got close to their campsite, Jim pulled into a grocery store to purchase food and drinks for the next few days. Big put Kadie on a leash and took her for a walk as the rest of the team joined Jim in the grocery store. They were walking down the aisles and filling the shopping cart when Swede spoke up, "Hey Dawg, what kind of dog food do you prefer, canned or crunchy?"

Dawg smiled and replied, "Which elbow would you rather have dis-located, your right one or your left one?"

The team laughed as Jim said, "Swede, since you brought it up, can you run outside and ask Big if he needs dog food for Kadie?"

"No problem," Swede said as he headed for the door. He was back in a few minutes and said Big had brought enough dog food with him and wouldn't need any for about two weeks. The team finished shopping, paid for the groceries and headed for the campground.

They pulled into the campground at 7:15 P.M. It wasn't crowded at all, so they found an isolated spot on the edge of the campground that was next to the lake. Everyone brought their own tent so they didn't have to share with someone else who snored or farted like Swede. After the tents were pitched, some of the guys grabbed their fishing poles and headed for the lake. They bought a lot of sandwich meat and chips at the grocery store, so everyone was on their own for making a sandwich for dinner. Jim and Mike got a fire going in the designated fire pit and set up the lawn chairs around the camp fire.

The guys got back from fishing around 8:30 with several nice walleyes. They cleaned them in the cleaning shack and put them in the cooler for the next night's dinner. After telling fish stories for a few minutes, Jim decided it was time to talk business.

"Mike and I introduced ourselves to the other campers while you guys were fishing. None of them were camping here when Billy disappeared and didn't recognize his photo. The wife of the camper in that small Airstream camper right over there said she stays in the camp ground during the day while her husband goes fishing, and she is going to keep an eye on our tents while we are gone. She does go for a walk every morning and takes a nap in the afternoon, and she can't watch them all the time, so don't leave any valuables in your tents when you leave in the morning."

Jim continued, "Now if we haven't found Billy in a week, I may ask Doc to come up next week so we can leave one person at the campsite during the day while the rest of us are conducting the search. That way we won't have to pack up and take everything with us in the morning and someone will always be here in camp. We can trade off so everyone gets a chance to spend one day in camp. That person will be able to do some fishing during the day as long as he can keep the tents in eye sight, and will have dinner started when we all get back to camp for our nightly meeting."

"That sounds good to me," Dawg said. "Besides, I would like to see old Doc and find out what he's been up to."

"You need to see a doc," Wiz commented.

Everyone laughed as Dawg spoke up, "Well, you need to take a bath, so choose your next words carefully or you just might end up in the lake."

"You'll have to catch me first," Wiz said. Dawg looked at Wiz for a few seconds, started growling, then jumped up from his lawn chair as Wiz took off on a dead run.

"Where are you going?" Dawg yelled at Wiz. "I'm just getting up to pee." Everyone was laughing as Dawg walked over to a tree, unzipped his pants, turned sideways, lifted his leg closest to the tree and started peeing on the tree just like a male dog would do.

"Now I know where he got the name 'Dawg'," Mike commented.

"Bad Dawg," Jim said as everyone was laughing out loud. "It's a good thing it's dark outside or someone might call in and report you for indecent exposure. Now you two knock it off and get back here so we can discuss the mission."

They both returned and high-fived each other before sitting down. Jim passed out the maps he had made back in the U.S. He divided each map into four parts and each team was assigned to cover the area in their sector. Then he pulled out some new 'Missing' posters that the team hadn't seen yet. Jim spoke as he was passing out the posters, "These new posters are a little different than the other ones you got earlier. They have a 'Reward' on the bottom of them. Billy's parents thought people would be more eager to give us information if they were going to get compensated for it. His parents don't have a lot of money, but they have put up a $10,000 reward for information that helps us find Billy. Also, there is a photo of his jeep and his dog, Kota, on the poster. Someone might not remember seeing Billy, but they may remember seeing the jeep or the dog. So, when someone gives you information about Billy, you will need to get their name, address and phone number so we can contact them later if their information leads to us finding Billy. Is everyone clear on that?"

"Clear," was everyone's response.

"Also," Jim said, "make sure you keep track of every place you stop. Write down the name of the place, the name of the person or persons that you spoke with if you get a name, and if you were allowed to place a 'Missing' poster at the location. Any questions?" Hearing nothing, Jim said, "I know some of you will want to work out in the morning before you head out, and others may want to do some fishing, so you are on your own as to when you leave camp each morning, but everyone try to be back around 1800 hours every night so we can brief on what we found and our plans for the next day. Now, if everyone has a beer, I'd like to make a toast. Everyone raised their beers as Jim said, "To a successful hunt."

"To a successful hunt," everyone replied and took a drink of their beer.

"Now, if no one has any questions or comments, I'm going to turn in for the night," Jim said. Hearing nothing, Jim said, "Good night everyone."

"Good night, Jim," was the response.

# Chapter 8

Mike woke at 6:00 Sunday morning and stepped out of his tent. The picnic table had fresh fruit, yogurt, cereal, milk and orange juice on it and Jim was making a pot of coffee on the camp fire.

"Good morning, Grim Dawg," Jim said to Mike.

"How did you know my old nickname was Grim Dawg?" Mike asked.

"I think Karen told me that once," Jim said. "I didn't tell the others since we already have one 'Dawg' in the group. The coffee will be ready in about two minutes."

"That gives me just enough time to bleed the weasel," Mike commented.

"Don't forget to wash your hands," Jim said.

"Yes, Mom," Mike said as he was quick-stepping towards the men's restroom.

Mike returned in a couple of minutes and Jim handed him a cup of coffee. Mike took a long drink and said, "not exactly Rich's Brew quality, is it?" Jim gave Mike a dirty look and Mike quickly said, "But still very good coffee."

Jim smiled and said, "Thanks for the nice compliment."

"You are very welcome," Mike replied. "So, are we the first two up?" Mike asked.

"Not hardly," Jim replied. "You were the last one up. The rest of the team is either fishing or jogging. They should all be back within the 30 minutes."

"Wow," Mike said. "I get up at zero six hundred hours and I'm the last guy up?"

"That is correct," Jim said. "I think everyone turned in early last night and got some good sleep. I don't think all of them will be up this early every morning, because I think some of them will try fishing at night and some of them will eventually have a drinking contest around the camp fire, so you could very well be the first one up one of these mornings."

"Hey, I wouldn't mind trying some night fishing also, and I never pass up a drinking contest," Mike said.

"Well, then you may be the last one up every morning," Jim said with a laugh.

"So, what is our game plan for today?" Mike asked.

"We are going to the convenience store first, since that is the last known location we know for sure that Billy was at. We will find out all we can there, then we will visit all of the gas stations, bait shops, grocery stores, restaurant, bars, souvenir shops, etc. in Vermillion Bay and see if anyone recognizes Billy's photo and can give us some information about him."

"What time do you want to leave?" Mike asked.

"Let's shoot for seven," Jim said. "You probably should go shower now before everyone gets back and uses up all of the hot water."

"Did you shower already?" Mike asked.

"I did," Jim replied. "And there was plenty of hot water, but I don't know how big the hot water heater is in the shower house, and I wouldn't take a chance on it."

"So, what if I use up all the hot water and the rest of the guys get cold showers?" Mike asked.

"No offense Mike, but they are tougher than you and I don't think cold showers will bother them as much as it would bother you. Besides, they can go for a quick swim in the lake if the hot water runs out."

"A swim this early in the morning?" Are some of the guys Navy Seals?" Mike asked.

"No, just tough guys," Jim replied.

"Dawg thought about going to Seal training and I have no doubt he was tough enough to make it through, but he wasn't a great swimmer and really didn't like the water that much, so he stayed in the Army. He went through Ranger school at Fort Benning and later entered the 'Best Ranger' competition. It's an annual competition of two man 'Buddy' teams that compete against each other for the coveted title of 'Best Ranger'. Have you heard of it?" Jim asked.

"I have heard of it, but really don't know anything about it. Tell me more."

"Okay," Jim said. "Best Ranger competition is a grueling, 3-day event that is designed to place extreme demands on the team's physical, mental and technical abilities. These guys are the toughest of the tough, and the attrition rate is usually around 60 percent, so only four out of ten of these tough guys even make it through the course. The teams get very little rest between events, so endurance plays a big part in the competition also. They get points for each event, and in the end, the team with the most points wins the completion."

"So, what are some of the events?" Mike asked.

"Well, I was stationed at Fort Benning one year when they had the completion and watched the teams compete for several hours on Saturday and Sunday. Some of the events I can remember were; the buddy run, parachute jump, road march, grenade assault course, rifle range competition shoot, obstacle course, night land navigation, night obstacle course and water obstacle course. I know there were more events than that, but that's all I can think of at this time."

"So how did Dawg do?" Mike asked with great enthusiasm.

"Well, Dawg and his partner were leading the competition with only a couple of events left when his partner fell and broke his leg. Dawg tried to carry him, but it was a bad break and the guy needed medical attention, so they had to drop out of the competition. Dawg was recognized as having the highest point total ever after completing 95 percent of the events, but he didn't get the coveted 'Best Ranger' title like he wanted.

"Wow!!!!" Mike said. "So, it's probably not a good idea to pick a fight with Dawg?"

"Not unless you want your butt kicked," Jim replied. "After a couple of guys on our team were killed, we soon realized that there is no second place in combat. You win, or you die. It's that simple. So, when we weren't on a mission, we trained very, very hard and always took our assignments seriously. I'm sure you know who Dan Gable is?"

"Of course," Mike said. "What a great wrestler and coach."

"Well, I remember watching Dan Gable wrestle at Iowa State when I was a young boy. He was undefeated throughout his college career, until his last match at the NCAA finals. He ended his collegiate career with a 118-1 record. That final loss motivated him even more and at the 1972 Olympics, he won the Gold medal without giving up a single point to any of his opponents."

"Wow... are you serious?" Mike asked.

"That is a fact," Jim said. "I have read articles from coaches and other wrestlers that said Gable was the hardest working person they have ever known. They say he worked so hard at practice and pushed himself so long that occasionally someone would have to carry him off of the mat because he was totally exhausted. Well, Dawg was a lot like Dan Gable as far as work ethic and always giving 100 percent. Very, very few people have a commitment to exceed like those two people. I'm really glad Dawg was able to come with us, because the team looks up to him so much and we always feel safer when he is around. Well, I see some of the runners coming back now, so you better go shower before they get here."

"Will do," Mike said as he grabbed his towel and shaving kit and headed for the men's shower room.

Dawg, Swede, Big and Shades were the four guys that went running, while Wiz and Boom decided to go fishing. The four runners finished running about 100 yards from the camp site and were walking towards camp. Wiz hollered to them from over at the edge of the lake and held up a stringer with four nice walleyes on it. All four of them turned and walked towards the lake to see the fish. After a couple minutes of fish stories, all six of them headed for camp. As they got closer to camp, Jim said, "Hey, those are some nice walleyes. Who caught them and what were you using?"

"Boom said, "Wiz and I each caught two using crank baits. I had another couple of hits, but missed them. We're going to go clean them after we get a cup of coffee."

"Great," Jim replied. "There is fresh fruit and yogurt on the picnic table if you are hungry."

"Swede and I are going to stop at the first choke and puke we see and get some pancakes and eggs," Dawg said.

"We are?" Swede asked.

"Yeah, we are," Dawg said. "I'm driving."

"Well, I'm glad you told me before I filled up on healthy food," Swede said as everyone laughed.

Wiz and Boom got some coffee and headed for the fish

cleaning shack. Big and Shades sat down to eat and Dawg and Swede grabbed some clean clothes and their shaving kits and headed for the shower room.

Mike got back from his shower and grabbed another coffee and some yogurt. The others returned in a few minutes and everyone was gathered around the picnic table. "The first team back needs to get the fire started," Jim said. "I will leave a tablet of paper on the picnic table for a grocery list. If you think of something you want to eat or drink, write it down on the list and Mike and I will pick it up before we return to camp each day."

"We need more beer," Dawg said.

"Come on, Dawg," Jim replied. "We brought 6 cases of beer and two bottles of liquor with us across the border. Unless someone stole it during the night, we should have plenty of alcohol."

"It's just that I would sure hate to run out of beer during a drinking contest," Dawg said.

"I don't think that is going to happen for at least a few days," Jim replied. "But if beer is on sale when we stop for groceries, we will pick up a couple more cases."

"And how about some schnapps or whiskey?" Swede added.

"You are on your own for the hard stuff. I'm not going to spend all of our community grocery money on booze," Jim said.

"I figured that's what you would say," Swede said. "But I had to ask."

"Okay," Jim said. "Call me if you get some 'hot' information, otherwise we will discuss what everyone found out tonight at our MUM. Let's roll, Mike."

They climbed into Jim's pickup and headed out of the camp ground as Mike spoke up, "What the hell is a MUM?"

"Mission Update Meeting," Jim replied. "In Afghanistan, we usually referred to our meetings as a 'BOB' for battle operations briefing, or 'BUB' for battle update briefing, but since we are on a mission and not in a combat zone, we will be using MUM while we are up here."

"Cool," Mike said. "I have always loved the way the military uses acronyms. I just want you to know that I'm going to have to 'TAD' before too long."

"Now what is 'TAD'," Jim asked.

"Take A Dump," Mike said.

"Got it," Jim said with a laugh. "Our first stop is the convenience store in Vermillion Bay. Can you wait that long?"

"I sure hope so," Mike said with a smile on his face.

They arrived at the convenience store after about a 10-minute drive. Jim pulled up to the gas pump as Mike jumped out and headed for the 'Men's' room. After filling with gas, Jim went inside and started talking to the convenience store employees. He showed them the reward poster and explained that Billy used his credit card in their store on Sunday, June 3rd. None of the employees remembered Billy even after looking at the photo. Jim got permission to hang the poster up in the store and said to make sure to call his phone number on the poster if anyone recognizes him or remembers anything about him. They agreed, and Jim and Mike left the convenience store and headed for the other businesses in town.

They stopped at three grocery stores, three gas stations, two restaurants, two bait & tackle shops, two souvenir stores, two bars and the city hall. They spoke with as many people as they could, but no one remembered seeing Billy. They put up several 'Reward' posters and Jim circled his phone number as the primary number to call. They hoped to get a call from someone that remembered seeing or talking to Billy. It was now lunch time, so they ate lunch in a local restaurant and showed the poster to everyone in the restaurant, but still no luck.

They spent the afternoon driving to resorts around Vermillion Bay and talking to the resort employees. Again, no luck. They asked where someone might pitch a tent and go camping around there and were told of a few camp grounds besides the one where they were staying. They marked them on the map to check out the following day. It was now time to head back to camp for the daily MUM.

They were the first ones back at the camp site, and Jim got out the turkey fryer and propane tank for cooking the walleye.

"What can I do to help?" Mike asked.

"Why don't you grab your fishing pole and go down to the lake and try to catch a couple more walleye for dinner," Jim said.

"Now that is one mission I have been looking forward to," Mike said as he grabbed his pole and headed for the lake.

The teams started showing up a few minutes later and everyone was back by 6 P.M. Jim hollered at Mike to come back and Mike returned with two nice walleyes on a stringer.

"Nice fish," Big said to Mike.

"Thanks," Mike replied. "I think we could catch some bigger ones if we had a boat."

"Hey, Doc has a boat," Dawg said excitedly. "If he is going to come up next week, he might as well bring his boat with him."

"Great idea. If we need him, I'll ask him to bring his boat along and see what he says," Jim commented.

"Sounds good," Dawg said. "I'll go help Mike clean these two and we'll be back in a few minutes."

"Make it quick," Big said. "I'm getting hungry."

"You're always hungry," Dawg said. "Your nickname should have been 'Hungry'."

Everyone was laughing as Mike and Dawg headed to the fish cleaning shack. The guys all chipped in cutting the walleye fillets into chunks, dipping them in eggs and then into the breading. The bowl was nearly full of breaded walleye when Mike and Dawg returned.

"Those two will make sure we have plenty of walleye for everyone," Jim said.

"I'm hoping we don't eat everything we cook tonight," Big said. "I'm looking forward to a cold walleye sandwich for breakfast tomorrow morning."

"Then don't eat six helpings for dinner tonight and you will have some left over for breakfast tomorrow morning," Dawg said.

"Wow. That is Brilliant. How did someone like you think of that?" Big asked.

"You better sleep with one eye open tonight," Dawg said, "If you don't want to end up in the lake."

Everyone was laughing as Jim spoke, "Okay guys, the oil is hot. Let's start cooking fish." After the cooking was finished, Wiz said a prayer and they all sat down to eat. The meal consisted of walleye, veggies, chips and beer.

"Wow, this walleye is delicious," Mike said. "Now I see why you guys come up to Canada fishing every year."

"Well, the walleye is one part of it," Jim said. "But mainly we come up for the camaraderie, the beautiful country, the fresh air, and just to get a break from the things that stress us out back home."

"And..." Swede commented, "I really enjoy the fact that I can grab another beer without my wife saying, 'Do you really think you need another beer?'" Everyone laughed.

After the meal was over, they cleaned up and got a campfire going for the meeting. They sat around the campfire and each team got to brief on their findings. Each team gave the same report that no one recognized the photo or remembered seeing or talking to Billy.

"Well," Jim said. "That is disappointing, but it was only the first day. I'm surprised no one remembers his jeep or Kota. You don't see an Alaskan Malamute that looks like a wolf every day. You think someone would remember seeing the dog. Between all of us, we did talk to a lot of people and put up lots of posters, so hopefully someone will see a poster and remember something and give us a call. Maybe tomorrow will be a better day. Anybody else have something to say?"

Hearing nothing, Jim said, "Okay, since we need more walleye for dinner tomorrow night, I suggest we do some fishing before it gets dark and get some more fish in the cooler."

"Hooah," Dawg said with a first sergeant voice as everyone agreed and went to grab their fishing poles. It was about 30 minutes before dark and the fish were biting. They caught enough walleye for another meal, then cleaned the fish and drank a few beers around the camp fire before heading into their tents for some shut-eye.

# Chapter 9

Monday morning started out about the same as the day before. Some of the guys went for a run while others went fishing. A couple of guys tried a cold walleye sandwich and really liked it. Big ate three of them and might have eaten a fourth one if they hadn't run out of walleye. The teams had all left the campsite by zero seven thirty.

Jim and Mike stopped at several resorts and a couple of small towns in their sector, but no luck. They put up several 'Missing' posters and hoped they would get a phone call in the next day or two. Wiz and Boom finished up visiting all of the businesses in a small town and stopped at a resort after eating lunch. The resort owner came out of the office and greeted them. "Good afternoon, gentlemen. Can I help you with something?"

"Hello, Sir," Wiz said. "Are you the owner of this resort?"

"I am," he said. "My name is Sam Williams."

"Nice to meet you Mr. Williams. I'm John Jamison and this is my friend Fred Fiddelke." They shook hands as Wiz continued. "A good friend of ours is missing and we are trying to find him. Could you take a look at the photo and see if you recognize him?"

Wiz handed the missing poster to Sam and he immediately said, "Yes, this man was here. He rented a boat and trailer from me. My grand-daughter is spending the summer with us and she fell in love with his dog." He turned around and yelled, "Missy, can you come here for a minute?"

Missy was there in a matter of seconds. "What is it, Grandpa?" she said.

"These men are looking for their friend. Take a look at the poster and tell them what you know."

He handed Missy the poster and right away she said, "That's Billy and Kota. Are they all right?"

"We sure hope so," Wiz said. "So, you remember them?"

"I sure do. Billy was so nice to me and Kota was the sweetest dog I have ever met. I have photos of them on my phone. I'll show you." She pulled up the photos she had and showed them to Wiz and Boom.

"Great photos," Wiz said. "Do you know where they were going to camp or go fishing?"

"No, we never talked about that. I played with Kota while Billy talked to grandpa. When it was time for them to leave, Billy told me I had a kind heart and gave me this necklace." She pulled the necklace out from under her T-shirt and showed it to them. "I didn't want them to leave, but Billy said I could play with Kota again when he returned the boat and trailer. I was really looking forward to seeing them again, so when the two foreigners showed up to return the boat and trailer, I was really sad. I sure hope Billy and Kota are all right."

Wiz and Boom immediately picked up on the two foreigners returning the boat and trailer but didn't want to say anything with Missy present so Wiz replied, "I'm sure they are fine. Probably just having so much fun up here that they forgot to come home."

Just then, Missy's grandma yelled for her. "Better go see what your grandma wants," Sam said.

"Okay grandpa," she said. "Good luck finding Billy and Kota. I'll keep them in my prayers," she said as she turned and ran to find her grandma.

"You sure have a nice grand-daughter there, Sam," Boom said.

"Yes, thank you," Sam said. "She is really special."

"So, two foreigners returned the boat and trailer.

"Yes. They were driving his jeep and said they were returning the boat and trailer for him. I asked where he was and they said he was fishing."

"Did you by chance get their names?" Boom asked.

"No, but one of the guys signed the bill. I told him I would make him a copy and he said he was in a hurry and had to go. I have the bill inside, but I remember that the fellow just scribbled a signature and there is no way you can make out a name from it."

"I would like to get a copy of the bill before we leave," Boom said.

"Not a problem," the resort owner replied.

"Do you remember what these two guys looked like?" Wiz asked.

"Yeah, I remember they were little guys with dark complexions. And they didn't speak English very well either," Sam replied. "When Missy saw the jeep, she came on the run to see Kota, but Billy and Kota weren't with them. She asked about Kota and one of the men shrugged his shoulders like he didn't have any idea what she was talking about. She finally said, 'the dog. Where is the dog?' The man just shrugged his shoulder again and walked away from her. She got out her camera to take a photo of the men, but they didn't want to be in any photos and quickly turned their heads and got into the jeep and drove away."

"Did you recognize their accent?"

"No, but I would guess it was a middle-east accent. I could tell English wasn't their primary language."

"Anything else you can remember about them?" Wiz asked.

"They looked out of place to me," the owner replied. "They didn't look like your typical fishing people that we usually get around here. They had on nice clothes and fancy sandals and they were in a big hurry. They just wanted to drop off the boat and trailer and get on their way."

"But they were driving Billy's jeep?" Wiz asked.

"Well, I don't know who the jeep belonged to, but it was the same vehicle that your friend Billy was driving when he rented the boat and trailer. I always write down the vehicle license number before I rent something out and it was the same vehicle."

"Did anyone say where they were camping or where they were fishing?" Wiz asked.

"Well, your friend Billy asked me some questions about Canyon Lake, but that's it. He didn't say where he was camping or anything like that. He just asked me if Canyon Lake was a good Muskie lake and where the boat dock was located."

"Anything else you can think of?" Boom asked.

"Not right now," Sam said. "I talked with Billy for a few minutes while Missy was playing with Kota, but we mainly just talked about fishing. He asked about this lake and I told him it was a good Northern lake, but there were better walleye lakes around than this one."

"Well, thank you for your help. I would like a copy of the bill and I also need your contact information for the reward money," Wiz said. "And, I would like to talk to your grand-daughter one more time if that is all right with you?"

"I'll get you a copy of the bill and have Missy come back out to see you. My contact information is on the bill. Let me know if I can be of any further assistance."

"Please call the number on the poster if you think of anything else," Wiz said. "We may be back later if one of the other guys thinks of something he wants to ask you."

"No problem," the owner said as he went into the office. Missy came out and Wiz asked her if she still had the photo of the men that brought the boat and trailer back. She looked on her phone and found the photo. You couldn't see the men's faces, only their profiles and the clothes they were wearing. Wiz asked her to send him the photo and gave her his cell phone number. She did and Wiz had the photo on his cell phone in a matter of seconds.

Just as the download was complete, Sam returned from the office. "My copy machine is not very good, so I'm giving you the original as it may be easier to read," the owner said.

"That's great. Thanks again. You have been very helpful," Wiz said. "And we will be glad to bring you the reward money if your information helps us find Billy."

"Glad to help. Good luck finding your friend," Sam replied.

They shook hands and Wiz and Boom got into their vehicle and drove away. They hit a couple more resorts on the way back to camp, but no luck at either one of them. They were the first ones back at camp, so they got a fire going and started cutting up the walleye fillets. The rest of the team showed up a few minutes later. Wiz and Boom didn't say anything to the others as they arrived, because they knew Jim liked everyone getting the information at the same time, so they told Jim they had some good information and wanted to hold the meeting before they started cooking dinner. Jim agreed and everyone got their notepads and gathered around the camp fire.

Wiz and Boom went first and told everything they learned from the resort owner and his grand-daughter. The team was really excited at first, but their mood changed when they heard about the foreigners bringing the boat and trailer back. Wiz had downloaded the photo from his phone to his laptop and passed his laptop around so everyone could look at the photo of the two men.

"Look at the photo closely," Jim said, "And comment if you see anything that might be of help to us."

Dawg was the first to look at the photo and said, "The fellow on the right is wearing a multi-colored shirt that would be easy to identify, and both of them are wearing sandals. My guess is that they are about five feet seven inches tall and weigh about 150 pounds." He passed the laptop to Swede.

Everyone looked at the photo and made a few comments, but without seeing the men's faces, they knew positive identification would be difficult. "Do you think the resort owner or his grand-daughter would be able to recognize the men if they saw them again?" Swede asked.

"I didn't ask them, but my guess is that they could," Wiz said. "We know the men have Billy's jeep, so that should be our main focus."

"Good point," Jim said. "Billy and Kota could be dead and buried, or at the bottom of a lake, but we know these foreigners have Billy's jeep, or at least had it when they returned the boat and trailer."

"Something smells fishy to me," Dawg said. "And I'm not talking about Swede's fingers, either."

Everyone chuckled, but the mood was too serious for any humor. Dawg continued. "Billy does several years in Afghanistan looking for bad guys, lives through numerous fire-fights, mortar attacks, ambushes, etc., and then just happens to run into a couple of terrorists in Canada, on a fishing trip by himself. It just doesn't sound right to me."

"Okay," Jim said. "First of all, we don't know these are bad guys. I'm sure we are all a little prejudice after what we went through and are thinking the worst right now. Maybe these guys were in the campsite near Billy and he asked them to return the boat and trailer."

"Yeah, and my grandmother taught Audie Murphy how to shoot," Dawg said. "Billy wouldn't let two people he didn't know drive his jeep and return something that he was renting. I know that for a fact. And since he told Sam's grand-daughter that she could play with Kota when he returned the boat and trailer that tells me something is very wrong with this scenario. Does anyone agree with me?"

"I agree with you one hundred percent," Shades said. "Even if for some reason, Billy asked these men to return the boat and trailer, he would have written a note to the resort owner thanking him and explaining why the other two men were returning the boat and trailer. I'm sure of that." Everyone agreed that Billy wouldn't have let two men he didn't know drive his vehicle and return the boat and trailer without calling the resort owner or sending an explanation note with the two men.

"So, what's the plan now?" Dawg asked.

"Well, since the resort was the last place we know Billy was, we redraw the map with the resort at the center point and divide the map into 4 equal parts like before, then tomorrow morning each team will start at the resort and fan out in their assigned quadrants. And when you show the poster of Billy, his jeep and Kota, make sure to ask if anyone has seen Billy's so called 'friends', two middle east looking fellows."

"Hey, Jim," Wiz said. "I can go into town and make color photos of the backs of the two foreigners for everyone to take with them. Even though we can't see their faces, maybe someone will remember the multi-colored shirt the one guy was wearing."

"Good idea," Jim said. "Why don't you go now and grab a bite to eat on the road. You might have to go to Dryden to find a print shop that is open all night. Someone from another team needs to go with you, so we don't have 2 tired people on the same team tomorrow."

"I'll go with him," Shades said.

"Great," Jim replied. "You guys stay alert driving because a lot of moose cross the roads at night. We'll probably do a little fishing after dark, so some of us might still be up when you get back." Wiz and Shades climbed into a vehicle and headed for Dryden. "I think it's a good idea for all of us to show the photo of the foreigners and have the photos when we head out tomorrow morning," Jim said. Everyone agreed. They all helped setting up the fryer and getting ready for dinner.

Dinner was great, and after everyone was finished, Swede asked, "Did anyone bring a charcoal grill?"

"I have one in the back of my pickup," Jim replied.

"Well, I would like to grill brats for dinner tomorrow night if everyone is okay with that."

Everyone was nodding their heads in agreement when Dawg spoke up, "I love brats, but I have to tell you these two things. First, I love cold beer with my brats, so we better stock up on beer tomorrow if we are eating brats tomorrow night. And secondly, brats do to me what onions do to Swede, so Swede may get a little payback in the vehicle the day after."

Everyone laughed as Swede spoke up, "I guess I have it coming to me."

"You dog-gone right you have it coming," Dawg replied.

Jim said, "Swede, you buy the brats in town that you want to grill and I'll pay you for them out of the grocery fund tomorrow night. And pick up a couple more cases of beer just to be safe."

"Now you're talking," Dawg said. "I'm going to skip lunch tomorrow so I will be extra hungry tomorrow night just in case Mike wants to challenge me to a brat eating contest."

"Everyone looked at Mike and Mike could see that all of the guys were shaking their heads telling him it would be a bad idea to accept Dawg's brat eating challenge. Mike looked at Dawg and said, "I'm not a big brat eater, but I will challenge you to a beer drinking contest tomorrow night."

Dawg smiled at Mike and let out a loud 'Yahoooooo," like he had just won the lottery. Everyone was laughing and Dawg said, "I have beaten every one of these guys in a beer drinking contest already, so when I beat you tomorrow night, I will become the undisputed, undefeated, heavy weight beer drinking champion of the world," as Dawg raised his arms and jumped up and down like Rocky Balboa.

"Down Boy," Jim said as everyone was laughing. "Looks like I will be driving on Wednesday while Mike is either passed out or puking out the window. Dawg, will you do me a favor? When Mike passes out, I want you to drag him into his tent and don't leave him outside all night where the mosquitoes will eat him alive after the fire burns out."

"Will do," Dawg said.

Jim could see that Mike had a worried look on his face so Jim said, "Mike, you didn't know what you were doing. You made a rookie mistake and you're going to feel bad because of it. We never go back on a challenge, so just accept the fact that you are going to feel like crap the next day and don't worry about it."

Instead of just sitting there quietly, Mike said, "I'm not worried about a hangover. I'm worried that I may not be able to pick Dawg up and put him in his tent when he passes out."

"Whoaaaaaaa," everyone said as they turned towards Dawg.

Dawg looked at Mike and said, "You've got balls, Mike. I like that. Now if you don't mind I'm going to drink a few beers tonight in preparation for tomorrow night's contest."

The rest of the night was quiet with everyone sitting around the camp fire and discussing theories of what happened to Billy and why two foreigners were driving his jeep. Mike asked the question, "What if we find these guys and they won't talk to us or act like they don't know anything?"

Jim said, "Don't worry about that Mike. We have ways of making people talk. We just need to find them and we can convince them to talk."

Mike was very curious about how they could get people to talk, but he could see that Jim didn't want to talk about it now, so he let it go. He decided he would ask Jim about it later when they were alone. None of the guys went fishing that night as they all preferred to sit around the camp fire and talk about theories of what happened to Billy. They were going to have brats for dinner tomorrow evening, so they didn't need to catch any more fish tonight or in the morning. They finally decided it was time to get some sleep and all of them were in their tents by midnight.

# Chapter 10

It was raining hard Tuesday morning when the team started waking up, so none of the guys went running or fishing like they had been doing. Wiz and Shades gave color photos of the foreigner's shirt to the teams and everyone decided to eat breakfast at a truck stop or café after they got on the road. So, after shaving and showering, everyone pulled out of the camp site eager to get back to their mission.

They had new territory to cover and most of them felt they would get some more leads having the information the resort owner had given them yesterday. Jim and Mike passed out several of the 'Missing' posters and talked to a lot of people, but no one recognized Billy, his jeep, Kota, or remembered seeing two foreigners that fit the description of the two men driving Billy's jeep.

The rain finally stopped just before lunch time. Jim and Mike had a great meal at a small-town café and talked to all of the people in the café. No luck. They stopped at several other businesses, resorts and camp grounds, but still no luck. It was late afternoon and time to head back to camp. "I really thought we would have some luck today," Mike said to Jim.

"I did too," Jim replied. "I'm just hoping one of the other

teams had better luck than us and we get some good information tonight at the meeting."

Jim and Mike were the first ones to arrive at the campsite. The afternoon sun had dried up most of the rain, so the lawn chairs and picnic table weren't as wet as they thought they would be. The fire wood was damp, so Mike dumped a bag of charcoal in the fire pit to help get the fire wood started. He also put a bag of charcoal in the grill and lit it. "I have a feeling we are going to have some great brats tonight, "Jim said.

"Yeah, "Mike replied. "And I have a feeling I'm going to find out how much beer Dawg can drink after we eat those brats."

"Oh, I don't think you will," Jim said.

"Why not?" Mike said with a surprised look on his face.

"Because you will be passed out long before Dawg quits drinking beer," Jim said with a laugh.

"Thanks for your confidence in me," Mike said to Jim.

"No problem," Jim said. "Just don't over-do it tonight, Mike. You don't have anything to prove, and I don't want to have to run you to the nearest hospital for alcohol poisoning or anything like that. Do you understand?" Mike shook his head in agreement. "Now, since you didn't go over the rules on the contest, I can recommend that we put a one-hour time limit on it, that way you guys aren't drinking beer all night long. What do you think about that?"

"Hey, that would be great," Mike said. "Do you think Dawg will agree to that?"

"Sure," Jim said. "He's still going to kick your butt, but this way you both won't be up all-night drinking and feel quite as bad tomorrow."

The rest of the teams started pulling in and Jim decided to again have the meeting before they ate dinner. Everyone was anxious to hear what information the other teams found out, so they gathered around the camp fire and Jim got the MUM started. "Okay, any team with some new information gets to go first. Who had some luck today?" Jim asked.

Everyone was waiting for someone to start talking, but no one did. "No one got any new leads today?" Jim asked. Again, no one responded. "Wow," Jim said. "I really thought that we would have some luck today. Tomorrow, just keep moving further from the resort in your sector. Anyone have any comments they would like to share?"

Wiz was the first to speak. "Jim, I'm going to be realistic here and feel I need to say this. Those two guys with Billy's jeep could be anywhere. Maybe they drove the jeep to Alaska. Maybe they sold it and flew home to Pakistan. Maybe it's now at the bottom of one of these lakes. Now that we know that two unknown foreigners were driving Billy's jeep, I think we should contact the Canadian authorities with our new information and let them put out an APB with the jeep's license plate number.

"I have already thought about that," Jim said, "and was planning to discuss it with all of you tonight. I don't know the Canadian laws, so I'm not sure we can legally be here in Canada asking people about our friend and offering them reward money to help us find him. We are visitors in a foreign country and I would hate for them to take over the investigation and send us home."

"I never thought about that," Dawg said. "Maybe we need some legal advice to determine if it is okay to be doing what we are doing."

"Those are my thoughts as well," Jim said. "How about if Mike and I drive to Dryden tomorrow and talk to a lawyer before we do anything?"

"I think that would be the smart thing to do," Dawg said. Everyone agreed.

"Okay, one more thing," Jim said. "We have a lot of work ahead of us and I don't want two guys hung over and sick tomorrow."

"Hey, you're not going to cancel the drinking contest are you?" Dawg asked.

"No," Jim said, "but I would like to put a one-hour time limit on it. Whoever drinks the most beer in one-hour wins the contest. Is everyone okay with that?"

Everyone agreed except Dawg. He finally spoke, "I was looking forward to throwing Mike in his tent later tonight, but I understand your concern and I accept the new rules. Let's get those brats on the grill so we can eat and get the contest started."

Dawg went to the cooler and grabbed a cold beer.

"Hey, the contest hasn't started yet," Swede said out loud so everyone could hear.

"I know," Dawg replied. I'm just thirsty."

Everyone was laughing as Mike shook his head and said, "Trying to psych me out isn't going to work, Dawg."

Dawg just looked at Mike and growled. "He's getting his game-face on," Jim said to Mike. "Just so you know that Dawg takes competition very seriously and has never lost a challenge since I have known him."

"Well, thanks again for the words of encouragement, Coach," Mike said to Jim.

"You're very welcome," Jim said with a smile.

Swede had bought a variety of different brats and everyone was excited to see how they tasted. "The coals are hot," Jim said. "Let's get those brats on the grill." The brats were great and everyone complimented Swede.

"So, who has a suggestion for dinner tomorrow night?" Boom asked the group.

"How about Gus burgers?" Shades replied. Everyone agreed.

"Okay Shades," Jim said, "Since you brought it up, you stop and get the groceries and I'll pay you for them tomorrow night. And better get some chips and dip to go with them."

"Will do," Shades replied.

"Now if everyone is ready, I say we get the main event started," Jim said as everyone started to cheer. "Wiz, would you do the introductions, and Big, will you keep track of how many beers each of them drinks during the contest?" Jim asked.

Dawg quickly said, "Jim, you probably should get someone that can count past ten."

"Ten thousand comedians out of work and you're trying to be one," Big said to Dawg. Everyone laughed as Big went on, "Just throw the empty beer bottles in a pile by your feet so we can all see them." Everyone agreed.

"Let's get it started," Jim said as he placed a full cooler of cold beer on the ground between Dawg and Mike.

Wiz stood up and said, "Ladies and Gentlemen, tonight's drinking contest is for the world championship. Drinking out of the red lawn chair, from some small town in Colorado, weighing in at 250 pounds of pure muscle, the man that is more animal than he is human, the undefeated beer drinking champion of the world, Ron 'Mad Dog' Hardin." All of the guys booed loudly and threw paper cups at Dawg.

Dawg stood up from his lawn chair and gave the crowd an evil look as he barked like a dog. Before he sat down, he looked at Mike and growled. Everyone was laughing as Wiz continued. "And his opponent, drinking out of the blue lawn chair, from the great state of Iowa, weighing in at a flabby 220 pounds, Mike 'the Underdog' Grimm." Everyone cheered and clapped loudly as Mike pulled out a small U.S. flag and waved it to the crowd.

"Drinkers," Wiz said. "At this time, lock and load one 12-ounce bottle of beer in your drinking hand." Both men leaned forward and grabbed a bottle of beer from the cooler. "Clear on the left?" Jim raised his beer and nodded his head. Wiz continued, "The left is clear. Clear on the right?" Wiz looked to his right as Shades lifted his beer and nodded his head. "The right is clear. The drinking pit is now clear. Remove the caps off of your beer bottles. Drinkers, COMMENCE DRINKING!" Wiz said in a loud voice as everyone was cheering.

Dawg downed the first beer in 12 seconds, threw the empty bottle on the ground, grabbed another and downed it, and grabbed a third beer and downed it as Mike was finishing his first beer. Dawg was two beers ahead of Mike after the first three minutes of the competition. "You got to be kidding me," Mike said. "This guy isn't human."

"Hey, Wiz told you that in the introductions. You really have to listen better, Mike," Jim said with a smile.

"Wow," Mike replied. "Karen tells me that all the time." Both of them laughed.

At the halfway point, Mike was getting full of beer and asked for an official count. "Dawg, twelve, Mike, five," Shades replied.

Mike knew it was hopeless so he stood up and said, "Dawg, there is no way that I can even drink another seven beers in the next thirty minutes to tie you, so I am going to withdraw from the competition and go take a 5-minute pee."

Dawg stood up and hugged Mike and whispered to him, "Don't quit your day job."

Mike smiled as Wiz grabbed Dawg's hand, raised it up above his head and said, "The winner, and still world beer drinking champion, Ron 'Mad Dawg' Hardin." Wiz then raised a beer bottle to Dawg's mouth like a microphone as Dawg said, "Yo, Adrian, it's me, Mad Dawg."

Everyone was laughing as Mike and Dawg headed off to drain their bladders on trees out of light from the camp fire. The rest of the night was pretty quiet and everyone was in their tents by eleven o'clock.

# Chapter 11

Jim was up before six Wednesday morning and decided to grab his fishing pole and see if the fish were biting. It was a beautiful morning with the sun just starting to rise over the tree tops in the East. Jim was standing on shore and casting lures when he noticed a Bald Eagle flying majestically around the edges of the lake looking for breakfast. He was watching the eagle while he was casting and retrieving his lure. He cast the lure out and just as he started to reel it in, WHAM, something hit the lure like a Great White Shark. Jim yanked back and set the hook. The rod was bent in a C-shape and Jim knew he had hooked a big one. The fight only lasted for about 15 seconds when suddenly the line broke. "Damn" Jim said out loud as Dawg walked up behind him.

"Man, you had a nice one on the line," Dawg said. "I wish I could have seen that one."

"What do you think it was?" Jim asked.

"Had to be a Muskie or a big Northern," Dawg replied. "That was a big fish."

"Well, now we know there are some big ones in this lake," Jim said.

"Yeah. And if Doc brings his boat up with him, we should

be able to catch some of those big boys," Dawg said with a suggestive look on his face.

"If we don't find Billy today, I will call Doc tonight and ask him to come up this weekend," Jim said.

"That sounds good to me," Dawg said. "I'm going to do some pushups and sit-ups and then go for a run in a few minutes if you want to go along?"

"I might as well," Jim said. "I can't catch any fish without a lure and I left my tackle box back in my pickup. I'll be back here in five minutes."

Dawg was on the end of the dock doing pushups when Jim returned. It reminded him of the Karate Kid training on the posts by the water. Jim did a few exercises and stretched a few minutes and they both left on the morning run.

The rest of the team was up and sitting around the camp fire when they returned. "Coffee will be ready in a couple of minutes and we have a little bit of fruit and yogurt left," Mike said as they reached camp.

"Got any biscuits and gravy?" Dawg asked.

"I'm afraid not," Mike replied.

"Well, then Swede and I will be stopping at the local café for breakfast this morning," Dawg said. "I like to eat biscuits and gravy the morning after a beer drinking contest. The grease helps soak up any beer that is still in my stomach."

"Why don't you just eat a stick of butter?" Wiz asked.

"You got one?" Dawg said.

"Hey, don't be teasing the dog, Wiz," Jim said with a smile on his face. "He's been known to bite, and I don't want you guys losing all of your money by challenging him to eat things, so I'm going to stop this right now." Everyone was laughing as Dawg shrugged his shoulders, grabbed his towel and shaving kit and headed for the shower.

"That guy sure is entertaining," Mike commented when Dawg was out of hearing distance.

"Yes, he is," Wiz said. "He is a lot of fun to be around when nothing is going on, but he is one intense individual when it's time for business."

"Amen to that," Jim said as the rest of the team shook their heads in agreement.

"Hey guys, I think I'm going to put off driving to Dryden today and talking to a lawyer." Jim said.

"Why is that?" Wiz asked.

"Well, if we don't find Billy today, I'm going to call Doc tonight and ask him to come up this weekend. Doc's brother is a lawyer, so I'm going to ask Doc to call his brother and see what he says about what we are doing. I've met his brother and he is a great guy. If he doesn't know the answer, he can probably find out on line or call one of his lawyer buddies and get the answer. Also, who knows what a Canadian lawyer will charge us, and more importantly, what would we do if he said we had to go home?"

"Good point," Boom said. "And I noticed that you brought it up while Dawg was in the shower. Any reason for that?"

"Hey, you guys know what Dawg thinks of lawyers," Jim said. "He was in a good mood this morning and I didn't see any reason to get him all riled up."

"Thank you for that, Jim," Swede said as everyone was chuckling. "I have to spend the day with him and it can be a REALLY long day when Dawg is in a bad mood. But, if Dawg finds out we discussed something without him that could make him more upset than you talking about a lawyer."

"Wow," Jim said. "You are exactly right. I'm heading for the shower right now and will tell him before he leaves."

"Are your rabies shots up to date?" Wiz said with a laugh as Jim was heading for the shower.

"Good one," Jim said as he walked away.

Jim told Dawg about asking Doc to talk to his brother and Dawg was okay with it. The teams were all positive that they would get some new leads today and were anxious to get started. The last team pulled out of the camp site around seven thirty.

They covered a lot of ground in the morning and spoke with a lot of people, but still no luck. Jim and Mike had lunch in a small café and were heading to the next town when Jim's cell phone rang. "Hello, this is Jim."

"Hi Jim. My name is Mary and I'm calling about the 'Missing' poster.

"Well, hi Mary," Jim replied. "Do you have some information for me?" Jim asked.

"Well, I remember talking to the person on the poster outside the grocery store in the town of Pineville about three weeks ago."

"And you're sure it was him?"

"Yes, I'm positive. I was parked next to his jeep and he had the back windows rolled partially down so his dog could get some air. I commented on what a beautiful dog it was and asked him the dog's name. I can't remember what he said, but I remember it was an Indian name."

"That is great. Anything else?" Jim asked.

"Well we talked for a couple of minutes and he asked if there was a good restaurant in town. I told him that the local café was closed for the day, but 'Tuff Guyz Bar and Grill' had good food. He asked me directions, then thanked me and left."

"So, you don't know if he went there or not?"

"Well, I do know that he went there, because on my way home I drove past Tuff Guyz and saw him getting out of his jeep and walking towards the front door."

"That is great information, Mary. Thank you very much. I

need to get your name and address for the reward money in case your information leads us to finding him. Better yet, I would like to meet with you when we go to Pineville if that is okay with you?"

"Sure. Just give me a call when you get to town and I'll meet with you," Mary said.

"That sounds great. We should be there in about an hour and I'll call you when we get to town."

"Okay, I'll see you in a bit," Mary said.

"Thanks again. Good bye," Jim said.

"Good bye," Mary replied.

Mike had the map out and was looking for Pineville. He found it in Wiz and Boom's quadrant. Jim pulled the vehicle over and asked Mike to drive so he could make a couple of phone calls. Mike agreed and they switched places and headed towards Pineville. Jim called Wiz on his cell phone. Wiz answered, "Hello Jim, what's up?"

"Hey Wiz, I just got a phone call from a lady in Pineville that spoke with Billy outside a grocery store. She said he asked for a good restaurant and she recommended a place called Tuff Guyz Bar and Grill. She said she saw his jeep parked there on her way home. Have you been to Pineville yet?"

"Yes, we were in Pineville yesterday," Wiz replied. "And Boom and I went into Tuff Guyz and asked some questions. No one knew anything and the guys weren't very friendly to us."

"Did you leave a poster with them?" Jim asked.

"I did," Wiz replied. "Do you want us to go back there?"

"No. Mike and I are headed that way. We're going to meet with the lady that spoke with Billy when we get to town. I'll call if we need you."

"Okay. Keep me posted," Wiz said.

"Will do," Jim replied. "Out here," Jim said.

Out here," Wiz replied.

Mike drove for about 45 minutes when they saw a road sign that said Pineville was 10 miles away. Jim called Mary on the phone and they agreed to meet in the parking lot of Tuff Guyz. Jim told her they would be in a black Chevy Silverado pickup with Iowa license plates on it. She said they would be easy to find and she would meet them there in a few minutes.

Jim and Mike arrived first and were standing outside the pickup when Mary pulled in next to them. After introductions, Jim asked her to join them for a cup of coffee and a piece of pie in Tuff Guyz. She didn't think they would have any pie, but agreed to join them for a cup of coffee. She also mentioned the fact that the bartender was the owner and he was a former hockey player. He was a tough guy known for fighting which explained the name, 'Tuff Guyz'.

It was dark and dreary inside, the floor was sticky and the place smelled like stale beer. There were about 6 people drinking beer at the bar and a couple more shooting pool. Mary said that most of them were locals and were probably on vacation or laid off and collecting unemployment. They got a booth and the bartender walked over and asked what they wanted to drink.

"Have you got any pie?" Jim asked.

"We're not that kind of place," the bartender replied.

"Then how about three cups of coffee?" Jim said.

"We're not a coffee shop either. There is a café a few blocks down the road and that's probably where you should go," the bartender said and turned to walk away.

"Wait a minute," Jim said. "We want to ask you something?"

The bartender turned around and faced them. "What do you want?" he said.

"A friend of ours is missing and we were told he was in here about three weeks ago," Jim said. "Here is the 'Missing' poster with his photo on it. He was in here late one afternoon and probably got a food order to go. He might have been wearing a black flat brimmed hat like Tom Laughlin wore in the movie, 'Billy Jack'. We are looking for information that may help us find him and his parents have put up reward money for anyone that helps us find their son. Do you remember seeing him?"

The bar tender looked at the poster and said, "Nope, never saw him."

"Would someone else have been working that day that he stopped in here?" Jim asked.

"No. I'm the owner and I work every afternoon by myself until my help comes in at 5 P.M."

"Well, is it okay if we talk to the rest of the people in here and hang up a 'Missing' poster?" Jim asked.

"No. I don't want you bothering my customers, but I will put up the poster for you," the owner replied.

"Well, we have been told that he was in here, so maybe someone at the bar remembers him or spoke with him," Jim said.

"Did this lady tell you that?" the owner asked. "Do you know that her name is 'Crazy Mary'? You can't believe anything she says, so if she is the one that told you he was in here, you are wasting your time. Now, I have to get back to work," the owner said as he turned and walked away without the poster.

They decided to leave, and on the way out, Jim took the poster to the bar and handed it to the owner. "Thanks for agreeing to put the poster up," Jim said. The owner took the poster and didn't say a word as the three of them walked out. Once outside, Jim said to Mary, "Is the local café still open?"

Mary looked at her watch and said, "Yes, it's open for another couple of hours."

"Well, I would like to buy you a cup of coffee and piece of pie at the café if you have time?"

"That sounds good to me," Mary said. "It's only about three blocks away, so if you want to follow me I will lead the way."

Jim and Mike followed her to the café. Lunch was over, so it wasn't crowded at all. They got a booth and ordered coffee and pie. They made small talk for a few minutes, then Jim said, "I hope you don't mind me asking, but why did the owner call you 'Crazy Mary'?"

"It's a long story," Mary replied.

"Well, we're not in any hurry," Jim said.

She looked at Jim and sighed. A few seconds later she started to talk. "I graduated from high school here in Pineville about 25 years ago. I fell in love with a man and we got married. I got pregnant right away and had a beautiful son later that year. Well, my husband had a wild side that I didn't know about and was committing home burglaries with a bunch of hoodlums he knew from high school. I didn't know about it and he never told me because I would have left him if I had found out. They eventually got caught and he was sentenced to five years in prison. I divorced him and was moving on with my life. I got a good job and my son was growing up healthy and happy. He was the love of my life. We had so much fun together," she said as tears started running down her face. She paused for about a minute as she got some tissues out of her purse and wiped the tears.

She started again, "One winter day we had a terrible snow storm. My son had just turned four years old and we spent the evening watching TV and playing games. We had a small dog that my son just adored. They were good buddies and the dog always slept on the bed with my son. Around ten o'clock, I let the dog out to pee and could see it was really nasty outside. The dog was only out for a couple of minutes and came back covered in snow. I got an old towel and wiped him dry. Then, I tucked my son into bed in his room and the dog jumped up on the bed with him. My son said his nightly prayer, then I kissed him goodnight and left his room. I checked all of the doors to make sure they were locked, and went to bed in my room."

"I woke up about seven the next morning and made some coffee. I decided to let the two of them sleep in since it was Saturday and I didn't have to go to work. There was still a bad snowstorm outside so we were going to spend the day inside playing games and watching more movies. I thought the dog might have to pee, so I opened my son's bedroom door to see if the dog wanted to go outside. I didn't see the dog, and at first, I thought maybe he was sleeping on the floor, so I walked around the bed and still didn't see the dog anywhere. I turned the light on in the room and my heart nearly stopped as I saw an empty bed."

She hesitated for a few seconds and had a terrified look on her face as she continued, "I thought maybe they woke up and heard me in the kitchen and decided to play a joke and hide from me, so I started yelling for them. I started looking under beds, in closets, in the bathroom, in the garage, in cupboards, every place that a small boy would be able to hide. But I didn't find them. I grabbed my coat and went outside in the blizzard looking for them around the house. I was yelling for them as loud as I could and my neighbors heard me. One of them came outside to see what was wrong and helped me search the backyard, and the other neighbor's yards. Nothing. He finally called the police and requested help. They showed up within a few minutes. My neighbor went door to door and got the other neighbors to help in the search. We looked for several hours, but didn't find a thing."

The police wanted to call off the search, but I wasn't about to quit looking. I was very cold and they were worried about hyperthermia and frost bite, so they carried me into my house as I was yelling and crying uncontrollably. The wanted to take me to the hospital, but I refused to leave the house, so they called my doctor and he agreed to make a house call. He wanted to give me a shot to help me settle down, but I refused. I wanted to go back outside and continue the search. The police needed to get a report from me and I tried to tell them what happened, but I was crying so hard and my voice was nearly gone from all of the yelling, that I just couldn't answer their questions. They finally held me down while the doctor gave me a shot and I passed out a few minutes later."

"I woke up a few hours later with the police and several of my relatives in the house. There was a search party outside looking for my son and they had brought in a search and rescue dog to help. They returned to the house at dark and hadn't found anything at all. I started crying again and screaming for them to get back out there and keep looking. They said they were calling off the search until morning and I started putting on my coat and was going to look for him all night if that was what it took. They stopped me and told me that no one could survive outside for that long and that if he had gone outside he was probably dead. I dropped to the floor crying and said that if he was dead, I didn't want to go on living. They had me committed to a mental hospital and I was there for about six months before I was well enough to go home."

Jim and Mike just sat there quietly until Jim finally said, "Wow. That is a tragic story. So, did they ever find your son," Jim asked.

"They never did," Mary replied. They thought that maybe he was abducted, but his dad was in prison and there was no evidence to support that theory. And, in the spring when the snow melted, they found the dog in a ditch about a mile from my house. He had been hit by a car, but he still had his collar on and the vet made a positive identification. Their theory was that my son got up in the middle of the night to let the dog out to pee. The dog didn't come back right away, so my son went outside to get him. He got too far from the house and couldn't find his way back. He died of exposure and later some wolves carried his body off and ate him in the woods."

"Wow," Mike said as his eyes were tearing up. "My heart goes out to you and what you have been through."

Mary thanked Mike and gave him a hug. "You are a very kind man with a good heart, Mike," she said. "But the story isn't over quite yet. A few years ago, my ex-husband was killed in a vehicle accident near Toronto. He had gotten out of prison and found work there. There was another person in the vehicle with him and when they ran a background check on the other person, they discovered he was using a fake identification, so they couldn't identify the body. They got approval to run a DNA test on him and it turned out to be my son."

Jim and Mike were so absorbed in the story that they didn't know what to say. They just looked at Mary and waited for her to continue.

"The police later got the truth from my ex-husbands brother. He had gotten into trouble with the law and agreed to tell them the story of what happened for a reduced sentence. They accepted his plea bargain. He told them that his brother had offered him a bunch of money if he abducted my son and kept him until my ex-husband got out of prison. His brother agreed to the kidnapping and decided to do it at night during a snowstorm so no one could see his footprints. My husband told him where I hid the spare door key so he could sneak into the house. He knew my son would wake up as soon as he went outside in the cold, so he taped his mouth shut. He took the dog with him, and about a mile from the house, he stopped the car, took the dog outside, killed him with a hammer and threw him in the ditch to look like he was hit by a car. Well, everything worked perfectly and we would never have known the truth if they hadn't been killed in the vehicle accident and someone decided to do a DNA sample on my son."

"Wow," Jim said. "That is one incredible story. And that explains the name, 'Crazy Mary'.

"Yeah, that's it. They printed the full story in the local papers, but there still are a few people around here that call me, 'Crazy Mary'."

"Well, Mary, you didn't do anything different than any loving parent wouldn't have done. I'm sorry people are so hurtful," Mike said.

"I agree with Mike," Jim said. "I can't imagine the suffering you went through losing a small child and not knowing what happened to him. I'm glad you finally found out the truth and know that none of it was your fault."

"Thank you both so much," Mary said. "I still have a hard time with the fact that the love of my life was taken from me at such a young age, and that I suffered for many, many years before finding out the truth.... but I am a strong Christian now, and have learned to accept what happened. I now try to be the best person that I can be and hopefully will see my son again one day in Heaven."

"You sure have the right attitude, Mary," Mike said. "I'm sure you will be rewarded for your pain and suffering if you keep your faith."

"Thanks, again, Mary said. "I sure wish I could help you find your friend."

"Well, you have given us some good information. I would like to ask you one more question? Do you remember what day of the week it was and roughly what time of day it was when you met Billy?

"I usually get groceries on Wednesday, so that is probably the day of the week. And I think it was around four thirty in the afternoon because the café closes at four o'clock," Mary replied.

"Excellent," Jim said. "Thank you so much for calling us and meeting with us today. We will handle it from here, and if your information helps us find Billy, we will be back with some reward money for you."

"That would be nice, but that's not why I want you to find your friend," Mary said.

"We know that, Mary. You are a nice person and if we can help you in any way please don't hesitate to call," Jim said.

"I will keep you in my prayers," Mary said.

"That would be great," Jim replied. "We have to go now. You have a great day." They all left the café together and Mary hugged both of them before they got into their vehicle and drove away.

Jim pulled into a parking lot a few miles out of town and parked the vehicle. "Okay, today is Wednesday, so it was 3 weeks ago today that Billy was seen going into Tuff Guyz. I'm going to call the team and we are all going to eat dinner at Tuff Guyz tonight and see if we can get some answers."

"That sounds good to me," Mike said.

Jim called Boom first. "Boom answered, "What's up, Jim?"

"Boom, we got a good lead today. Have you bought the ingredients for the Gus Burgers yet?"

"No, I was going to buy everything later on our way to the campground," Boom replied.

"Okay, we have a change of plans," Jim said. "We are going

to eat dinner in Pineville tonight, so you can hold off and buy the groceries tomorrow. I'll explain everything to you when you get here. We'll all meet in the parking lot of the local café on Main Street. You are the closest of anyone, so go ahead and finish what you are doing before heading this way. Plan to be here between 4:30 and 5:00."

"Okay, We'll see you soon. Out here," Boom said.

"Out here," Jim replied.

Jim called the other two teams and gave them the same message. Everyone was in the café parking lot by twenty minutes to five. Jim got everyone together and told them that Billy was seen going into Tuff Guyz, but the owner wouldn't give them any information or let them talk to any of the customers.

"We are going to do the 'Fort Benning Bar Routine'," Jim said. "Dawg and Swede, you guys go in first and drink beer at the bar. The owner is also the bar tender, and he is an ex-hockey player that was known for fighting. Some of his old hockey friends hang out in the bar, which explains why he named the place, 'Tuff Guyz'. Wiz and Boom, you guys go in about 15 minutes later, sit at a table close to the back door and get a pitcher of beer so the bartender won't have to come back to your table very often. Don't ask any questions about Billy and maybe the owner won't recognize you."

"Big and Shades, you go in about 10-15 minutes after Wiz and Boom and sit at a table near the bar. Mike and I will be the last ones to go in and we are going to sit by the pool table and play pool as soon as we can get on the pool table. Remember, you only know the guy you are with and don't know the rest of the team. And don't use your real names even if someone asks you for it. Wiz, you act like you have had too much to drink and when you see me take off my ball cap, you walk up to the bar and ask the bartender to see the 'Missing' poster you left in the place yesterday. If he shows you the poster and lets you talk to the people in the bar, then have Boom help you and the rest of us will just sit tight."

"Now, If he refuses, which I'm pretty sure he will, then you start getting loud and more demanding and we'll play it by ear. Dawg, you and Swede will be right there at the bar so you may be the first ones to step in if the bartender starts something." Jim looked at the team and could tell they were getting their game faces on.

"Boom, you cover the back door and don't let anyone leave and come back in when trouble starts. They might be returning with a gun. Let them leave if they want, but don't let them back in. Big and Shades, your main job is to keep the bartender's friends from jumping Wiz, Dawg or Swede when the action begins. Mike and I will be playing pool and our main job is to keep others from grabbing pool cues and using them as weapons. Mike, are you okay with this?"

"I'm okay," Mike said.

"Great," Jim said. "Does anyone have any questions?" Hearing none, Jim said, "Okay, focus on the mission and think about what you are doing. Don't drink too much, don't start anything, and try not to hurt anyone too badly when trouble starts. No blows to the head or knees to the nuts if they can be avoided. And Dawg, please be on your best behavior and don't hurt anyone too badly. Now, is everyone clear with the plan?"

"Clear," was the response. "Shades, do you have your badge with you?" Jim asked.

"I sure do," was Shades reply.

"Good, keep it handy because you may need to show it if someone wants to call the law," Jim said. "Okay, Tuff Guyz is about 3 blocks down this road on the right side of the street. Dawg and Swede, take off. Let's get this party started."

Dawg and Swede drove to the bar and went inside. There were two empty seats at the bar, so they sat down and ordered beers. Wiz and Boom came in a few minutes later and sat at the table closest to the back door. The owner had a waitress working the floor and she got the pitcher of beer they ordered. The owner recognized Wiz and Boom and quietly said this to his three buddies sitting at the end of the bar, "Those two guys that just ordered a pitcher of beer were the ones that were in here yesterday asking questions about the Indian fellow that was here about three weeks ago. Apparently, he is missing and they are looking for him."

"You mean the guy you called, 'Tonto' and spit in his food before you gave it to him?" one of the guys said as they all laughed.

"Yeah, that's the one," the owner said.

"You don't think your spit killed him do you, Rocco?" one of the guys said to the owner.

"Maybe," the owner said as they all laughed out loud.

Dawg and Swede both acted like they were talking to each other and didn't hear the conversation, but they heard every word. It was really hard for Dawg to stay calm after he heard the owner had spit in Billy's food, but he knew he had to follow the game plan and just hoped he would get a shot at the owner a little later.

Big and Shades were the next ones to go in and they sat at a table near the bar just as planned. Shades was talking to the waitress about where he could go do some dancing, and she said there was a dance hall about 20 miles away and they had bands on weekends. She was planning to go with some friends on Saturday night and maybe they would dance with Shades and his friends if they showed up. Shades said he had to talk to his friends, but he was pretty sure they would go for it and he would see her on Saturday night. Shades paid for the beers and gave her a nice tip. She smiled and walked away.

Jim and Mike came in a few minutes later and sat by the pool table. They got a couple of beers from the waitress and laid two quarters on the pool table to challenge the guys that were playing pool.

"We're playing for beers," one of the guys said to Jim.

"Sounds good," Jim said. "You guys want to play partners?"

"Sure," just as soon as we finish this game," one of them said.

Jim nodded to them and took a drink of his beer. He softly said to Mike, "Let them win and we'll buy them some beers. I want to check out the people in here for a while before we make our move." Mike nodded approval.

The two guys finished their game and Jim racked the balls for the next game. "Partners for beers?" one of the guys said.

"You got it," Jim replied. During the game, Jim was looking over everyone that was inside the bar and trying to get a read on them. He was hoping that none of them were off-duty police officers or lawyers. He couldn't get a good read on one table of four men, so after he shot and missed, he decided to walk over to them and see what he could find out.

"Hi guys," he said as he walked up to the table. "My friend and I are up here fishing, but we aren't having any luck. I would gladly buy you guys a round of drinks if each of you would give me your opinion on where we could go to catch some fish." They all looked at each other and nodded approval. Jim said, "I'm Bob and the guy shooting pool in the blue jean jacket is my friend, Brad. We're from Minnesota and we own a construction company." Jim held out his hand and all of them shook hands with him and said their names. "So, what do you guys do for a living?" Jim asked.

"I own a small resort a few miles from here," one of them

said. "Stan drives a truck for a living. Earl works for a logging company, and Brent here doesn't do much of anything," he said as all of them laughed.

"Well, I want Brent's job," Jim said as they chuckled and smiled back at Jim. "Hey, it looks like it's my turn to shoot, so I'll be right back to get the fishing spots from you and buy you guys some drinks."

Jim felt a lot better now that he knew what all of them did for a living. After he missed his shot, he returned to the table and all of them gave him the name of the lake where they thought he could catch some fish. He thanked them, then asked the waitress to get them a round of drinks and he would pay for it. They got their drinks and waved to him as he was looking over the pool table for his next shot.

Just as the pool game ended, Dawg went by and looked at Jim, then looked at the Men's room. He did it twice, so Jim knew Dawg wanted to talk to him in the restroom. Jim took his shot and missed, then told Mike he had to pee and headed for the restroom. Inside, one of the guys in the bar was in there with Dawg, so they waited for him to leave. As soon as the man left, Dawg spoke to Jim, "The bartender recognized Wiz and Boom. He said they were in here asking questions about the Indian fellow that the bartender named 'Tonto' and then spit in his sandwich before giving him his food order."

"That son of a bitch," Jim said as his face got red.

Dawg was washing his hands and said, "I just wanted you to know in case you need to use that information later." "And, I want first shot at him if trouble breaks out."

"You got it, Dawg," Jim said. "Just don't hurt him too badly. He's not worth going to jail over."

"I'll try to hold back," Dawg said.

"No, you WILL hold back," Jim said. "I can't afford to lose you, old buddy. Do I have your word on that?"

"Okay, you have my word that I won't hurt him as badly as I would like to," Dawg said.

"Okay, now you go back to the bar and hopefully nobody will notice we were in here at the same time." Dawg left the restroom and headed back to the bar. Jim remained in the restroom for a couple more minutes, then went back to his pool game. They had lost another game, so Mike bought them a couple of beers and was racking up the balls for the next game.

"We lost another one?" Jim said.

"These guys are really good," Mike said.

"Hey, you guys aren't professional pool players, are you?" Jim asked.

"Hell no," one of them said. "We're both mechanics at the Chevy dealership in the next town. We went to high school with the owner of this place and are in here nearly every night."

"So, who is the owner of this place?" Jim asked.

"The bartender owns this place," the man said. "His name is Rocco Adams and he played semi-pro hockey. He is one tough son of a gun."

"Wow," Jim said. "And I suppose those guys at the bar are his old hockey buddies?"

"Some of them are," the guy said. "The ones at this end of the bar played hockey with him and the ones at the other end are more of his friends from high school. I don't know the two men in the middle."

"Okay, well this is our last game, gentlemen, and we plan to get one of those beers back from you."

"I doubt it," the other guy said. "You might as well call the waitress and order that third round now," as both of them laughed and high-fived each other.

"You might be right," Jim said. "But let's play the game and see what happens."

Well, they were right. Jim bought them another round of beer and sat down next to Mike. Jim kept his pool cue with him and Mike had his leaning against the table. The other two guys decided to take a break from pool and order a pizza from the waitress. Jim decided it was time and he stood up and removed his hat and ran his hand through his short hair a few times as he was talking to Mike. Wiz saw the signal and staggered to the bar. Jim put his hat back on and waited to see what was going to happen.

"Hey, beer tender," Wiz said out loud as he got to the bar. "Where is the poster of our missing friend that I left with you yesterday? I want to show it to some people."

"I think somebody took the poster with them," the owner replied.

"Did they recognize our friend and take the poster so they would have the phone number?" Wiz asked.

"How the hell do I know," the owner said as his buddies snickered. "And besides, I wouldn't let you talk to my customers about the poster anyway."

"And why not?" Wiz said.

"Because he was a lousy, stinking Indian and I wish more of them would go missing," the bartender said as his buddies all laughed.

Wiz got loud and yelled, "HEY, THAT'S NO WAY TO TALK ABOUT MY FRIEND." Everyone in the place stopped what they were doing and were looking and listening to what was going on at the bar.

"Listen buster," the bartender said. "You yell in here again and I'll make you wish you never set foot in this place. I told you the Indian wasn't in here so shut your mouth and sit down before I knock you down."

His buddies were snickering and one of them said, "You want me to throw him out, Rocco?"

"Yeah, you might as well," Rocco said.

As the man was getting up off of his bar stool, Dawg jumped up and got between him and Wiz. "You will have to go through me to get to him," Dawg said.

"Hey, what's he to you?" the guy asked.

"He bought me a beer the other day and I owe him one," Dawg said.

"Well, just so you know, the three of us played hockey with Rocco and when one of us fights, we all fight," the man said with a big smile on his face as Rocco and his buddies were laughing.

"You mean I may have to fight all of you ladies?" Dawg said as the guy he was talking to threw a punch at his head. Dawg ducked under the swing, punched the guy in the stomach so hard it knocked the wind out of him then picked him up and threw him into the wall. This only took a couple of seconds and one of his buddies got up and came at Dawg. He tried to tackle Dawg and take him to the floor, but Dawg grabbed the guy by the head and brought his knee up into the man's chest. This raised him up off of the floor a few inches and he crumbled into a heap.

The last guy picked up his barstool and was heading for Dawg when Swede stuck out his leg and tripped him. Dawg kicked the guy in the stomach as he was getting up, then lifted him up and threw him into the closest bar table, which just happened to be where Big and Shades were sitting. They were ready for it and both jumped up from the table as the guy came crashing into it.

Suddenly, a man behind them screamed out in pain as he crashed to the floor. Everyone turned and looked as Mike spoke excitedly, "he had a knife and was heading for Dawg. I hit him in the shin bone with my pool cue."

There on the floor next to the guy that was screaming in pain was a hunting knife. Dawg walked over and picked the knife up, then grabbed the guy by the hair and lifted up his head. "Don't ever pull a knife on anyone unless you need it for self-defense. You could have killed me and gone to prison for the rest of your life, or I might have killed you. You might be in pain now, but it will eventually go away. This guy saved you from prison or death." He let loose of the guy's hair and then stomped on the guy's right hand before walking away. The guy was really screaming now and Dawg was sure he broke some bones in the man's hand.

Dawg walked up to the bar, raised the knife above his head and slammed the blade into the bar top as hard as he could. The owner grabbed a club and said, "That's it. You get out of my place right now or I will beat you with this club."

"Now you listen to me," Dawg said. "If you swing that club at me, I will take it as an aggressive action to do me physical harm, and I will take the club from you and break several bones in your body. I just want to make sure you understand that before you try anything stupid."

Jim decided it had gone far enough and he needed to step in. "Hold it," he said. "Everybody settle down right now before someone ends up in the hospital. I was in here earlier today, and left a 'Missing' poster with you. Where is the poster?" Jim asked.

"I don't know," the bartender said. "Maybe someone took it."

"Okay, Tuff Guy. Give me your trash can behind the bar, or I will send this big guy back there to get it." The bartender hesitated and looked at Dawg.

"He's giving you a choice," Dawg said. "I hope you don't give the trash can to him so I have to go back there and get it. I really do."

The bartender quickly grabbed the trash can he had behind the bar and handed it to Jim who was now standing at the end of the bar. Jim turned the trashcan upside down and emptied the contents on the floor. The wanted poster was in the trash. Jim picked it up and looked at it. Someone had drawn a noose around Billy's neck and written foul language on the poster. Jim looked at the bartender and said, "Rocco, you are a liar. You know if I show this poster to this big fellow here, he's going to hurt you really bad."

"I can explain," Rocco said. "The poster was sitting on the end of the bar and some guy drew that stuff on it. When I saw what he had done, I threw the poster away."

"Sure you did, Rocco," Jim said. "So, let me ask you this, do you remember seeing our friend when he was in here three weeks ago?"

"Listen, I have already told you that I don't remember him. So, if Crazy Mary is the only person you have that says he was in here, then you are wasting my time."

Jim stepped forward and said, "Well Rocco, three people called me after seeing one of the 'Missing' posters we left in town. Mary only said she saw him walking in the door as she drove past. The other two both said they were friends of yours, but they were calling for the reward money. They said he came in here and ordered some food to go. AND"...... Jim said loudly, "both of them said you don't like Indians so you spit in his food order before you gave it to him."

Dawg slammed his fist on the bar so hard it knocked over three partial beers that were sitting on the bar.

"Who told you that?" Rocco said.

"I'm not going to tell you their names," Jim said, "but they were in here when it happened."

"You'll never get anyone to admit that in person," Rocco said.

"Is that a fact," Dawg said as he walked over to the first guy that confronted him. The guy was sitting up against the wall Dawg had thrown him into and had a look of pain in his eyes. Dawg asked him, "Are you all right?"

"I'm not sure," the guy said.

"Well," Dawg said, "I'm going to ask you a question and if you lie to me, I'm going to grab your arm and dislocate your elbow, which they tell me is extremely painful."

"Are you crazy?" the man said out loud.

"Some people sure think so," Dawg said.

"Someone call the law," the man said.

"No need for that," Shades said as he pulled out his badge. "I'm a law enforcement officer."

"Great," said the man on the floor. "Arrest this man for assault and battery."

"I'm afraid I can't do that," Shades said. "I watched the whole thing go down and he was only acting in self-defense. I would testify to that in a court of law. And now I have to pee, so if I were you, I would tell this man the truth so he doesn't hurt you while I'm in the Men's room." Shades then walked past a group of people and into the restroom.

"Okay," Dawg said as he looked at the guy on the floor. "Did our friend whose photo is on the poster come in here?"

"I can't remember," the man said.

Dawg reached over and grabbed one of the man's arms. The guy tried to pull it back, but Dawg was stronger and knocked the guy over onto his stomach and pulled the man's right hand up to about the middle of his back. "I'm not very good at this," Dawg said, "so I may dislocate your shoulder instead of your elbow.

The man was yelling, "Stop, you're hurting me," but Dawg didn't let up one bit.

"Now let me say this before I ask you the question a second time, I was sitting at the bar when those two fellows back there walked in. Rocco told you that they were friends of the Indian guy that was in here a few weeks ago. I heard everything, and I want you to repeat what was said or I am going to raise your hand up towards your head until something breaks or pops out of its socket. Do you understand me?"

"I understand," the man said.

"Good," Dawg said. "Now, tell everyone in here what was said at the bar when my friends came in about an hour ago."

"Okay," the man said.

"You say nothing to them," Rocco yelled.

"Rocco, if you yell at him again, I will let him go and put you in this same position. So, please yell at him again and see what happens." Dawg looked at Rocco, but Rocco didn't say a word.

"Well, young man," Dawg said. "Tell us what was said at the bar tonight and if you tell the truth, I will let you go without hurting you. You have my word on that."

"Okay," the guy said. "When your friends came in, Rocco said they were in here yesterday asking questions about the Indian guy that was in here a few weeks ago. All three of us that were sitting at the end of the bar tonight were in here that night sitting in the same places. Your friend came in and sat at a table and ordered a couple of burgers to go. Rocco doesn't like Indians and called him, 'Tonto'. When his food order was ready, Rocco took it behind the bar, opened the lid so we could all see it, removed the top buns and spit on both of the burgers. We all laughed and he put the buns back on top and took the order over to your friend. The Indian fellow had no idea what had happened and even gave Rocco a nice tip."

"Then what happened?" Dawg asked.

"That's it. Your friend got up and left. Rocco made some jokes about Indians for a couple of hours after he left but that was it. I never saw him or heard anything about him again until tonight when your friends came in."

"Are you sure nothing happened to my friend after he left here?" Dawg asked.

"I'm sure," the man said. "No one followed him outside or anything like that. He left and I never saw him again."

Dawg released the man's arm and let him roll over on his back. "Stay on the floor until I tell you it's okay to get up," Dawg said to the guy. He nodded, okay.

"So," Dawg said while looking at the other two guys laying on the floor, "Both of you guys were also in here that night as well," he said as he looked at the other two men laying on the floor. "I'm going to ask you the same question that I asked your friend, and you know what will happen to you if you don't tell me the truth, right?" Both of them nodded that they understood.

The man closest to Dawg spoke first, "Everything he said is one hundred percent true. I have nothing to add."

Dawg looked at the other guy and he said, "That's exactly what happened. I haven't seen your friend since that night and have no idea what happened to him."

"One more question," Dawg said. "Have you seen Rocco spit in food at other times or was this the first?" Neither one of them said anything at first, so Dawg yelled, "I WANT THE TRUTH AND I WANT IT RIGHT NOW."

"Okay, we have seen him spit in food several times," the closest guy said. "If he doesn't like someone, or they complain about something, he spits in their food. He thinks it's the tuff guy way of showing that he is the boss."

Dawg looked at the other guy on the floor and he nodded and said, "That is correct."

Dawg turned to look at the owner and said, "Rocco, you cowardly, low life son of a bitch. Please walk out from behind that bar and take a swing at me. I'll give you all the money in my wallet which is around a hundred dollars if you do it."

"No way," Rocco said. "I just want you guys to leave."

Just then, Shades walked out of the Men's room and said to Dawg, "I'm afraid I have to leave. Mr. Dawg, do you want to press charges on these guys for attacking you?" It was hard for Dawg and Jim to hide the smiles from their faces as they looked at each other.

Dawg finally said, "No, I don't think I will press charges at this time, but I would like you to write a report of what happened in case I have problems with these fellows at a later time."

"Will do," Shades said. "You have a nice day, Sir," he said to Dawg.

"Thank you, officer," Dawg replied. Swede got up and followed Shades out the front door. "Just a few more things before we leave," Dawg said to the crowd. "You people that live around here and eat in here on occasion have probably had your food spit in from time to time. I want you to tell your friends what you heard in here today and let them know not to eat here anymore."

Dawg hesitated for a few seconds then continued, "Also, this friend of ours that is missing, has some very powerful parents. We are his old army buddies, so we were the first ones to come up looking for him. If we don't find him, his parents will send up some really bad asses to look for their son. I know those guys won't be as nice as we have been to you. I'm sure they will come in here and ask some more questions. And, if they ask you a question, you had better tell them the truth, because if they even think you are lying to them, you will wish you never set foot in this bar."

"And," Dawg said, "We have a report that some mid-east looking men were seen driving our friend's jeep. They are small men with dark complexions, black hair, and speak with an accent. They were wearing sandals and one of them had on a bright, multi-colored shirt, but they could be wearing something else by now. Have any of you seen some men that match this description?"

No one spoke up. "Okay, if you see one of them or remember anything that may help us find our friend, call the phone number on the poster. There is a reward and we will be glad to give it to you if your information helps us find our friend. I'm going to leave a few copies of the 'Missing' poster in here with Rocco, whose nickname is now 'Spitty'. So Spitty, if I come back in here and one of these posters is not hanging up, I won't be as nice as I was today. Does anyone have any questions or comments before we leave?" No one made a sound.

"Okay then," Dawg said. "All of this talking has made me hungry, so my army buddies and I are going to leave and go get some good food that no one has spit into. You all have a nice evening and thanks again for the information." Dawg headed for the door and the other guys followed. Shades was sitting in the pickup and Big was standing with Kadie in the grass by the parking lot.

Jim waited until everyone was there and then spoke, "Good work in there guys. Dawg, that's the most I have heard you talk at one time since I met you."

Everyone laughed as Dawg said, "Yeah, sometimes I tend to talk a lot when I get worked up.

"Well, you did great, Dawg" Jim said.

Dawg then spoke, "I want to thank Mike for covering my back when that guy pulled a knife on me. Mike, I owe you one. Let me know if I can ever help you with anything and I will be there."

"Thanks, Dawg," Mike said, "But I was just doing my job."

"Well, thanks again, you can watch my back anytime," Dawg said as he grabbed Mike and gave him a man hug.

Jim said, "Okay, let's stop the mushy stuff right now before you two end up getting a room." Everyone laughed as Jim continued, "Mike and I will stop at that fried chicken place and get a couple of buckets of chicken to eat back at camp if everyone is okay with that?" Everyone nodded approval. "Okay then, let's get out of here before someone gets our license plate numbers." They all got into their vehicles and headed down the road.

"So, what is the story behind the name, 'Fort Benning Bar Routine'? Mike asked Jim as they were driving down the road.

"Well," Jim said, "One time the team was attending some training at Fort Benning, Georgia between missions and a bunch of soldiers were badly beaten one night at a bar off post. It was the third time a group of soldiers were beaten at this bar and the Post Commander was planning to place the bar 'Off Limits' to all soldiers. One of the young soldiers that was beaten happened to be Dawg's nephew that I told you about earlier. The team visited the young man in the hospital and he told us that his buddies and he were jumped in the parking lot as they were walking to their cars. He said they didn't do anything wrong, weren't loud in the bar, didn't pick any fights or anything. He had no idea why the men jumped them."

Jim continued, "the men that jumped them were wearing black ski masks to hide their faces and hit the soldiers with baseball bats. The soldiers suffered several broken bones in their hands, wrists and arms. One of the soldiers was hit in the knee and the bat shattered his knee cap. He needed surgery and it was doubtful that he would be able to remain in the Infantry. The police were called to the scene, but the men in the ski masks had left or taken their masks off and of course, no one saw anything or knew anything about the incident."

"Knowing Dawg, you know he doesn't handle things like this very well. He felt he needed to find the men that were beating soldiers with baseball bats and put an end to it. He did some checking and found out that the beatings had all taken place on a Saturday night. He talked to all of the soldiers in the hospital and they remembered a softball team coming into the bar and drinking beer with a bunch of their buddies. A couple of the soldiers said that they danced a few dances with some young ladies but the ladies had asked the soldiers to dance and assured them that they didn't have boyfriends. Dawg guessed that was the motive. The local guys were probably looking over the young ladies and trying to get the nerve to ask them to dance when the ladies asked the soldiers to dance."

"Well, as you can imagine, Dawg came up with a plan and the next Saturday night we executed it. Dawg had a few 'Army Buddies' at Fort Benning and got them to help us out. Two of them were M.P.'s (Military Police) and Dawg wanted them in uniform with their pistols just in case things got out of hand. Dawg had four guys on our team dress in softball uniforms and go into the bar and start drinking. He had another four rent some wigs and beards and look like some of the locals. They went in and a couple sat at the bar and another couple were shooting pool. Then he had four of our young soldiers go into the bar and have a few beers. As we expected, the young ladies asked the four soldier boys to dance and they gladly danced with the ladies. They even went so far as to ask the ladies to join them at their table and bought the ladies several drinks. This really pissed off the locals and they kept giving the soldiers the evil-eye every chance they could."

"I think I know what is going to happen next," Mike said with a smile.

Jim smiled and continued, "As all of this was going on inside of the bar, Dawg and about fifteen soldiers were outside hiding in the parking lot. One of the guys had worked as a locksmith and had a device to get into locked cars. They started going through the vehicles in the parking lot and found the baseball bats the teams had been using. A couple of the bats had blood on them and the M.P.'s kept those bats for evidence. The M.P.'s also took photos of the vehicles, the bats, and the license plates of each vehicle. When it was finally time for the soldiers to leave the bar and head back to post, they took their time saying goodbye to the ladies. The plan was for the soldiers to take their time leaving, because when the locals saw that the soldiers were getting ready to leave, a few of them left the bar ahead of the soldiers to get the bats out of the vehicles. The soldiers hugged the young ladies and exchanged names and phone numbers right in front of the locals and the team could see the locals were getting madder by the minute. One of soldiers that was dressed like a biker saw one of the locals quietly passing out black ski masks to the others."

"The ones that went out early to get the baseball bats were jumped by Dawg and the other soldiers when they opened the trunk of the vehicle. The team took them around to the other side of the building and Dawg somehow convinced them to confess to jumping the soldiers and hitting them with baseball bats. Dawg had some fake blood and poured it on one of the guys so he looked like he was bleeding all over. Then Dawg told him to hold his arm like it had been broken or he would break the guys arm for real. The guy faked a broken arm and Dawg thru onion water into his eyes to make them water. Dawg told him to fake like he had the piss beaten out of him or Dawg would make it happen for real."

Jim could tell Mike was really enjoying the story and he continued. "When the four soldiers came out of the bar, they were followed by ten locals who asked them to stop and talk. The four soldiers stopped and saw ten guys wearing black ski masks. The locals told the soldiers they were not welcome here and wanted them to leave and promise that they would never come back. Of course the soldiers wouldn't do that, and the leader of the group yelled for his friends with baseball bats to join them. You should have seen the look on the locals faces when a group of soldiers showed up rather than his friends with the bats. The soldiers surrounded the locals so they couldn't run away and Dawg walked into the circle with the guy that was faking being injured. The first thing Dawg said was he wanted all of them to put their hands on their heads so they could see that no one was pulling a gun or knife out of his pockets. They all did as Dawg requested."

"Next, Dawg showed them the bloody guy and said he had a signed statement from him giving the names of all the guys that had hit the soldiers with baseball bats. Immediately the leader yelled for someone to call the police. Dawg said they were already there and had the M.P.'s step forward into the circle. Next Dawg told them to take out their driver's license and hand them over to the M.P.'s so they could write down everyone's names. The leader told them not to do it and Dawg knocked him to the ground and put his face down into the gravel while pinning his arm behind his back like he did to the fellow in Tuff Guyz. He gave the locals 10 seconds to have their driver's license out or he was going to break the guys arm."

"And as you can imagine, the guy screamed, 'Do as he says'

and they all got out their licenses and were handing them to the M.P.'s. The M.P.s then called the local police to the scene and explained everything to them. Dawg convinced the locals to confess to the police when they arrived because he had a list of their names and would hunt them down if they refused to confess. They all confessed and the police took them to jail and filed charges. There was never another incident at the bar where soldiers were attacked as far as we know. The end," Jim said.

"Wow, great story," Mike said. "So today in the bar was nothing unusual for Dawg?" Mike asked.

"Not even close," Jim said. "I think Dawg is mellowing out in his old age," Jim said as he and Mike both laughed.

# Chapter 12

The guys had a nice camp fire going when Jim and Mike showed up with the chicken. Everyone grabbed some chicken, potato chips, and a cold beer and placed their lawn chairs around the fire for the meeting. Jim let everyone eat for a few minutes before starting the meeting.

"First of all, everyone did a great job today, so let's have a toast to that," Jim said.

"Here, here," Shades said as everyone clinked beer bottles with the others and took a long drink of beer.

"And Dawg," Jim said, "Thank you for not losing it and hurting someone today."

"Well, you don't know how badly I wanted to hurt Spitty," Dawg said. "But I decided to hurt him in his pocket book rather than hurt him physically by telling everyone in there that he spits in their food when he is mad about something. Word will get around town and his food business should take a big hit."

"That was perfect, Dawg," Jim said. "But what about the part where you said Billy had some very powerful parents and if we don't find him they are going to send some really bad-asses up to look for him?"

"Oh yeah," Dawg said. "Well, I just wanted to leave them something to think about after we left."

"Well done, Dawg, well done," Jim said as he patted Dawg on the back. He continued, "I guess my only concern is that Spitty might decide to get revenge on us. We insulted him, embarrassed him and hurt his business. Maybe he has some more hockey buddies or relatives that he can talk into coming after us. And if he happened to look out the window and saw us in the parking lot talking to Shades, he might figure out that Shades was with us and wasn't a real law man after all. If we ever do this again, Shades, you should get into your vehicle and drive a block or two away so no one sees us together.

"Got it," Shades said. "And it probably would be a good idea to park all the vehicles a block or two away so they couldn't get our license plate numbers when we left," Shades added.

"Another good idea," Jim said.

"Hey, I just thought of something," Swede said. "They have Jim's phone number on the poster. They could have someone call and say they have some information about Billy and want to talk to us. We would naturally go to meet with them and could walk right into an ambush."

"Well, that sure is a possibility," Jim said. "If I get any calls, I'll set up our meeting in a crowded place of business and all of us will go rather than just two. Better to be safe than sorry. Also, I have some shotguns and deer slugs in my truck and want every team to take one of the shotguns and a couple of boxes of ammo with them tomorrow, just in case. Any other comments on our little visit to 'Tuff Guyz?"

Hearing nothing, Jim continued. "Well, really all we learned today was that Billy was in there, Rocco spit in his food, Billy paid for it and left. Is there anything else that I'm missing?"

"And Dawg isn't anyone to mess with," Swede said as everyone nodded.

"Yeah, but we already knew that," Jim said as Dawg growled and barked a few times.

"And Mike is a great wingman and might have saved a life today," Dawg added.

"Here's to Mike, our newest team member," Jim said as everyone raised their beer bottles and drank a toast to Mike.

"So, I think we need to concentrate on finding the foreign guys that returned the boat and trailer. Let's brainstorm some ideas on where they may be staying."

Wiz was the first one to speak and said, "Well, it's been three weeks since they returned the boat and trailer and they may have left the country by now.

"That's true," Jim said. "But, they probably didn't take the jeep with them. Tomorrow morning, I will contact the Canadian law enforcement people again and see if they have any new leads on the vehicle. So, for now, let's just say that the foreigners are still here in Canada."

Shades said, "Well, since the guy that owned the resort said they didn't look like normal fishermen and they were wearing nice clothing, they could be staying at a hotel/motel in the area rather than a resort."

"That's a good point," Jim said. "Wiz, will you find all of the hotels/motels in a 50-mile radius of Vermillion Bay and we will start checking them out. Any other ideas?"

Everyone was thinking when Mike spoke up, "Maybe there are some remote cabins up here, or lake houses that can be rented out for the month or even for the whole summer."

Everyone was shaking their heads in agreement as Jim said, "That's a good idea, Mike. We have been driving by lake houses with 'For Sale or Rent' signs on them. We need to start stopping at them from now on. And, we need to stop at all the local realtor offices in towns and give them one of the 'Missing' posters. Maybe they rented something out to the foreigners. Good thinking guys. Any other ideas?"

Hearing nothing, Jim said, "Well, we now have some new areas to look at, so tomorrow morning, we will start from the resort where the foreigners turned in the boat and trailer and check all hotels, motels, lake houses, remote cabins and realtor offices and see if we can get some new leads."

"How do we check for remote cabins?" Swede asked.

"I think the best way will be to ask resort owners, local business owners, realtors, and bait shops if they know of any remote cabins in the area that can be rented out. Tell them a friend of yours is an author and is looking for a remote cabin to rent because he likes to do his writing in quiet, secluded places," Jim said.

"Got it," Swede said.

"And see if you can get a map of the area that shows lake houses and cabins" Jim added. "Maybe the realtor offices will have some maps we can get from them. Any more thoughts on the subject?" Okay, then I'm going to call Doc and see if he will come up here this weekend instead of going to the ranch. And yes, Dawg, I will ask him if he will bring his boat."

Dawg lifted his hands like a dog's paws and whined like a begging dog.

"Dancer can't come up without a passport so maybe he can team up with Angela since she has the summer off from her teaching job."

"I have a question," Swede said.

"Go ahead," Jim said.

"Can I trade places with Dancer?"

Everyone laughed as Jim said, "So who would like to trade

places with Dancer and work with Angela every day?" All hands went up. "Well, at least I know all of you are straight," Jim said. "But the answer is 'No', since Dancer can't get into Canada."

"Awwwwwww," came the reply from the group.

"Okay guys," Jim said. "I'm going to walk down by the lake and call Doc, then make my daily call to Billy's parents, and then I will call Angela and ask her if she will work with Dancer when he gets there. I'll be back in a few minutes and let you know what everyone says." Jim walked off towards the lake.

The phone call to Doc went well. Doc would drive up this weekend with his boat. After they hung up, Doc was going to call his lawyer brother and ask him the questions Jim wanted to know. The call to the Littlebears went well also. They didn't have any new information so Jim gave them an update on the incident at Rocco's place. He left out a lot of details of the fight and of course that Rocco spit in Billy's burgers as he didn't want to upset them any more if possible. Angela was at the ranch so Jim spoke with her for a few minutes. She would be glad to work with Dancer and show him around town. He made one more call to Dancer to let him know that he would be working with Angela rather than Doc, and that Billy's parents said he could stay with them at the ranch. Dancer was fine with this and would arrive at the ranch on Sunday afternoon.

Jim returned to the camp site and briefed the team on the phone calls. He could tell a lot of them were still pumped up from the incident at Tuff Guyz and he guessed they would probably drink a lot of beer before going to bed, but he was tired, so he again thanked everyone for their efforts and retired to his tent for the night.

# Chapter 13

Jim guessed he was the first one up Thursday morning and decided to go for a run by himself and let the guys sleep in a little. It was only 6 A.M. and he had heard the guys laughing by the camp fire until after midnight, so he knew most of them would be tired and hung over when they woke up. He did some stretching exercises and took off for an early morning jog. He was about a half-mile from camp when he saw another runner coming towards him. It was Dawg. He was heading back to camp after running a few miles. Jim hollered, "Good morning," to Dawg as they passed.

Dawg saluted Jim, then barked a few times and picked up the pace a little as he was now in the home stretch. Jim thought about how Dawg had handled himself in the bar yesterday and was sure glad that Dawg was able to make the trip.

Jim got back to camp as Dawg was walking back from the shower with only a pair of running shorts on. Jim was in great physical condition, but he didn't look a thing like Dawg. Dawg had the body most body builders would envy, and he had never used any steroids. In Dawg's earlier days, he was almost obsessed with working out and something inside drove him to be stronger and tougher than others.

"Good morning, First Sergeant," Jim said to Dawg.

"Good morning, Sir," Dawg replied. How was your run?" Dawg asked.

"It was good," Jim said. "I had some time to do some thinking about the mission and I was trying to think outside the box and come up with some new thoughts as to where we can find Billy."

"I do the same thing every day," Dawg said. "Did you come up with anything?"

"Nothing new," Jim said. "I keep thinking that someone around here has some information that will help us find him, and we either haven't found that person yet, or he isn't talking."

"I have the same feeling," Dawg said. "And I tend to believe that we just haven't found the person that is going to give us the information. I really believe that our new search of looking at hotels, lake houses and cabins will give us some new leads on the foreigners."

"I sure hope so," Jim said. "I can't accept the fact that if we don't find Billy, his parents would sell the ranch and spend the rest of their lives in Canada searching for their son. That breaks my heart."

"Don't worry, Jim, we aren't going to let that happen," Dawg replied. "I can stay up here until the snow flies if needed, and I'm sure others will take turns and help with the search as often as they could. Since my wife left me, I really don't have anything to go home to, so I don't mind spending some time up here looking for my good friend."

"Wow. Just hearing you say that means a lot to me, Dawg. The team and I could trade off and help you for a couple of weeks at a time. I don't want you up here alone, but as long as at least one other person was with you, I would feel a lot better about it," Jim said.

"I am okay working alone, but I understand your concern

and always enjoy company, so that works for me. I really think we will get a good lead in the next week or two and we will be able to find Billy or get an answer as to what happened to him."

"I sure hope you are right," Jim said.

The others were starting to get up and join Dawg and Jim around the camp fire. Everyone was up by seven, and Jim could see that they were all tired and hung over so he just had to say, "Okay, mandatory 5-mile run this morning. Get your gear on and be ready to go in 5 minutes."

A loud moan came from the group as Swede said, "Nice try, Tunes, but you can't make us go for a run anymore and we all know that."

"You are exactly right," Jim said. "I was just checking to see how hung-over you guys really were. So, who drank the most beer last night?"

Everyone pointed at Dawg. Jim said, "So Dawg drank the most beer and he was up running before six this morning?" Everyone looked at Dawg and just shook their heads in amazement.

"Holy crap, Dawg. You drank all that beer and still got up and went running this morning?" Shades said.

"Hey, I felt fine," Dawg said. "I quit drinking shortly after midnight so I got plenty of sleep and felt the need to exercise this morning."

"Well now I know why you never competed in the Olympics," Shades said. "You couldn't pass the hormone test to prove that you were one hundred percent human."

Everyone laughed. Dawg smiled and said to Swede, "How soon are you going to be ready to go? I'm hungry for biscuits and gravy and I start getting mean if I have to wait to get fed."

"Oh crap. I hate working with a mean dog," Swede said as he grabbed his clean clothes and took off on a run for the shower rooms.

Everyone was a running a little slow that morning, so some of them didn't get out of the camp site until around eight o'clock. Jim and Mike headed for Dryden to speak with law enforcement officials about Billy's jeep and to get some more 'Missing' posters printed up. The rest of the guys were going to start stopping at realtor offices and checking out lake houses and cabins for rent. They all had a good feeling that this would give them some new clues.

It was a long day for everyone. Jim and Mike were the first ones back to the camp site at five-thirty. They got the camp fire going and threw some charcoal in the grill. Boom was bringing back the ingredients for Gus Burgers tonight, so there would be some good eating. Jim hadn't told Mike what was in a Gus Burger since Mike hadn't asked him. He was hoping Mike wouldn't ask so he could see how he reacted to his first one. The teams started rolling in and everyone was there by six o'clock. Jim decided to have the meeting before they started grilling burgers.

Jim was surprised that no one had any luck that day. He hadn't gotten any phone calls either, so even though he was discouraged, he had to stay positive. "Well, we got a lot of 'Missing' posters in circulation today," Jim said, "And we just started covering the realtor offices and rental properties, so maybe we will get a phone call tonight or tomorrow morning. Mike and I picked up a bunch of new posters today, so be sure to take plenty with you when you leave in the morning. Also, the Canadian law enforcement people are going to put out an APB on Billy's jeep and see what they can come up with. They checked with customs, and the jeep did not cross back into the U.S., or board a plane or ship for another country, so they believe that it's still here in Canada. Any comments on this subject?" Jim asked.

"Maybe we should start working longer days," Dawg said. "Leave camp by seven in the morning and don't come back until seven at night. That would give each team an extra two hours of searching each day and maybe an extra couple of hours will help us reach the people we are trying to find."

"Well, that's a team decision," Jim said. "How many here think we should start working longer days and cover more ground?" Everyone put their hand up. "Okay," Jim said. "I think that is a great decision. We only have ten days left before some of us have to start heading home, so we need to hit it hard while we have everyone here. And by the way, Dawg has agreed to stay up here and continue the hunt if we haven't found Billy within the next ten days. I don't want him up here alone, so if any of you can come back up for another week or two this summer or fall, that would be greatly appreciated. If we haven't found Billy by next Sunday, I will make up a list and you can sign up for a week or two at a time when you get the go-ahead from your spouse or employer."

The team could see that Jim was a little choked up as he continued, "we feel that if some of us remain in Canada and keep looking for Billy, his parents won't sell the ranch and move up here to continue the search. Let's face it, if eight of us can't find him, his mother and father probably won't be able to find him either. But you heard what his dad said, and you know he meant what he said, so we really have to keep looking as long as possible. Any more discussion on this?" Jim asked.

No one said a thing. "Okay then, the coals are hot, so let's get cooking some Gus Burgers."

"I'll grill the burgers," Boom said.

"I'll help with the condiments," Wiz said as everyone laughed. He continued, "You guys just relax and drink a couple of beer while we do the cooking."

"Sounds good to me," Dawg said. "Just don't burn the burgers, Boom. I like mine a little pink."

"Wow. Cooking instructions from a guy who I've seen eat things that would make a Billy-goat puke," Boom said.

"Hey, I'm just trying to become more sophisticated in case I decide to start dating again," Dawg said.

"I hope you're not thinking about getting back with your ex-wife?" Boom asked.

"Da Bitch," everyone said as Dawg rolled his eyes and shrugged his shoulders.

"I might consider it if she gets down on her knees, apologizes for her mistakes and begs me to come back," Dawg said.

"You have a better chance of winning the lottery," Boom said as everyone kept laughing.

"And you have a better chance of getting your butt kicked if you burn my burger," Dawg said.

"Okay, Dawg. I'll make sure your burger isn't burned too badly." Boom said.

"I'm just saying you have a better chance of getting a nice tip if the burger is exactly the way I requested it," Dawg replied.

"Since when have you ever tipped anyone?" Boom asked.

"Back in 1997 when my ex-wife and I were out with another couple," Dawg said.

"Da Bitch," everyone said as the whole group laughed.

Gus Burgers were burgers with a fried egg on top of them. No one could remember who first made them, but the team all liked eggs, and one day when they were grilling burgers, someone got out a frying pan and started cooking eggs. He put a fried egg on top of every burger and the team just loved them. Someone said they were called Gus Burgers back home and the name stuck. When the burgers were just about done,

Wiz got out a frying pan and started frying eggs. The team made sure Mike got a lawn chair with his back to the grill so he wouldn't see Wiz frying eggs.

When the burgers were done, Wiz put an egg on top of every burger and Boom put them in buns and stacked them on a serving tray. They also put out chips and dip, some veggies and cheese and hollered at the guys to come and get it. Everyone grabbed a burger or two and some of the other stuff as they passed through the line. Mike grabbed a burger and lifted the top bun to put some mustard and ketchup on it when he noticed the fried egg sitting on top of his burger.

"What the hell is this?" Mike said with a laugh.

"What does it look like?" Boom said.

"It looked like a fried egg," Mike replied.

"We have a winner," Boom said as the group laughed.

"Have you ever had a Gus Burger?" Wiz asked.

"Not that I can remember," Mike said.

"Well then if you like eggs and you like burgers, you are in for a real treat," Wiz commented. "Most of us just put a little salt and pepper on top of the egg, some put ketchup or cheese on top and Dawg puts hot sauce on his."

"I think I'll just try a little ketchup on this first one and see how it goes," Mike said. He filled his plate, returned to his chair and everyone was watching as he tried his first bite.

"Well, what's the verdict, Mike?" Boom asked.

Mike replied, "Let me take one more bite, before I answer." He took another bite, chewed it for a while, swallowed it and said, "They are totally awesome," as the group cheered and continued eating.

"Another satisfied customer," Boom said and everyone continued eating.

When everyone was finished eating, Mike said, "Gus Burgers are awesome, but I have one recommendation for the next time we have them."

"And just what is the recommendation, Mike?" Boom asked.

"Well," Mike said, "I like bacon with my eggs, so how about putting a couple strips of bacon on top of the egg?"

Everyone looked at each other and Dawg finally spoke, "Pool Cue, you are a genius," as the whole group cheered.

"Okay," Boom said. "Let's have them again next week and put bacon on top of the eggs." Everyone agreed.

The rest of the night was pretty mellow, just sitting around the camp fire and shooting the breeze. Jim had an idea he wanted to ask the team about. He spoke up and said, "I want to bring up a suggestion and see what you guys think about it. You remember Mary, the lady that called and had spoken with Billy and gave us the tip about seeing him walk into Tuff Guyz? I told you guys the story she told Mike and I about losing her son. I just can't imagine the pain she went through for all those years. She seems like a wonderful person and I would like to ask her to help us. She is a cook at a local school and has the summer off, plus she grew up around here and knows the territory pretty well. We could all chip in a few bucks and pay her something for helping us. I would really like to give her the reward money if it happened to work out. What do you guys think about that?" Jim asked.

"I think it's a great idea," Mike said.

"Anything to help us find Billy," Swede said.

Everyone agreed so Jim got up and walked away from the camp fire to give her a call. He returned a few minutes later and said she agreed to help and that Mike and him would pick her up in the morning. Jim said he was going to call Billy's parents and then turn in for the night. Everyone agreed that they could use some sleep after staying up late the night before.

Billy's parents didn't have any new information so the call didn't last very long. Everyone was in their tents by ten o'clock.

# Chapter 14

Everyone was up by six o'clock Friday morning and most of them went for a morning run. Mike and Swede didn't feel like running, so they grabbed their fishing poles and headed for the lake. The runners were back by six-thirty and Mike and Swede headed back to camp.

"Any luck?" Shades said as they got to camp.

"We each caught a couple of small ones, but let them go," Swede said. "I think we will have some better luck when Doc gets here with his boat tomorrow afternoon."

Everyone was in a hurry to get showered and out of camp by seven, since that was what they agreed on. They could pick up some breakfast on the road. Jim called Mary after Mike and him were on the road and told her they would meet at the local café for breakfast before starting out. She agreed and they met up at around seven-thirty. Jim told Mary about their plan to start visiting realtor offices and checking lake houses and cabins that could be rented out. Mary knew where some of the realtor offices were in the surrounding towns.

Mary mentioned her uncle talking about a secluded 'Party Cabin' that he had been to once for a friend's bachelor party. He told her it was a beautiful cabin with several bedrooms and a private drive. He said that if his friends wouldn't have put signs out along the road, he never would have found the cabin. Jim asked her if she could call her uncle and get some more information on the cabin. She didn't have his phone number, but she could call her cousin and get the number from him.

Mary called and talked to her cousin for a few minutes and got her uncle's phone number. Jim pulled into a resort and asked Mary to call her uncle. She did, and her uncle answered the phone. They talked for a few minutes and finally Mary said some friends of hers were looking for remote cabins and remembered him telling the story about the bachelor party he went to at a remote cabin a few years ago. Her uncle said his friend rented the cabin from a guy that worked in a realtor office in Vermillion Bay, but he couldn't remember the name of the office or the realtor. Mary thanked him for the info and said good-bye. Jim turned south and headed for Vermillion Bay.

Jim and Mike had covered all the businesses in Vermillion Bay and remembered stopping at a couple of realtor offices, but they only asked about Billy and didn't ask about renting any cabins or lake houses to some foreign guys.

"I'm not sure if we should ask if they rented anything out to some foreign guys," Mike said.

"Why is that?" Jim asked.

"Well, these guys don't know us, and if they did rent something out to some foreigners, they might not want to tell us that. I think we would be better off telling them we are looking for a remote cabin or Lake House for our friend, the writer, and see what they have to offer."

"You know, I think that's a good idea, Mike," Jim said. "Let's try it your way first, and if we don't get any leads, we can always bring up the foreigners later.

"Sounds good," Mike said.

They arrived at the first real estate office and went inside. The office didn't handle any rental property there, but said they thought the other real estate office in town had an agent that handled some rental properties for some clients. They asked about the foreigners but no one had seen them. They left another poster and headed for the other real estate office.

At the other office, they were told that an agent named Phil handled rental properties for some clients and that he should be back to the office in a few minutes. They decided to wait and sure enough, Phil showed up in a few minutes. The receptionist informed him that these three people would like to speak with him and he invited them into his office. Phil shook hands with everyone and said, "What can I do for you today?"

"Well, we work for a well-known author in the United States that wants to rent a secluded cabin in this area to write his next book. He likes privacy, so something remote and quiet is what we are looking for," Jim said.

"Well, I have a client that owns a really nice secluded cabin, but it is large and pretty expensive," Phil said.

"Large is okay," Jim said, "because his wife may come up and stay with him from time to time, and when he finishes his book, he throws a big party and would probably have the party at the cabin if it was big enough. And he has lots of money, so the cost in no concern."

"What is the name of this author," Phil asked.

"I'm afraid I can't tell you that," Jim said. "He is well known, and if word got out he was staying at the cabin, reporters, T.V. stations, fans, etc., would show up and he wouldn't like that at all. All of these people will be invited to his party when he finishes the book, but he wants to remain anonymous until that time."

"I think I have a cabin that would be perfect for him, but it is rented at this time. How soon does he need it?" Phil asked.

"Sometime this fall," Jim said. "He didn't give us an exact date."

"Well, the current renters have it until the first of October, so it may work out just fine," Phil said.

"Great," Jim said. "We need to take a look at it first, and then if we like it we will give you a deposit or we can pay you for October and November if you wish."

"Just let me tell you the price for renting the cabin is $2,500 per month," Phil said.

"No problem," Jim said. "If we like the cabin, I will give you $5,000 for two month's rent when you give me a receipt."

"Wow. That would be great, but the renters that are there now have requested privacy, so I'm not sure how they would feel about letting someone look at it," Phil said.

"Well, we're not going to pay for something without looking at it," Jim said.

"I understand," Phil said. "They did say that they wanted a twenty-four-hour notice if something came up and someone had to visit the cabin, so I can call them now and see about showing it to you tomorrow if that works for you."

"That would be great," Jim said.

Phil looked up the renter's cell phone number, then picked up the phone and dialed. After a few seconds, he said, "Mr. Nazari, this is Phil in the real estate office. How are you today, sir? I'm fine, thank you. The reason I'm calling is that I have some people here that want to rent the cabin this fall after you leave and they would like to take a look at the cabin tomorrow if at all possible."

Jim got a strange feeling in his gut when he heard the man's name was Nazari. He looked at Mike and Mary and he could tell they were thinking the same thing as him.

Phil continued, "Yes I know you requested privacy, Mr. Nazari, but these people will not rent the cabin unless they get to look at it first. I really must insist that they be allowed to look at the cabin. I am giving you a twenty-four-hour notice like you requested, so we won't be there until tomorrow morning around ten o'clock." Phil listened for a few seconds then said, "Yes sir. It will be a quick tour and we will be finished and gone within thirty minutes." He listened for a few more seconds then said, "Great. Thank you, sir. We will see you at ten o'clock tomorrow morning." He hung up the phone. "We are all set," Phil said. "How about we meet here at 9:30 tomorrow morning and you can follow me to the cabin?"

"Or we can just meet you there," Jim said.

"No offense, but you probably wouldn't find it even if I gave you directions," Phil said. "The road back to the cabin is not on any maps. It is an old logging road and people have a hard time finding it if they don't know exactly where they are going. It's just better if you follow me."

"Okay, we'll meet you here at nine-thirty," Jim said.

"Great," Phil said. "I have to run now. I'm showing a house in fifteen minutes. I'll see you in the morning."

"We'll be here," Jim said.

"Okay," Phil said. "You all have a great day."

"You too," Jim said as Phil hurried out the office door.

Jim, Mike and Mary left the office and got into Jim's pickup. "I wish he would have given us the address,' Jim said. "I would have driven over there today just to see if the guys in the cabin could be the guys that were driving Billy's jeep."

"I think it's a long shot," Mike said. "I really think that the guys that were driving Billy's jeep are long gone, but it's sure worth checking out."

"You're probably right," Jim said. "I'm not going to get too excited until we get a good look at them. Well Mary, can you think of any more cabins we can check out?"

"No," Mary said, "that's the only cabin that I can think of, but I do know a realtor in the next town to the east, so if you want, we can pay him a visit and see if he can give us some information on some other cabins."

"Sounds good to me," Jim said. "Let's head that way."

They drove to the town and visited with the realtor, but it didn't produce any leads. They had lunch in a nice restaurant, then visited a couple more realtor offices in surrounding towns before heading back to Pineville to take Mary home. They got to Pineville around six o'clock, dropped Mary off at the café and headed for camp. "She sure is a nice lady," Jim said. "I really hope she finds love and doesn't have to grow old all by herself."

"I agree," Mike said. "I would like to introduce her to a couple of single friends of mine if she didn't live so far away. Are any of the guys on the team single, besides Dawg?" Mike said with a laugh.

"I don't pry into other people's lives, but I think Dancer is the only other one that doesn't have a wife or girlfriend," Jim said.

"Well, I don't think she is Dawg's type, do you, Jim," Mike said.

"You never know about old Dawg," Jim said. "She isn't a thing like his ex, but then again they didn't make it, either. Believe it or not, Dawg is a very kind-hearted person. Someone gave him a tee-shirt years ago that said, 'I'm 51% nice guy, 49% monster. Don't push it.'"

"That's good," Mike said with a laugh.

"And it describes Dawg very well," Jim said.

"Since we need to stop at that country mart grocery store and get some lunch meat and bread for dinner tonight, how about grabbing a couple of heads of lettuce and some salad dressing also?" Mike asked.

"Sure," Jim said. "I haven't eaten a salad in a week, so it actually sounds pretty good."

They stopped and bought groceries and arrived at the camp site around seven thirty. The whole team was there sitting around the camp fire waiting for the evening MUM. They decided to eat first since some of the guys were hungry and it wouldn't take long for everyone to make up their own sandwiches and salad. When they finished eating, Jim got the meeting started. No one had any leads other than Jim and Mike. They told the guys the whole story and all of them thought it had great potential. Jim asked Shades if he had heard of the name 'Nazari' before and Shades said that it was a common surname in Afghanistan.

"I thought of something today I want to get your opinion on," Jim said. "Doc will be here tomorrow night when we get back to camp. We could take turns leaving someone in camp like we discussed earlier, OR, we could have one more team helping with the search if we used Doc and Mary. Mike and I worked with Mary today and she is great. She gave us the lead on the cabin we are checking out tomorrow morning. And we haven't had any problems with any of our tents or coolers this past week, so I think we would be okay not to leave anyone here in camp like we have been doing. What do all of you think about that idea?"

"You mean I could actually work with a real human being," Swede said as the group all laughed.

"Better choose you next words carefully," Dawg said to Swede as he growled.

"It sounds good to me," Shades said.

"Everyone was shaking their heads and concurring except Dawg, so Jim said, "Are you okay with this Dawg?"

"No problem here," Dawg said. "I think we should trade off team mates every day. I would like to get to know Pool Cue a little better, and spend a day with the rest of the guys and give them some tips on women."

Everyone laughed and shook their heads as Jim said, "Dawg, are you okay working with Mary for a day also?"

"I guess I can act civilized for one day," Dawg said.

"That means no licking your balls or humping her leg," Swede said as everyone laughed.

"Hey, one day with me and she will throw rocks at you, Swede," Dawg replied.

"Okay, you two knock it off," Jim said. So, everyone is in agreement that we use Mary and Doc to make another team and rotate team members every day?" Everyone agreed. "Okay," Jim said, "We will start the rotation Sunday morning. The driver of the vehicle will keep his same territory and the riders will switch off every day."

"How is our beer supply holding up," Dawg asked.

"We're down to about four cases," Wiz said.

"Better pick up some more beer tomorrow," Dawg said.

"Got it," Jim replied.

"Hey Tunes," Shades said. "Do you still play the guitar?"

"Yeah, whenever I get the chance," Jim replied.

"Why didn't you bring your guitar along?" Shades asked.

"Didn't want my nice guitar to sit in a hot pickup all day," Jim said. "I really need to buy an old guitar that I can take with me for times like this."

"Well," Shades said. "Today we stopped at a pawn shop in one of the towns we visited and they just happened to have a used guitar for sale. We remembered that tomorrow is your birthday, so we all chipped in and bought it for you." Shades grabbed the guitar and handed it to Jim.

"Wow. Thank you guys very much."

"How about you play some oldies that we can sing to?" Swede asked.

"Sure," Jim said. "As long as Dawg doesn't start howling and get us thrown out of the camp ground."

"Very funny," Dawg said.

"I bet I know Dawg's favorite band," Mike said.

"Who might that be?" Dawg asked.

"Three Dawg Night," Mike said as everyone laughed out loud.

The guys all high-fived Mike as Dawg grinned and said, "Good one, Pool Cue."

Jim tuned the guitar and started playing oldies. The guys were all singing along and having a great time. Some of the other campers came over and the guys invited them to join them. Before long, everyone in the camp ground was there listening to Jim and the guys sing some great oldies. One of the campers had a request for the Elvis song, 'I Can't Help Falling in Love with You'. It was their anniversary and that song was sung at their wedding. Jim knew that Shades did a great Elvis impersonation, so he asked Shades if he would sing the song. Shades agreed, and to everyone's surprise, he did a fantastic job.

About halfway through the song, the man asked his wife to dance, and they held each other and slow danced for the remainder of the song. When the song ended, the man gave his wife a big kiss and everyone clapped and congratulated them. The team got to know some of the other campers and made a lot of new friends before the night was over.

Jim had to pee so he handed the guitar to Dawg and said he

would be right back. Dawg grabbed the guitar and strummed a chord and started to sing, "I like to go swimmin' with bull-legged women, and dive down between their legs...... but I know I'm in trouble if their backside blows bubbles, so I surface and just swim away."

The guys laughed loudly as Jim was walking back to the camp fire. "What's so funny?" Jim asked.

"Dawg sang a song from 'Jaws' and changed the words a little," Swede said.

"I can believe that," Jim said, "but we need to keep the noise down and let the other campers get some sleep. Again, thank you guys for the guitar. It really means a lot to me. Now I'm going to put it away. We can still talk and drink beer, but let's keep the noise down for the rest of the night."

Everyone was tired from the day's activities and called it a night by 10:30. Jim didn't sleep well that night as he had a gut feeling that the foreigners could be the guys that were driving Billy's jeep. He wished the girl would have gotten a photo of their faces so they could make a positive identification, and he knew he needed some physical evidence to prove that they were the ones. He fell asleep thinking about what the next morning would bring.

Jim was the first one up Saturday morning and waited for Dawg to get up so they could go for a run. Swede got up and took Kadie for a walk just as Jim and Dawg were leaving on their run. The guys returned, showered, and everyone was headed out of the camp ground by seven o'clock.

Jim and Mike met Mary at the café and had breakfast together before they left. Jim asked Mary about being a part of the team and working with someone different every day and she said she would be happy to do whatever she could to help. They were running a little early, so they made a stop at a small town that was in their territory and passed out some posters. They were back on the road in a short time and the next stop was the realtor office in Vermillion Bay. The office was open, but Phil wasn't there yet, so they sat in Jim's vehicle outside and talked. Jim reminded them not to say anything about the foreigners. They could ask questions about the cabin, but Jim would do all of the talking about the foreigners if he decided to bring it up.

Phil pulled in right on time. They exchanged greetings and Phil told them to follow him to the cabin. Mike was taking notes and Jim was calling off mileage on the odometer every time they made a turn. They turned off of the main road onto what looked like a deer trail. Mary had her camera along and took a photo of the trail right where they turned off of the main road. They traveled for about 5 more miles and turned off onto another grass covered road that was barely wide enough for their vehicles to get through. Jim called off the miles on the odometer and Mary took another photo of the location where they made the turn. They drove for a few more minutes and finally arrived at a clearing where a large, beautiful two-story cabin was sitting right on the shore of a big lake. They parked their cars next to a small Volkswagen vehicle and got out.

"Now, could you have found this if I only would have given you directions?" Phil asked.

"Probably not," Jim said. "This place sure is remote."

"The owner was a wealthy man who wanted his privacy, much like your boss," Phil said. "He used it for a few years, then got cancer and died suddenly. In his will, he said the family was to keep the cabin and not sell it. No one in the family wanted to live here or even vacation here, so they just rent it out."

"Well, let's take a look at it," Jim said as the group started walking towards the front door. When they were nearing the front door of the cabin, two men came out and met them.

"Good morning, Mr. Nazari," Phil said as he stuck out his hand. Mr. Nazari shook hands with Phil as Phil said, "These are the people that want to look at the cabin."

Mr. Nazari was a foreigner with dark skin and black hair, but he was a stocky man and probably weighed close to 200 pounds. The men in the photo were much smaller than him. Mr. Nazari shook hands with everyone and nodded. He saw the camera Mary was carrying and he said, "No photos. No photos." Phil saw Mr. Nazari was getting upset so he asked Mary to put the camera back in the vehicle. Jim said he would take it back for her, and as he was carrying the camera to the vehicle, he snapped a couple of photos over his shoulder without anyone noticing. He put the camera in the vehicle and returned to the group. Phil said he had some photos of the cabin in his office and he would give them to the group when they returned to the office.

You could tell that Mr. Nazari was upset, but he quickly regained his composure and invited them into the cabin. He had an accent, but his English was pretty good. The other man was smaller than Mr. Nazari, but he was older and had gray hair. The two men in the photo had black hair, so Jim was sure that these two men were not the people that were driving Billy's jeep when they turned in the boat and trailer. Mr. Nazari did not introduce the gray-haired man, so he did not speak or shake hands with anyone.

They went into the cabin and looked around. It was beautiful inside. You could tell the owner was wealthy and didn't cut any corners. "Look at the size of this living room," Phil said. We don't get good television reception out here, so the large screen TV is hooked up to a DVD player and as you can see there are over 1,200 videos here in the collection. There are several leather couches and recliners in here when it's time to relax. The fireplace is gas so you don't have to bring in firewood. There is a large kitchen in the next room," Phil said as he was leading the group. "All of the appliances are new within a year or two. There is a smaller kitchen table in here and a large dining table in the next room. There are two large bathrooms, one on each floor."

"Very nice," Jim said. "Do you recommend the cabin, Mr. Nazari?" Jim asked.

"Yes, it is very nice," Mr. Nazari answered.

Jim was hoping he could get Mr. Nazari to talk a little more, but that question wasn't the right one. "Let's see the bedrooms," Jim said.

"All four bedrooms are upstairs," Phil said as he started up the oak cased stairway. Mary, Mike and Jim started up the stairs and Jim noticed that Mr. Nazari and the other man followed very closely. The bedrooms were very large and had a lot of closet space. Phil stated that the mattresses were new and everyone that stayed there commented on the wonderful sleep they got while staying at the cabin.

There were two bedrooms on one side, a large bathroom in the middle, and two bedrooms on the other side. After looking at the first two bedrooms and the bathroom, Phil said, "The other two bedrooms are basically the same as the first two, so you probably don't need to see them."

Mary had been quiet so far but she finally spoke up, "Hey, how do we know you're not trying to hide something from us?"

"You're funny," Phil said as they went to the third bedroom.

Jim immediately noticed that someone was living in that bedroom also. He didn't say anything as they went to the fourth bedroom. Jim could see someone was staying there as well, so he commented, "How many people are staying here?"

"Four people," Phil said.

"So, where are the other two people?" Jim asked. Phil looked at Mr. Nazari for the answer. Mr. Nazari just looked back at Phil as if he didn't understand or didn't want to answer the question. After a few seconds of silence, Jim spoke up, "Mr. Nazari, where are the other two people that are staying here at the cabin?"

"What business is that of yours?" Mr. Nazari answered.

"Whoa," Jim said. "I'm so sorry if I offended you. I just wanted to ask them if they liked the cabin as much as you do."

Mr. Nazari stared at Jim for a few seconds as if to intimidate him, then he answered, "They both like the cabin very much. Now, we have business to attend to, so I must ask all of you to leave."

"Yes, it's time to go," Phil said. "Thank you very much for allowing us to see the cabin." Mr. Nazari nodded and started for the stairs. The gray-haired fellow waited for the last person to start down the stairs, then he followed them out the door. Phil thanked them again, then the two men stood in the front yard and watched as the group got into their vehicles and drove away.

Jim backed up his pickup and started following Phil away from the cabin when Mary quickly spoke up, "Where is the photo of the two men that the girl took at the resort?" Mike handed the folder to Mary and she quickly opened it. "I thought so," Mary said. "I saw a multi-colored shirt in one of the closets that matches this shirt perfectly," she said.

"You did?" Jim said excitedly.

"Yes, it was in the third bedroom we looked at. I opened the closet to see how much room they had in them and I saw a shirt with this same pattern hanging in the closet."

"You're sure of that?" Jim asked.

"Yes, I'm positive now that I see this color photo," Mary said. "I wanted to be a fashion designer when I was younger and have a good eye for patterns and colors. If this isn't the shirt that the guy was wearing in the photo, it is an exact duplicate."

"Wow," Jim said. "I'm so glad you went with us and looked in that closet, Mary."

Mary got a big smile on her face and said, "Glad to help."

"Hey," Mike said, "Doc is bringing his boat up today, so we could launch the boat on the lake and just happen to troll by the cabin and take some photos."

"Good idea, Mike," Jim said. "And I have some other ideas to discuss with the team later. My guess is that the shirt hanging in the closet is the shirt in the photo and the two guys that we didn't get to see today are the two guys that turned in the boat and trailer."

Mike and Mary both agreed with Jim. You could feel the excitement in Jim's vehicle as they talked about Mr. Nazari and the gray-haired man. They finally arrived in Vermillion Bay and pulled into the parking lot of Phil's office. Phil signaled them to come inside. They followed him into the office and Phil said, "Mr. Nazari called me on my cell phone just after we left the cabin. He doesn't want any more visitors to the cabin while he has it rented. So, I'm glad you got to look at it, because I cannot show it again until after he leaves at the end of September."

"Did we offend him in some way?" Jim asked.

"He didn't say," Phil replied. "He just said that he is going to demand privacy for the rest of the time he has it rented and if he wants anyone to come to the cabin, he will invite them. He also said he is going to put up a new gate across the road that turns to the cabin so people won't accidently drive back to the cabin. There was a gate across the road years ago, but it has been broken for many years. Mr. Nazari is going to buy a new gate and replace it."

"And you gave him permission to do that?" Jim asked.

"Yes of course," Phil replied. "It is a private drive and he is going to pay for it himself. I'm glad he is going to do it. So, here are the brochures on the cabin. Would you like to reserve it now, or do you want to speak to your boss first?"

"We don't know the exact dates yet," Jim said. "So, I think we better let him look at the brochure and give us the dates before we do anything."

"Okay," Phil said. "My contact information is on the brochure and here are a few of my business cards for the three of you. Let me know what your boss says and I will reserve the cabin for him."

"One more thing," Jim said. "I see the name of the lake is on the brochure. Are there any resorts or public boat docks on the lake? I'm just curious of how busy the lake will be with other fishing boats."

"There are no resorts on the lake," Phil replied. "There is a public boat dock on the south side of the lake, but it is not well maintained and is seldom used. I have never fished the lake so I can't say whether or not it is a good fishing lake. Most lakes in Canada are very good fishing lakes, so my guess is it probably has some big fish in it."

"Okay, thank you for your time and we will be in touch with you," Jim said.

"You all have a nice day," Phil said as the group left the office.

It was lunch time, and Mary knew a good restaurant in the area, so they headed there to get a bite to eat. Jim wanted to discuss his ideas on how to get a positive identification on the two guys from the cabin with Mike, but he didn't want to involve Mary, so he kept quiet.

After lunch, they stopped at a couple more towns and visited the realtor offices, restaurants, convenience stores, bait shops, etc., and left a 'Missing' poster at each place. It was late afternoon, and Jim headed for Pineville to take Mary home. The team had decided to eat at a steakhouse later that night rather than cook a meal and Jim invited Mary to join them. Jim thought she would like to meet Doc and the other guys in the team and Mary readily accepted the invitation. When they got to the café in Pineville, Jim thanked Mary again and said he would see her at the restaurant at seven-thirty. Jim and Mike watched as she got into her car and drove away.

Jim planned to hold the MUM when Doc showed up at camp and then head for the restaurant. You couldn't predict how long it might take to get through customs at the border, so Doc couldn't give them a definite time when he would arrive. They turned into the campsite and Jim saw a new Chevy Suburban parked there that had a nice boat and trailer attached to it. He knew Doc was already there.

Big and Shades were already back and were drinking a beer with Doc as Jim and Mike pulled up. Doc stood up and saluted as Jim was getting out of his pickup. "At Ease, Soldier," Jim said as he and Doc hugged each other. "How are you my good friend?" Jim asked.

"I'm doing well, thanks," was Doc's reply. "And how are you doing, Tunes?" Doc asked.

"Well, it's been a long week, but we finally got a good lead today and things always go better when you arrive," Jim said.

"So, this must be Mike?" Doc said as he held out his hand to Mike.

"Yes, nice to meet you, Doc," Mike said as they shook hands.

"How do you like hanging out with these wild men, Mike?" Doc asked.

"They are a great group of guys," Mike replied.

"Apparently, you haven't met Dawg," Doc said with a laugh.

Jim quickly commented, "Well Doc, we had a little trouble in a bar a couple of days ago, and Mike hit a guy with a pool cue that was coming up behind Dawg with a knife."

"Wow," Doc said. "So, not only have you met Dawg, you have been in a fight with him. I'm guessing I'm going to hear all about this bar fight later tonight."

"I'm sure you will," Jim said.

Wiz and Boom pulled in next and exchanged hugs and greetings with Doc. Dawg and Swede pulled up a few minutes later. Dawg got out of the truck and started singing, "Doctor, Doctor, give me the news, I got a bad case of clap from you."

Everyone was laughing as Doc and Dawg did a man hug and patted each other on the back. "Still the same old Dawg," Doc said.

"Who you calling old?" Dawg said as he barked out loud.

The guys talked and drank beer for about 30 minutes before Jim decided to start the MUM. "Let's have our meeting so we can head into town and get something to eat. Mary has agreed to join us for dinner, so all of you please be on your best behavior," Jim said.

"Well, I guess that means Dawg doesn't get to go," Swede said.

Everyone laughed as Jim said, "Dawg can go as long as he promises to be a 'Good Dawg'."

"Aw crap," Dawg said. "I am really hungry for a good steak, so I will agree to be good."

"Could you put that in writing?" Swede said.

"Okay, knock it off guys, we need to start the meeting," Jim said.

They went around the campfire and each team gave an update on the day's activities. None of the three teams got any good leads that day. Jim and Mike were the last ones to talk. They carefully told the whole story of how Mr. Nazari wasn't friendly, the gray-haired guy didn't speak, how Mary spotted the colored shirt in one of the closets and how Mr. Nazari had called Phil after they left and told him he would not allow any more visitors and was going to put a gate up across the drive to make sure no one drove up on the cabin, even by mistake.

The team was very excited about the information and felt they finally had a good lead that could give them some information on what happened to Billy. Jim said, "I came up with a plan today and want to go over it with you guys. It is open for discussion, so speak up any time you have a comment. Tomorrow morning, three guys would launch Doc's boat in the lake by the cabin and try to get some photos of the four men that are staying in the cabin. We really want to see photos of the two men that weren't at the cabin today. If they are the same size as the men in the photo the girl took, I think we have our men. Mike and I can't go since they know our faces. Doc, you need to go to run the boat and Shades, you need to go because they may speak Dari if you get close enough to hear them. Since Mike and I won't be with you, you could actually pull up to their dock and strike up a conversation with them if you see them outside. Tell them you heard they caught a big walleye and wanted to see it or something like that. Make up an excuse for why you pulled up to their dock. Dawg, Wiz and Big, I want you guys with me as we sneak in close to the cabin and put up some Trail Cams. We will also have a couple of cameras with us and will try to get some photos of the foreigners if we see them outside of the cabin. Okay, we need one more guy to go in the boat?"

"I'll go," Swede said.

"Great," Jim said. "That leaves Boom and Mike to go into the town nearest to the lake and start asking questions about the foreigners. Someone besides the resort owner had to see these guys. I don't see any need to leave early in the morning as these guys will probably sleep in, so let's have another meeting in the morning to go over everything one more time, and we'll do an equipment check at that time also. Any questions or comments?" Hearing nothing, Jim said, "Then let's head to town and get a thick, juicy steak." Dawg let out a howl as everyone got into their vehicles and headed for town.

It was a nice evening. The team was motivated about finding the cabin with the foreigners in it and everyone really enjoyed talking with Doc and Mary. The restaurant had a small bar attached to it so after eating everyone moved into the bar. They were the only ones in the bar and it was nice and peaceful. Shades checked out the juke box and found some great songs on it. He played a few of them and started dancing around when the first song started playing. He walked up to Mary, held out his hand and said, "May I have this dance?"

Mary said, "It would be an honor," and got up and danced with Shades. After the song ended, the team clapped as Mary and Shades returned to the table.

Jim commented, "Mary, you are lucky that one of our team members called Dancer didn't get to come to Canada with us because he would want to dance with you on every single song."

"Wow," Mary said. "I love to dance, but not to every song. I really like visiting with all of you and getting to know you guys better."

"Well, we feel the same about you, Mary. I'm so glad you called and we got to meet you. And the tip on the cabin might just prove to be the one that leads us to Billy. I would like to propose a toast," Jim said as everyone raised their glasses. "To our newest friend and team member, 'Mary'."

"To Mary," everyone said as they clinked glasses and took a long drink. Mary's face was red and you could see she was a little embarrassed by all the attention she was getting, but Jim felt she was happy to have made some new friends and be part of a group of people that liked her for who she really was.

It was a nice night and everyone seemed to be having a great time. Dawg was coming back from the restroom when the song, 'Who Let the Dogs Out' started playing on the jukebox. Dawg started dancing and jumping around and everyone stood up and clapped. Dawg got more into it and really put on a show. Jim couldn't remember when the group had laughed that hard. Even the bartender was clapping and laughing his butt off.

It was nearly midnight and they finally decided to call it a night. The team walked Mary out to her car and she hugged all of them and thanked them for a wonderful night. Jim told her they were going to check out the cabin in the morning, so they wouldn't need her tomorrow. He would call her and let her know what they found out and if they needed her next week. Mary got into her vehicle and drove away.

The team got back to the camp site a few minutes later and Jim reminded everyone that they had an eight o'clock meeting to check equipment and go over the plan. They all agreed and headed for their tents to get some sleep.

# Chapter 15

Dawg was the first one up Sunday morning and was doing pushups and sit-ups when the rest of the team came out of their tents. Everyone was working out or taking showers by seven-thirty. They had coffee, juice, yogurt or fruit for breakfast and everyone was ready for the meeting at zero eight hundred. Jim could sense the excitement in the air and it reminded him of Afghanistan. They went over the boat mission first. Doc, Shades and Swede were going in the boat. They loaded fishing poles, tackle boxes, a cooler full of sandwiches, drinks, two cameras with telephoto lens, and a shotgun loaded with deer slugs. Everyone had their fishing licenses and Doc had the boat registration. They decided they would pull up to the dock to ask the foreigners if they had caught any fish in the lake and what they were using for bait. Everything was good to go and the three of them pulled out of the campground in Doc's Suburban pulling Doc's boat.

Jim, Dawg, Wiz and Big were going to park their vehicle a couple of miles from the cabin and sneak in close to see what they could find out. They were going to check out the terrain surrounding the cabin, and set up some Trail Cams. The trail cams were the ones that hunters used to see what animals were passing through their hunting area. They were activated by movement and didn't have a flash to scare anything away. The team hoped to get some close-up photos of the foreigners if they went into the woods.

Mike and Boom had a map of the area surrounding the cabin and were going to visit the four small towns that were closest to the cabin. They had the missing posters and the photo of the foreigners with the multi-colored shirt and hoped someone would recognize the jeep or the shirt and give them some information. They were going to take Kadie with them since Big was going to be sneaking in with Jim and the others. Mike and Boom were both dog lovers and were happy to take her along. Jim said it was time to go, and everyone got into their vehicles and pulled out of the camp ground.

Doc and his team arrived at the boat launch around 9 o'clock. It was run down and looked like it wasn't used very often. Doc guessed the fishing must not be very good in the lake or the boat dock would have had more traffic and the weeds and small saplings wouldn't have gotten as big as they were now. They got the boat launched and decided to troll around the lake shore until they found the cabin. Jim had described the cabin to them in detail and showed them the approximate cabin location on a map, so they were sure they could find it even if there were other cabins on the lake. Doc was driving the boat and watching the depth finder trying to keep them in about 14 feet of water. The bottom of the lake had good rock structure, and Doc guessed there were walleye in the lake, but the sun was shining bright now and walleye have sensitive eyes and head for deep water when the sun comes up. Of course, the guys would like to catch some fish, but if they were going to pull into the cabin and ask about catching fish, it would be best if they weren't seen catching any.

Jim found a good spot to park his vehicle on the logging road and the team unloaded their gear and took off for the cabin. They walked in the woods, but close to the road so they could see any vehicles coming from or going to the cabin. Jim was carrying a shotgun loaded with deer slugs just in case they happened to surprise a mother bear with a cub. They were going slow and trying to make enough noise that he didn't think they would sneak up on anything. It took a little over an hour, but they finally arrived at the cabin. They split up into two-man teams, Wiz was with Jim, and Big was with Dawg. They were going to circle the cabin, putting up Trail Cams and getting photos of the foreigners if they got the opportunity. There was a vehicle parked outside the cabin and Jim confirmed that it was the same vehicle that was there yesterday. The team was well trained in surveillance and moved slowly and methodically through the woods surrounding the cabin. They stopped every now and then to get a photo of the cabin from different angles. They were going to meet back at the rendezvous point in two hours, so they had plenty of time to do some snooping and pooping as they call it in the Infantry.

Each team had placed one Trail Cam in the woods and was looking for a good place to put up a second Trail Cam when they heard voices coming from the direction of the cabin. They quickly moved to the edge of the woods where they could see four men standing in front of the cabin, talking and smoking. Wiz zoomed in and got some good photos of all four of the men. Jim had binoculars and zoomed in on the two men that were not at the cabin the day before. He was excited when he saw that they did resemble the two men in the photo that the young girl had taken. After talking for a few minutes, the two young men headed for the boat dock while Mr. Nazari and the gray-haired man got into the vehicle and drove away.

Jim guessed they were probably going into town to see about buying a gate to put across the road to the cabin. The two young men got into a boat that was tied up at the dock, started the motor and headed out into the lake. Jim guessed no one was in the cabin, so he called Doc on his cell phone to tell them to come to the cabin as soon as possible. Doc had trolled past the cabin once already, but not seeing anyone outside, he went on past. He quickly turned the boat around and headed back to the cabin. He saw the other boat from a distance, but they were going the other way so he didn't get a good look at the men in the boat.

Doc pulled his boat up to the boat dock outside of the cabin like Jim told him to do. Jim called Dawg and Big and asked them to go back to the woods along the road to the cabin and call him if a vehicle was heading towards the cabin. He didn't want Mr. Nazari to turn around and come back to the cabin while they were out in the open. If the two men in the boat returned, Doc would warn them. When Dawg and Big were in position, they called Jim. Jim and Wiz left some of their gear in the woods, but came out wearing back packs and were going to say that they were hiking in the woods and had gotten lost. They needed directions and could use something to drink as they were out of water. They walked up to the cabin and knocked on the front door. No one answered. Jim tried the door and it was locked. They walked around to the back door, and it was locked also. The windows were all covered with blinds or curtains, so they couldn't see inside. Jim thought about breaking in, but didn't think this was the right time for that.

There was a small shed in the back yard and a trash can next to it. There was nothing in the shed except a lawn mower and some garden tools. Jim was hoping to steal their trash and go through it piece by piece to see what he could find, but the trash can was empty. Wiz spotted a large fire pit in the backyard next to the woods. They went over and sure enough, they had been burning all of their trash. Maybe it was because no one came to the cabin to haul away the trash, or maybe it was because they didn't want anyone going through their trash and finding something that could incriminate them. The ashes were cool, so Jim started digging through the ashes. He found a few small items he couldn't recognize, so he put them into a plastic bag and put the bag in his back pack to look at later.

Jim's cell phone vibrated and he answered it. It was Doc. The two men in the boat were headed back to the dock. Jim and Wiz were in the back yard so they couldn't see the boat coming. They quickly retreated back into the woods and then started moving in the wood line so they would be able to see the confrontation at the boat dock. They got to where they could see the dock through the brush and waited to see what was going to happen.

Doc had pulled his boat up to the cabin's dock, but all three of the men remained in the boat. The other boat was coming towards the dock wide open and only slowed down as they started getting close to the dock. When they got to the dock, one of the men spoke with a strong accent and said, "What are you doing here? This is a private dock that goes with the cabin."

The team had already decided they were going to act like a bunch of red-neck southern boys and Swede was going to do most of the talking. Swede said, "Well howdy there partners. I'm Billy Bob and these are my two cousins; Leroy and Pooch. We ain't catching any fish in this here lake and was wondering if you could give us some tips on what has been working for ya'll?"

The two foreigners looked at each other and one of them spoke to his friend in their native language. The other smiled at his friend, then got serious as he looked at the team and said, "We don't fish, so we can't help you."

"Well then what are those fishing poles doing in your boat?" Swede said with a big smile. "I know you just don't want to tell us because you're afraid we will catch all the fish in the lake if you tell us what they are biting on, am I right?" Swede asked.

"No. You are not right. We tried fishing, but didn't have any luck," the man said to Swede. "Now I must ask you to leave before my friends come back."

"So, you have some friends here also? Well, we would like to talk to them. Maybe they are friendlier than you fellers and will tell us how we can catch some fish."

"No," said the man. "You must go."

"Now you hold on a minute little man," Swede said. It seems to me that for some reason, you don't like us. We just stopped by to ask you what the fish were biting on. That's all. Now, with you telling us we have to leave, that tells me you fellows either don't like us, or you have something to hide. Now which one is it?"

The men looked at each other again and spoke back and forth in their foreign language a couple of times. Finally, the one man spoke to Swede, "We are sorry if we offended you, but we have some other people with us that insist on privacy. If they come back and find you here, they will be upset with all of us."

"Well, we would like to meet these friends of yours and we will tell them that you asked us to leave but we refused, that way they can't get upset with you. And we really don't care if they get upset with us," Swede said as Doc and Shades laughed out loud. Swede was eating a ham sandwich before they pulled into the dock and took a big bite of it in front of the two men. "You fellers want a ham sandwich and a beer? We got plenty."

"No, we are not hungry. You must leave now," the man said to Swede.

"You just keep your drawers on," Swede said to the man. "Where are you fellows from anyway?"

The two men spoke to each other in their own language a few times before the man said to Swede, "If you don't leave right now, we will call the law and have them arrest you."

That was the wrong thing to say to Swede as he answered, "You go ahead and call the law. This is a public lake and we didn't do anything wrong. We came in here to ask you fellers a question and you have been nothing but rude to us. I'm feeling like maybe I should jump in your boat and throw both of you into the lake. Go ahead and call the law and we will be glad to tell them our side of the story. It's clear to me that either you fellows hate Americans or you are hiding something here. And I don't plan to leave until you tell me the truth. So, go ahead and call the law. I've never been arrested in Canada before, so that would give me something to talk about back home. But, let me warn you, that if I spend the night in jail and have to pay a fine, I know where you guys are staying and I will be back to even the score. Do you understand me?"

The man in the other boat could tell Swede was serious and the look on the man's face went from anger to fear. He finally said, "I am very sorry. We do not want any trouble. We have been catching fish trolling with crank baits just before sunset. This time of the day, we find a deep spot in the lake, anchor the boat and then jig with minnows or leaches. That is all that we know."

"I'll be damned," Swede said. "You knew how to catch fish all along but just wouldn't tell us. Well, I got some friends back home that never tell their fishing secrets either, so I guess I can't blame you. Just one word of advice, try to be friendlier to people from now on. If I wasn't in such a good mood today or if I had a bad hangover, I would have thrown you both into the lake a long time ago. We're going to leave now, so you fellers stay out of trouble and don't take any wooden nickels," Swede said as Doc fired up the motor and was backing away from the two men in the other boat.

Just as Doc put the boat in forward and was turning towards the middle of the lake, Swede yelled to the two men who were now standing on the dock. "One more thing before we go," he said. The men on the dock looked as Swede, Doc and Shades all turned around, dropped their pants and mooned the two men on the dock. The three of them were laughing and high-fiving each other as Doc opened up the motor and sped away.

They followed the shore line north for about a half mile when Swede signaled Doc to cut the motor. They were out of sight of the cabin and Swede and Doc wanted to know what the two men were saying to each other. Doc shut the motor off and they threw out the anchor to try some jigging. "So, what did they say to each other, Shades?" Doc said.

"Well, the first time they spoke, one of them said that we were some real hillbillies and the other one said he thought idiots would be a better word. The second time they spoke, they were getting upset and one of them said, 'And some people wonder why we like to kill Americans.' And the third time they spoke, one of them said that if their boss came back and saw them talking to us, they would be in big trouble, so they agreed to tell us how to catch fish and maybe that would get us to leave."

"Wow," Swede said. "So, they actually said, 'and some people wonder why we like to kill Americans?'"

"They sure did," Shades said.

Doc's cell phone rang and he knew it would be Jim. "Hello," Doc said.

"Whose idea was it to moon them as you were leaving?" Jim asked as everyone laughed. "I think Dawg must be rubbing off on you guys," Jim said. Doc laughed, then told Jim what the foreigners had said about killing Americans. Jim didn't laugh after that comment. He paused for a minute, then told Doc to fish for another hour and then troll back by the cabin and get some more photos if the other men are back by then. After that, they were to load the boat and head back to camp for the meeting. Jim wanted to get all the information and then let the team go over courses of action on what to do next.

Jim called Dawg and told him to meet in the woods behind the cabin. Dawg and Big took their time moving through the woods and met up about 20 minutes after making the call. Jim briefed them on what Doc had told them. Dawg said that they had placed a Trail Cam on the road leading to the cabin so they could tell when a vehicle drove to or left the cabin. They decided to search the timber surrounding the cabin for an hour to see if they could find the jeep or any clues at all. They would meet back in the spot they were at in one hour and walk out together.

Their search of the woods found a lot of mosquitos and wood ticks, but no jeep or anything else that may have belonged to Billy. They met back up when the hour was over and started walking back to Jim's vehicle.

Doc trolled the boat back past the cabin as they were leaving, but no one was outside and the car wasn't there either. They returned to the boat ramp, loaded the boat and headed for the camp site.

Jim called Mike and Boom and told them to head for camp as they were going to have a meeting when everyone got back. They quickly finished passing out the remainder of the 'Missing' posters and headed for camp.

Everyone was back at camp by two o'clock and Jim got the meeting started. He let Shades tell the story about talking to the two men in the boat. You could see how serious everyone got when he told them what the man said about killing American's. No one laughed much when Swede told them how they mooned the men as they were leaving. A few of the guys snickered, but no one laughed like they normally would have done. Jim told about walking up to the cabin and all of the doors were locked and the windows were all covered so he couldn't see inside. He told how they burned their trash, so there was nothing to go through. He remembered they went through the ashes and found a few pieces of things, but he doubted they would do any good.

Jim decided they might as well all take a look at what they found in the ashes, so he took the plastic bag out of his backpack and emptied the contents into a paper cup. He then filled the cup with water and swished the contents around a few times. He put some paper towels down on the picnic table and poured the cup out onto the paper towels. The guys were picking up the pieces and trying to figure out what they were.

Suddenly Mike said, 'Hey Jim, this looks like it could be a name plate that goes on a dog collar. I'm going to get the photo of the dog tag that Billy had made for Kota." Mike handed the piece of metal to Jim and headed for the pickup. Jim really couldn't tell by looking at it, so he handed it to Dawg. Dawg was looking at it as Wiz handed him a steel brush he had gotten from his tool box. Dawg brushed the piece of metal as best he could but he still couldn't tell for sure.

Wiz came back with a magnifying glass and handed it to Dawg. Dawg looked at the piece of metal, then asked Mike for the photo. He looked at the photo, then back at the piece of metal. He looked up at the group and they could see he now had his game face on. "I think this is Kota's dog collar," he said. "Those bastards are in for a world of trouble and I'm just the guy that is going to make it happen."

"Now settle down, Dawg," Jim said.

"Wiz, you take a look at it with the magnifying glass and see if you confirm what Dawg just said."

Wiz looked at it for a few seconds, then looked at the photo and said, "Well, this could be it. The name of the dog is gone, so we can't be 100% positive, but the company logo that is on the photo is here on the metal. Since we are pretty sure the two young men are the ones that returned Billy's jeep, and Mary said the multi-colored shirt in the closet was a perfect match for the shirt in the photos, and now we have the remnants of a dog collar that was made by the same company as the one Billy had made for Kota, I would have to say that we have enough evidence to do whatever is needed to force these men to talk."

Everyone was nodding their heads in agreement when Dawg said, "So what is the plan, Jim?"

"We need to discuss different courses of action and then choose the one we like best," Jim answered.

"Well, I think we need to do something tonight," Dawg said. "If they tell Mr. Nazari what happened at the boat dock, he might think we are on to him and they could pack up and leave before we got back to them. They probably paid cash for the cabin and gave the realtor false names, so we wouldn't be able to track them down. Anyway, that's what I think," Dawg said.

"You bring up a good point, Dawg," Jim said. "Doc, do you or any of the guys in the boat think they might feel threatened by you and leave early?"

Swede answered first, "I don't think so. They called us rednecks and I'm sure they think they are smarter than us. And since we left when they told us how to catch fish, my guess is they think we got the information we were after and will never be back."

"I agree," Doc said. "They might have felt threatened while we were there, but my guess is they are laughing at us now."

"Yeah, I agree with that," Shades said. "When the one guy said to the other, 'And some people wonder why we like to kill Americans,' that tells me they are terrorists and were not intimidated by us in the least. I think they were more afraid of Mr. Nazari and what he would do if he came back and saw them talking to us."

"Well, since they are the only lead we have right now, we can't take the chance of losing them. If they left in the middle of the night, I really doubt we would be able to find them again. We need to do something to ensure they don't leave until we get a chance to talk to them. What are your thoughts on this, Dawg?" Jim asked.

"I recommend we put one team in a tent just inside the woods by where the vehicle is parked next to the cabin," Dawg said. "And another team about two miles down the road in another tent. If they start loading the vehicle and it looks like they are going to leave, the guys can call the team in the second tent and they can put a log across the road and stop them from leaving."

"I like it," Jim said. "Except I would rather take them at the cabin then on that narrow trail road, so I say we put both teams in the woods by the cabin and if they start loading the vehicle and it looks like they are going to leave, we stop them right there and take them back inside the cabin. We have plenty of shotguns and I if we get the jump on them, it should be a piece of cake."

"I like it," Dawg said, "but why don't we just jump them tonight when they are outside of the cabin and get it over with?"

"What if all four of them don't go outside tonight?" Jim said.

"We can come up with some ways of getting them to go outside," Dawg said. "Don't you worry about that."

"What do the rest of you think about taking them tonight?" Jim asked.

"I'm for it." Swede said.

"Me too," Shades said.

"If we take them tonight, we can keep them awake all night long and keep waking them every time they start to fall asleep," Doc said. "You know how people tend to talk when they get really, really tired. They will tell you anything you want to know if you promise to quit waking them and let them get some sleep."

"That's good point, Doc," Jim said. Everyone agreed to move in tonight, except for Mike. Jim noticed that Mike hadn't said a word and decided to ask for his thoughts. "So, Mike," Jim said. "What do you think about all of this?"

"I'm not sure," Mike said. "What you are talking about could be described as kidnapping or holding a person against their will. What if these guys are not the ones we are looking for and had nothing to do with Billy's disappearance? And you already told me that you have ways of making people talk, so that could be considered torture. I don't want to go to prison for being an accessory to what you guys might do to them."

"I totally understand what you are saying, Mike, and I'm sure the rest of the team does as well. We really need one person to stay in camp and watch our things, and I was going to recommend that you be the one to do it," Jim said.

"Hey Mike," Wiz said. "We don't plan to hurt anyone. We have developed a few techniques to trick people into thinking that we are torturing them when we really aren't."

"Like what?" Mike asked.

Wiz looked at Jim and Jim replied, "Mike, what I am going to tell you is confidential, so you say nothing about this to anyone, you understand?"

"I understand," Mike replied.

"One time when we were in Afghanistan, we were on patrol with a larger American unit and got ambushed. They killed a couple of our men with small arms fire right off the bat during the initial attack. We immediately took cover behind a large rock pile only to find out that the Taliban had planted a bunch of IED's behind the rock pile hoping that we would go there to seek cover. The IED's were the small personnel kind, designed to blow off your legs, but not to kill you. The Taliban knew that we never leave a fallen comrade behind, and they enjoyed hearing men scream in pain, so they often built small IED's for this purpose."

Jim continued, "Well, several of the soldiers stepped on the IED's before we figured out what had happened. The medic in the unit was one of the men killed by small arms fire when they first opened up on us. Doc went into action and was doing everything he could to keep the wounded soldiers alive. The soldiers were all carrying a tourniquet, but many of them had both legs severely damaged and Doc was having to put a tourniquet on each leg. We gave Doc all of the tourniquets we had, but he ran out before he finished the last soldier. This guy was in bad shape and was going to bleed to death in a couple of minutes if Doc didn't stop the bleeding. Well, to make a long story short, Doc was wearing a paracord bracelet and took it apart and used the paracord to make a tourniquet. He saved the guys life and later when Doc went back to the states on leave, he visited the guy in the hospital."

"The guy was getting a prosthetic leg within the next week and was very excited about it. Doc had been thinking of an idea of making a video to help get captured enemy soldiers to talk and asked the guy for a favor. The soldier would have done just about anything for Doc and readily agreed. Well, they asked the head hospital administrator and he had to get approval from the Pentagon, but eventually they got approval to make the video. Since Doc's friend was missing a leg, they took a similar looking leg from a cadaver to make it look like the guy had two good legs. They wrote the script and got a film crew to come into the hospital to shoot the video. In the video, they show the guy handcuffed to a chair wearing only a T-shirt and a pair of shorts. They used makeup to make the cadaver leg look like his good leg and had them taped together up under the guy's shorts."

"Well, the man was supposedly caught selling secrets to the enemy and refused to talk. They told him they would put a tourniquet on his leg and it would cut off the blood supply below the tourniquet and the living tissue in his leg would start to die without a fresh supply of blood. The man still refused to talk, so they put the tourniquet on his leg. Remember now, this was a cadaver's leg and not his real leg. Well, as the tissue in the leg started to die, the pain kept getting worse and worse and the man started screaming his head off. The film crew did a close-up of the man's face as he was screaming and yelling in pain while the film crew removed the makeup from the cadaver leg and added some makeup to make the leg look really bad."

Jim could see Mike was listening intently as he continued. "The camera then moved down and showed a close up of what the leg now looked like after the blood supply was cut off for about two hours. The leg was really ugly, and when the man couldn't stand the pain any longer, he started telling everything he knew. The video later shows the man lying in bed without a leg and he says he wishes he would have talked sooner so they would have removed the tourniquet and he could have kept his leg. He ended up giving the information anyway, so his hesitation cost him his leg."

"Well, they did some editing on the video and had it narrated in Dari. When we used it in Afghanistan, we tied the person up to a chair with his arms behind him. We showed him the video of what we were going to do to him if he didn't tell us what we wanted to know. Often, they refused to talk, so we gave them an injection to put them to sleep for a few minutes. While they were asleep, we took a baseball bat and hit them on the chin bone like you did to the guy in the bar. You have seen first-hand how painful that can be. Then we placed a fake tourniquet on the man's leg. It was a real tourniquet, but it was loose and not cutting off any blood supply. When the man wakes up, he instantly feels the pain in his leg from the baseball bat and starts screaming. He sees the tourniquet and thinks it has cut off the blood supply to his leg and the tissue in his leg is dying."

"Well, as you can imagine, they usually tell us everything we want to know if we remove the tourniquet. We remove the tourniquet and give them an injection that they think is to get the blood flowing again. Actually, the injection is for the pain in their leg and once they feel the pain in their leg is going away, they think everything was legit. We promise to put the tourniquet back on if they refuse to answer any questions or lie to us about anything. We have had great success with this and plan to use this on the foreigners if they refuse to talk. Now, is this technique legal to use in a foreign country? Of course not. But we are up here to find our friend and that is what we intend to do. We don't want to kill them and don't even plan to hurt them if they answer all our questions. So, Mike, how do you feel about this now?"

"Well, I feel a lot better about it….. But why don't we just contact the Canadian officials and let them handle it?" Mike asked.

"Well Mike, we just think that we have a better chance of making those men talk than the Canadian court systems would," Jim answered. "What if the foreigners get good lawyers and are allowed to go free like O.J. Simpson, Amanda Knox, or Casey Anthony? I read that over 90 percent of American's believe all three of these people were guilty, yet all of them were acquitted of murder charges. And maybe these men in the cabin have rich families or can get money from their terrorist organization. I'm afraid that if these men were set free by the Canadian court system after we had enough evidence to prove them guilty, we would have to take action into our own hands and then we could end up in prison for the rest of our lives because the Canadian courts failed to convict them or had to let them go on a technicality."

"Mike," Jim said, "we plan to get them to confess what they did to Billy and we are going to record their confessions. After we get a full confession and find Billy's body, we will turn the men over to the Canadian officials. You can stay at camp while we do this, so you are not a part of it in any way. If we were to get into trouble over this, we all will say that you stayed in camp, knew nothing about what was happening and had no part of it. Now, what are your questions or comments?" Jim asked as he looked Mike straight into his eyes.

"I understand what you are doing and why you are doing it. Thanks for explaining it to me. I am okay staying at the camp or doing whatever you want me to do. I'm a part of this team and you have my full support."

"Booyah," Dawg said as he hugged Mike and lifted him off of the ground. The rest of the team shook hands with Mike and gave him a man-hug as Swede opened the cooler and started passing out beers.

"Only one beer since we have a mission later," Jim said. "And I recommend some of you get some sleep if you can. We will work in shifts, so some of us can get some shut-eye in the cabin's bedrooms while others are questioning the foreigners and keeping them from sleeping. Big, do you want Kadie to go with us or do you want to leave her here with Mike?"

"I want her with me," Big said. "And I can take her out in the woods around the cabin and see if she alerts to any decomposing flesh."

"Good idea," Jim said.

Mike spoke up and said, "Hey, I can go into town and bring you guys meals at the cabin if you want me to?"

"I never thought about food," Jim said. "I would rather give you the food money and have you buy a bunch of groceries tomorrow and take them to the cabin. I don't want a vehicle driving in and out several times a day."

"That makes sense. And you will have a nice refrigerator, freezer, oven and microwave at the cabin so you will be able to eat like kings," Mike said.

"We eat like kings now," Dawg said as everyone laughed.

"Hey, how about if I leave a notepad on the picnic table and you guys can write down anything you are hungry for," Mike said. "I'll try to get everything on the list."

"That's a great idea," Swede said. "I would like some homemade pancakes for breakfast and you better pick up some Diet Pepsi and Mountain Dew."

"And get some pork products," Dawg said. "I feel like eating bacon right in front of them."

"No problem. Just put it on the list," Mike said. "How long do you think you will be at the cabin?"

"My guess is a couple of days," Jim said. "But it could be longer or shorter than that."

"One more question?" Mike said. "Are you going to do all four of them at the same time, or put them in separate rooms and do them one at a time?"

"Well, this is a unique situation for us," Jim said. "We normally just have one person so we don't need to worry about others. We can do two at a time and will have to decide which two to do first. Mr. Nazari knows the most, but he looks like a tough old bird and he might not talk even if he thinks it will cost him both of his legs. The young men will talk easier, but they might not know everything. What do you think Dawg?" Jim asked.

"I say we go for Nazari first," Dawg said. "I think he may hold out longer than the others, but he will talk eventually. They all do. I would hate to start with one of the young men because they might not know what happened to Billy. What if Nazari had his gray-haired assistant kill Billy and never told the young guys about it? They could be saying they don't know anything and maybe that is the truth. So, we could keep pushing them to talk after they had already told us everything they know. I say we do Nazari's legs first and if he doesn't talk, then we go to his arms. We have never had to go that far before and we have gotten some men a lot tougher than Nazari to talk. I think it's a combination of the pain and the fact that they don't want to go through the rest of their life missing limbs or being confined to a wheel chair."

"You bring up a bunch of good points, Dawg. Anyone else want to comment on who to do first," Jim asked.

"I agree with Dawg," Swede said. "The others may be afraid to talk for fear of what Nazari will do to them later. Nazari does not have to worry about anyone killing him if he talks. I say we do Nazari first." Everyone agreed with that, so Nazari would be the first one in the chair.

"Here's another idea," Big said. "Since they don't know Shades can speak their language, we put all of them in a room together and have Jim call a meeting outside. We leave Shades in the room to watch them. They may say something to each other about Billy not knowing that Shades can understand every word they are saying."

"Better yet," Wiz said. "I brought some small tape recorders.

I could hide a tape recorder in the room and then everyone could leave. They would surely talk to each other if no one was in the room."

"I like it," Jim said. "But they might suspect a tape recorder if we go into a room before them. I think we could have someone break into the cabin from the back while all of them were out front and plant a tape recorder before we take them back into the cabin. Then we leave them alone for a few minutes and see what they have to say."

"You know, I really like brain-storming with you guys," Jim said. "You keep coming up with great ideas and our plans keep getting better and better."

"Hooah to that, Jim" Dawg said as the team all echoed a loud, "HOOAH."

"Okay, we will leave them alone in a room with a hidden tape recorder and listen to the recorder before we start with the tourniquets," Jim said. "We might get lucky and get enough evidence on tape that we won't have to use the tourniquets on them."

"Aw, come on Jim," Dawg said. "You know how much I like watching them wake up in pain and see the tourniquet on their leg. You can't take that from me," Dawg pleaded.

"Sorry Dawg," Jim replied. "We're not going to do the tourniquet routine unless we need it." Dawg drooped his head and made a soft whining sound like a puppy missing his mommy.

"Hey Doc, how many syringes of each drug do you have?" Jim asked. "I have ten of each," Doc answered. "Ten syringes that will put them to sleep for several minutes, and ten syringes that will take away most of the pain from the sore chin bone. My favorite part is after they spill their guts and the pain medicine starts to wear off. Their chin bone starts to hurt like hell and eventually they realize they were tricked."

"I love that part also," Dawg said. "I want my shift to be after Mr. Nazari talks, because I want to be there when the pain medicine starts to wear off. I think I'll make up a big bowl of popcorn and just sit and watch him suffer while I eat popcorn and enjoy the entertainment."

"Normally I would say that was sick," Wiz said, "but coming from you Dawg, I've heard a lot worse."

"Yeah, I'm really mellowing out in my old age," Dawg said.

"You mean to tell me that you've mellowed out since you put on the show in Tuff Guyz three days ago?" Wiz asked.

"Hey, I think I was pretty mellow in there," Dawg said. "You don't know how badly I wanted to go behind the bar and hurt old Spitty. And if Mike hadn't stopped the guy with the knife before he got to me, who knows what could have happened. Unless he cut my throat or stabbed me in the heart, I probably would have killed him in self-defense."

"Hey, once again Dawg, I'm very proud of the way you stayed calm and handled yourself in the bar," Jim said. "And we're going to need you to remain calm during this next mission also. Even if we get a confession that they killed Billy and buried him in the woods somewhere, you must remain calm. We will think it through and do what the team decides to do. I don't want you slapping someone so hard that you accidently break their neck or something like that. I'm serious about this Dawg. If you don't think you will be able to control yourself if we find out that they killed Billy, then you stay here at camp with Mike."

"Hey Jim, I'm going to the cabin," Dawg said. "You know that. I'm not going to kill anyone unless it is in self-defense. You have my word on that."

"Your word is as good as gold," Jim said. "We all just need to keep our heads and do what is best. If we get a confession, we will find Billy's body and then the team will decide how and when we give the foreigners to the Canadian law enforcement officials."

"Hey, I have another question," Mike said.

"Go ahead Pool Cue," Dawg said to Mike.

"Are you planning to leave all of your vehicles hidden in the woods?" Mike asked. "What if someone finds the vehicles and sees them there for a couple of days straight? They could possibly steal them, or get the license plate numbers and turn them in to the local law enforcement officials, which would mean someone might come to the cabin looking for the owners of the vehicles."

"That's a great point," Dawg said. "We can't take the vehicles to the cabin as that would really look suspicious if the realtor or anyone else drives up to the cabin. And we shouldn't leave them in the woods for a couple of days either. What do you say, Jim?"

"Mike brings up a good point. I think we should leave someone else here at camp with Mike. We really don't need eight of us at the cabin. Would anyone like to stay here with Mike?" No one volunteered. "I know you guys all want to be part of the action and I admire you for that, but we need one more person to stay here for the first night. We will rotate people tomorrow. Doc, can the two people that stay here use your boat and do some fishing in the lake?"

"They sure can," Doc said.

"So," Jim continued, "The person that stays here with Mike tonight can do some fishing in Doc's boat and we will change out people tomorrow."

"Kadie and I will stay here with Mike tonight," Big said, "And we will swap out with someone tomorrow so I can take Kadie into the woods around the cabin and see if she alerts to something."

"Okay, thanks Big," Jim said. "So tonight, all of us will crowd into a couple of pickups driven by Big and Mike. They will drop us off near the cabin and drive back to camp. That way all of our vehicles are here in camp. If we have an emergency at the cabin, we can use our cell phones or the foreigner's car. I don't think they will mind. Mike, you bring Big and Kadie over to the cabin around eight tomorrow morning. Big can help you get groceries on the way to the cabin. You can drive up to the cabin parking lot and we will come out and unload the groceries. Big will stay at the cabin and one team member will go back to camp with Mike. Any questions or comments on this?"

Hearing nothing, Jim said, "Okay, then let's talk about how we are going to get the jump on them," Jim said. "I think they will probably go outside this evening and sit at the picnic table and smoke, drink tea, whatever. It's a nice day today, so they probably will want to get out of the cabin. And, maybe they all decide to go fishing before the sun sets since they told us that was a good time to catch fish. We have to assume that they have pistols on them and will not hesitate to use them. If they did kill Billy, then they won't be afraid to kill the rest of us if they get the opportunity. We have to take them by surprise and don't give them a chance to draw their weapons."

"I agree," Dawg said. "If we are going to break into the cabin and set up a tape recorder, then why not have the whole team go into the cabin and we can jump them when they come back inside."

"That would get us up close and personal with them," Jim said. "And they wouldn't have time to draw their weapons if we jump them as soon as they come back into the cabin."

"But.... What if they come back in one at a time?" Wiz said.

"Then we jump them one at a time," Dawg said.

"Then we have to be concerned about being very quiet, and what if they send one of the guys in to make tea and he doesn't come back. Will they get suspicious and think something is wrong?" Wiz asked. "That's a good point," Jim said. "Since we don't know what they are going to do or where they are going to be, we need to go over some different scenarios."

"I agree," Dawg said. "I think the best plan would to be a combination of some guys in the cabin, and some guys outside. We wait until all four of them are outside, then four guys sneak into the cabin from the back. The other three hid along the side of the cabin. If all four of them return to the cabin at the same time, the outside guys rush to the front door and follow the last guy into the cabin. The four guys inside get the drop on them as the other three come at them through the front door. We tackle them and handcuff them, rather than point a gun at them and tell them to put their hands in the air. If they have committed murder, they may go for a handgun and we would be forced to start shooting. We have superior fire power with our shotguns, but we need them alive to tell us what happened to Billy."

"Okay, Dawg, what if only one guy goes back into the cabin?" Jim asked.

"Then we take him down quietly," Dawg replied.

"And if by chance he screams like a girl before you get your hand over his mouth?" Jim asked.

"Then the three guys outside spring into action as the three others inside come running out the front door," Dawg replied.

"Wiz, how far would you say the picnic table was from the front door of the cabin?" Jim asked.

"It was pretty close," Wiz replied. "I would say 20 feet."

"And how far would you say it was from the north edge of the cabin to the picnic table?" Jim asked.

"It's quite a bit farther, I would say around 50 feet," Wiz replied.

"So, we could be on them and taking them to the ground

within a couple of seconds," Jim said, "and that is plenty of time if we catch them by surprise. But if someone yells or something happens and we give away the element of surprise, they would have plenty of time to draw their pistols and start shooting. My biggest concern is the same as it was in Afghanistan, I just don't want any of our team seriously injured or killed. All of us are up here as volunteers, so we don't have to do this mission. Does anyone here think we should contact the Canadian officials and let them handle this?" Jim asked.

"Hell no," Dawg said. "It's like you explained to Mike. We can't take the chance that these guys could go free without telling what happened to Billy."

"I want each one of them to answer the question of what happened to Billy," Boom commented.

"This is our mission, and we need to carry it out to the end" Swede said.

"We need to do this," Shades commented.

"I wouldn't have come up here if I thought we were going to give the mission to the locals," Doc added.

"Let's finish what we started," said Wiz.

"Let's git er done," Big said as some of the guys laughed.

"I'm totally for it," Mike said as Jim was nodding his head in approval.

"I knew what the answer was going to be before I asked the question," Jim said. "I just wanted everyone to have the opportunity to comment on it."

"I just had an idea," Doc said. "If we launch my boat back into the lake by the cabin, we could have Mike and Big drive the boat past the cabin when all of them were outside. We will call them and let them know when everyone is outside of the cabin. As they go past the cabin, they honk the horn, wave, hold up a fish, or whatever to get the foreigner's attention. When all of them are looking at the boat, we rush them and take them down. I think the distraction gives us an extra second or two and that should be all the time we need."

"Bingo," said Jim.

"Excellent idea," said Dawg as everyone agreed they now had the master plan.

"Okay," Jim said, "It's three o'clock. We may be up all night, so I recommend taking a short nap if you want, but before you do, write down what type of sub sandwich you would like for dinner. I am going to drive into town and will pick up a bunch of sandwiches for later tonight. We will have an equipment check at five o'clock and review the mission once again before we head out. Any questions or comments?" No one spoke up. "Okay, I'll see all of you in two hours."

# Chapter 16

Everyone was sitting in their lawn chairs at five o'clock when Jim started the meeting. They did a quick equipment check and everything that they needed in the boat was present and accounted for. They went over where each person would be positioned, and their assignments. They decided to change the plan and put everyone inside the cabin except Boom. He would be outside hiding around the corner of the cabin. Boom would have a shotgun, and the last person to leave the cabin would have a shotgun. They decided that person would be Jim.

They would execute the plan when all four of the men were sitting or standing at the picnic table. Dawg would lead the charge from the cabin and take down the two men closest to the front door. He planned to ram the person closest to him and knock him to the ground, then tackle the next closest person. Swede and Shades would be right behind Dawg and they would tackle the third and fourth men and take them to the ground. Wiz would be close behind and jump on the first man that Dawg had knocked to the ground. Jim would be the last man coming out of the cabin and he would be carrying the shotgun. Boom would come running from the edge of the cabin with a shotgun as soon as Dawg exited the cabin.

Big was going to drive Doc's vehicle with the boat, and Mike was going to drive Jim's pickup. They would drop the team off in the woods about a mile from the cabin. The team would sneak through the woods to the cabin while Big and Mike were launching the boat. When they reached the cabin, they would position themselves in the surrounding woods so they could see the cabin from every angle. When all four of the men were outside the cabin, the team would meet in the woods behind the cabin and sneak up to the back of the cabin.

They would break into the back of the cabin as quietly as they could and Boom would position himself at the corner of the cabin. At this point, Jim would call Big in the boat and tell him to head for the cabin. Jim and the team would be watching the men through the cabin windows and waiting for the boat to arrive. When the boat arrived and Big and Mike started yelling and waving to the men, Jim would give the "Go" signal and Dawg would lead the charge.

The drive to the cabin was quiet and everyone had their game faces on. Big and Mike finally arrived at the destination and brought the vehicles to a stop. The team exited the vehicles, grabbed their equipment and were moving out in less than two minutes. Big and Mike drove away heading for the boat ramp. The team moved slowly and quietly through the woods and were at the cabin in about thirty minutes. No one was outside at the time, so they took up multiple positions in the woods and began the waiting game.

Big and Mike got to the boat ramp and launched the boat. They make one pass around the lake shore line to locate the cabin, then slowed down and started trolling the shoreline north of the cabin. Around seven o'clock they caught their first fish. It was a nice sized walleye and they put it into the live well and continued fishing.

Soon after, the two young men went outside the cabin and sat down at the picnic table. They were smoking and just enjoying the fresh air. About 20 minutes later, Mr. Nazari and the gray-haired man joined them. Jim decided to leave Big in the woods where he could see the men sitting at the picnic table. Jim put his cell phone on vibrate and Big was told to call Jim's cell phone if any of the men went back into the cabin or started walking around the cabin. Jim didn't want to risk one of the men going back into the cabin while they were breaking into the back of it.

The team quickly snuck up to the back of the cabin and using a crowbar, pried open the back door with very little noise. They quickly went inside and called Boom. Boom left his position quietly moved through the woods in back of the cabin. From there, he quietly walked to the edge of the cabin. Wiz was watching through the window and signaled to Jim that Boom was in place.

Jim called Big and told him they were inside the cabin. Big turned the boat around and headed for the cabin. They decided to troll past the cabin close to the dock and then hold up the walleye for the men at the picnic table to view. As they came into sight, the men all heard the boat motor and turned to see what was coming their way. Jim alerted the team in the cabin and they all moved to the front door and waited for Jim to give the signal. Jim was watching out the window next to the front door, and when Big and Mike held up the walleye and started yelling at the foreigners, Jim said, "NOW."

"Dawg swung open the front door and moved out like an NFL linebacker playing for a new contract. All four of the men were sitting down at the table, so Dawg hit one of the young men that was closest to him so hard it knocked him into the gray-haired man sitting next to him and both men fell backwards off of their seats with their legs still under the picnic table. Dawg pounced on both of them as Swede and Shades took down the two men on the other side of the picnic table, which was Mr. Nazari and the other young man. Wiz jumped on one of the men Dawg had pinned down and Dawg let him go and grabbed the other man with both hands. Jim and Boom were there now pointing the shotguns at the foreigners as they were yelling and trying to make sense out of what just happened to them. Shades passed out the handcuffs and all four men were cuffed with their hands behind their backs.

They searched the men and found pistols on all four of them, but no identification. They gave the pistols to Boom and Jim said, "Okay, let's take them inside." As they were being led inside, Jim gave the thumbs-up sign to Big and Mike and they waved back and headed for the boat ramp.

Inside the cabin, Jim said to take the foreigners into the kitchen. Jim and Wiz carried the small kitchen table out of the kitchen and into the dining room leaving the kitchen chairs. Four of the kitchen chairs were placed up against the kitchen wall and the four men were told to sit down in the chairs. All four of the men were yelling and talking to each other in their language when Jim finally screamed, "SHUT UP," as loud as he could yell.

Everyone was quiet as Mr. Nazari spoke up, "What is the meaning of this? You have broken our rights and invaded our privacy. I will see to it that all of you go to prison."

"Okay, listen up," Jim said. "All of you remain silent until we ask you to speak. Do you understand?"

Mr. Nazari quickly spoke up with his foreign accent and said, "You do not tell us what to do. I demand that you release us immediately or all of you will go to prison."

Jim quickly replied, "I'm only going to say this one more

time so you better pay attention. You will speak ONLY when we ask you to speak, or when we give you permission to speak."

Mr. Nazari said, "We will not listen to anything you tell us to do and we will speak whenever we want to speak." He continued, "I demand that you release us this very moment or I promise to make you pay for doing this to us."

Jim rolled his eyes and said, "Dawg, would you please shut him up."

"With pleasure," Dawg said as he walked up to Mr. Nazari, pulled a dirty handkerchief out of his pocket and stuffed it into Mr. Nazari's mouth. The others were yelling at Dawg and calling him names as Mr. Nazari was coughing and gagging and trying to spit the handkerchief out of his mouth.

Jim said in a loud voice, "Everyone shut up and listen to me. I will have him remove the handkerchief from your boss's mouth if everyone agrees to keep quiet."

The men kept yelling and Jim continued, "Who has the pork and the duct tape in their ruck sack?"

"I do, "Swede said.

"Please give it to me," Jim said as Swede pulled it out of his ruck and handed it to Jim. "Now," Jim said. "If you don't shut up, I'm going to stuff pork in your mouths and duct tape your mouths shut. It is your call and you have 15 seconds to decide."

The men all looked at each other and spoke in their own language as Jim looked at his watch and said, "Five, four, three, two, one." Amazingly, the room was quiet. Jim continued, "Mr. Nazari, we will remove the handkerchief from your mouth if you agree to be quiet also. If you agree and promise to be quiet, then nod your head."

Mr. Nazari was gagging and badly wanted the handkerchief removed, so he reluctantly nodded his approval. Dawg removed the handkerchief as he was coughing and gasping for air. Jim waited a few seconds and then began to speak. He told them the story of their missing friend and how they had come to Canada looking for him. He told about the resort owner seeing the two young men bring the boat and trailer back with Billy's jeep. He told about the photos the girl had taken and how the shirt in the closet matched the shirt one of men were wearing. He told about the partial dog tag they found in the ashes of the fire and how it was identified as being the tag Billy had purchased for his dog, 'Kota'. He finished talking and paused a few seconds while the team studied the looks on the men's faces. Jim finally said, "Mr. Nazari, let's start with you. Tell us where we can find our friend, Billy."

Mr. Nazari looked at Jim and said, "I have no idea what you are talking about."

"Oh, really?" Jim said. "Then maybe you didn't know that these two young men with you were driving Billy's jeep and returned the boat and trailer Billy had rented."

Mr. Nazari shrugged his shoulders and said, "I have no idea of what you are talking about."

"Okay," Jim said. "Then I will ask one of the young men that were in Billy's jeep a question." He looked at the young man closest to Mr. Nazari and said, "Tell me how you happened to be driving our friend's jeep?"

The young man spoke in a whisper and Jim couldn't make out what he was saying.

"Speak louder so we all can hear you," Jim said.

The young man continued to whisper as Dawg got in the man's face and said, "Speak up Boy." The young man spit in Dawg's face and then laughed out loud. Dawg wiped his face off with his sweatshirt and then turned to Jim and said, "Request permission to talk to this young man?"

"Permission granted," Jim said to Dawg. Dawg looked at his

partners and said, "Will you guys put duct tape on the mouths of these other three guys while I have a talk with this young man that spit in my face? I just want to make sure that they all hear what I am going to say."

The team quickly duct-taped the three men's mouths shut and signaled to Dawg that they were finished. "Thank you guys," Dawg said to the team.

"You are quite welcome," Swede answered.

"Glad to help," Wiz added.

Dawg looked at the man that spit in his face and grabbed him firmly by the throat. This cut off his air supply and you could see the look of panic on the man's face. "Dawg said, "Okay, everyone listen closely to what I have to say. Here's what is going to happen to the next one of you that spits in any of our faces. We are going to take you out into the woods, take all of your clothes off and handcuff you to a tree. Your back will be against the tree and we will tie your feet to the tree also. I will stick a big piece of ham in your mouth and duct tape your mouth shut so you won't be able to spit out the ham or call for help."

Dawg could tell the man was needing air, so he released his hand on the man's throat and let him get some air. After a few seconds, he grabbed the man's throat again and continued to speak. "We are going to leave you in the woods all night long, but before we leave you, we are going to hang a necklace made out of meat around your neck, and cover your penis with honey. I'm told bears really like honey. Well, it's going to be really dark in the woods, so you won't be able to see all of the different animals coming to get some of that food that you have for them. I have done this to suborn people before, but not in Canada. I can tell you that the survival rate in Afghanistan is around twenty percent, but there are more bears here in Canada, so I doubt the survival rate is that high up here. And the mosquitoes are really going to feast on you until the wild animals start coming in around midnight." The man's face was beat red and he couldn't go much longer without air, so Dawg again removed his hand as the man was gasping for air.

"Now," Dawg continued, "This may sound like a cruel thing to do to you, but I am positive that you are lying to us and we really want to know what happened to our friend. So, I want all of you to nod that you understand what will happen to you if you spit in any of our faces."

All four men were vigorously shaking their heads up and down. "Excellent," Dawg said. "Now, we will start with the other young man and see if he is ready to talk." Swede removed the duct tape from the man's mouth as Dawg pulled a chair up in front of the man and sat down. "What is your name?" Dawg asked.

"Mohammed," the man answered. "What country are you from?" Dawg asked.

"Afghanistan," the man answered.

"What are you doing here?" Dawg asked.

"We are on a fishing trip," the man answered.

"Why were you driving our friend's jeep?" Dawg asked.

"He asked us to return the boat and trailer for him and we did," the man replied.

"And why did he ask you to return the boat and trailer?" Dawg asked.

"He was busy and had a meeting he needed to attend. He let us use the boat and trailer for two days before we had to turn it in."

"So, where did our friend go?" Dawg asked.

"He didn't tell us. Your friend and the man with him both left in the other vehicle."

"Whoa," Dawg said. "Our friend had another man with him?"

"Yes," the man said.

"And you're telling me that our friend left with this other man and neither of them came back?"

"That is correct," Mohammed replied.

Dawg turned and looked at Jim with a puzzled look on his face. Jim dug into his ruck sack and pulled out a 'Missing' poster and walked up to the man. "Is this a photo of either of the men you are talking about?"

The man looked at the photo of Billy and said, "No. That man does not resemble either of the men that gave us the jeep and left in the other car."

Dawg then showed the photo of Billy to the other three men and asked them, "Have you seen this man?" All of them shook their heads to signify, 'No'.

Dawg then asked another question, "So where is the jeep?" The man hesitated, and looked at Mr. Nazari, "Look at me when I'm talking to you," Dawg said. "Do you want me to grab you by the throat like I did to your friend?"

"No, please," the man said. "I don't know what happened to the jeep after we brought it back to the cabin."

Dawg looked at the others and said, "Does anyone here know what happened to the jeep?" Mr. Nazari was shaking his head up and down, so Jim removed the duct tape from his mouth so he could speak.

Mr. Nazari said, "The men came back and got the jeep during the night. They must have had a spare set of keys and didn't want to wake us up. When we got up the next morning, the jeep was gone."

"So how do you know someone didn't steal the jeep while you were sleeping?" Dawg asked.

"I guess we don't know for sure," Mr. Nazari said. "The men in the jeep asked us to take the boat and trailer back to the resort

## THE HUNT FOR BILLY JACK

for them. We didn't want to do it, but they said we could use the boat for two days before we had to return it and they would leave the jeep with us to pull the trailer. They told us where to take the boat and trailer back and they really wouldn't take no for an answer. They told us we could drive the jeep for a few days until they came back to get it. We finally agreed. They left, and a few days later when we saw the jeep was gone, we just assumed the men came and got it during the night."

"Well," Jim said, "I'm hoping that you can give us the names these men, or maybe a photo of them, or at least the license plate number of the vehicle that they were driving when they left the cabin?" Mr. Nazari looked at Jim and shook his head to signify 'no'. "Well, can any one of you give us some information about the men or the vehicle they were driving?" Jim asked. They all shook their heads to signify 'no'.

"So, you want us to believe that these men trusted you with a jeep, and a boat and trailer, and you never got their names or any information from them?" Jim said. The men all sat quietly and didn't say a word. "Well, I think you are hiding something from us," Jim said, 'And that makes me very upset. Now, I hope you understand that we are very serious here. What Dawg said about spitting on us is totally true, so if you think we are just messing with you, please spit on me and see what happens."

Jim asked the team to remove the duct tape from the mouths of the other two men. When they finished, Jim put his head about a foot in front of Mr. Nazari's face and said, "Go ahead and spit on me if you think we are just joking about what will happen to you." Mr. Nazari gave Jim a dirty look but didn't spit or say a word. Jim went to all of the men and gave them the opportunity to spit in his face. None of them did.

"Okay," Jim said. "I know all of you would like to spit in my face, so you must believe us when we told you what would happen if you spit on any of us. Well, just let me say that we don't think you are telling us everything you know about our friend, his jeep, and the dog. So, we are going to step away from you for a few minutes and discuss some methods we have to get you to talk."

Wiz had signaled to Jim earlier that he had the recorder running, and Jim wanted to see what they said to each other when they were alone in the room. He also wanted to ask Shades what they said when they first jumped them and brought them inside the cabin. Jim told the team to get out some rope and tie the men's handcuffs to their chairs and also their feet to the legs of the chairs to make sure they stayed put during their meeting. He then said to move them apart so they couldn't whisper to each other. He needed them to speak loud enough for the recorder to pick up what they were saying. He knew the men thought no one in the group could understand Dari, so he was sure they would talk to each other in their native language. After the men were tied to their chairs and the chairs were spaced a few feet apart, Jim said, "Now you guys stay here until we get back." Some of the guys were laughing as they all left the room.

Jim had Boom stand in the next room with a shotgun, and placed him so he could see the men through the door opening. Boom wasn't close enough to hear them, but he could see them through the open door and they could see him holding a shotgun. Jim and the rest of the team went outside and sat at the picnic table to talk. As soon as they were seated, he asked Shades what the men had said earlier. Shades said at first the talk was that they couldn't believe what had happened to them. Then it turned to anger and how much they hated Americans and what they were going to do to us when they were set free. The only thing that stood out was that when they were inside Mr. Nazari threatened them and said his people back home would kill their families if they talked."

"Wow," said Jim. "Do you have that on tape?"

"Hopefully," Shades said. "The tape player was already turned on, but there was a lot of background noise, so I'm not sure how clear it will be."

"Well," Jim replied, "the main point is that we know they have a secret that is so important that Mr. Nazari has threatened to kill their families if they talk. We're going to give them a few minutes to talk things over inside, then move them into a different room so Shades can listen to the tape player and find out what they were saying."

"Do you want me to set up the other tape player in the room where you are going to move them into?" Shades asked.

"Good idea," Jim said. "We need to record as much as we can."

"How about we break out those sub sandwiches we brought along and eat now before we continue with the interrogations?" Swede asked.

Dawg spoke up, "I was hoping we could eat in front of them."

Jim looked at Dawg and said, "Let me guess, you got a double ham sub with bacon on top?"

"Good guess," Dawg said.

"Well, how about this?" Jim said. "We move them into the other room and have Dawg stay with them so he can have his fun and eat in front of them all he wants. The rest of us will return to the picnic table and listen to the tape while Shades interprets it for us."

"That sounds good to me," Doc said. "I am curious to find out what they are saying while we are out here."

"Okay," Dawg said. "But I want to be briefed on what they said as soon as everyone finishes eating. Can you send someone in to relieve me so I can join you out here and be briefed on everything they said?"

"Will do," Jim said. "Shades, why don't you go inside and find a good spot to hide the tape recorder in the dining room. After you have it ready, come and get us and we will pick up the guys and move them into the dining room and talk to them for a few minutes. Then we will tell them we need another meeting, and we will come back out here and listen to the tape while we eat our sandwiches. Dawg, I'm sure you are going to eat like a pig in front of them and I'm sure they are going to curse you and say some terrible things about you on the tape."

"Can't be any worse than what my ex-wife used to say about me," Dawg replied.

"Da Bitch," everyone said," with a smile on their face.

"I just don't want you to have your feelings hurt when Shades tells you what they said about you," Jim said.

Dawg looked at Jim and imitated the little Vietnamese boy in the 'Green Berets' movie, "You funny, Peter Son, Ha, ha, you funny." Everyone chuckled as Jim slapped Dawg on the back. Shades came out the door and signaled that the tape recorder was in place. Everyone got up and went back into the cabin.

When they got into the kitchen, Jim said, "We are going to move you into the dining room because it is bigger than this kitchen." Dawg and Swede each grabbed one side of the chair Mr. Nazari was sitting on and picked it up and carried in into the dining room. They returned and got the others as well. They placed the four men's chairs up against a wall in the dining room facing the big dining table. The team turned the dining room chairs of the big table around and sat down facing the men on the wall.

"Well, have you men decided to tell us the truth about what really happened, or do you want us to start the torture process?"

Jim asked. No one said a word, so Jim continued, "I just want you to know that we have a unique way of getting people to talk. We have found that everyone talks when the pain level gets high enough that they can't stand it any longer. So, the bottom line is that you are eventually going to tell us everything we want to know. It's going to be up to you as to if you tell us now, or if you tell us when the pain level gets so bad that you can't stand it anymore."

"Now, if you think you are tough and we won't be able to get you to talk, then you are wrong. We have dealt with people a lot tougher than any of you, and all of them talked. If you pass out from the pain, we will throw cold water on your face and wake you up. We don't want you to die, because then we can't get any more information from you. Now, I want all of you nod your head if you understand everything that I have just said."

They all nodded that they understood. "Good," Jim said. "In a few minutes, we are going to take one person at a time out of this room and into another room for questioning. All four of you will get your turn in the other room, so just be patient. The thing about doing it this way is that none of you will know which one of your friends tells us what we want to know. We are not going to tell you who talked, so you cannot punish that person for talking. We are going to question all four of you, and if one of you tells us what we want to know, we will not torture anyone until we can verify that he was telling the truth. If none of you talk, then we will start the torture process and I promise that it will be the worst night of your life. Are there any questions?" No one spoke up.

"Okay then," Jim said, "We are going to have another meeting outside while we eat dinner. Dawg will stay in here with you. You can talk things over between each other if you want, but when we finish dinner and start asking you questions, you better tell us the truth, the whole truth, and nothing but the truth, or we're going see how much pain you can endure before you finally tell the truth." He looked at each of them and finally said, "Well team, let's eat. I'm starving."

Everyone left the room except Dawg. He found a TV tray in the kitchen and set it up right in front of the four men. Then, he opened his ruck sack and took out this giant sub sandwich, chips and a can of Budweiser. He placed them on the TV tray and said, "You guys don't mind if I eat in front of you, do you?"

Mr. Nazari looked at him and said, "Yes, we would prefer that you eat in the other room if you don't mind."

Dawg looked at him and replied, "Well, I do mind. But, if you tell me right now what happened to my friend, I will go eat in the other room."

"We have already told you everything," Mr. Nazari said loudly.

Dawg looked him right in the eyes and said, "I'm getting really tired of your lies. If you lie to me one more time, I'm going to grab you by the throat and choke you until you piss in your pants. Do you understand?" Mr. Nazari looked at Dawg and shook his head to acknowledge that he understood. The men started speaking to each other in their own language as Dawg opened up his sandwich to show them the ham and bacon. He asked if anyone was hungry and wanted part of his sandwich.

Mr. Nazari said, "We are hungry, but we do not eat pork. We have some food in the refrigerator that you could give us."

"If I get your food for you, will you tell me what really happened to our friend?" Dawg asked.

Mr. Nazari started to speak, then decided he better shut up to avoid a choking.

"Smart man," Dawg said. "I'll let you guys talk it over and decide which one of you is going to tell us everything we want to know when the team comes back in a few minutes. Now I'm going to enjoy this fantastic ham and bacon sub right here in front of you." Dawg took a big bite of the sandwich and said, "Oh man that is good. You guys really are idiots, you know that? You eat camel, dog, possum, and probably even skunk, but you won't eat pork." He took another big bite and purposely let some of the ham hang down outside of his mouth. They men watched him in disgust and spoke to each other. Dawg was sure they were cursing him and he enjoyed it.

He finally finished eating just as Swede came in and said, "Okay, Dawg, Jim wants to talk to you, so I'm here to take your place."

Dawg got up and said, "Let me know if Mr. Nazari lies to you while I am gone and I will choke him when I come back."

"Will do," Swede said as Dawg walked out of the room.

Dawg joined the rest of the team at the picnic table. "So, what did they say to each other?" Dawg asked as he sat down.

"They mainly cursed us and were thinking of ideas on how to get loose," Shades said.

"Well, wait until you listen to the next tape where I ate the ham sandwich in front of them. I'll bet there will be a lot more cursing," Dawg said.

"Did they say anything about Billy?" Dawg asked. Shades looked at Jim, then back at Dawg and said, "We're not sure, but one of them said they need to make up a story so all of them say the same thing, and Mr. Nazari told them not to mention the body no matter what happens to them. He said that if one of them mentions the body, the Americans would kill them or they would go to prison for the rest of their lives. He reminded them that if someone talked, his people back in Afghanistan would kill their whole family."

Dawg's face got serious and he said, "So there is a body,

somewhere? Well, I know the plan was to keep them up all night with questioning and hold the tourniquet off until morning, but I recommend we question them one more time tonight, and if they won't talk, we separate them and get started. And, since we still have over an hour of daylight, why don't we call Big and have him bring Kadie over and they can get started walking the woods around the cabin?"

Jim looked at the others and asked, "Does everyone agree that we call Big and we start tonight rather than wait until morning?" Everyone agreed.

Dawg spoke up again, "Let's question them all together like before, then leave them alone one more time and tape what they say. After we listen to the tape, we separate them and question them one at a time. If no one talks, we show them the video and get started." Everyone agreed to the plan.

Jim called Big and told him to come over right away and bring Mike and Kadie with him. He told Big that the men mentioned a body and the team wanted Kadie to start sniffing the woods behind the cabin right away. They could search until dark, and then return to the camp ground for the night and come back in the morning. Big agreed and said they would be there as soon as possible.

"So, how are we going to get the tape recorder out of the dining room?" Dawg asked. "They were doing a lot of talking while I was with them, so I think we should listen to the tape and see if we get any new information before we proceed."

"How about we give them a bathroom and smoke break?" Jim said. "We untie them and handcuff their hands in front of them, and put handcuffs on their ankles so they can't run, then bring them outside and let them pee and smoke while we remove the tape player?"

"Normally I wouldn't let them smoke and would let them

piss themselves," Dawg said. "But since we need to get them out of the room, I guess that would work. They might get suspicious if we keep moving them from one room to another all the time."

"That's exactly what I thought," Jim said. "We'll get the tape recorder while they are taking their break, then listen to the tape after we get them back inside and tied to their chairs."

"Let's do it," Dawg said. "I'm anxious to hear what nice things they said about me."

Everyone looked at Dawg and laughed as Jim said, "Now, are you sure your feelings won't be hurt if they said some bad things about you?"

"I'm not sure," Dawg said as he whimpered like a little puppy. "I've been told that I don't take criticism very well." The guys all laughed and shook their heads as they walked into the cabin.

Jim explained to the four men that they were going to get a smoke and bathroom break outside behind the cabin. He explained to them about the handcuffs and what would happen to them if they tried to escape. He didn't want anyone in a boat to see them outside, so they went out the back door and stood in the back yard behind the cabin. When all of them were outside, Wiz removed the tape recorder and hid the other one in the same exact place. After about 15 minutes, Jim moved them back inside where they were again cuffed behind their backs and tied to the chairs.

# Chapter 17

Boom was outside watching the perimeter as Big and Mike pulled up to the cabin. Boom told them what the men said about a buried body and the team wanted Kadie to search the woods until dark. Boom told them to use the back door of the cabin when they returned. They agreed and headed off into the woods.

Boom went back inside the cabin. Jim and Dawg questioned the men again and their story was the same as before. Nothing had changed. After the questioning was over, Jim and the guys went outside for another meeting. They double-checked the handcuffs and rope to make sure they were secure, then left them alone in the room so they could talk freely without Dawg watching over them. Boom remained in the next room with a shotgun, just to be safe.

Outside, they listened to the tape as Shades interpreted everything they said. The team guessed right, the men called Dawg every bad name in the book and Mr. Nazari told the young men that all Americans were like Dawg and the world would be a much better place after they finished killing all of them. Then, they made up a story so all of them would say the same exact thing when they were questioned individually. They thought that if everyone told the same exact story, Jim and the men would have to believe it and would eventually turn them loose.

When they were questioned individually, they would admit that they were paid five hundred dollars in American currency to take back the boat and trailer. And that the two men that paid them said they had to dispose of something before they came back and got the jeep. They also were going to say that the vehicle the men left in was a red KIA with U.S. license plates. They decided to say that the men were both in their forties, one of them had black hair and wore a baseball hat. He was of medium build and probably about five feet ten inches tall. The other man was blonde and was taller, probably around 6 feet three inches tall.

They were all excited and believed they were much smarter than the Americans. They were sure that if all of them told the same story, the American's would set them free and start looking for the two men in the red KIA. They went over the story details a few more times until they felt all of them had it memorized.

The team went back inside and sat in front of the men like before. Jim was the first to speak, "Okay guys, you had a smoke and pee break and a chance to discuss everything between yourselves. So, which one of you is going to tell us the truth about what really happened?" No one said a thing, so Jim said, "You guys are really starting to piss me off, so to save us some time, let me tell you something. We know you made up a story and each of you are all going to tell us that you got paid $500 to return the boat and trailer."

You could see the look of surprise on the men's face as Jim continued. "We know you are going to tell us the two men left in a red KIA with U.S. license plates. We know you are going to say one of the men was about five feet ten inches tall and had dark hair, and the other man was blonde and about six feet three inches tall. We know you are going to tell us that the men said they were going to return and get the jeep after they disposed of something. We also heard Mr. Nazari threaten to kill your families back in Afghanistan if you told about the body. We heard you make up the story and rehearse it so everyone would tell us the same thing. We heard you say that if all of you told us the same story, we would have to believe it and would let you go. We heard you say that you thought you were smarter than us.... So, tell me, now who do you think is smarter?"

For the first time, Jim saw real fear in the faces of the men. They knew the team somehow heard everything they had said and their plan had just gone south in a real hurry.

Mr. Nazari said to the others in Dari, "Do not say a thing to them no matter what happens. I promise you that we will get out of this if no one talks."

Jim looked at Shades and said, "If they had any brains at all, they would have figured out that at least one of us can speak Dari. What did he just say, Shades?"

"He told the others not to say a thing no matter what happens and he promised he would get them out of this if none of them talks."

The men in handcuffs all looked at their leader, Mr. Nazari for him to say something, but he didn't say a word. "Well," Jim said, "Wiz, change of plans, I think it's time to show them the video right now. How about setting the projector on the table and shooting the video on that wall? We can turn their chairs so they can all see it clearly."

"You got it," Wiz said as he started taking the equipment out of his backpack. Dawg and the others started moving the chairs as Wiz was hooking everything up. You could see the fear in the men's faces and Jim knew he could get them to talk before daylight tomorrow morning.

Wiz gave Jim the thumbs up that the video was ready to go and Jim looked at the four men and said, "Now, listen to me closely. We are going to show you a video of what we are going to do to you if you don't tell us what we want to know. Again, we really will do this to you, and again, the pain will get so intense that you will tell us everything we want to know. So, with that, Wiz, please start the show."

The four men sat and watched the video of a man who was being questioned, but would not talk. The team gave the man a shot to put him to sleep, then placed a tourniquet on his right leg above the knee. After the man woke up, he was in a lot of pain and asked about the tourniquet. They told him it was cutting off the blood supply to his leg and the tissue in his leg would soon start to die without adequate blood supply. The man still refused to talk and the pain continued to get worse and worse. The man was sweating and breathing heavy and yelling out in pain, but he still wouldn't talk.

Finally, the man just couldn't stand the pain any longer and told them everything they wanted to know. They removed the tourniquet, and rushed the man to the hospital, but it was too late. His leg had to be amputated. They later showed the man in a hospital bed with his right leg cut off above the knee. He was crying and said he wished he would have talked sooner and kept his leg, because he ended up talking anyway when he couldn't stand the pain any longer.

You could see how serious the men were taking the video and one of the young men was fighting back tears. The video then went to a double amputee and he was interviewed in a prison cell. He said he was a tough guy and could tolerate a lot of pain, but after he didn't talk with tourniquets on both of his legs, they started putting a tourniquet on his right arm and he decided to tell them everything. They removed the tourniquets on his legs, but by the time they got him to a hospital, it was too late and both of his legs had to be amputated.

Before the film ended, Jim was on camera saying that they had one-hundred percent success with the tourniquet technique. Some of the people held off talking a little too long and had to have their legs amputated, but everyone talked eventually.

The film ended and the room was totally quiet as Jim spoke, "We have decided to do two of you at a time since we have two video cameras. We will be recording everything so we can later enjoy watching each of you suffer over and over again. And, by the way, the only hospital we know of is in Dryden, which is about a two-hour drive from here, so the chances of saving your leg after you talk will be rather slim unless you talk within thirty minutes of the tourniquet being placed on your leg."

Mr. Nazari suddenly yelled, "They are lying. They will not do this to us. They are just scaring us and trying to get us to talk. Do not tell them anything."

"Well, Jim said, "He is right about one thing. We are trying to get you to talk. But, he is wrong saying that we will not do that to you. We would really like someone to tell us the truth so we don't have to torture you. But, believe me when I say we are going to torture you and see how much pain you can endure before you talk. I really hope you talk before you lose your leg, but that is totally up to you. So, who wants to volunteer to go first and second?" Jim asked.

No one said a thing, so Jim said, "Well then, I am going to recommend that we take Mr. Nazari into one of the upstairs bedrooms, and young Mohammed into one of the other bedrooms and we get this show on the road."

Just as they were going to start carrying the men upstairs,

Mike walked in the back door and yelled for Jim. Boom stayed with the foreigners while the rest of the team left the kitchen and met Mike by the back door. Mike said, "Kadie alerted to something in the woods. We removed the leaves and sticks and it looks like a fresh grave. We brought Big's SUV, so the shovels are back at camp in Jim's pickup. It's nearly dark and the mosquitos are already worse than I have ever seen in my entire life. Big is putting Kadie in the SUV and will be here in a minute."

"Damn," Jim said as he closed his eyes and shook his head.

"Forget about the tourniquet technique," Dawg said. "Let me take one of them down to the lake and hold him under water until he is ready to talk. After I drown a couple of them, the others will surely talk."

"No," Jim said. "We don't know for sure that it is a grave or that Billy's body is buried in it. We will continue with the plan. Just then, Big walked into the cabin and joined the team. "What do you think is buried out there," Jim asked Big.

"Well, it's hard to say," Big replied. "It might be a person, but it could also be a deer, or maybe even Kota. I could tell by the way Kadie responded that something is buried and decomposing in that spot. But, since I can't say for sure, I would hate for any of us to dig it up tonight and get eaten up by mosquitos just to find out it was an animal."

"Okay," Jim said. "We'll wait for daylight to dig it up and see what is down there. You guys go on back to camp and get some sleep. Why don't you be back here around seven tomorrow morning with the groceries and the shovels?"

"Okay," Big answered. "So, how are things going here?"

"We just showed them the video and are about to take two of them at a time into separate rooms and start the tourniquet technique," Jim replied.

"Sweet," Big said with a smile on his face. "Well, you guys have fun and we'll see you in the morning."

"Okay. Thanks for coming over right away," Jim replied.

"No problem," Big said.

"You guys be careful tonight," Mike said as they walked out the door.

"We will," Jim said as he closed the door behind them. He then turned to the team and said, "Let's not tell them that we know that something is buried out back and we are going to dig it up in the morning. I have a feeling they are going to tell us what is buried out there before the night is over."

"Wiz, Swede and I will be with Mr. Nazari in the south bedroom. Dawg, Shades and Doc, you will have Mohammed in the far north bedroom. Boom, will stay with the other two men in the kitchen. Make sure the video cameras are up and running before you start the questioning. Doc, after you give young Mohammed a shot to knock him out, come to our room and give Mr. Nazari a shot. Is everyone clear on what to do?"

"Clear," was the answer from all of them.

"Then let's go to work," Jim said.

They went back inside and Dawg and Swede carried Mr. Nazari and his chair upstairs and put him in the south bedroom. They returned and carried Mohammed upstairs and placed him in the north bedroom. The teams split up and went to the bedrooms they were assigned and started questioning the two men. Mohammed must have believed Mr. Nazari when he told them the Americans were just scaring them and would not actually do what they showed in the video, because he refused to talk. So, after about 20 minutes not getting any answers from him, Dawg held him down while Doc gave him an injection that knocked him out. Doc then took the other syringe to the south bedroom for Mr. Nazari.

Jim had him wait a few minutes before he gave Mr. Nazari the injection. After Mr. Nazari was out, Doc returned to the north bedroom where Mohammed was out like a light. Shades had put the fake tourniquet on Mohamed's right leg just above the knee and Doc gave Dawg the okay to hit Mohammed in the chin bone. Dawg had brought a piece of steel pipe in his ruck sack specifically for the job. He hit Mohamed with the pipe three times below the knee. He hit him hard, but not hard enough to break the bone. The pipe would sometimes break the skin and cause bleeding, so they might have to put a band aid or a small bandage over the cut to keep the blood from showing through the pants. They waited for a minute but there was no bleeding from Mohammed's leg. Dawg then went to the other bedroom and did the same thing to Mr. Nazari.

About fifteen minutes later, Mohamed's shot wore off and he started to gain consciousness. He immediately felt the intense pain in his leg and started to scream. He looked down and saw the tourniquet and realized that they had actually done what they said they were going to do. He cursed them loudly between screams. Mr. Nazari gained consciousness a few minutes later to the same feeling of pain. He heard Mohammed screaming and noticed the tourniquet on his leg. He was shocked the American's were actually doing what they said they would do.

After a few minutes of cursing and screaming, Jim put duct tape on Mr. Nazari's mouth so he could hear what Jim was going to say to him. Jim told him he would remove the tourniquet on his leg as soon as Mr. Nazari was ready to tell them what had happened to their friend. Jim told him that when he was ready to tell the whole truth, to nod his head and Jim would remove the duct tape. But, as soon as the duct tape was removed, Mr. Nazari would have to start talking and tell them what really happened. As soon as he told them what happened to Billy, Jim would remove the tourniquet and his leg would be saved. Mr. Nazari's face was bright red and he was sweating profusely, but he refused to nod his head at least for the time being.

Back in the other bedroom, Doc put duct tape over Mohammed's mouth and told him the same thing Jim had said to Mr. Nazari. Mohammed was trying to be strong, and Doc could sense he was starting to give in to the pain. Doc told Mohammed that if he didn't talk within ten minutes, they were going to put him to sleep again and put a tourniquet on his other leg. When he woke up the next time, the pain would be twice as bad as it was now, and would continue to get worse as the living tissue in his legs started to die from lack of blood.

Ten minutes went by and Mohammed still was refusing to talk, so Doc gave him another shot. He was out cold in a couple of minutes and they placed another fake tourniquet on his left leg and Dawg hit him with the pipe three times below the knee. He also hit him twice more in the other leg just to increase the pain level. Doc went down to the other bedroom and called Jim out into the hallway. He told Jim what they were doing and Jim decided to hold off on knocking Mr. Nazari out until Mohammed gained consciousness. After Mohammed was fully awake, Doc would come down to Jim's room and give Mr. Nazari his second shot. Jim thought Mohammed might feel more comfortable talking if he knew Mr. Nazari was unconscious and couldn't hear anything he said.

Jim removed the duct tape from Mr. Nazari's mouth so Mohammed would be able to hear Mr. Nazari yelling in pain when he woke up. A few minutes went by before Mohammed started to wake up. The first thing he did was scream like a little girl. The pain by now was unbearable and Mohammed was afraid he was going to lose both of his legs. He heard Mr. Nazari yelling in the other room and Doc told him he was

# THE HUNT FOR BILLY JACK

going to give Mr. Nazari another shot to knock him out, and he would be back in a couple of minutes. Mohammed begged Doc to release the tourniquets and Doc told him that he only had a few minutes left before permanent damage occurred to his right leg. Doc turned and walked to the other bedroom.

In the south bedroom, Doc gave Mr. Nazari his second shot and he was out cold in a few minutes. After he was unconscious, Swede picked up the pipe to hit him in the leg and Jim said, "I don't think we need to hit him in the leg right now because I think Mohammed is going to tell us everything we want to know." Swede looked at him with sad eyes, and Jim said, "Wait a minute. My bad. Put the tourniquet on his left leg and hit him twice for the fun of it."

Swede got a big smile on his face and said, "Thank you, Sir."

Jim replied, "You're very welcome."

Swede hit Mr. Nazari twice in the chin bone as Doc said, "That is going to hurt like hell when he wakes up."

Swede again smiled and said, "That's the plan, Stan," as they all snickered and headed out the door to the north bedroom.

In the north bedroom, Jim told Mohammed that he would release both tourniquets and give him a shot for pain if he told them everything he knew. Mohammed had reached his pain threshold and agreed to talk. Jim told him that Mr. Nazari was unconscious so he wouldn't be able to hear anything that Mohammed said and told him what would happen to him if he lied to them. Mohammed agreed to tell the truth about everything. Jim released both tourniquets and Doc gave Mohammed a shot in both legs for the pain.

The pain in his legs started to go away as Doc was massaging both of his Mohammed's calves to appear like he was trying to increase circulation. Doc told Mohammed that his legs would be fine as long as he told the truth and warned him that the tourniquets would go back on if they felt he was lying to them about anything. He also told Mohammed that he would not tell Mr. Nazari anything that Mohammed told them. He said all of them were going to tell the truth eventually, so if Mohammed wanted to keep his legs, he had better talk now or the tourniquets would be put back on in a matter of seconds.

Mohammed agreed to tell everything and Jim started the questioning. "We found a grave out back and are going to dig it up in the morning. What will we find in the grave?" Jim asked.

"You will find the body of a dead woman," Mohammed answered. "She was a whore and we brought her here for our pleasure. She stayed with us a couple of days and then wanted to leave. Mr. Nazari gave the order to kill her rather than let her go."

"Who killed her?" Jim asked.

"Hahta, the gray-haired man. He is Mr. Nazari's body guard and does most of the killing."

"So, what about our friend, what happened to him?" Jim asked.

"I never saw your friend, so I don't know what happened to him," was the reply.

"Okay," Jim said. "I don't believe you, so I'm going to put the tourniquets back on."

"No," Mohammed yelled. "I am telling the truth. I never saw your friend. You must believe me," he said as tears rolled down his cheeks.

"Then what about the dog?" Jim asked.

"The men that gave us the jeep also gave us the dog," Mohammed said.

"Now wait a minute," Jim said. "We heard you make up the story about the two men."

"Yes, we made up the story about what the two men looked

like, but there really were two men here. They gave us the jeep, the boat and trailer and the dog. They were American's. One was really thin and had dark circles around his eyes. He looked like a heavy drug user. The other man was fat and bald."

"Could you recognize the men if you saw them again?" Jim asked.

"Yes, I'm sure of it," Mohammed answered.

"Are your legs feeling better?" Jim asked.

"Yes, they are starting to feel better," Mohammed answered.

"Well, you keep telling me the truth and they will feel even better than they do right now. But if you lie to me, I will put the tourniquets back on and the pain level will be much worse than before," Jim said.

"I will tell you the truth about everything," Mohammed said. "Please don't put the tourniquets back on my legs," he pleaded.

"Well, it's really up to you," Jim said.

"So, what happened to the dog?" Jim asked.

"We tied the dog up outside the first night because Mr. Nazari didn't want him going to the bathroom in the cabin. When we woke up the next morning, he was gone. He pulled so hard on the rope that he broke the collar and ran off. We burned the collar with the trash that day."

"And what about the jeep?" Jim asked.

"Well, the men never came back to get it like they said they would and Mr. Nazari started getting nervous. One day he ordered us to drive it deep into the woods and get rid of it. Hahta followed us in the car and we found a deserted logging road about 30 miles from here. We picked out a good spot and abandoned the jeep. We took off the license plates and filed off the VIN so no one could trace it. We also left a sign inside it that said anyone could have the jeep if they wanted it."

"Could you take us to the place where you left the jeep?" Jim asked.

"Yes," Mohammed answered. "I remember where we turned off onto the logging road and I could find it eventually."

"Let's go back a little bit. Why are you really here in Canada?" Jim asked.

Mohammed hesitated and didn't want to answer the question. He looked down at the floor and was not talking. Jim got out of his chair and picked up the tourniquets. Tears started running down Mohammed's cheeks as Jim grabbed his right leg and started putting the tourniquet back on it.

Mohammed said, "Okay. Okay. I will tell you. We were going to sneak into the United States and meet up with some fellow countrymen that are there now making bombs. We were going to plant the bombs in several shopping malls and kill as many American's as we could."

Jim looked at Dawg and then back at Mohammed. Then he looked at Shades and said, "Make sure we are getting this on video." Shades checked the recorder and gave Jim a thumbs-up that everything was working. Jim looked back at Mohammed and said, "So, when were these mall bombings going to take place?"

"The day after your Thanksgiving holiday," Mohammed answered.

"Oh, my God," Jim said. "Black Friday. The busiest shopping day of the year." Jim stood up and walked around the room for a minute. He wondered if Billy had discovered this information and someone killed him to keep him from talking. He couldn't get over the magnitude of this. This plot could kill more people than were killed on nine-eleven. And most of them would be women and children. This was pure evil and Jim had a hard time containing his anger. He sat back down and looked at Doc and Shades before he continued the questioning.

"So, tell me more about your mission," Jim said.

"One of our countrymen was going to meet us here at the cabin in September. He would show us how to sneak across the border into the U.S. We would meet up with everyone else somewhere in Minnesota and split up into groups. Each group would be assigned a major mall in the city that they were assigned."

"Do you know which cities the groups were going to place the bombs at?" Jim asked.

"Minneapolis, Des Moines, Omaha and Kansas City," Mohammed answered."

Jim shook his head as he knew many of his friends and family could be at a mall in Des Moines on Black Friday. "Go on," he said to Mohammed.

"We were going to scope out the malls and come up with the best ways to sneak explosives into the malls, and the best places to plant the bombs to maximize the casualties," Mohammed said. "After the bombs went off, we were to meet up back in Minnesota and stay there until we felt it was safe to sneak back into Canada. We would hide out in Canada for a while until they told us it was safe to fly home."

"And where is home?" Dawg asked.

"Kabul, Afghanistan," Mohammed answered.

"Is there anything else you can tell us about the mission?" Jim asked.

Mohammed shook his head and said, "That is all I can think of at this time."

Jim looked at Shades and said, "Shut off the recorder. I want the rest of the team to hear the recording and process this information before we continue. Doc, since you and Shades already know what is on the tape, I want one of you to stay here with Mohammed and the other one with Mr. Nazari. I want Dawg with me as we decide what to do next."

They both nodded approval as Jim grabbed the recorder and headed downstairs. Dawg yelled for Wiz and Swede to follow them. Jim wanted Boom to hear the recording also, so they double-checked the hand cuffs and knots and made sure the two men in the kitchen were secure before they left the room. There was a small room in the back of the cabin that had been used for an office and that is where Jim set up the recorder. The men pulled up chairs and Jim played the video. When it ended, Jim could see the shock in the men's faces as he asked, "What are your comments?"

Wiz was the first to speak and said, "Wow. So, we have discovered a plot to place bombs in malls and kill American shoppers on Black Friday?"

"That is what Mohammed told us," Jim replied. "I believe he was telling the truth, but how do we know for sure?"

"My suggestion is we take the two men in the kitchen upstairs and give them the tourniquet technique and hear what they have to say," Dawg said. "I'm guessing the other young man will talk rather than lose his legs, and if he says the same thing as Mohammed, then it is probably true."

"I agree," Wiz said. "I think Mohammed was telling the truth. He wouldn't make up a story like that."

"What are your thoughts on this, Swede?" Jim asked.

"I agree with Wiz and Dawg. If one of the other men gives us the same story as Mohammed, then it probably is true. Tomorrow morning, we can dig up the body and hopefully find Billy's jeep. If Mohammed was telling the truth about the woman in the grave and we find the jeep, then I would bet he was telling the truth about bombing the shopping malls as well."

"Good point," Jim said. "So, we all agree to give the two men in the kitchen the tourniquet technique and see if their story matches that of Mohammed." Everyone agreed. "And in the morning, we dig up the grave and send a couple of guys with Mohammed to find Billy's jeep?"

"That sounds like a good plan to me," Dawg said as everyone shook their heads in agreement.

"I think our chances of getting someone to talk are better with either of the men in the kitchen than with Mr. Nazari," Jim said, "But since Mr. Nazari is just gaining consciousness from his second leg hit, we might as well at least question him and see what he says." Everyone agreed and they walked out of the room and headed upstairs as Boom returned to the two men in the kitchen.

In the south bedroom, Mr. Nazari was just starting to gain consciousness and the pain in both of his legs was really severe. He woke up screaming as the group joined Mr. Nazari and Shades in the bedroom. Mr. Nazari saw everyone and started yelling at them in Dari. Jim looked at Shades and said, "Let me guess, he's saying some things about us that are not very nice."

"Good guess," Shades said. "And he is saying things about our mothers, and our country, and how happy he will be when Allah rids the earth of all Infidels."

"Okay. Whatever," Jim said. "Dawg, do you think you can get Mr. Nazari to stop yelling so we can question him?"

"I'll bet that I can," Dawg said as he stepped forward and grabbed Mr. Nazari by the throat and pinched off his air supply. Dawg then looked him right in the eyes and said, "We want you to quit yelling and answer some questions for us. If you keep yelling, I'm going to stuff pork into your mouth and tape it shut until you are ready to talk. And, I just want to remind you that the tissue in your legs is craving blood right now, and if you refuse to tell us what we want to know, the tissue in your legs will soon start to die. A short time after the tissue starts to die, an infection called gangrene will start to develop. Once gangrene sets in, you will have to have both legs amputated to save your life."

Now, if you still refuse to talk, we will put tourniquets on both of your arms and you will eventually lose both arms as well as your legs. They tell me the pain is unbearable, and when you wake up in the hospital without any army or legs, you get really depressed, and then, when you are well enough to leave the hospital, you get to spend the rest of your life in prison. So, are you going to answer questions now or do you want me to get the pork? Blink your eyes if you are going to answer every question truthfully and I will release my grip on your neck."

Mr. Nazari was just about ready to go under from lack of oxygen but blinked his eyes and Dawg released his neck hold and let him get some oxygen. He was gasping for air as Jim said to him, "Now Mr. Nazari, if you are ready to talk, we will release the tourniquets on your legs and give you a shot for the pain before we start the questioning. However, if you lie to us about anything, the tourniquets will go back on and you will lose your legs. Do you understand what I am saying?"

Mr. Nazari shook his head up and down. "And are you ready to answer all of our questions truthfully?" Jim asked.

He again shook his head up and down and said faintly, "Yes, I will talk. Please remove the tourniquets and give me the shot for pain." Jim removed the tourniquets as Doc administered a shot into both of his legs and started massaging Mr. Nazari's calves to make him think he was helping to get the blood circulating in his legs.

The pain killer started working in a few minutes and Doc finally said to Mr. Nazari, "You are lucky. There isn't any permanent damage to either of your legs. Please tell us the truth, because if we put the tourniquets back on, the pain will be even greater and the infection will start sooner. The tissue in your legs will not be able to go as long without oxygen as it did the first time. Do you understand?" Doc asked. Mr. Nazari nodded that he understood.

Jim started the questioning and said, "We have discovered a grave in the woods behind the cabin and are going to dig it up in the morning. What will we find in the grave?"

Mr. Nazari answered, "I think you will find your friend's body."

Jim was surprised at that answer and said, "What do you mean by 'You think we will find our friend's body?'"

Mr. Nazari continued, "When I told you the two men in the car were going to dispose of something before they came back and got the jeep, well, they later told me they buried a body in the woods behind the cabin. I'm guessing it is your friend."

"So, why didn't you tell us this earlier?" Jim asked.

"Because," Mr. Nazari said, "I was afraid that if I told you about the body, you would think we had something to do with it."

"And did you have anything to do with it?" Jim asked.

"No. We had nothing to do with the murder of your friend," Mr. Nazari answered.

"Or anyone else?" Jim asked.

"Mr. Nazari hesitated and looked at Jim closely before he answered, "We have not killed anyone."

"Okay," Jim said. "Next question. What are you doing here in Canada, and don't tell me you are here on a fishing trip or I will put the tourniquets back on and we will leave the room?"

Mr. Nazari answered, "We are here to meet up with a bunch of fellow countrymen and help them get back to Afghanistan."

"And that is all?" Jim asked.

"Yes, that is all," Mr. Nazari answered. Some of our people lost their passports and cannot get back to Afghanistan. Our leaders sent us here to help them get home."

"So, you weren't here to commit any terrorist acts or cross the border into the Unites States?" Jim asked.

"Of course not," Mr. Nazari replied. We are here to help our friends get back to Afghanistan. We have done nothing wrong and I wish we never would have met the two men a few weeks ago. None of this would have happened if we didn't agree to take back the boat and trailer."

"Okay, tell me what these two men looked like," Jim said.

"One of them was tall and thin and we all agreed that he looked like a heavy drug user," Mr. Nazari answered. The other man was short and fat."

"So, how did you meet these men?" Jim asked.

"They just showed up at the cabin one day. They asked us to return the boat and trailer for them and we said no. We argued for several minutes and they finally offered to pay us five hundred dollars to do it for them. We agreed to do it because they were starting to get frustrated with us and we didn't want any trouble."

"So, they left the jeep, the boat and the trailer with you and left in another vehicle?" Jim asked.

"That is correct," Mr. Nazari answered.

"Did they leave anything else?" Jim asked.

"Not that I can think of," Mr. Nazari said.

"Any animals or anything like that?" Jim asked.

"Oh yes, they left the dog whose photo was on the poster," Mr. Nazari said. "I forgot about that. We had him tied up outside and he broke his collar and ran off. We have not seen him since."

Dawg then asked, "Are you sure you didn't eat the dog?"

"Of course not," Mr. Nazari answered. "We are civilized

people. We would not do that. We all have clean records and none of us has ever hurt anyone. We were sent here to help our people get back to Afghanistan, like I said before."

"So," Jim said, "these people you were going to meet and help get back to Afghanistan, had they been in the United States or had they committed any crimes?"

"Not that I am aware of," Mr. Nazari answered. "They were here in Canada for a meeting and then did some fishing. While they were fishing, their boat hit a rock and sank. They had their passports with them in the boat and they were lost in the lake."

"So, you were sent here to help them get new passports so they could go home?" Jim asked.

"Yes," Mr. Nazari answered. "They don't speak English, so we were sent to help them."

"And how long have you been here in Canada now?" Jim asked.

"About four weeks now," Mr. Nazari responded.

"So, where are these friends of yours at now?" Jim asked.

Mr. Nazari hesitated and Jim said, "Let me say this again. If I find out that you lied to us about anything, I will let Dawg here take you out and handcuff you to a tree for the night like we talked about earlier. I think that after the young men see your body in the morning, they will tell us everything we need to know."

Mr. Nazari looked at Jim with hate in his eyes and said, "I'm not afraid to die for my cause."

"And what is your cause?" Jim asked.

"To rid the planet of all Infidels," Mr. Nazari said.

"I know that Infidel means non-believer, so you think it's all right to kill people just because they don't believe in the same thing as you?" Jim asked.

"We are Allah's people," Mr. Nazari said. "And to make

the world clean again, you non-believers must convert or be eliminated."

"Mr. Nazari, you are a very sick man, and I'm finished talking to you," Jim said.

"Doc, put him to sleep again and place the tourniquets back on both of his legs. After he is unconscious, we will move him and Mohammed down stairs and bring the other two up to see what they have to say."

Mr. Nazari started cursing at the top of his voice and Jim asked Dawg to put some duct tape over his mouth. Dawg asked if he could shove a piece of pork in his mouth first. Jim approved, so Dawg forced a large piece of ham into Mr. Nazari's mouth, and then duct taped his mouth shut before he could spit it out. Dawg then held him still while Doc gave him another shot to knock him out. He was unconscious in a few minutes and Jim told Dawg to hit him in the chin bones a few more times to increase the pain when he gained consciousness. Dawg smiled as he picked up the pipe and hit Mr. Nazari three times in each leg. Doc placed the fake tourniquets back on his legs before Dawg and Swede picked up Mr. Nazari's chair and carried him down to the kitchen.

When the young man in the kitchen saw Dawg and Swede carry in the unconscious Mr. Nazari, a look of fear went over his face and he asked, "What did you do to him?"

Dawg replied, "We tortured him until he passed out from the pain."

The young man said excitedly, "You must remove the tourniquets from his legs while he is passed out. He cannot talk while he is unconscious and it may be too late to save his legs when he wakes up. Please, I beg of you to remove the tourniquets now."

"I will remove the tourniquets if you promise me you will

tell the truth when we question you," Dawg said. The young man didn't answer and Dawg said, "Mr. Nazari already told us about the body buried out back, about where you left the jeep, about the dog and about the two American men. We just need you to tell us what happened, and if your story matches the story he told us, we will stop with the torture and start looking for the evidence to prove the story is true."

The young man thought Mr. Nazari must have talked or else they wouldn't know all of this, so he agreed to tell the truth. Dawg removed both of the fake tourniquets from Mr. Nazari's legs like he promised. He also removed the duct tape from Mr. Nazari's mouth so the others would hear Mr. Nazari yelling in pain when he woke up. Then, Swede and Dawg grabbed the chair the young man was sitting in and carried it upstairs to the south bedroom. After this, they carried Mohammed downstairs and carried Hahta up to the north bedroom where Mohammed had been.

The young man had already agreed to talk, but Jim wanted to make sure the gray-haired man was unconscious before he began questioning the young man. So, they started asking Hahta some questions in the north bedroom. He refused to answer, so Jim told Doc to give him a shot and knock him out so Hahta would be unconscious while they questioned the young man in the south bedroom. Doc gave Hahta the shot and he was unconscious in a few minutes. Dawg then put a fake tourniquet on his right leg and hit him on the right chin bone three times with the pipe before they walked to the south bedroom.

Shades signaled to Jim that the recorder was running and Jim wasted no time in getting started. He told the young man that Hahta refused to talk, so they gave him a shot to put him to sleep and put a tourniquet on his right leg. Jim guaranteed the young man that Hahta would start screaming in pain shortly after he gained consciousness. Jim also told the young man that the same thing would happen to him if he refused to talk or didn't tell them the truth.

The young man looked at Jim with tears in his eyes and said, "I am not afraid to die, but I do not want to live without my arms or legs. My main concern is for my family. If Mr. Nazari finds out I talked, he will have his men kill my whole family back in Afghanistan. He has done this to others and he promised to do this to us if we talked."

"I understand your concern," Jim said. "I would be scared for my family as well if I had a boss like Mr. Nazari. But, let me tell you this, Mr. Nazari has already talked, and so has Mohammed. If your story matches their story, we won't put the tourniquet on your leg. We will dig up the grave and try to find the jeep tomorrow morning. If what you told us is true, you will not be tortured and Mr. Nazari cannot tell his thugs to kill your family since he also talked. Do you understand?" Jim asked.

The man shook his head and said, "Yes."

"Okay, let's get started," Jim said. "First question, what is your name?"

The young man replied, "My name is Abdul."

"Okay, Abdul, why are you here in Canada?" The young man's face showed both fear and indecision as he wasn't sure how much Mr. Nazari had said. Jim said, "You told us you would talk if we released the tourniquets on Mr. Nazari's legs. We did as you asked, so now you have five seconds to start talking or Dawg will go downstairs and put the tourniquets back on both of his legs. And when Dawg gets back upstairs, we will put a tourniquet on your right leg so you will know what intense pain feels like. One, Two, Three, Four," Jim said as the young man interrupted him and said,

"Okay. I will talk. We were sent here on a mission."

"What was the mission?" Jim asked.

Tears started running down the young man's cheeks as he continued, "We were going to sneak across the border into the U.S. and plant bombs in shopping malls," the young man answered.

"And when were you going to detonate the bombs?" Jim asked.

"The day after your Thanksgiving holiday," the man answered.

"And how were you going to get the explosives to make the bombs?" Jim asked.

"We have people already in the U.S. that are making the bombs. These people are well-known bomb experts and cannot risk getting killed or captured, so we are going to be the people that plant the bombs in the shopping malls."

"And were you going to put the bombs in four malls located in Minneapolis, Des Moines, Omaha and Kansas City?" Jim asked.

The young man looked at Jim with relief in his eyes as he knew that Mr. Nazari had already told them everything.

"Well, as you can probably figure out, that is what Mr. Nazari told us" Abdul answered.

"So, you confirm that it is true?" Jim asked.

"Yes," the young man said. "He told you the truth."

"Okay," Jim said, "Next question. We found a grave in the woods behind the cabin and will be digging it up in the morning. What are we going to find in the grave?"

"You will find a body of a young woman," the man said. "She was a whore and we brought her here for sex. When she wanted to leave, Mr. Nazari thought she might talk or try to blackmail us so he decided to kill her rather than let her go."

"So, who killed her and how?" Jim asked.

"Hahta killed her with a knife," the man answered.

"And what about the piece of dog collar we found in the ashes?" Jim said.

"The men that left the jeep and boat also left a dog," the man answered. "We tied him up outside and he escaped during the night. We burned the dog collar with the trash to get rid of the evidence."

"And what happened to the jeep?" Jim asked.

"We took it in the woods and abandoned it," Abdul answered.

"Why did you do that?" Jim asked.

"Because the two men never came back to get it like they said they would and Mr. Nazari didn't want it here anymore in case the men were criminals and the police were looking for the vehicle."

"So, you abandoned the jeep in the woods?" Jim asked.

"Yes," the man answered.

"Close to this cabin?" Jim asked.

"No, I would say about 50 kilometers from here," the man answered.

"Do you think you will be able to find the jeep for us tomorrow?" Jim asked.

"I think so," Abdul replied. "It might take a while, but I should be able to find it if it is still there."

"What do you mean, 'If it is still there'?" Jim asked.

"Well, we left a note inside of the jeep that whoever finds it can keep it," the man answered. "So, it might be gone by now."

"Did anyone go with you in the jeep?" Jim asked.

"Yes, Mohammed was with me in the jeep," the man answered.

"And how did you get back to the cabin?" Jim asked.

# THE HUNT FOR BILLY JACK

"Hahta followed us in the car and gave us a ride back."

"Okay, tell me about the men that left the jeep and asked you to take the boat and trailer back for them?" Jim asked.

"Well, we knew they were not nice people," the man replied, "because when we didn't want to take the boat and trailer back for them, they wouldn't take no for an answer. We started getting scared that they might start trouble, so we agreed to do it for them."

"What did they look like?" Jim asked.

"One of them was tall and thin with long, greasy hair. The other one was short and fat," the man said.

"What color hair did they have?" Jim asked.

"The skinny one had long, blondish hair and the short one had dark hair," the man replied.

"Did the short one have long hair also?" Jim asked.

"No, his hair was short, and when he removed his hat to swat at some bugs, he was bald on top."

"How old would you say these men were?" Jim asked.

"I don't know," the man answered. "They were not old, but their faces showed age. Mr. Nazari thought they probably were drug users."

"And can you remember what type of vehicle the men were driving?" Jim asked.

"I'm sorry, but I don't remember," the man said.

"Do you remember the color of the vehicle and what country the license plates were from?" Jim asked.

"The vehicle was black and had U.S. plates on it," the man answered.

"Okay," Jim said. "One more question. Do you have any idea what happened to our friend?" he said as he held up a poster with Billy's photo on it.

The man looked at the photo and said, "No. I don't know.

I never saw this man and don't know what happened to him. I swear that is the truth."

"Is there any chance that he could be buried in the grave behind the cabin?" Jim asked.

The man started to answer, then paused for a few seconds to gather his thoughts. He finally said, "Mohammed and I dug the grave and buried the whore in the grave. But, I suppose there is a chance that someone could have dug it up later and buried another body there. Mr. Nazari often has Hahta do things for him without telling us, so I cannot say for sure. All I know for sure is that Mohammed and I dug the grave and buried the whore there."

"Tell me more about yourself, your family, the men you work for, and how you got mixed up with them?" Jim asked.

"I came from a small family," Abdul replied. "I was the only boy and had two younger sisters. We lived in a mud shack near the city of Kabul. My family didn't have money, and one winter we were cold and hungry and didn't know if we would survive. My father had been injured many years earlier and was crippled. He could only walk with crutches. One day, some men came to our house and offered us food and money if my father joined them. My father knew they were Taliban and he didn't want to join, but we desperately needed food and money, so he finally accepted their offer."

"My father was trained to make bombs, and later I was trained to be a fighter. I ran errands and did all kinds of things for them when I was young. One day they asked me if any of my neighbors were sympathetic to the Americans. I told them that I thought one of my neighbors probably was because I overheard him saying bad things about the Taliban to my father. I was a young boy and didn't know enough to keep my mouth shut. Well, a few days later, this neighbor disappeared and we never saw him again."

"One day, my father asked me if I said anything to the Taliban about our neighbor and I told him what I had said. He cried and told me to never say anything like that again. I wanted to apologize to the man's family, but my father said I could not. He said I would just have to live with it for the rest of my life."

The man hesitated and Jim said, "Go on."

The man continued, "When I got older, I was assigned to a small group of fighters. Mr. Nazari was the leader of our group. He gets orders from someone higher up and tells us what to do."

"What type of things did you do?" Jim asked.

The man hung his head. He knew he was probably going to go to prison for the rest of his life. He understood when he joined the Taliban that on any given day he could be killed or go to prison. He now realized that day was finally here. Chances of escaping were very slim. The American's were professionals and were very good at what they did. He didn't want to accept defeat, but he couldn't think of anything else to do, so he might as well talk and keep his legs.

"We did whatever Mr. Nazari told us to do," the man said. "We had training on many different things such as; weapons, bomb making, planting IED's, how to torture people to get them to talk," with this he looked at Jim.

Jim smiled back at him and said, "Basic terrorist training 101," as the others in the room chuckled. "What else?" Jim asked.

The man looked down at the floor and shook his head, "That is all I can think of at this time."

"All right then," Jim said. "I think we are done with you for the night. We will finish questioning Hahta, and then wait for morning to dig up the grave and go find the jeep. We still don't know what happed to our friend, so maybe tomorrow one of you will remember something that might help us find him. If not, then tomorrow is going to be a bad day for all of you."

The men walked out of the room and down to the north bedroom where Hahta was still unconscious. Jim told the team members in the room what the young man had said and they discussed the next day's activities. The group was thrilled that they had discovered a plot to bomb malls in the U.S. on Black Friday, but at the same time were upset that they hadn't found out any good information on Billy. It was around ten o'clock and Jim said he had to make a phone call to Billy's parents and Angela and give them an update before it got too late. He went outside to the picnic table to make the call.

The phone call to Billy's parents went well. Jim didn't tell them about the grave out back and withheld a lot of information on the foreigners, but did tell them they had some good clues and he should know more when he called tomorrow night. Angela and Dancer weren't there, so Jim called Angela and told her the same thing he told the Littlebears. He called Angela rather than have Mr. Littlebear call her because he wanted to find out if she and Dancer had found out anything back home. They had not, but Dancer said he had a lead he was working and would keep Jim informed if he found anything.

Jim returned to the house around ten thirty. Hahta had gained consciousness and was screaming in pain. Jim got to the north bedroom where Hahta was screaming and asked Dawg to duct tape Hahta's mouth shut. Dawg did so and Jim started the questioning process with Hahta. Dawg removed the duct tape so Hahta could answer the questions, but Hahta just yelled and cursed the men and would not answer even one question. Jim came to the conclusion that Hahta was a tough old man and could take a lot of pain. Jim and the men were tired. It had been a long day and tomorrow might be even longer depending on what they found in the grave. Jim decided to stop for the night and start again in the morning. They carried Hahta and the young man back downstairs and put them in the dining room with Mr. Nazari and Mohammed.

Jim called a meeting and everyone went back to the office. Since the foreigners knew about the tape recorder, they decided to tape the men's mouths shut for the night so they couldn't talk to each other. This would also muffle the yelling and screaming and let the team get some sleep. They would take turns pulling guard duty on the men. They drew cards to see who got to sleep on the beds and Doc, Shades, Swede and Boom were the winners. Jim, Dawg and Wiz would sleep on the couches or in the recliners in the Great Room. Since there were seven of them, each man would pull a one-hour shift on guard duty and wake the next man when his shift was up. A few of them went outside to drink a beer and unwind before they turned in for the night.

# Chapter 18

The night was uneventful. Everyone was up by 6:00 o'clock Monday morning and they untied the foreigners and let them go outside for a smoke and pee break. Their legs were still very sore and they could barely walk. When they went to rub their legs, they felt the pain on their chin bones and could not understand why it hurt so much. Doc told them that the blood vessels in their legs were near the front of their legs and when the tourniquets were put on them, the tissue in the front of their legs was deprived of oxygen and was badly damaged. He said the tissue would repair itself and the pain will go away in a few days. It was hard for some of the guys to keep a straight face as Doc was feeding them this story, but none of the foreigners were asking any questions. They seemed to be living in the moment, smoking cigarettes and being allowed to stagger around the backyard.

Big and Mike showed up just before seven. They had a lot of groceries with them and the team quickly got out the frying pans and started frying bacon as they ate cinnamon rolls and drank coffee or juice. They wanted to eat breakfast first and let the sun come out and drive the mosquitos away before they started digging up the grave. There were some old lawn chairs in the shed and the guys brought them out and let the foreigners sit down in the backyard and soak up some sun. Shades was left to watch them in case they said anything important in Dari.

After they had unloaded the groceries, Jim noticed that someone had purchased a bunch of fruit, raisins, dates, nuts, and other items the foreigners would like to eat. Jim was going to ask Big to pick up some food for the foreigners, but with everything that happened the day before, he had totally forgotten to mention it. He was glad that Mike had a big heart and had thought about it when they were shopping. Mike walked into the kitchen and grabbed a big serving tray and started loading it with the fruits, nuts and raisins. He said, "Hey Jim is it okay if I give the foreigners some food and juice?"

Jim smiled and said, "You bet. Thanks for picking up the special food for them. You're a good man, Mike."

"I wish someone would tell Karen that," Mike said with a smile on his face.

"She knows," Jim said. "But she just doesn't want to say anything for fear you might let it go to your head."

"Oh, so that's it?" Mike said as he and Jim both laughed.

Mike took the food and juices out to the foreigners and they were thrilled to finally get something to eat and drink. They were all sitting in lawn chairs and gently rubbing their legs to promote circulation. Mike told Shades he would bring him some breakfast when the bacon and pancakes were ready. Shades gave Mike the thumbs up approval as Mike headed back to the cabin.

The team ate a great breakfast and discussed the day's activities. Dawg, Mike, Shades, Big and Kadie would take the two young foreigners and go look for Billy's jeep. They would take two vehicles and handcuff the foreigners in the back seat. Dawg would sit between them to make sure they behaved. They wanted to let Kadie search the area where they found the jeep just in case something was buried nearby. They would tow the jeep back to the cabin if they couldn't get it to run.

Jim, Doc, Boom, Swede and Wiz would stay at the cabin with Mr. Nazari and Hahta and dig up the grave in the woods behind the cabin. After breakfast was over, the team that was going to look for the jeep showered and put on clean clothes and was leaving the cabin at 9 A.M. The rest of the team that was going to dig up the grave decided to wait and shower later after the digging was done.

They decided that Mr. Nazari and Hahta should go with them, so they handcuffed them together, grabbed the shovels, a tarp, and headed out. They had to move slowly as Mr. Nazari and Hahta's legs were very sore, but the grave was only a few minutes from the cabin and Big and Mike said they had marked it well before they left last night, so it should be easy to find. When they got to the grave site, they handcuffed Mr. Nazari and Hahta to a tree and Wiz got the video recorder going while the rest of the men started digging. Jim wanted everything to be on video so they could verify their story later when they turned the men over to the authorities.

They only dug for a few minutes when they discovered an arm buried in the dirt. They put down their shovels and started using their hands to remove the dirt from around the body. It took about 15 minutes for them to be able to lift the body out of the grave. The body was starting to decompose and smelled really bad, but they could see it was the body of a young woman like the young men had told them they would find in the grave. The team kept digging deeper for several more minutes until they hit rock and were sure that nothing else was buried in that spot.

Before returning to the cabin, Jim walked over to Mr. Nazari and Hahta and just stared at them for a couple of minutes. He finally said, "Mr. Nazari, please tell me the story behind this young woman's body being buried behind your cabin?"

Mr. Nazari looked at Jim and said, "I have no idea of what happened to her or how she ended up buried out here." Jim raised his shovel up like a baseball bat and swung it at Mr. Nazari's head just as Mr. Nazari ducked. The shovel hit the tree with such force that it knocked off a big chunk of bark. Mr. Nazari yelled out, "What are you doing? We don't know anything about this body and I will testify to that in court."

"I'm so sick of your lies that you might not live long enough to testify in court," Jim said with anger in his voice. "I know you are not afraid to die for your cause, so I'm still thinking about the best way to make you suffer before you die. Maybe leaving you handcuffed to a tree for several days will do it, I'm not sure. But if you keep telling us lies, then I'm sure you are going to lie in court and there's no sense in turning you into the authorities for you to tell more lies and waste everyone's time and money. If you don't start talking and help us find our friend, then you are no good to us and you don't deserve to go on living. Do you understand me?" Jim asked.

Even though Mr. Nazari had said he wasn't afraid to die for his country, he really didn't feel that way. He thought all along that the American's were bluffing and he would be turned over to authorities, then the Taliban could hire great lawyers and he would eventually be set free. He was a rich and powerful man back in Afghanistan. He had a good life and didn't want it to end anytime soon. He now realized that Jim was serious and might actually kill them rather than turn them over to the authorities. He now feared for his life and didn't know what to say.

Jim looked him in the eyes and said, "No matter what this young woman did, she didn't deserve to die like this. You have no right to take the life of another person unless it is self-defense. Now I'm fed up with your lies and I'm not going to take any more of them. Do you fully understand me?"

Mr. Nazari looked at Jim and said, "I understand."

Jim continued, "And how about you Hahta, do you understand what I have just said?"

Hahta looked at Jim, then turned his head and looked away. Jim waited for a few seconds, then swung the shovel and hit Hahta in the chin bone below his right knee. Hahta yelled out in pain and Jim said, "I can do this all day if that's what you want. Now, I'm going to ask you until you answer me, and every time you refuse to answer, I going to hit you in your sore legs with the shovel. And if you keep screaming, we will tape your mouth shut and wait for you to acknowledge by shaking your head."

"So, old man Hahta, do you understand that I am fed up with your lies and am not going to tolerate them anymore? Hahta looked at him but did not say a word. Jim swung the shovel and this time hit him in the chin bone on his left leg. Hahta again screamed out in pain as tears ran down his cheeks. He quit screaming in about 30 seconds as Jim looked him in the eyes again and said, "Do you understand that I'm not going to tolerate any more lies from either of you?"

Mr. Nazari finally spoke, "Yes we both understand what you are saying."

"Well, I'm afraid I have to hear Hahta say it or I'm going to start rotating the blows between both of you. So, Hahta, if you don't want to talk, I will start hitting Mr. Nazari every other time and maybe when you see your boss in pain, you will acknowledge what I have said. And, I think it's Mr. Nazari's turn coming up next, so Hahta, do you understand what I have been saying that I'm not going to take any more lies from either of you?"

Hahta looked at Jim but did not say a word. Jim raised the shovel to strike his boss as Mr. Nazari yelled out, "Hahta, I order you to acknowledge him right now."

Hahta looked at his boss and then at Jim and said, "Yes, I understand."

Jim lowered the shovel and said, "Well good. I'm happy that both of you are going to tell the truth from now on and we won't have to torture or kill you. Now, one of you tell me the story behind this young girl being buried here."

Mr. Nazari spoke up and said, "She was a whore that we brought here for our pleasure. We caught her stealing money and when we confronted her about it, she cursed Allah. Her punishment was death. We dug the grave and buried her. End of story."

Jim looked at Mr. Nazari through teary eyes and said, "You aren't the law and you don't have the right to decide who lives and who dies. This young girl might have been living a life of sin, and may have gone to jail if she was caught, but she didn't deserve to die. You are making it awfully hard for me to let you go on living." Jim just stood there quietly for a couple of minutes, then said, "Let's go back to the cabin."

The other team members already had the young woman rolled up in the tarp and picked it up and headed for the cabin. Jim released the handcuff that was around the tree and signaled for the foreigners to follow the men carrying the tarp. Their legs were now very sore and it took them several minutes to make the trip, but they finally arrived at the cabin and sat down in the lawn chairs in the backyard. Jim decided to wait until the rest of the team got back from looking for the jeep before deciding what to do next.

Dawg, Mike, Shades, Big and Kadie were with the two young men looking for the jeep. It took them awhile, but they finally found it. It was hard to believe, but no one had bothered it at all for the two weeks that it had sat in the woods. Dawg worked on trying to get it started while Big and Mike walked Kadie in the surrounding woods. Since they didn't have the keys to the jeep, Dawg had to get under the dashboard and by-pass the ignition switch. He finally got the right wires connected and the jeep started. He honked the horn a few times to signal Big and Mike to return. They showed up in a few minutes and said Kadie didn't alert to anything, so they decided to head back to the cabin. They marked the area with a pile of rocks in case they decided to come back and do a better search of the area. Mike drove the jeep and was the middle vehicle on the return trip.

The jeep was nearly out of gas, but they didn't want to stop and fill up with no license plates on it, so they kept going and made it back to the cabin running on fumes. The rest of the team was sitting in the backyard soaking up some sun and they joined them there. It was comfortable in the backyard and Jim wanted to hold the meeting there, so he asked Mike if he would watch the foreigners while they had a meeting. Mike agreed and the team helped take the foreigners inside and handcuff and tape them to the chairs. They gave Mike a shotgun and returned to the backyard.

Jim filled the team in on what they found in the grave and the shovel incident he had with Mr. Nazari and Hahta. Then, Dawg told them about finding the jeep and having to hotwire it to get it started. Jim didn't like the fact that they now had a dead body and murderers at the cabin. He didn't want to turn the foreigners over to the Canadian law enforcement officials until they found Billy, but he was getting nervous and wasn't sure what to do. He planned to recommend that they contact H3 at the Pentagon and get his advice. H3 was the nickname for

Lieutenant General Hewlett, the 3-star general and task force commander that they worked for in Afghanistan.

General Hewlett was the smartest man and the best leader the team had ever worked for and they all had the utmost respect for him. He was going to the Pentagon when he left Afghanistan to try to get a fourth star before he retired, and he had given Jim and Dawg his personal cell phone number and told them to call him if they ever needed his help. Jim thought now was the time to call him and decided to see what the team thought about it.

"I've been doing a lot of thinking on what we should do next," Jim said, "And my recommendation is to call H3 and tell him the whole situation and get his advice. What do you guys think about that?"

Dawg spoke first, "That is a great idea. I think he was going to be the head of the anti-terrorism division and since we uncovered a plot to kill civilians in the Unites States, it's our duty to inform him of what we discovered."

"I agree," Shades said. "He will know what to do with these losers."

"Sounds good to me," Swede said as the rest of the team was nodding their approval.

"Okay," Jim said. "I will give him a call a little later and see what he recommends. Now, I have some news I want to share with all of you. This morning after we returned to the cabin from digging up the grave, I got a phone call from Dancer. He met some guy in a bar one night that knew Angela's brother. The guy told Dancer that Angela's brother had found out she was dating Billy and he was furious about it. The guy thought that Angela's brother was afraid that if Angela got married to Billy, she would cut him off from all the money she had been giving him."

"The story gets better," Jim said. "The guy in the bar also

said that a week later, one of his friends overheard two local drug-users talking about getting out of a bill they owed to a drug dealer. They didn't have the money they owed for drugs and the dealer offered them a job. He said if they took care of someone for him, he would forget about the money they owed him. They did the job for him and were celebrating that their debt was now paid in full." Jim could see the team was now deep in thought going over this new scenario, so he continued.

"There's still more. Dancer didn't want to say anything to Angela about this, so he started looking into it on his own. One day they ran into Angela's brother so Dancer now knew what he looked like. Dancer started trailing her brother when Angela wasn't around and one day he saw him meeting with two guys that he thinks were the two drug-users that were celebrating in the bar. He couldn't get close enough to make a positive identification, but he is pretty sure it was the same two guys."

Jim could see the look on everyone's faces as Dawg spoke up, "So could they be the two men that dropped off Billy's jeep here at the cabin?"

"I know it's a long shot, but it doesn't sound like the foreigners know what happened to Billy, so we need to start looking into the two drug dealers and Angela's brother to see if we can get some real evidence." Jim answered. "I asked Dancer to get some photos of the two men and send them to Wiz. When we get the photos, we will put them on the laptop and mix them in with a bunch of other photos we get off of the internet and see if the foreigners can identify the two men they say dropped off Billy's jeep.

"That sounds like a great place to start," Wiz commented. "If the foreigners pick out the two drug dealers in the photos I show them, I think we will be able to get them to tell us what happened and where we can find Billy."

"I agree," Jim said. "Dancer is going to try to find out where the men lived and get a photo for us as soon as possible. If we get a positive ID on the men, I would like Dawg and Swede to go back to South Dakota and assist Dancer in getting these men to talk. My guess is they probably aren't tough guys and will start talking with a little encouragement from Dawg."

Wiz then said, "Didn't one of the young men say that the two Americans left the cabin in a black SUV?"

"That's a good point, Wiz," Jim said. "They could have been driving a rental or maybe they borrowed a car from a friend, but I will ask Dancer to find out what vehicles they drive and get a photo of the vehicles also."

"So, let me go over this scenario," Dawg said. "Angela's brother is a drug dealer and didn't want Angela to marry Billy, so he tells two drug-users that if they kill Billy, he will forget about the money they owe him for drugs. They find out Billy is going fishing to Canada and decide to kill him up there. The two drug users make a road trip up to Canada, kill Billy, and return home. After they kill Billy, they hide the body and decide to give the jeep, boat, trailer and dog to the foreigners. This will buy them some time and if the foreigners go back to their own country, there will be no witnesses to point the finger at them. Does anyone have anything else to add to this?"

"I know it seems like a long shot," Jim said, "But if we can get a positive identification on the photo or one of them has a vehicle that matches a black SUV, then I will think we are on to something."

"If your scenario is true," Wiz said, "Then the two men had to cross through customs a day or two after Billy did. If one of the men has a vehicle that matches the black SUV description, we can get the license plate number off of the vehicle and check with Customs to see if and when that vehicle crossed into Canada and returned to the Unites States."

"Good point," Jim said. "If we get a positive ID on the photos of these two guys, I have no doubt that Dawg can get them to talk and tell us exactly what happened to Billy and where we can find his body."

"Wow," Shades said. "All along we have been thinking the foreigners killed Billy, but maybe they had nothing to do with it and would have snuck into the U.S. and killed thousands of people if the two men hadn't left the jeep and boat here at the cabin."

"Pretty amazing," Jim said. "But don't forget they are already guilty of murder and planned to murder many more."

"Oh, I don't feel any sympathy for them," Shades said. "It just struck me as amazing the way the Big Guy up in heaven had all of this play out."

"Amen to that," Jim said as the rest of the group agreed. "I think I'll call Dancer right now and see what he says." Jim pulled out his cell phone and made the call.

Dancer answered, "Hey Jim."

"Hey Dancer," Jim said. "I'm sitting here with the team and I have you on speaker phone so don't say anything you might regret later."

"You got that old coon dog with you? Dancer asked.

Dawg growled and barked a few times as Jim said, "Yeah, he's taking a break from chasing rabbits and is laying down right next to us."

"Probably licking his balls," Dancer replied.

Everyone laughed and said 'Hi Dancer' and Dancer answered, 'Hi guys'.

Jim continued, "We wondered if you had an update for us."

"Well, I just got through telling Angela about everything

and she is pretty upset. She gave me the nick-names of the two drug-users and I am going to try to find them and get some photos for you."

"Hey Dancer," Wiz said. "Is Angela there with you now?"

"She's in the next room," Dancer replied.

"Would you ask her what type of vehicle her brother drives and what color it is?"

"Sure," Dancer said, "Let me walk into the next room and ask her now." A few seconds later they heard Dancer say, "Hey Angela, what type of vehicle does your brother drive?"

They heard Angela in the background say, "As far as I know, he still drives an old Chevy Blazer."

"What color is it?" Dancer asked.

"It's black," Angela replied.

"Did you guys hear that?" Dancer asked. "He drives a black Chevy Blazer." The team looked at Jim and everyone was nodding their heads to approve Dawg and Swede going back to help Dancer.

"Okay Dancer," Jim said, "Dawg and Swede are leaving here in an hour or so and will meet up with you at the local café tomorrow morning. We think the two drug users had something to do with Billy's disappearance. I would like you to get the license plate number off of Angela's brothers black SUV and check with customs to see if the vehicle crossed into Canada. I don't want you to take any photos of the two druggies, because if they did kill Billy, they have already committed one murder and may well commit another to keep them out of prison. Just see if you can find out their real names and where they live but don't contact them or get any photos today. Dawg and Swede will help you with that tomorrow."

"Okay. Sounds good to me," Dancer said.

"I will call later tonight and talk to you and Angela," Jim said.

"All right. You guys take care up there and I'll see Swede and the junkyard dog in the morning," Dancer said.

Dawg just shook his head as Jim said, "Thanks Dancer. We'll talk to you later. Out here."

"Out here," was Dancer's reply as they both ended the call.

"Okay Dawg, you and Swede go back to camp and load up your gear and head for South Dakota. Make sure you take a tape recorder with you and record any confession you get from the druggies. We may need it for later. I really can't see two drug users digging a hole to bury a body. That would be too much work. My guess is they threw Billy's body into a ravine or pushed him off of a cliff or something like that. You get the general location of where they left the body and Kadie should be able to find him."

Swede said, "If I would have known I was heading back today, I would have eaten some onion rings last night and had some fun on the long ride back."

The team laughed as Dawg said, "You're lucky you didn't eat any onion rings because you would have been riding in the pickup box."

"Whatever," Swede said as Dawg and him shook hands and did the 'man hug' thing with the team before going into the cabin and saying goodbye to Mike. They soon left the cabin and headed for the campsite to load up and start the drive back to the U.S.

Everything was at a standstill now until they talked to H3 and got a confession out of the drug-users. Jim decided to wait and call H3 the next day after he got an update from Dancer, so he gave the team the day off to go fishing or go into town and do some shopping or something. They had Doc's boat and the boat the foreigners were using, so several of them decided to do some fishing. Some of the guys wanted to go out for dinner and Mike volunteered to stay at the cabin and watch the foreigners. Boom said he would stay with Mike as he knew Jim wanted at least two people on every mission and would not approve of Mike staying at the cabin alone.

So, Jim said that if Mike and Boom pulled guard duty tonight, they could go into town tomorrow night while the rest of them pulled guard duty. Mike and Boom agreed. Jim called Mary to invite her to join them for dinner. She agreed to go and Jim told her to pick the restaurant and they would meet her there. Mary said she had such a good time the last time they went out that she picked the same place. They agreed to meet her there at six thirty. It was now 10:30 in the morning and Jim asked for one guy to stay with him so the others could take off. Big volunteered, so Doc, Mike and Wiz would go fishing in Doc's boat and Shades and Boom were going to go fishing in the boat that was left at the cabin.

Both groups caught a few fish and were back at the cabin by five o'clock. They took turns in the bathroom and everyone that was going out for dinner was cleaned up and ready to go by six o'clock. Mike and Boom had the team's phone numbers and would call if anything came up. Jim, Doc, Wiz, Shades and Big jumped into Doc's Suburban and headed for the steak house.

They got there a few minutes early and were sitting at the bar when Mary walked in and joined them. Mary was thirsty for margaritas and the team decided that sounded good to them so they ordered two pitchers of margarita's and everyone moved to the big table. It was a great night and everyone ate and drank too much. After eating, they returned to the bar and had a couple more drinks and took turns dancing with Mary. They were still laughing and having a great time when the bartender gave them 'last call'. They couldn't believe it was that late and decided they had better call it a night. They walked Mary to her car and she gave all of them a hug before she got in and drove off.

"She sure is a nice lady," Shades said as they were getting into Doc's Suburban.

"I noticed she danced with you more than anyone else," Jim said.

"I just really like her," Shades said.

"But you are a happily married man, right?" Jim said.

"Not anymore," Shades said. "I was gone so much that we grew apart and we both decided it would be better if we divorced and went our own ways. I'm sorry for not saying something earlier."

"Don't worry about that," Jim said. "That is your private life and you don't have to tell us something if you don't want to. I'm just sorry that things didn't work out between you two."

"Thanks, Jim, but it's okay," Shades said. "I'm a lot happier now and I know in my heart that there is someone out there for me."

"You are right about that," Jim said. "And I'm sure you will find her one of these days." Shades smiled and patted Jim on the shoulder.

They arrived back at the cabin and were glad to hear it had been an uneventful night. Mike had picked up some special food for the foreigners and had made them a nice dinner. Mike wanted to talk to the team before he left for the camp ground and Jim called a meeting in the back office. Mike told the team that Mohammed had requested to use the bathroom and Mike went with him. In the bathroom, Mohammed started to cry like a little girl and Mike asked him what was wrong. Mohammed explained that Mr. Nazari had told them he was going to put out the word for his people to kill all of his family and the family of the other young man, Abdul. Mr. Nazari was upset that the young men talked and now their families would be killed because of it. Mr. Nazari said they would all be tortured before they were killed to show others what happens to people when they talk.

Jim asked the team for their input on what to do about this. The only solution they could come up with at the time was to kill Mr. Nazari and Hahta to prevent them from talking, but they knew that murder wasn't an option. Jim agreed to tell H3 about this when he called him in the morning. He also told the team to keep thinking of ways to prevent Mr. Nazari's men from killing the young men's families and they would discuss it again tomorrow after Jim talked to H3. Mike, Big and Kadie left for the campground and the team once again make out the schedule for guard duty and turned in for the night.

# Chapter 19

The team was all up by seven o'clock Tuesday morning. Many of them went to the backyard to do some exercises before going on a run. Jim was hoping Dancer would call any minute with an update so he could give H3 the information on Billy when he called him. Jim exercised with the team in the backyard, but decided not to go on the run with them. He said he would have a big breakfast ready for them when they returned and he sure did. Jim had pancakes, sausages, juice, coffee and cinnamon rolls waiting when the team returned.

Jim didn't go on the run because he wanted to get his thoughts together and jot down some notes before he called H3. The team had searched the cabin, but did not find any forms of identification for the men, so he couldn't give H3 their names for them to look up in the terrorist data base.

Jim still hadn't heard from Dancer, so he decided to call him and see if he had any new information. Dancer said he had met Dawg and Swede for breakfast and they had come up with a plan. He said he would call later with an update. Jim decided he would call H3 now and fill him in on the story. It was now 9 A.M. and he knew H3 had a habit of going into the office early and getting all the important things done early like the old TV commercial used to say, 'In the Army, we do more things by 9 A.M. than most people do all day'.

It was a beautiful day and Jim decided to make the call outside of the cabin while sitting at the picnic table. His phone was charged up and he had written down everything he wanted to tell H3 to make sure he didn't forget anything. It was a few minutes after nine o'clock and Jim placed the call. General Hewlett answered. He had gotten his $4^{th}$ star and Jim congratulated him on that. The team would now refer to him as 'H4'.

After a couple of minutes of small talk, Jim got to the reason for the call. Jim went over everything from the time he got the call from Billy's dad to the present day. H4 listened intently and took notes. After Jim had told the whole story, H4 said he was going to call a special meeting and would call Jim back when the meeting was over. The call ended, and Jim was relieved that H4 was now informed and would be calling him back and telling him what to do next.

Jim went back inside the cabin and called a meeting in the back office to bring the team up to date on the phone conversation with H4. They were glad to hear their former task force commander had received his $4^{th}$ star and now was a full-fledged General. One star is a Brigadier General, two stars is a Major General, three stars is a Lieutenant General and four stars (now the highest) is a General Officer. There was a five-star General rank, 'General of the Army', but it was retired in 1981 with the death of General Omar Bradley.

The team agreed to drink a 'toast' later that evening to General Hewlett's promotion and Jim continued to fill the team in on the rest of the conversation. He figured it would take H4 a couple of hours to conduct the meeting and call him back with the details of how to proceed. Mike and Big showed up at the cabin with Kadie and Jim filled them in on the conversation with H4.

They needed more food, so the team made out a grocery list of things they wanted and Jim asked who wanted to go to town and do the shopping. Doc, Shades and Wiz all wanted to go and Jim gave them the rest of the grocery money as they were walking out the cabin door. They were gone about two hours and the team heard them pull into the cabin parking lot and went out to help them carry in the supplies.

Wiz had purchased a volley ball net and a volley ball and everyone was anxious to get the groceries unloaded and put the net up. The team had played a lot of volley ball when they were stationed in the U.S. and were all pretty good at it. Wiz had purchased a can of white spray paint so they could paint the boundaries of the volley ball court in the grass. This would help avoid many arguments as to whether the ball was 'in' or 'out'.

They quickly put the groceries away and set up the volley ball net and painted the boundaries. They brought the foreigners outside and hand-cuffed them to each other in the lawn chairs so the person on guard duty could play or watch if he so wanted. Wiz was the best volley ball player and everyone knew it. He was only six feet three inches tall, but he could jump like a jack rabbit. He could dunk a basketball with two hands behind his back and blocked a lot of shots in volley ball when he was playing in the front row by the net.

While everyone was hitting the ball back and forth over the net, Jim's phone rang. His first thought was that H4 was calling back and he walked away from the group as he answered the phone and said, "Hello, this is Jim."

"Hey Jim, this is Dawg. How is everything going up there?"

"Hey Dawg," Jim replied. "Things are going well. I called General Hewlett this morning and he got his forth star already."

"That's great," Dawg replied. "I knew he would get it before he retired. Tell him congratulations from me the next time you talk to him."

"I will do that," Jim said. "He asked about you, and I told him you came up here with us but went back yesterday to help follow up on a lead."

"And that is the reason for the call," Dawg said. Dancer got the license plate number from Angela's brothers black SUV and contacted Customs. They just called back and said the vehicle crossed into Canada on June 3$^{rd}$ and crossed back into the U.S. on June 5$^{th}$. The owner of the vehicle was not with the two men, but the men had a letter from the owner giving them permission to drive his vehicle to Canada for a short fishing trip. Customs kept a copy of the letter in their file. The letter gave Jason Smith and Gordon Williams permission to drive the vehicle owned by Jack Paulsen into Canada."

"So, it looks like our theory was correct," Jim said.

"It sure does," Dawg said. "And, when Swede and I got into town last night, we decided to drink a few beers before we went to bed."

"Imagine that," Jim said with a laugh.

"Well," Dawg continued, "We hit a few of the local bars and at one of the places we saw a couple of guys that looked like the two drug-users the foreigners had described to us. I had my camera in the vehicle and brought it in and got a few photos of the two guys as they were shooting pool. Swede and I even challenged them to a game of pool and drank a couple of beers with them. We introduced ourselves and they said their names were Jason and Gordon. This morning at breakfast, I saw Shades the photos and he confirmed that they were the two men he had seen with Angela's brother. I'm going to email the photos of the two men to Wiz as soon as we hang up. I will wait for you to get back to me with a positive ID from the foreigners before I go any further."

"And what are your plans if we get a positive ID?" Jim asked.

"I plan to have a nice chat with the two men and get them to tell me where we can find Billy," Dawg answered.

"Be careful," Jim said. "Don't hurt them in any way and be sure to get their confession on tape. Wiz will mix the photos you send us with a bunch of other photos and I will call you back as soon as we get a positive ID."

"Sounds good. I'll be waiting for your call," Dawg said.

"Okay, thanks Dawg. Out here," Jim said.

"Out here," Dawg replied.

Jim walked back to the team and called a meeting in the back office. They could see the foreigners out the back window, so no one needed to stay outside with them. He told the team what Dawg had said and asked Wiz to get his laptop and let everyone look at the photos of the two men as soon as he got the email from Dawg.

Wiz got his laptop out and opened it up just as he received an email from Dawg. He showed the team the photos of the two men and Jim asked him to search the internet and find similar photos of men to mix in with the photos of the drug-users. Wiz went to work on creating a line-up of similar photos and the rest of the team returned to the back yard.

They played a little volley ball for about 20 minutes before Wiz walked out of the cabin and gave them the 'thumbs up'. He had hooked his laptop to the projector in the kitchen and was ready to show the presentation. They took the foreigners into the kitchen and told them they were going to show a slide show of photos and wanted them to identify the men that had left the jeep with them. Wiz started the show.

The seventh photo in the slide show was of Jason Smith and

right away they recognized him. "You are sure this is one of the men," Jim asked.

Mr. Nazari was the first to speak, "If it's not him, then it must be his twin brother."

"Does everyone agree that this is one of the men?"

Everyone was nodding their head in agreement as Mohammed said, "Yes, he is wearing the same cap that he was wearing when we met him." The others agreed. Wiz went to a few more photos and no one recognized them. He then showed a photo of Gordon Williams and the group all agreed that he was the other man. Wiz then showed a photo of both of them together and all four of the foreigners agreed that they were the two men that left the jeep, boat, trailer and dog with them.

Jim walked outside and called Dawg and told him they had a positive identification on the two men. Dawg said he would call Jim back when he had some information about Billy. Jim again told Dawg to be careful and they ended the call. Shades had gone through the DVD's in the living room and picked out several movies that he thought the team would enjoy watching. He laid them on the table and the group agreed that they would like to see 'The Patriot', so everyone went into the living room and Shades loaded the movie in the DVD player.

Jim came back inside and said he didn't like watching a movie without popcorn, so Mike jumped up and headed for the kitchen. A couple of minutes later you could hear the popcorn popping in the microwave. Mike threw in another bag when the first one was done and brought out some small containers so the guys could each have their own bowl of popcorn. Jim thanked Mike and said, "I'm sure glad you were able to come with us."

Mike smiled and replied, "It has been an experience I will never forget."

"I can believe that," Jim said as everyone laughed and Wiz started the movie.

About half-way through the movie, Jim's phone rang. He quickly grabbed his notepad and headed outside before he answered the phone. It was H4. He told Jim that the president of the U.S. was informed of the situation and set up a special task force to handle it. The task force wanted to catch the terrorists that were making the bombs and planning to target the shopping malls in the United States on Black Friday.

The plan was to send some government agents to the cabin to take over the operation. They would hold the terrorists there at the cabin until the guy showed up to sneak them into the U.S. They would arrest him and try to get him to identify the bomb makers that were in the U.S. They had already gotten approval from the Canadian government, so the special agents would be leaving first thing in the morning and would be at the cabin by noon tomorrow. The agents would work with the Canadian authorities on turning in the body of the dead hooker.

Jim told H4 about how Mr. Nazari has told the two young men that their families in Afghanistan would be tortured and killed because they had talked and Jim asked if there was anything that could be done to prevent this from happening. H4 said the government had money put aside for a 'witness protection' program and he would put in a request to meet with the Director as soon as possible. If approved, the families would receive enough money to move to Pakistan or a remote village in Afghanistan where Mr. Nazari's men would not be able to find them.

The families might not want to move, and that was up to them. But they would be told that someone wanted to have them killed and the U.S. would pay for the move and give them money to start a new life somewhere else. Also, H4 said to give the agents all of the evidence they had, which included the taped confessions and the recording from the tape players. Jim agreed. H4 also said the President expressed deep appreciation for what the team had done and wanted to personally thank them after this ordeal was over. Jim said they were glad to help and the conversation was over.

Jim went back inside and let the team finish watching the movie before calling a meeting in the back office and filled the team in on the conversation with H4. The team was glad the agents would be taking over and they could move back to the campground. They were concerned that they only had four days left before they had to head home and they didn't want to leave without accomplishing their mission of finding Billy. Jim assured them that Dawg could be a very persuasive person and would probably get a confession out of the drug-users before the night was over. They team agreed and decided to play a little volley ball before dinner.

They brought the foreigners outside with them and again hand-cuffed them to the lawn chairs. This time they decided to split up into teams and play a real game. The stakes were high as the losing team had to make dinner. Since Wiz was a ringer, he got his choice of two other players on his team. He chose Shades and Jim. That left Doc, Big, Mike and Boom on the four-man team. They decided it would be a best of three tournament and each team won one of the first two games.

The tie-breaker was a close game with the four-man team winning by two points. It was a good workout for all of them and Big went into the cabin and came out with a cooler of beer. They agreed on brats for dinner and fired up the grill in the backyard. They took the handcuffs off of the foreigners and let them walk around and go to the bathroom if they needed. They were all limping badly and someone made the comment that he didn't think any of them could make a run for the woods even if they wanted. Everyone laughed.

Mike made a nice meal for the foreigners and then joined the team at the picnic table. Beer was always good, but it just seemed to be a little better when consumed with a good brat. They finished eating just before dark and were drinking another beer when Jim's phone rang. It was Dawg. He had gotten a confession out of the drug-users. He said they admitted to shooting Billy in the head with a pistol when his back was turned, then they tied a couple of concrete blocks to his body and sunk the body in a lake. They didn't know the name of the lake, but said it was the same lake that the cabin was on where they dropped of Billy's jeep.

Dawg then gave the description of how the murder went down. The drug users were at a convenience store when they saw Billy drive through town. They jumped into their vehicle and followed him to the boat ramp on the lake. They sat in their vehicle and waited for Billy to get the boat into the water. They acted like fishermen and were standing on shore casting lures into the lake as Billy tied the boat up to the dock and parked the jeep.

As Billy was walking to the boat, one of the guys faked a heart attack and dropped to the ground. Billy ran to help and was bent over helping the guy when the other man walked up behind him and shot Billy in the head. They said that Billy died instantly and didn't suffer at all.

Next, they lifted Billy's body into the boat and motored out into the lake. They followed the shoreline past the cabin and then tied two concrete blocks to Billy's body before they pushed it over the side of the boat and into the water. They estimated the location where they sunk the body to be about two football fields north of the cabin in 24 feet of water. Dawg got choked up a couple of times while telling Jim the details and Jim had tears in his eyes as Dawg finished the story. Dawg said he had the confessions on tape and the pistol used to shoot Billy. Dawg planned to hold the two men until he got word that the body had been found. Jim thanked him and they ended the call.

H4 had told Jim to call if he got any new information and Jim decided he needed to make the call. H4 answered and Jim filled him in on everything Dawg had just said. H4 expressed his sympathy and said for him and the team to be strong. He also said he would send a couple of divers along with the agents to find the body and that the agents would handle the paperwork for taking Billy's body back into the U.S. They ended the call and Jim walked back into the cabin to pass the information to the team.

Jim was keeping a couple of bottles of Templeton Rye whiskey in his duffle bag and decided it was time to break them out. He brought them into the living room and the team could tell by the look on his face that he had some bad news. Jim took the cap off of the first bottle and took a long drink before handing the bottle to Doc. Doc took a drink and passed it to Shades. No one spoke as the bottle went around the room and everyone took a drink before handing it back to Jim.

"I've got some bad news," Jim said. "Dawg got a confession out of those worthless drug-users and they admitted to killing Billy and dropping his body into the lake." Everyone hung their heads and some eyes teared up as Jim continued, "This is the lake they dropped Billy's body into, and H4 is going to send a couple of divers with the agents that are coming here in the morning."

Jim took another long drink from the bottle, then handed the bottle to Doc to again pass around the room. "H4 sends his sympathy to all of us and wants us to stay strong. He said the agents will handle the paperwork to allow us to take Billy's body back into the U.S."

Doc was the first to speak and said, "So did Dawg turn the druggies into the authorities or is he going to handle it himself and make it look like an overdose?"

"Well," Jim replied, "He is holding them captive overnight until we find the body. We want to make sure they gave us the right lake. Without a body, they could say Dawg tortured them into talking and they made up a lie to stop the torture. It's very important that the divers find the body tomorrow so Dawg can turn the men into the authorities."

"And what about Angela's brother?" Wiz asked.

"Dawg has it on tape that her brother hired the drug-users to kill Billy. He probably already has a long criminal record and this should send him to prison for the rest of his life."

Big spoke up, "Jim, I would really like to have 10 minutes alone with Angela's brother before we turn him over to the authorities."

"We all would, Big," Jim answered. "And I'm sure Dawg feels the same way we do. My guess is Dawg will inflict some pain on him before he turns him over to the authorities. We are going to hold off saying anything about this to Angela or Billy's parents until we find the body."

The team finished the bottle of whiskey and Jim cracked open the second one and sent it around the room. It took a few minutes for the alcohol to hit them, but eventually they started talking about old times and some of the humorous things that happened to the team when Billy was with them.

They told some great stories about pulling practical jokes on each other and remembered some of the times when Billy had pulled a joke on each of them. The team laughed and cried as each of them took turns telling stories about Billy. Each story started off with the line, "You remember when……."

They must have told stories for two hours straight before one of the foreigners yelled that he had to go to the bathroom and brought them back to the present.

It was nearly midnight and everyone was ready to get some shut-eye. They let the foreigners use the restroom and have a smoke break before handcuffing them to the chairs for the night. They drew names for guard duty and Shades got the first shift. The rest of them went to bed or climbed into a recliner to get a few hours of sleep.

# Chapter 20

Everyone was up by seven o'clock Wednesday morning. Mike and Boom took the foreigners to the backyard and were serving them breakfast. Wiz was in the kitchen making bacon and eggs for the team. The mood was very somber knowing Billy was killed because Angela's drug-dealing brother was afraid his sister would quit giving him money if she married Billy. The team wanted to deal with Angela's brother themselves, but they knew Jim wouldn't have any part of it, so they hoped Dawg would inflict some pain on him before he turned him over to the authorities.

It was a quiet morning. Some of the guys were playing cards and the others were watching a movie when Jim's cell phone rang. It was one of the agents. Four agents and two divers were in two vehicles heading for the cabin. Their ETA was 1130 hours. Jim told them he would meet them in town rather than give them directions to the cabin. They were hungry, so Jim gave them directions to the local café and said he would meet them there for lunch.

Jim and Mike went to the café early and reserved a table for eight people. The agents showed up and after some quick introductions, everyone had a nice lunch. They couldn't talk business in the café, so nothing was said about the mission. When they arrived at the cabin, the divers took their gear to the boat and headed out. Their mission was to find Billy's body and they wanted to get started right away.

The foreigners were in the backyard and Mike went out to watch them while the meeting took place inside the cabin. The team had packed their gear and cleaned the cabin while Jim and Mike were in town. The agents wanted to see the videos of the confessions and listen to all of the tapes before the team left. They had several questions and took a lot of notes. They got the name of the realtor that rented out the cabin and planned to meet with him in a day or two.

The meeting had gone on for about two hours when they heard the boat motor pulling up to the dock. Everyone needed a break, so they all walked down to the dock to talk to the divers. The divers had a body bag in the boat and the team helped them carry the body bag up to the front yard of the cabin.

They laid the body bag in the grass and one of the agents said, "I know this is going to be hard on you, but we need someone to make a positive identification that this is your friend." The agent partially unzipped the body bag so the team could see the person's head. The head was bloated and pale and something had chewed on the face, so it was hard to make a positive identification.

Jim spoke up and said, "Billy had a tattoo of an Indian warrior on his right arm." The agent unzipped the bag a little further to expose the body down to the waist. He reached inside and pulled the stiff right arm out of the bag. There was the tattoo. It was Billy all right. The hunt was over.

This wasn't what the team hoped to find, but it was what they had expected. Jim said, "That's him," and the agent zipped up the bag.

Some of the team members walked away from the bag to be alone for a few minutes and others just kneeled on the ground next to Billy. The agents went back into the cabin and said they would continue the meeting when everyone was ready. It took about 30 minutes for all of the team members to gain their composure and return to the cabin. Jim gave the agents the folder with Billy's photos, birth certificate, DD 214 and a few other documents in it to help the coroner fill out the death certificate.

They finished the meeting and the agents wanted the team to introduce them to the foreigners before they left. Everyone went into the back yard and Jim told the foreigners that these four men would be taking over and were now in charge. Jim showed the agents the tarp with the young girl's body in it and the agents said the task force had already made arrangements with the Canadian government to pick up the bodies of Billy and the female in a couple of hours. The head agent said he would call Jim when Billy's body was ready to be picked up and taken back to the U.S. He was told it would probably be two days from now which would be Friday. The team shook hands with the agents and got into their vehicles and drove away.

No one spoke much on the drive to the camp ground. They had a two-day wait before they could get Billy's body and drive back to the U.S. Jim didn't want to call Billy's parents, but he knew it was his job and he had to make the call. He also had to call Dawg, Angela, Mary, and his family back home. When they got to the campground, everyone unloaded their gear and gathered around the picnic table to discuss the day's activities. Jim said he had several phone calls to make and told the team to call home and tell their families that they would be home this weekend.

"What about Billy's funeral?" Doc asked.

"That will be up to his family," Jim said. "I hope they will have the funeral next weekend so we can go home for a week before going back to South Dakota."

"So," Doc said, "What's the plan for tonight?"

"Anyone have a suggestion?" Jim asked.

"I vote we go back to the steakhouse," Shades said.

"So, you can invite Mary to join us?" Doc added.

"Hey, I'm planning to go out with Mary tonight, whether we go to the steakhouse or not. I just thought you guys might want to see Mary again before we head home on Friday."

Doc had a smile on his face as he said, "I would like to have one more dance with Mary before we head home. So, Mr. Shades, do I have your permission to dance one more time with the lovely Mary?"

"As long as it's a fast dance," Shades said as everyone laughed.

"Is everyone okay with going to the steakhouse and bar tonight?" Jim asked.

Everyone nodded approval and Jim said to Shades, "You better call her before she makes other plans."

"I already called her and we have a date for tonight," Shades said. "I just have to call her back and tell her I couldn't find a baby-sitter so the rest of the team will be there also." Everyone laughed again and Jim was glad the mood had lightened up and the team was looking forward to going out to dinner and seeing Mary later tonight.

Jim said, "I'm going to take a lawn chair and go sit down on the dock and start making phone calls." Everyone was glad it was Jim and not them that had to make the call to Billy's parents and Angela. No one said a word as Jim grabbed a lawn chair and walked towards the lake. It was a beautiful day and Jim sat on the dock for a few minutes and enjoyed the sunshine and fresh air before he started making calls.

Jim decided Dawg should get the first call and dialed up his number. Dawg's cell phone rang once and Dawg answered, "Hey Jim, what's going on up there?"

"Hey Dawg, it's been a rough morning. The agents and divers showed up at the cabin around noon and the divers found Billy's body at the bottom of the lake within two hours. The only way we could identify him was the Indian warrior tattoo on his right shoulder. He had been shot through the head just like the druggies said. The agents are having his body and the body of the young female picked up this afternoon and we are supposed to be able to get Billy's body and the death certificate on Friday. So, we will be back in South Dakota on Friday night or Saturday morning."

Dawg didn't say a word and Jim knew he was hurting inside. Jim finally said, "Billy was like a brother to all of us, Dawg, and we are all hurting. I know you would like to kill the drug-users and Angela's brother, but you know you can't do that. None of them are worth going to prison over."

"You are right, Jim" Dawg said. "Besides, death would be too good for them. I would rather they go to prison for a long time and some tough guy takes them for his girlfriend."

"There you go," Jim said. "I trust you will do the right thing and turn them over to the authorities?"

"You have my word I will turn them over to the authorities," Dawg replied.

"Thanks, Dawg," Jim said.

"Hey, Jim, you better hold off calling Angela and Billy's parents until we find her brother and take him into custody."

"That's a good point, Dawg," Jim said. "Do you have his name and address?"

"I do," Dawg said. "His name is Jack Paulsen, and we were told he goes by the nickname, 'Weasel'. I know where he lives and Swede and I have a plan to capture him. I'll call you as soon as the plan is executed," Dawg replied.

"Okay," Jim said. "You be careful, Dawg."

"Safety first," Dawg said.

"Safety first," Jim replied. "We'll talk later. Out here," Jim said.

"Out here," Dawg replied.

Dawg's plan to get Angela's brother was to get him to come to the home of the drug-users and jump him when he was inside the house. The drug-users told Dawg that Weasel kept a .357 pistol in his blazer, so last night, Swede picked the door lock on the blazer, found the pistol and removed the firing pin. He then put the pistol back in the blazer and locked the doors so Weasel couldn't tell someone had entered the vehicle.

At the drug-users house, Dawg told Jason to call Weasel and tell him that a drug-using friend of his was at their house wanting drugs and they didn't have any extra to sell him. Dawg said to tell Weasel that the guy had a lot of money and was flashing several hundred-dollar bills around. He said to tell Weasel to bring some drugs with him and that he better bring his pistol just in case the guy didn't want to pay for the drugs. Weasel would ask if they knew the guy and trusted him and Jason would say yes.

Jason placed the call and Weasel was at the house in 15 minutes. Swede was playing the part of the drug-user while Dawg was hiding in the kitchen. Swede answered the door and invited Angela's brother into the house. The two drug-users were sitting on the sofa in plain sight when Weasel entered the house.

"What's going on here?" Weasel asked.

"This is Pooch. He is an old friend of ours and wants to buy some drugs," Jason said. "We are all out and decided to call you and see if you had any you would sell."

Weasel made a face and said, "What the hell is wrong with you guys? I have no idea what you are talking about. Pooch could be an undercover cop for all I know. I'm going home."

"Hey Weasel, he's cool," Jason said. "We've done drugs with him several times."

"I don't care," Weasel said. "I will talk to you guys later when Pooch is gone."

"Hold on," Swede said. "These guys said you would have some drugs and you're not leaving until I get some of them. I have money and I will pay you for them."

Angela's brother quickly pulled the pistol and pointed it at Swede. "Back off, Big Guy. I could kill you right now if I wanted. Now, you get out of here and I don't ever want to see you again. Do you understand?"

Swede looked closely at the pistol and could tell it was the one without a firing pin. He had put a small white dot on the end of the barrel and he could see the dot. Knowing the gun didn't have a firing pin in it, Swede said, "Hey Dawg, this guy doesn't want to give us any of his drugs."

Dawg walked out from the kitchen wearing plastic gloves, and you could see the look of panic in Angela's brother's eyes as he moved the barrel of the pistol from Swede to Dawg. "Why didn't you tell me there were two of them?" he yelled at the two drug-users sitting on the couch. He looked at Swede and then at Dawg and said, "Stay right where you are or I promise I will shoot both of you."

Dawg made a mean face and said, "I want you to know that I don't like being threatened by anyone, and especially a worthless piece of crap like you. Now, hand over that pistol or I'm going to take it from you."

"You just try taking it from me," Weasel said.

Dawg replied, "Well, if that's the way you want it," and he took a couple of steps towards Weasel. Without hesitation, Weasel pointed the gun at Dawg and pulled the trigger. Nothing happened.

Dawg stopped a few feet from Weasel and said, "Don't tell me your gun is empty?" as he laughed out loud. Weasel pointed the gun at Dawg and pulled the trigger several more times but nothing happened. Dawg started towards him and Weasel raised the pistol and tried to hit Dawg with it but Dawg blocked the blow with his left arm and punched Weasel hard in the stomach with his right fist.

Weasel fell to the floor. He was still holding the pistol, so he dropped the magazine out of the pistol to see if the gun was loaded. As he went to pick up the magazine, Dawg smashed Weasel's right hand with the heel of his combat boot and broke several bones in Weasel's hand.

Weasel screamed in pain and Dawg just smiled and said, "Here, let me load the pistol for you." Dawg picked up the pistol, loaded the magazine and chambered a round. He then handed the pistol to Weasel and said, "It should work now." Weasel grabbed the pistol with his left hand pointed the barrel at Dawg and pulled the trigger. Nothing happened. Weasel pulled the trigger again and again, but nothing happened.

Dawg kicked Weasel in the chest and knocked him over. As Weasel was trying to get up, he placed his left hand on the floor and Dawg now smashed his left hand with the heel of his combat boot. Weasel was now screaming in pain with two broken hands as Dawg picked up the pistol and put it in a plastic bag.

Dawg then said, "Believe me Weasel, I would like to continue breaking your bones, but I think I will quit now and call the police." Dawg removed the rubber gloves from his hands, took out his cell phone and dialed 911. He told the operator what had happened and she said the police were on their way.

The police showed up a few minutes later and Dawg and Swede told their story. They had a tape player recording everything and played the voice recording of the drug-users telling how Weasel had promised to forget their drug bill if they killed Billy and how they went to Canada and did it. The police were there for about an hour getting statements and evidence before they were satisfied they had everything they needed. Dawg and Swede were told not to leave South Dakota until the District Attorney gave his approval. They agreed and everyone left the house and went on their way.

Dawg called Jim and gave him the news that all three of the men were handed over to the authorities. Jim asked if all of the men were okay and Dawg replied, "Angela's dumb brother, Jack, pulled a gun on me and I had to break his hand. Then, he grabbed for it again and I had to break his other hand."

Jim laughed and said, "I knew you were going to do something."

Dawg then asked, "So how does a guy go to the bathroom and wipe his butt with both of his hands in casts?"

Jim laughed again and said, "I guess old Weasel is going to find out isn't he?"

"I guess he will," Dawg replied.

"So, Dawg, do you want to tell Billy's parents and Angela or do you want me to call them?"

"I think it would be better if I told them in person," Dawg responded.

"I agree," Jim said. "Why don't you get everyone together and tell them tonight after dinner. I will call later and give my condolences and answer any questions they might have for me.

Tell them that we still plan to be given Billy's body on Friday and we will be heading to South Dakota as soon as we get the body."

"I will tell them," Dawg replied.

"Thanks for doing this, Dawg," Jim said.

"I'm just glad Swede and Dancer will be there in case I have trouble getting the words out," Dawg replied.

"Be strong my friend," Jim said.

"I'll try," Dawg replied.

"Out here," Jim said.

"Out here," Dawg replied.

Dawg and Swede went back to their hotel rooms and Dawg called Dancer first. Angela was with him, so he couldn't say anything but told Dancer they wanted to have a meeting at the Littlebear ranch at seven o'clock. Dancer confirmed that Angela and him would be there.

Dawg then called the Littlebears and asked them if they could all meet at the ranch tonight at seven o'clock. They agreed. It was nearly five-thirty now, so Dawg and Swede decided to get cleaned up and grab a quick bite to eat before they left for the ranch.

Dancer and Angela were already at the ranch when Dawg and Swede pulled in a few minutes before seven. They all met in the living room and Mrs. Littlebear offered them a beer or wine. Dawg thought Billy's parents must know they are going to get some bad news because they had never been offered alcohol at the ranch before tonight. Everyone had a drink and they talked for a few minutes before Dawg decided it was time.

Dawg stood up and told the whole story. There wasn't a dry eye in the room when he finished. Angela was crying so hard it hurt Dawg's heart to see her in such pain. Shades was sitting next to her and she put her head in Shades chest and Shades wrapped his arms around her and hugged her. Billy's father had tears running down his cheeks as he was holding his wife in his arms and trying to be strong for her.

After a several minutes, Mr. Littlebear spoke, "We need to start making arrangements for the death ritual. I will contact my people tonight and try to set a date for next Saturday, nine days from today."

Dawg said, "We are here to help you with anything you need. Just tell us what you would like us to do?"

"Thank you, Mr. Dawg," Billy's father said. "I'm sure we can use your help, and I will let you know what you can do in the next day or two."

Just then, Dawg's cell phone rang. It was Jim. He wanted to talk to Billy's parents and Angela. Dawg passed his cell phone around and all three of them talked to Jim for a few minutes. After the call ended. Mr. Littlebear asked everyone in the room to bow their heads as he said a prayer.

"Oh, Great Spirit, who dwells in the sky, hear me now. Thank you for guiding these men on a successful hunt. My son, whom I love more than life itself has been taken from this earthly world and his spirit will soon be traveling to your world. I ask that you give me the strength to go on living without him. Guide me through this pain, and help me live my life with clean hands and straight eyes, so when my life fades, as the fading sunset, my spirit will come to you without shame and I may be with my son again in the afterlife."

When the prayer ended, Mr. Littlebear said, "I need to be alone now. You may stay as long as you want, but I need to be alone and continue speaking to the Great Spirit." He then gave everyone a hug before he walked out of the cabin.

Mrs. Littlebear said he would go down by the creek and finish talking to the Great Spirit before he came back to the cabin. She assured them he would be all right, then she gave everyone a hug before they left her alone in the cabin.

Angela invited all three of the guys over to her house because she didn't want to be alone. They agreed to spend the evening with her and picked up a few of bottles of wine on the way there. Angela had a nice little ranch house and she showed them a scrap book full of photos of her and Billy. They talked, looked at the photos and drank wine until midnight. Dawg, Swede and Dancer got up to leave and Angela started crying again. She didn't want to be alone and Dancer agreed to stay there and sleep on the couch. Dawg and Swede left as Angela was filling up two wine glasses.

# Chapter 21

Wednesday had been a very long day for everyone and Dawg and Swede both agreed to sleep in Thursday morning. They made plans to meet for breakfast at seven-thirty in the hotel restaurant and Dawg was already there at seven-fifteen when Swede showed up. "Morning, Dawg," Swede said as he ordered a cup of coffee from the waitress.

"Morning, Swede," Dawg replied.

"How much sleep did you get?" Swede asked.

"I think about four hours," Dawg answered. "How about you?"

"About the same," Swede replied.

"So much for sleeping in," Dawg said with a chuckle.

"I know you live for this kind of excitement, Dawg, but since I retired from the military, I now prefer the less-stressful civilian life," Swede said. "Yesterday was hard on me, and I'm looking forward to going back home."

"I understand," Dawg said. "I really hope that someday I will mellow out and be able to enjoy living a quiet, peaceful life."

"Wow," Swede said. "I never thought I would hear you say that."

"Well, I'm not talking in the near future," Dawg said. "I said 'someday', like maybe in 30 or 40 years."

"Yeah, okay," Swede said. "I'll believe it when I see it."

After finishing breakfast, they decided to call Dancer and Angela and see how they were doing. Neither of them answered their cell phones, so they guessed both of them stayed up drinking until daylight and were sleeping like logs. "So, what's the plan for today?" Swede asked.

"I don't have anything planned," Dawg replied. "Jim's niece, Amber, is a nurse in Sioux Falls and I thought about calling her and seeing if she wants to have dinner with us tonight, but I'm open for suggestions as for what to do for the next nine hours."

"Dinner with Amber sounds great. Why don't you call her and see if she is available?" Swede asked. "Maybe she will have some suggestions on what we can do today?"

"Sounds like a plan," Dawg said as he dialed Amber's phone number. Amber didn't answer, so Dawg left her a voicemail message to call him back if she was available for dinner. Just as Dawg finished the voicemail message, the waitress showed up at the table with a fresh pot of coffee.

"Miss, we have the day off and are looking for something interesting to do in Sioux Falls. What do you recommend?" Swede asked.

"Well, there is a very nice zoo in Sioux Falls if you like that sort of thing," she replied. "I have taken several friends and relatives there and we always have a great time."

"That sounds good to me," Swede replied. "Thank you very much."

"You are quite welcome," she replied before turning and walking away.

"So, how do you feel about going to the zoo and visiting some of your relatives?" Swede asked.

"It sounds good to me," Dawg replied.

"Maybe they will have a silverback gorilla you can wrestle," Swede said with a laugh.

"No more wrestling gorillas," Dawg replied. "The last time I wrestled a silverback, I dislocated his shoulder and the zoo keepers were really upset with me."

"Sure you did," Swede said as they both laughed.

Up in Canada, Jim and the team were sitting at the camp site picnic table finishing a great breakfast of walleye, eggs and hash browns. They had all gone fishing the night before and caught so many walleye, they had to release several of them after they reached their possession limit. They had one more day in Canada before they were to pick up Billy's body and return to the U.S., so they planned to do some more fishing. They heard about a nearby lake that was full of big Northern Pike and they wanted to check it out. Since walleye don't bite well during the hours of bright sunlight, they might as well check out this other lake and be back before sunset to catch some more walleye.

Just as they finished eating, Jim's cell phone rang. "Hello, this is Jim."

"Good morning, Jim. This is General Hewlett."

"Good morning, Sir," Jim replied.

"How are you guys doing?" the General asked.

"We are doing about as well as can be expected, Sir," Jim replied. "Billy was like a brother to us and there is a lot of pain, but he is in a better place now and we have to learn to accept it."

"Well, I know how you feel and how hard it is to understand," General Hewlett replied. "I have lost a lot of close friends over the years and it never seems to get any easier. General George Patton once said that it is wrong to mourn soldiers that have died, rather we should thank God that such men lived. That's how I feel about my friends that were killed and I hope you can feel the same way about Billy. Had Billy not gone to Canada on a fishing trip, we may not have discovered the terrorist plot to set bombs in shopping malls in the U.S. I look at Billy as a real-life hero and would gladly speak at his funeral if his family would like that. Please tell his parents that I would be honored to say a few words about Billy if they approve."

"I will tell them, Sir," Jim replied. "I have no idea of what an Indian 'burial ritual' is like or what takes place at these events, but I will tell them you offered to speak if they want that sort of thing."

"Thank you," H4 replied.

H4 continued. "I just spoke with the Canadian authorities, and they are going to release Billy's body to you at zero nine hundred tomorrow morning. They have notified Customs and will give you the paperwork you need to cross back into the United States."

"That is great, Sir," Jim replied. "Thank you so much for all you did to make this possible."

"Glad to help," General Hewlett said. "You guys did a great job finding Billy and uncovering a terrorist plot that could have killed thousands of Americans. I have to go to a meeting now, but I plan to see all of you at the funeral and I would like to speak to the whole team the day before the funeral or the morning of the funeral. I will be in touch with you and let you know when and where we can meet. And let me know if the family would like me to say a few words about Billy."

"Yes, Sir. I will let you know what they say. We are all looking forward to seeing you at the funeral," Jim said.

"Thanks, Jim. You take care and I'll see you soon. Out here," General Hewlett said.

"Out here," Jim replied.

After ending the call, Jim said to the team, "We can pick up Billy's body and head for home at nine o'clock tomorrow morning."

"Hooah," the team replied.

"And," Jim said, "H4 is going to the funeral and wants to meet with all of us."

"You better warn Dawg in advance so he can be on his best behavior when we meet with H4," Shades said.

"Now, does anyone here think Dawg has a best behavior?" Jim asked. Everyone shook their heads and laughed.

"I do miss that old coon dog when he's not around," Doc said.

"Kind of like you miss the gout or the stomach flu?" Big said as the whole group laughed out loud.

The rest of the day was spent fishing and telling stories about Billy. Everyone was anxious to go home and see their family and friends. It had been a long two weeks since they left home and the mission didn't end the way they wanted. They caught a lot of Northern Pike at the small lake they went to and headed back to the camp site around mid-afternoon. They stopped at a liquor store and bought a few bottles of nice wine to go with dinner since Mary was planning to join them for a fish fry at the camp site.

After leaving the liquor store, Jim's cell phone rang. A person thought they saw the dog on the 'Wanted Poster'. Since it was nearby, Jim told the others that he and Mike would go check it out and they would meet the others at camp a little later.

The call came from a lady at another campsite and they arrived at the location in about 10 minutes. They quickly found the lady that called and she explained to them that a stray dog kept coming around the campsite looking for food. She said he was friendly to children, but very cautious around adults and easily spooked if there was a loud noise or sudden movement. She said she had just seen him and started walking through the campground with Jim and Mike.

She suddenly stopped and said, "There he is." The dog was being petted by a young boy. Jim had brought one of Billy's shirts along with him and was carrying the shirt in his hand. He asked Mike and the lady to stay there and he would slowly approach the dog by himself. He started slowly walking towards the dog and he could see the dog was watching him closely.

"Hi Kota," Jim said in a friendly voice. The dog's ears went up and Jim spoke again, "Hi Kota, are you a good boy?" You could tell the dog responded to the word Kota and now was very interested in the adult that was approaching him. When Jim got within 20 feet of the dog, he took a knee and said, "Come here Kota, I have something I want you to smell." The dog slowly left the boys side and cautiously walked toward Jim. Jim kept talking to him, "Hi Kota, how are you doing big fellow? He held the shirt out in front of him and the dog finally reached the shirt and instantly started wagging his tail and making a whining sound. Jim started petting Kota and the two of them bonded in a matter of minutes.

Mike and the lady came over and both petted the dog. It looked like Kota was going to stay with Jim as long as he had the shirt with Billy's scent on it, so they started walking back to Jim's pickup and Kota walked with them. They thanked the lady and when they got to Jim's pickup, Jim opened the door and threw Billy's shirt on the seat in the extended cab. Kota jumped up into the pickup without hesitation. He had found something with the scent of his master and he wasn't going to let it get away.

Jim and Mike got into the pickup and drove out of the campsite. "So, are we taking Kota home with us?" Mike asked.

"Possibly," Jim responded. "But first I want to check something out."

"Check what out?" Mike responded as he was petting Kota and scratching his ears.

"You remember how much the little girl at the resort loved Kota?" Jim asked.

"I sure do," Mike said, "and her name was Missy."

"You have a good memory Mike," Jim replied. "Anyway, I want to see if her grandfather will let her keep Kota."

"Wow," Mike replied. "That sounds like a good plan, but the girl goes back to her parents during the school year and maybe her parents don't want her to have a dog."

"You might be right," Jim replied. "But I have a plan that I think will work."

"Well it looks like we are about to find out," Mike said as Jim turned into the driveway to the resort.

Sam Williams, the resort owner came out to meet the men as they were getting out of Jim's truck. "Hello there," Mr. Williams said.

"Hello, Sir," Jim responded. "We met you a couple of weeks ago, when we were here looking for our friend that rented a boat from you."

"Yes, I remember," Mr. Williams replied. "Did you find your friend?" he asked.

"Yes, Sir we did, but not like we wanted to find him. A couple of divers found his body at the bottom of a lake."

"Well, I'm very sorry to hear that," Mr. Williams replied. "My condolences to you and his family."

"Thank you, sir," Jim replied.

"Is your grand-daughter still here?" Jim asked.

"She sure is," Mr. Williams replied.

"Well, sir, I would like to ask you something and see what you think about it."

"Okay," Mr. Williams responded.

"We're heading back to the United States in the morning and we just found Billy's dog, 'Kota' less than an hour ago. We have him in the pickup right now, and since your grand-daughter really seemed to bond to the dog, I was wondering if you would want to take the dog or let her have the dog?" Jim asked.

"Well, Missy was sure fond of that dog, and I was thinking about getting another dog to have here at the resort," Mr. Williams said. "How about if you let the dog out and I get to see if Missy and the dog still connect like they did before?"

"That is a great idea," Jim replied. Mr. Williams yelled for Missy, and she was at his side in a couple of minutes.

"Hi, Missy," Jim said.

"Hello," Missy replied. "Hey, you are the guy that was looking for Billy and Kota," Missy said.

"That's right," Jim responded.

"Did you find them?" she asked.

"Why don't you look in the back of the pickup and see what is in there?" Jim replied. She went over to the pickup and Mike opened the door for her.

"Hi Kota," she quickly said as she hugged the dog and started petting him." Kota's tail was now wagging and you could see he was loving the attention Missy was giving him.

"Can he come out of the truck and play with me for a while?" she asked.

"You bet he can," Jim replied. Missy backed up and called to Kota and he jumped out of the truck and followed her. They went down by the lake and sat on the dock together and she petted him and hugged him the whole time.

"Well, it sure looks like they have a special bond," Mr. Williams said. "I will take the dog and he can stay here with me if Missy's mother won't let her take the dog home. Missy's dad died of cancer last year and he didn't have much of a life insurance policy to leave his family, so Missy's mother is struggling to make ends meet. I'm afraid she won't want the expense of having a dog no matter how much Missy will beg to let her keep the dog. So, if her mother won't let her bring the dog home, I can keep the dog here and that way Missy will be excited to come up here every summer if she knows Kota will be here," he said with a chuckle.

"That is great," Jim replied. "But there is one more thing. Since you and Missy gave us some information that helped us find Billy, we want the two of you to have five thousand dollars of the reward money."

"What?" Mr. Williams asked.

"Billy's parents put up a ten-thousand-dollar reward and we decided to split it with you and a lady that gave us information that helped us find Billy," Jim replied. "The information that you and Missy gave us helped us track down Billy's body and we are very grateful to you for that," Jim said.

"Wow," Mr. Williams said. "That is wonderful. I'm sure that if I give the money to Missy's mom and explain everything to her, she will let Missy keep the dog."

"That is a great idea," Jim said. "You are a good man, Mr. Williams."

"Oh, I'm just an old fart that truly loves his family," Mr. Williams replied. "Is it okay with you if I call Missy up here and tell her about this?" Mr. Williams asked.

"Please do," Jim replied.

"Hey, Missy, can you and Kota come here a minute?" Mr. Williams yelled. Both of them got up and came up the bank to where the men were standing. "Missy, I have something I need to tell you," her grand-father said. "Billy was killed in an accident and these men are looking for a good home for Kota. Do you think we could keep him and provide him with a loving home?"

Missy had a strange look on her face, because she was both sad about the death of Billy, and excited about the possibility of being able to keep Kota.

Jim could see she was at a loss for words, so he quickly spoke up and said, "Missy, Billy loved this dog very much and would have wanted him to go to a loving home. I'm sure he would want you to have Kota if you want him."

Missy quickly replied, "Of course I want him, he's the best dog in the world. I'm just not sure my mother will let me have a dog because they are very expensive."

"Well, I've got some good news for you Missy. Why don't you tell her, Jim?" Mr. Williams asked.

"Missy, Billy's parents put up a reward for information that helped us find Billy," Jim said to her. "The information you and your grandpa gave us helped us find him and we are giving you five-thousand dollars of the reward money."

Missy's face lit up and she said," Are you serious?"

"Yes, I'm serious," Jim replied. "The photo you gave us of the man with the multi-colored shirt helped us locate those men and they helped us find Billy's body."

Missy said, "I'm so sorry about Billy. He was a very nice man."

"Yes, he was, thank you, Missy," Jim replied. "And I know Billy must have really liked you, because he gave you the necklace you are wearing."

Missy grabbed the necklace and said, "Well the feeling was mutual," as all of them smiled.

Mr. Williams then spoke, "And if your mother won't let you

take Kota home with you, we will keep him here with us and you can come up when school gets out and spend the whole summer with him."

Missy quickly replied, "I want him to go home with me, but either way will be wonderful as long as I can spend some time with Kota."

"One more thing," Jim said, "if at any time you find out that you can't keep Kota, you give me a call and I will come and get him. Please don't give him to someone else or put him in an animal shelter."

"You have my word on that," Mr. Williams said.

"Well then, I guess it is all settled," Jim replied. "There is five thousand dollars in traveler's checks in this envelope." He handed the envelope to Mr. Williams and said, "Thank you again for the information and for providing Kota with a nice home."

Mike spoke up, "Should we leave Billy's shirt here with them?"

"Good idea," Jim said as Mike grabbed the shirt out of the pickup. "This has Billy's scent on it and having it around might make him feel more comfortable until he gets used to his new home," Jim said as he handed Mr. Williams the shirt. The men shook hands with Mr. Williams and Missy gave Jim and Mike a long hug before the two of them got into Jim's pickup and drove away.

"That was a very nice thing to do," Mike said to Jim.

"I'm sure Kota will have a loving home with them, and giving them half of the reward money just seemed like the right thing to do." Jim replied. "I talked with Mr. Littlebear last night and he asked my opinion on who should get the reward money. I thought about it a little and told him I thought it should be split fifty-fifty between Missy and Mary. He agreed, so I was planning on driving over here today anyway. So, the phone call on Kota was perfect timing," Jim said.

"It sure was," Mike replied. "I think God wanted Missy to have that dog."

"I think you are right," Jim said as they both smiled.

They arrived at the campground a short time later and the guys were drinking and talking to Mary. They started dinner as soon as Jim and Mike got there and had a very nice meal.

As soon as the meal was over, Shades said, "I have an announcement. Mary and I have grown very fond of each other and neither of us want to say good-bye and end our relationship. Mary is going to drive to South Dakota for the funeral and I'm going to ride with her. After the funeral is over, I will ride back to Canada with her and then fly home."

Doc was the first to speak and said, "I'm very happy you two found each other. You are both great people and I wish you all the best." Doc lifted his glass of wine and said, "May your lives be filled with happiness as your love continues to grow. To Shades and Mary."

"To Shades and Mary," the team responded as everyone took a drink before congratulating the new couple.

Jim spoke up and said, "I have an announcement also. Mary, as you know, Mr. and Mrs. Littlebear put up ten-thousand dollars of reward money for information that led us to Billy. I spoke with the Littlebears last night and we agreed that the reward money should be split between you and the girl that took the photo of the foreigner with the multi-colored shirt. Mike and I gave Billy's dog Kota to the girl and the reward money to her grand-father that owns the resort. This envelope contains five-thousand dollars of travelers' checks, and on behalf of the Littlebear family and the team, we are happy to present it to you."

Jim handed Mary the envelope as the team stood up and

clapped. Mary's eyes teared up as she took the envelope and said, "Thank you so very much."

"Thank you, Mary, for everything," Jim replied as the team all congratulated Mary and hugged her.

Jim got his guitar out and played some oldies as everyone sang along and took turns dancing with Mary. Shades had to get Mary home to finish packing for the trip and he said they would meet the team at the local convenience store at ten o'clock tomorrow morning and follow them back to South Dakota. Everyone agreed as Shades and Mary got into Mary's vehicle and left the campground.

The team decided to call it a night and as they were putting out the campfire, Doc commented to Jim, "You sure were right about those two."

"Well, I saw them looking at each other one night and could tell they had deep feelings for one another," Jim replied. "If Shades didn't invite her to the funeral, I was going to ask her and try to get them together. I think they are a great couple and I'm so glad they found each other."

"I feel the same way," Doc replied.

Back in South Dakota, Dawg and Swede finished touring the zoo and were headed back to the motel. Amber had called and was going to meet them for dinner. Amber's boyfriend, Justin, would be joining them and Amber recommended an Italian restaurant that was close to the motel where Dawg and Swede were staying. Amber would make reservations for six thirty, and they agreed to meet there at six o'clock for a couple of drinks before dinner.

It was a nice evening. The lasagna was the best Dawg and Swede had ever eaten, and Amber and Justin were super people. Dawg was glad that Justin was a nice young man and felt that he and Amber made a great couple. They finally decided to call it a night and said farewells as Dawg and Swede headed back to their motel.

# Chapter 22

Jim was the first one up Friday morning and decided to go for a run before the others woke up and climbed out of their tents. It was a nice morning for a run and Jim ran a couple of extra miles while thinking about everything that had happened during their two weeks in Canada. It had been an exciting adventure, he just wished it would have ended differently.

The team was up and cooking eggs and walleye when he returned to the campsite. After the meal was finished, they gave all of their left-over groceries to a couple of the other campers and said their good-byes. They were all finished showering and ready to roll by 8 o'clock. It was about a 30-minute drive to the morgue and they wanted to be there early.

They pulled out of the campground a few minutes after eight and Mike said to Jim, "This has been a trip I will never forget, but I'm sure looking forward to going home."

"I'm really glad you were able to go with us, Mike," Jim replied. "Not too many people would use up two weeks of vacation to help some guys look for a missing friend in a foreign country. And who knows what would have happened if you hadn't stopped that guy that pulled a knife on Dawg in Tuff Guyz. You probably saved someone's life that day and I want you to know that the whole team thinks the world of you. They have told me so. So, thanks again for going along."

"Well, thank you again for asking me to go," Mike replied. "Now, don't forget, you are going to help me think of a nice gift for Karen during the ride home."

"You got it," Jim replied. "As soon as we pick up Billy's body and hit the road, we'll talk about that. I have an idea and want to see what you think about it."

"Sounds like a plan, Stan," Mike replied as they headed down the road.

Things went well at the morgue and they had already decided to load Billy's government casket into Jim's pickup since he had a topper on it. They covered the casket with blankets and sleeping bags so it wouldn't be noticeable when they had to stop for food or fuel. They were on the road shortly after 9 o'clock and met Shades and Mary at the convenience store a few minutes before 10:00. After filling coolers with drinks and snacks for the long drive to South Dakota, the convoy pulled out of the convenience store and headed for the border crossing at International Falls.

It was a beautiful day and the scenery was magnificent. Jim commented to Mike, "There's a lot of things about Canada that I really like and I wouldn't mind living up here someday."

"Really?" Mike replied. "Why on earth would you want to live up here in this wilderness?" Mike asked.

"Well, the fresh air, the clean lakes, the big fish, the wild life, fewer people and no waiting in line are just a few things I can think of off the top of my head," Jim replied.

"Yeah, I can see how you would like it since you love the outdoors," Mike replied. "But as for me, I like having good reception for my cell phone, computer and T.V.'s. And I like taking the dog for a walk without having to worry about being attacked by a bear or a pack of wolves. I will choose Iowa over Canada any day of the week," Mike said.

"So, I guess we disagree on that just like we do on the Cyclones and the Hawkeyes," Jim replied.

"I guess so," Mike said, "and I'm really looking forward to you buying me a case of beer after the Hawkeyes beat your Cyclones in football this fall."

"Yeah, Okay," Jim responded. "You know Iowa State has one of the toughest schedules in the country and I really don't think the Cyclones will get to a bowl game this year… But, we always get motivated when we play Iowa and often play our best game of the year."

"That's so true," Mike replied. "How come you guys always play lights-out against us after losing to a much worse team the first or second game of the season?"

"We just really enjoy beating you guys and then listening to the local sports talk shows and hearing Hawkeye fans call-in with a list of excuses as to why they lost the game. 'Sound-Off' on Channel 13 was a classic last year," Jim said with a huge smile on his face.

"Yeah, whatever," Mike replied as they both laughed. "So, tell me Jim, is your whole family Cyclone fans?" Mike asked.

"No, not at all," Jim replied. "My Mom, my brother Kelly, my Uncle Fred and I are really the only ones."

"Now wait a minute," Mike said. "I remember seeing your sister, Renee wearing an ISU sweatshirt."

"You probably did," Jim replied. "When I found out she liked the Hawkeyes, I bought her an ISU sweatshirt for Christmas every year for 10 years in a row."

"So, did you get her to convert over to the Cyclones?" Mike asked.

"No, just spent a lot of money on sweatshirts," Jim replied as they both laughed out loud.

"Okay, now what is the idea you have for a gift I can buy for Karen to thank her for letting me go on this trip," Mike said.

"Well," Jim replied, "You know how Karen and my wife Patti are like the best sisters in the whole world, I was thinking that maybe the four of us could go on a cruise this winter?"

"Wow," Mike replied. "I was thinking about the four of us going to Los Vegas for a few days, but I think a cruise would be even better."

"Well, you think about it and we'll get online and do some searching for cruise packages when we get home. I know both of our wives would love it," Jim said.

"Yeah, and when they are happy, life just seems to be a lot better for you and me," Mike replied.

"Amen to that, good buddy," Jim responded as they both raised their coffee cups and touched them together in a toast.

There was a long line of cars and trucks waiting to cross the border into the United States when the convoy reached International Falls. Jim let Mike drive his pickup and he got out and walked to the Customs office with the paperwork for Billy. Customs told Jim that his group of people could come to the front of the line and didn't have to wait, so Jim called Mike and the others on their cell phones and told them to meet him outside at one of the crossing gates. The customs agents looked at the paperwork and did a quick check in every vehicle before waving all of them through. Jim thanked the Canadian officials and estimated it save them nearly two hours by not having to wait in line. It was approximately an eight-hour drive from International Falls, MN to Sioux Falls, SD and they should now get to the Littlebear ranch just after dark.

The team stopped for lunch and a couple of bathroom

breaks, but made good time and arrived at the Littlebear ranch at 8:15 P.M. Jim called a few minutes out to let them know they would be there soon. There were a lot of vehicles at the ranch and a large group of people came out of the house as the team was driving up the lane.

Mr. and Mrs. Littlebear and Angela hugged and thanked everyone first. Then came introductions to the rest of the people. They were mostly relatives and close friends of the Littlebears. After the greetings and introductions were finished, Mr. Littlebear's nephew, Tommy, asked the team to come with him into the machine shed so he could speak to them.

The machine shed had been cleaned out and there were tables and chairs set up throughout the building. Tommy asked everyone to sit down as he wanted to speak with them for a few minutes. Tommy began, "Billy's funeral will be next Saturday morning at 10 o'clock A.M. It will be held here on the Littlebear property, down by the creek. If the forecast calls for rain that day, it will be held here in the machine shed."

Tommy continued, "Friday night before the funeral, there will be a modern-day wake held here in the machine shed. There will be a stage and microphone for people to get up and share memories of Billy. Food and alcohol will be served. Saturday morning, the burial ritual will be about a quarter of a mile from here, on a hillside overlooking the creek. It will be a more traditional Native-American ritual, with chanting and bright-colored clothing and headwear. We will be sitting on the ground and several blankets will be placed on the ground for us to sit on. You are welcome to bring a pillow to sit on, but there will be no chairs. You may stand in the back if you do not wish to sit through the whole ceremony."

"We have reserved a block of rooms at two of the local motels and the contact information is on this paper I am passing out now." After everyone had a copy of the paper, Billy continued. "The Littlebear family hopes all of you will be able to attend next weekend and would like to know if any of you are unable to attend. They want to thank you for everything you have done and all of you will be recognized at the wake on Friday night. Does anyone have any questions at this time?"

Jim asked, "So is Billy going to be buried here on the family farm?"

"No," Tommy answered. "His parents thought about it, but decided to bury him on a nearby Indian reservation with other members of his family. His mother and father will be buried next to him when their life on earth is through. The actual burial is a sacred event and only immediate members of the family will be present when he is put into the ground. I know he was like a brother to you, but the family wants to keep the burial traditional and hopes that you understand."

"We understand," Jim said.

"Thank you," Tommy replied. "Now, the Littlebear family understands that you are anxious to get home to your loved ones, so you are free to leave. My phone number is on the paper you have in your possession, so please call me if you are unable to attend next weekend, or have any questions about anything."

Tommy shook hands with everyone and they headed for their vehicles. The group of people had gone inside the Littlebear house and had taken the casket inside as well. The team could hear the weeping and chanting from the house as they got into their vehicles and drove away.

# Chapter 23

Jim and Mike drove home to Iowa that night, but most of the team only drove for a couple of hours and got a room or pulled into a campground for the night and finished the drive home on Saturday morning. Jim dropped Mike off at his house in Norwalk just after midnight and headed for home. Patti was waiting up for him and they embraced for a long time when Jim walked into the house. They had a couple of glasses of wine as Jim relaxed and filled her in on the details of the trip.

It was nice to be home and the week went by fast. Jim and Mike decided to ride together to Billy's funeral and both of their wives were able to get time off work to go along. They left Des Moines on Thursday night after everyone got off work and spent the night in South Sioux City, Nebraska. They had a nice breakfast on Friday morning and were on the road to Sioux Falls, SD around eight o'clock.

While on the road, Jim got a call from H4 that he wanted to meet with the team at 5 o'clock that afternoon before they attended the wake. H4 had reserved a small conference room in the hotel for the meeting and expressed to Jim that only team members were to attend. Jim said he would call everyone to make sure they were there in time for the meeting.

The whole team was at the hotel by 3 o'clock in the afternoon and met in the bar for a couple of drinks before the meeting with H4. The women hit the pool and sauna for an hour, then were going shopping while the men were in the meeting.

About 10 minutes to five, the team made their way to the conference room. H4 was waiting inside and greeted them one at a time as they entered the room. After the greetings and man-hugs were over, H4 had everyone sit down and he got the meeting started.

"First of all, I just want to say that it pleases my heart to see all of you again. You guys saved a lot of lives in Afghanistan and I will never be able to thank you enough for everything that you did. President Obama was briefed on what happened in Canada and he approved an award for each of you. He asked me to personally thank you on behalf of a grateful nation. You once again saved many lives, only this time it was the lives of innocent men, women and children that would have been out shopping on Black Friday."

General Hewlett continued, "What I am going to say next is classified information. All of you must sign an agreement of secrecy before I can continue. Mike, since I do not know you or your security clearance, you are free to leave at this time."

"Sir," Jim said, "Mike is a member of our team and we all trust that he will not discuss classified information after he signs the agreement." H4 looked at the team and all of them were nodding their heads in agreement.

H4 said, "Dawg, do you trust Mike with classified information?"

Dawg immediately said, "Yes sir, I do. I would take a bullet for Mike."

"Wow," H4 replied. "Apparently, Mike has made quite an impression on you. That is great. Let me explain the secrecy agreement to everyone and then Mike can make the decision as to whether or not he wants to stay and hear the details of the mission."

H4 held up the agreement and said, "this secrecy agreement is very brief and to the point, but it is very powerful and breaking the agreement could result in a prison sentence." Everyone was listening intently as H4 began reading, "I do solemnly swear that the details of this mission are classified and I will not discuss any part of the mission with anyone other than my team members or supervisors. Failure to do so may result in criminal charges."

"So," H4 said, "Now it's time for you to take an oath and sign the secrecy agreement, or you must leave the room and not talk about what we have discussed so far." H4 started passing out the agreements and when all of the team members had a copy, everyone, including Mike, stood and raised their right hand as H4 read the oath. After the oath was read and repeated by the team, each one of them signed the secrecy agreement and H4 collected the documents and put them into a briefcase.

"Now," H4 continued, "Since you can't even tell your wives or families the details of the mission, we have come up with a story for you to tell your families. Our team has written an elaborate plan of what you will be doing in Canada and we will give you weekly updates for you to tell your loved ones when you communicate with them. You will tell them you are training/advising the Canadian Army on terrorist tactics. Since all of you are proven experts in terrorism, this should be easy for your families to believe. And, it's very close to what you really will be doing. Any questions at this time?" H4 asked.

Hearing nothing, H4 continued, "Our anti-terrorism task force came to the conclusion that there must be many more terrorists in Canada waiting to cross the border into the United

States. We came up with a plan, and with a few minor changes by the Prime Minister of Canada and the President of the United States, we now have a mission. The plan is for your team to go to Canada and find these terrorists. You will be broken into two teams, Jim will lead one team and Dawg will lead the other. Each team will have two Canadian agents with them. You will be training these agents on how to find terrorists."

H4 paused for a moment, then continued. "I made it clear to the Prime Minister of Canada that Jim and Dawg will be the team leaders and call the shots. If any one of the Canadian agents give you any grief, you call me and I will have them removed from the team. Just understand that if you elect to remove an agent from your team, they will be replaced with a new agent, and you may have to repeat some of the training to get the new agent up to speed. So, be very sure it's the best thing to do before you decide to have an agent removed from your team."

H4 continued, "The length of the mission will be one year. After that, the Canadians will take over the mission in its entirety. You will be paid very well since the Canadian government is paying for most of your salary. You will be given several nice vehicles to drive, and a couple of nice fishing boats as well. You will also be given credit cards to be used for all of your expenses. You will receive your orders from a task force that is being formed especially for this mission. The task force will be located in the Pentagon, and will be working closely with a counter-terrorism task force in Canada. Occasionally, you will be given guidance on where to look and what to look for, but most of the time you will be doing your own thing. The counter-terrorism task force in Canada will have helicopters available to you upon request. Are there any questions at this time?"

Hearing nothing, H4 continued, "Okay, I will be around

tonight but I will be leaving tomorrow shortly after the burial ritual. I will be glad to answer any questions you may think of later. We can talk in my room or go to my car if we are at the Littlebear's ranch. You have one week to make your decision. Here is another paper telling about the job of training the Canadian Army. This makes it look more official and will help you get the facts straight when you talk to your family. Please contact Jim with your answer, and I will contact him next Friday to see how many of you have accepted the mission. Are there any questions at this time?" No one said a word. "Okay then," H4 continued, let's get ready to go to the wake."

The wake was scheduled to begin at seven o'clock, and the team was all at the Littlebear ranch by six-thirty. There was a large crowd, and the mood was very somber and peaceful. At seven, Tommy Littlebear got up on the stage and got the event started. He said the night was not for sorrow, but to honor the memory of Billy by sharing stories with everyone. There would be plenty of time for weeping tomorrow during the burial ritual, so he again requested everyone to lighten up the mood, have a few drinks and get up on stage and share fond memories of Billy with others.

The wake turned out to be a great event. Every member of the team that served with Billy got up and shared a story. Some stories were so humorous, the crowd laughed for minutes, while others were more serious and showed the gentle, caring side of Billy. Some of Billy's relatives told stories of him as a little boy, and one of his cousins told how Billy once took a pet snake to school by hiding the snake in his shirt. The teacher called on Billy to stand up in front of the class and read a paragraph of the book she was reading to the class. Just as Billy was about to finish reading, the snake stuck his head out of Billy's shirt and a couple of girls in the front row screamed and ran for the door. Billy got into big trouble for that and was told he would be suspended if he ever brought another snake to school.

When the wake ended, the team decided to stop for a drink in the hotel bar before retiring for the night. A couple of the wives and girlfriends went also, so they waited for the ladies to retire to their rooms before they got a table and discussed the mission. H4 happened to come into the bar for a night-cap and joined them at the table. He told them that Mr. Littlebear wanted them to come to the ranch an hour before the burial ritual as he wanted to speak to the team in the machine shed before the other people showed up. H4 then answered a couple of questions the team had before heading to his room for the night. Most of the team was planning to commit to the mission, but a couple of them still hadn't make up their minds. It was nearly midnight and the team decided to call it a day.

The Great Spirit must have wanted Billy's death ritual to be outside, because Saturday was a picture-perfect day. The team showed up at the Littlebear ranch a few minutes before nine o'clock and headed for the machine shed. Mrs. Littlebear took the women into the house with her so the men could be alone in the machine shed. Mr. Littlebear had put a bunch of chairs into a circle and invited to team to have a seat. When all of them were seated, he began to speak.

"My wife and I cannot thank you enough for all that you have done for us. Although we are saddened by Billy's death, we know he will be in a better place after the death ritual when his soul goes to be with the Great Spirit. Billy kept his $400,000 life insurance policy after he got out of the military and his mother and I were named as beneficiaries. We have decided to give each of you $20,000 for your part in finding Billy and bringing his body home to us. There were ten of you on the team, and I have an envelope for each of you with a check for $20,000 inside. That leaves his mother and me with $200,000, and that is plenty of money for us to live out our time on earth. Please do not refuse to take the money, as you have all earned it and we insist that you take it. You are all wonderful men and it is easy for my wife and I to see why Billy loved you like brothers. Here are the envelopes, please take the one with your name on it," he said as he handed the envelopes to Jim.

Mr. Littlebear continued, "After the burial ritual, I probably won't be able to talk to you, so I want to hug each of you now before you leave the machine shed. You are always welcome here and if there is ever anything we can do for you, please do not hesitate to ask." The team all took the envelope with their name on it, and one by one hugged Mr. Littlebear before leaving the machine shed.

H4 was waiting for the team outside the machine shed. He could tell they were fighting back tears and he waited for someone to speak to him. Jim walked up to him and said, "Sir, no need to call me on Friday. Eight members of the team have committed to the mission. Doc and Mike will not be going with us. I would like to add two new people to the team if you approve. One of them is Mary, the lady from Canada that worked with us and helped us find Billy's body. The other is my brother-in-law, Red, a Viet Nam veteran that is retired and looking for something to do. Both of them would be a valuable asset to our team."

H4 looked at Jim and said, "Approved. Now let's walk down the hill and get a seat for the burial ritual."

As the team walked down the hill, Jim couldn't help but think of everything that had taken place over the last month. He had lost one of his brothers, and this saddened him deeply. But the reality of it was that if Billy had not gone to Canada fishing, the terrorist plot most likely would not have been uncovered, and hundreds if not thousands of innocent people would have died a few months from now. So, it helped to ease some of the pain knowing that Billy's death was not in vain.

And one more thing.... If the team had found four terrorists in Canada while looking for their friend, how many could they find if they were actually looking for terrorists? Jim looked around at all of his team members and smiled.... I guess they were going to find out.

# THE END